W9-CAV-163

THE APOSTLE

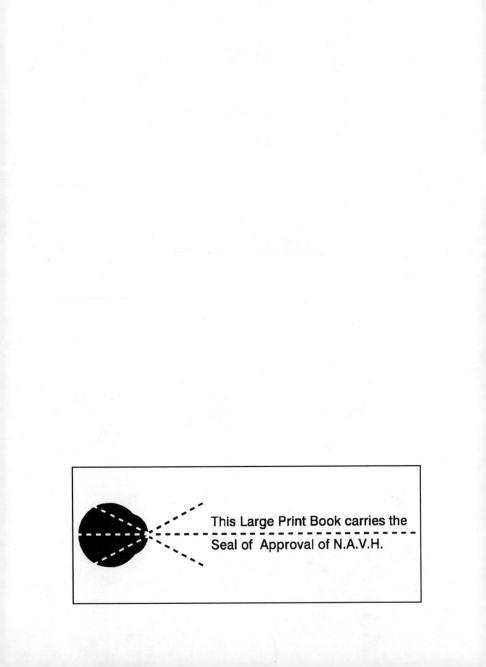

This Large Print Book carries the
Seal of Approval of N.A.V.H.

THE APOSTLE

A THRILLER

BRAD THOR

THORNDIKE PRESS

A part of Gale, Cengage Learning

GALE
CENGAGE Learning

Detroit • New York • San Francisco • New Haven, Conn • Waterville, Maine • London

GALE
CENGAGE Learning

Thorndike Press® Large Print Core.

The text of this Large Print edition is unabridged.

Other aspects of the book may vary from the original edition.

Set in 16 pt. Plantin.

Printed on permanent paper.

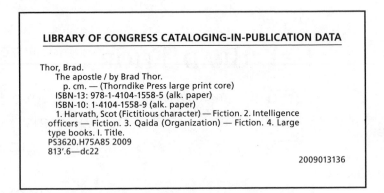

LIBRARY OF CONGRESS CATALOGING-IN-PUBLICATION DATA

Thor, Brad.
   The apostle / by Brad Thor.
     p. cm. — (Thorndike Press large print core)
   ISBN-13: 978-1-4104-1558-5 (alk. paper)
   ISBN-10: 1-4104-1558-9 (alk. paper)
    1. Harvath, Scot (Fictitious character) — Fiction. 2. Intelligence officers — Fiction. 3. Qaida (Organization) — Fiction. 4. Large type books. I. Title.
PS3620.H75A85 2009
813'.6—dc22

                         2009013136

Published in 2009 in arrangement with Atria Books, a division of Simon & Schuster, Inc.

Printed in the United States of America
1 2 3 4 5 6 7 13 12 11 10 09

In our nation's war on terror, a new breed of operator has emerged. Passionately dedicated to their craft, they ignore the trials and hardships of their profession and work tirelessly in the face of limited support and bloated bureaucracies to achieve one singular goal—mission success.

Motivated by a deep and undying love for their country, these operators willingly face intense danger so that America may remain free.

Once labeled "true believers," this term no longer applies. These warriors have become Apostles.

For James Ryan,
Warrior

People sleep peaceably in their beds at night only because rough men stand ready to do violence on their behalf.

— George Orwell

CHAPTER 1

Nangarhar Province, Afghanistan

Next to a stream of icy snowmelt from the Hindu Kush, a small caravan unloaded its contraband. Cases filled with weapons, money, communications equipment, and other gear were placed beneath a rocky overhang and covered with camouflage netting to keep them concealed from overhead surveillance.

A man in his late forties with deep Slavic features stood nearby and supervised. He had blue eyes, medium-length gray hair, and both the clothing and bearing of a local Afghan.

When his team of Pakistani smugglers was done, the man removed a stack of bills and paid them double what he normally did for bringing him into the country. It was a severance package. He wouldn't be using them again. This was going to be his final operation.

He made himself comfortable near a stack of rams' horns that marked a Taliban grave site and watched as the line of smugglers and pack animals disappeared back into the mountains toward Pakistan. Though he couldn't spot them, he knew there were men in the rugged hills above, men with sophisticated weapons — weapons he had provided to them — who were keeping him in their sights.

Twenty minutes later, three muddy Toyota Hilux double-cab pickup trucks appeared from the other end of the valley. The convoy splashed across the fast-moving stream and drove up to the overhang. As the trucks rolled to a stop, young men with thick, dark beards and Kalashnikovs jumped out.

Like the man next to the rams' horns, they were dressed in traditional Afghan clothing known as *salwar kameez* — baggy cotton trousers that stopped just above the ankle and loose-fitting tunics that ended just above the knee. They all wore winter coats that came to midthigh. Many slung warm wool blankets referred to locally as *patoos* over their shoulders to further ward off the cold. Upon their heads they wore *pakols,* the wide wool hat encircled by a thick, rolled brim made famous by the mujahideen during their war with the Soviets.

The men worked quickly and efficiently. Once the gear was loaded, the blue-eyed man climbed into the front passenger seat of the lead vehicle, the driver popped the clutch, and the truck lurched forward.

It was a painful, kidney-jarring ride along a rutted road that followed the snowmelt downstream into the valley. As the truck came down hard into yet another pothole, the men in the backseat erupted in a barrage of Pashtu curses.

The blue-eyed man tuned them out and stared through the spattered windshield. The landscape outside was windswept and barren. It was hard for him to believe that he had been fighting and running operations in this country for over twenty-five years. His blood had been spilled upon its soil on more occasions than he cared to remember and he had watched more men die than anyone ever should.

He loved and hated Afghanistan at the same time. It had taken far more from him than it had ever given. His body was in shambles, as was the small family he had managed to begin over the years during his short visits home. All he was left with in his life was a sweet, innocent boy who had been terribly disfigured.

The blue-eyed man blamed himself. He had known about his wife's alcoholism. He also knew that it grew worse when he was away. Even though he'd been trained to listen to his intuition, he had ignored it when it told him that the woman could no longer properly see to their child. Had he made other arrangements for the boy, had he found a responsible caregiver to see to him while he was away, the fire might never have happened.

But it had happened, and the father wore the guilt of his son's disfigurement across his shoulders much like the *patoos* across the shoulders of the Taliban fighters now riding alongside him.

He tried to forget his pain and to instead focus on his mission. It was one of the most audacious operations his intelligence service had ever considered. If it was successful, he could finally retire and would be so highly rewarded that he and his son would never want for anything else. That success, though, ultimately rested with the man he was about to meet. In the near distance, his destination finally came into sight.

The village, in Nangarhar's rugged Khogyani district, was mostly mud houses, with some made of stone, which were set along either side of the road.

It was austere and colorless, as much of Afghanistan was. Window and door frames were unpainted. Rough-hewn beams jutted out from beneath rooftops, and none of the buildings were more than two stories tall. Dust and children and hard-looking men with guns were everywhere. No women were visible.

They were there, of course; hidden behind the thick mud walls of their houses by Taliban husbands and fathers who forbade them to work, to go to school, or even to go outside without being completely covered and with a male family member accompanying them.

The convoy ground to a halt before a high wall set with two massive double doors. The driver of the lead vehicle tapped his horn three times in quick succession. A small panel opened in the gate and a pair of angry dark eyes peered out. Moments later the doors swung open and the convoy rolled into a typical Afghan compound known as a *kwala*.

When the blue-eyed man climbed out of the truck, he was greeted by one of the Taliban's most notorious, battle-hardened commanders. Mullah Massoud Akhund stood about five-foot-eight, a good three inches shorter than the blue-eyed man, but he had a commanding presence.

Massoud's eyes were the color of flint and possessed with the power to look right through a man. His heavy black beard was streaked with gray. He was only in his late forties, but a life of incessant combat had aged him beyond his years, giving him the appearance of a man twenty years older.

Placing his right hand over his heart in the traditional Afghan greeting, Mullah Massoud nodded slightly to his guest and said, *"Salaam alaikum."*

The blue-eyed man performed the same gesture and replied, *"Wa alaikum salaam."*

Massoud embraced his guest and held him tightly for many moments. The blue-eyed man had learned early in his career that a hug from an Afghan man was a sign of respect. The longer the embrace, the deeper the respect you were held in.

Finally, the commander broke off the hug. "It is good to see you again, Bakht Rawan."

CHAPTER 2

Many suspected that the blue-eyed man was Russian, but it was a topic Mullah Massoud did not like to discuss. There were still dormant animosities, even in his own village, over the long and bloody war the Afghans had fought with the Soviets. For this reason, Massoud addressed the man as Bakht Rawan and not by his given name of Sergei Simonov.

Their relationship stretched back more than twenty years. Before Massoud had joined the Taliban, he had been a fledgling Afghan intelligence operative and Simonov had been his mentor. His code name was Pashtu and meant "running luck," something Massoud felt his mentor possessed in abundance.

The pair politely inquired into each other's health, families, and affairs as Massoud gave orders to his men to unload the trucks. He then motioned for Simonov to follow him inside.

The Russian removed his hiking boots at the door and followed his host. The room was spartanly furnished with two long tables, a low bed, a small wooden desk, and a single chair. It would be more than adequate.

Two of Massoud's men brought in an ancient carpet and unrolled it along the floor. It was a red, elephant-foot pattern known as a Bohkara. Simonov could only imagine what such a rug would fetch in Moscow or St. Petersburg.

Other men entered bringing blankets, a pillow, a power strip, and an extension cord, which would allow him to run his electronic equipment off the compound's generator.

Satisfied that his guest was on his way to being situated, Mullah Massoud informed him that he would see him for tea in twenty minutes.

Simonov thanked his host and closed the door. From the leather holster beneath his tunic, he withdrew his 9mm CZ-75 pistol and placed it on the desk next to a suppressor from his coat pocket. Inside the compound, he had no need for any of his weapons. *"Ze talibano milmayam,"* he said aloud in Pashtu. "I am a guest of the Taliban."

The traditional code of honor among the Pashtun, known as *Pashtunwali,* dictated every aspect of their lives and was very explicit. One of the most important edicts of Pashtunwali dealt with hospitality and the treatment of guests. Once a Pashtun invited someone into his home, he was honor-bound to protect that guest at all costs, even if it meant fighting to his own death to protect him.

As Simonov unpacked his gear, he ran through the arguments Mullah Massoud had initially raised about the operation and how he would counter them if they came up again.

The bottom line was that the time was right for the Taliban to finally move beyond al-Qaeda.

In 1998, two years after seizing majority control of the country, the Taliban had molded Afghanistan into the purest Islamic state on the planet. Their ambassadors were shuttling back and forth to America and were close to signing a peace treaty with the Northern Alliance fighters — the last holdouts in Afghanistan against full Taliban control of the country. The Soviets were long gone, self-serving Afghan warlords were being dealt with, and the Taliban were on the brink of bringing stability to their war-ravaged nation. In short, they had achieved almost everything they wanted.

Then Osama bin Laden and his al-Qaeda organization carried out the bombings of the American embassies in Kenya and Tanzania. The Americans had responded by firing missiles into Afghanistan. Angered, Taliban leader Mullah Omar broke off peace talks and disengaged himself from the Americans. The war with the Northern Alliance picked up speed and things gradually deteriorated. Just when it looked as if things couldn't get worse, September 11 happened and the Americans invaded. In short, every problem the Taliban had could be traced to al-Qaeda. It was time for a divorce.

Mullah Massoud had always been smart enough to see al-Qaeda for what they really were — a liability. They were foreigners who put their global jihad ahead of everything else. They didn't care what happened to Afghanistan and its people in the process. Massoud, on the other hand, did, and that was why he had agreed to go along with Simonov's operation.

In typical Russian fashion it was elegantly simple. Simonov had found a way to deal al-Qaeda a death blow, but to make it look as if the Americans had been behind it. As the ineffective Mullah Omar drowned with the weight of the dying al-Qaeda organization tied around his neck, Mullah Massoud would step into the vacuum of power and would take over as supreme leader of the Taliban.

With the windfall they intended to reap from al-Qaeda's demise, they could purchase all the weaponry and hardware they needed. They would mount a devastating offensive against the Americans and their coalition partners and send them running from Afghanistan like whipped dogs. And what the Russians asked for in return for their help was a pittance.

The Russians had learned their lesson and had no desire to repeat the mistakes of the 1980s. Afghanistan had been a Soviet graveyard. This time, they wanted nothing to do with the governance of Afghanistan, only the ability to help increase and share in its prosperity. How the Russians would use their influence in the region was of no concern to the Taliban. As long as they stayed out of Afghan affairs, the relationship showed significant promise.

Simonov unpacked his satellite uplink equipment and reflected on how ironic it was that Russia was now funding and orchestrating instability within Afghanistan, exactly as America had done to the Soviets in the 1980s.

But the Russians needed to be very careful. Times had changed. America had many partners in Afghanistan, and if Russia's role in promoting insurgency was ever proven, the international repercussions would be extraordinarily severe.

He was still running these points through his head when he heard a crash as his door was kicked in.

The Russian reached for his CZ atop the desk, but caught himself and stopped. Standing at rigid attention in the doorway was Mullah Massoud's mentally challenged brother, Zwak.

He wore a blue hooded sweatshirt and boots two sizes too big. One of his pants legs was rolled up to just beneath his knee and he clutched an AK-47 to his side, the top of its barrel wrapped with blue tape. He had the "official" job of guarding the village well and watching for spies. Carrying the rifle was a source of pride and made him feel equal to the other warriors who fought for his brother.

Zwak was thirty-one years old, stood only a hair above five feet tall, and had a coarse, dark beard that followed his jaw line, exactly like his brother's. Each morning the two men shaved their upper lips together in a cracked mirror in the courtyard. When not searching for spies or guarding the well, spending time with his brother was Zwak's favorite thing to do.

Simonov had great respect for how Massoud treated his childlike brother. He never mistook the man's compassion for weakness. He knew that Massoud was anything but weak, and as soon as his country was rid of al-Qaeda, he would be the Taliban commander under whom the country would be united.

The Russian studied his visitor. An intent look of satisfaction spread across Zwak's face as he realized he had startled Simonov. He was exceedingly proud of his accomplishment.

Sergei approached and gave the man a military inspection, which Zwak took very seriously. He stood as straight as he could while the Russian examined his clothing and then his weapon.

Shaking his head, Simonov crossed the room to retrieve something from his pack. Zwak removed his boots and stepped inside to see what the Russian was doing.

When Sergei turned, he held in his hands a pair of white hi-top basketball shoes. Despite their hatred for the West and Western culture, the only thing the Taliban prized as highly as their rifles was basketball shoes.

Zwak couldn't believe his eyes. Simonov

smiled as he handed them to him. "Don't let anyone take these from you," he said, though he didn't believe there was anyone in Afghanistan dumb enough to rob the brother of Mullah Massoud.

Forgetting custom, Zwak dropped the shoes on the floor and slid his feet inside. They weren't a perfect fit, but they were much better than the oversized boots he had been wearing for as long as he could remember.

Zwak tested the shoes by bouncing up and down on his toes. His excitement registered in the smile on his face.

But as he remembered his purpose for coming to the room, his smile faded and Zwak was all business. "Tea," he said. "Tea now."

The Russian smiled back and said in Pashtu, "Tell your brother I will be there in a moment."

Snatching up his rifle, Zwak slung it over his shoulder and headed for the door. As he reached it he turned back around. Simonov assumed a thank you was coming. Instead, Zwak repeated, "Tea now."

"Soon," said the Russian, "tea soon," and he watched as the man left his room and stepped out into the courtyard to show off his new shoes to his brother's Taliban soldiers.

Walking over to his pack, Simonov withdrew a picture of his son, Sasha. It was the last photo that had been taken of the boy before the accident.

He pinned the picture to the wall above the desk and placing a kiss upon his fingers, pressed them against the photo. "Soon, Sasha. Soon," he said.

Grabbing a folder full of photographs, the Russian took a deep breath before heading toward the door. Everything depended now on whether Mullah Massoud was still 100 percent committed to his plan.

Stepping into the courtyard, Simonov prayed that the American he had selected would be the right bait for his trap. Time and the new president of the United States would tell.

CHAPTER 3

Kandahar Province
Monday (Three weeks later)

Dr. Julia Gallo sat on a dusty carpet and eyed the cracked mud bricks and exposed timbers of the tiny room. She didn't need to look at her interpreter to know that he was watching her. "Ask again," she said.

Sayed cleared his throat, but the question wouldn't come. They were in dangerous territory. It was bad enough that the young American doctor dragged him to the most godforsaken villages in the middle of nowhere, but now she was openly trying to get them killed. If the Taliban knew what she was doing, they'd *both* be dead.

The five-foot-six Afghan with deep brown eyes and black hair had a wife, three children, and a not-so-insignificant extended family that relied on him and the living he made as an interpreter.

For the first time in his twenty-two-year-old life, Sayed had something very few Afghans ever possessed — hope; hope for himself, hope for his family, and hope for the future of his country. And while what he did was dangerous, there was no need to make it any more so by taunting the specter of death. Dr. Gallo, on the other hand, seemed to have a remarkably different set of priorities.

At five-foot-ten, Julia was a tall woman by most standards, but by Afghan standards she was a giant. And although she kept her long red hair covered beneath an Afghan headscarf known as a *hijab,* she couldn't hide her remarkable green eyes and the fact that she was a very attractive woman. She was a graduate of the obstetrics and gynecology program at Rush University Medical Center in Chicago, and ten years her translator's senior. And while she might have shared Sayed's vision for the future of Afghanistan, she had her own opinions of how best to bring it about.

In a country where most parents didn't name their children until their fifth birthday because infant mortality rates were so high, Dr. Gallo and others like her had made a huge difference. Infant mortality was down more than 18 percent since the Taliban had been ousted. That meant forty thousand to fifty thousand infants who would have died under the old regime were surviving. She should have been thrilled, but for some reason she wasn't. She was unhappy, and that made her push harder to bring about change.

Gallo knew she wasn't just rocking the cultural boat on these visits out into the countryside, she was shooting holes in the stern and reloading, but she didn't care. The Taliban were a bunch of vile, misogynistic bastards who could rot in hell, as far as she was concerned.

"Ask her again," she demanded.

Sayed knew the answer and was certain Dr. Gallo did too. It was embarrassing for the women to have to answer, yet she pressed her point anyway. It was the setup for a message she had taken to proselytizing on a regular basis. Gallo had become a zealot in her own right, no different from the Taliban, and as much as Sayed admired her, this was going to be their last trip out of Kabul together. He would respectfully ask their NGO, CARE International, not to assign him to her anymore. He wasn't going to die because of her.

Dr. Gallo had always been complicated. She never spoke about her family or personal life, no matter how many hours they spent driving together or how many opportunities Sayed offered her. She either turned the conversation back to him, asking questions she already knew the answers to, or she simply sat in the passenger seat staring out the window. Sayed had given up trying to connect with her and now was done trying to understand her.

Two pairs of eyes lowered toward the floor as Sayed capitulated and asked the women Dr. Gallo's question once more. A long silence followed. The translator was tempted to fill the uncomfortable void, but Gallo held up her hand to quiet him. Finally, the elder of the two women responded in Pashtu.

Julia listened, and when they were finished, Sayed translated.

"They traded the girl to pay off her father's debt," he said.

"Like some sort of farm animal," Gallo replied. "Tell them they don't have to live like this. I don't care what kind of arrangement the men of this village have with the Taliban, women have rights, *even* in Afghanistan. But unless they know their rights, they can't begin to exercise them. The first step is for them to get educated. There is a school less than five kilometers from here. Why aren't they going to it?"

Sayed shook his head. "You know why."

Julia fixed him with her intense green eyes. "Because it's dangerous?"

The interpreter didn't reply.

"More dangerous than being beaten by your husband or sold off because your father's opium fields failed to produce?" Julia waited for an answer and when none was offered, she stated, "We need to explain to them that they have options."

"You say this even though the Taliban ride by on motorbikes and spray children and teachers who dare go to school with acid. It is easy for you to demand that these women exercise their 'rights,' as you say. But I'm sorry, Dr. Gallo," said Sayed as he stood. "I can't do this anymore."

"Can't do what?"

The young man didn't have the energy to explain. He had told Dr. Gallo repeatedly that what she was doing was dangerous for both of them.

"I'll wait for you outside at the car." Turning, he exited the room and closed the door quietly behind him.

Julia felt a stab of regret. Sayed was the best interpreter she had ever worked with. They had spent countless hours together in some of the wildest, most remote regions of the country. She had learned that she could trust him and he was invaluable to her. She had contributed money out of her own pocket to make sure he was paid better than any of the other translators CARE used, and she had also spearheaded the effort to get the organization to pay to send him to medical school. He couldn't leave her. Not now. She wouldn't let him. They had a long drive back to Kabul. She would talk to him. She'd promise to relax her rhetoric a bit.

Shifting her attention back to her patients, Julia employed her limited Pashtu medical vocabulary and completed the exam.

CHAPTER 4

Twenty minutes later, with the sun beginning to sink low in the sky, Dr. Gallo exited
the mud-walled *kwala* with her olive-drab
medical bag slung over her shoulder and
her hijab tightly wrapped around her head.
Afghan men, many with AK-47s propped
nearby, squatted in a circle chatting. They
fell silent and stared at the American woman
as she walked past.

Julia found Sayed leaning against the hood
of their faded Nissan Patrol smoking a cigarette. "Ready to go?" she asked.

Sayed nodded as Julia opened the rear passenger door, tossed her bag onto the backseat, and climbed in front.

Taking one last drag, Sayed tamped out
his cigarette on the bumper and slid the re-
mainder into the pack for later.

It took several slams before the latch
caught and his door would stay shut. After
starting the engine, the interpreter ground

the vehicle into first gear and pulled out.

Julia tried to read his face as he picked his way down the dusty road from the village. If Sayed felt any anger toward her, he didn't show it.

As she tried to come up with the right words to say, he beat her to the punch. "I'm going to ask to be reassigned."

Julia didn't know how to reply. After everything she had done for him, she felt betrayed. But she knew she was being selfish. She had met his wife and his children. She understood. She had been putting him at greater and greater risk. In all fairness, it actually said a lot about their friendship that he had kept going into the countryside with her for as long as he had.

With no words that seemed to suit the moment, she said what was in her heart. "I understand."

Sayed smiled again. "I will pray for you, Dr. Gallo, and for your work."

The redheaded American was about to respond when they came around a bend and she noticed three green Afghan National Army pickup trucks blocking the road ahead.

"Roadblock," said Sayed.

Julia retrieved her bag from the backseat with her ID. "Why would they have a roadblock out here? We're in the middle of no-where."

"I don't know," he replied, eyeing the soldiers manning the 7.62mm machine guns mounted atop the vehicles' roll bars. "We'll have to stop."

Julia nodded. Running the roadblock was out of the question. ANA soldiers were poorly disciplined and would open fire with the slightest provocation — stopping only when they had exhausted their ammo.

"Don't worry," he said as he rolled down his window. "I'm sure it's just routine."

Julia looked at the soldiers. They seemed keyed up, tense. "Keep the car running," she said quietly.

The interpreter nodded and fished his ID out of his pocket. As their vehicle slowed to a stop, they were surrounded by the heavily armed soldiers.

Sayed placed his hand over his heart, nodded, and bade the men, *"Salaam alaikum."*

No one returned the greeting.

A captain appeared at Sayed's window and snapped his fingers for his ID. The young Afghan complied and handed over his papers.

Without even looking at the documents, the captain ordered him out of the SUV. Julia put her hand upon his arm. *Something*

34

definitely wasn't right.

Sayed smiled at her and gently pulled his arm away. When he had trouble opening his door, the captain got angry and wrenched it open from the outside.

Sayed tried to explain that the door was unreliable, but the captain wasn't listening. He grabbed the young man by the back of the neck and threw him to the ground.

Inside the truck, Julia gasped and covered her mouth. *What was going on?*

Sayed tried to rise to his feet, but the captain kicked him in the ribs. Wheezing, the Afghan fell back to the ground.

Julia had seen enough. She began to open her door, but it was kicked shut by one of the soldiers, who then seated his rifle in his shoulder and pointed the muzzle right at her head.

Gallo turned her attention back to Sayed. She could see him through the open driver's side door, lying on the ground with his arms wrapped around his sides.

He tried to speak, but the captain ignored him and brought his boot back for another kick. This one landed under the interpreter's chin and snapped his head backward.

Julia screamed as Sayed fell unconscious and a stream of blood began to trickle from his mouth.

The captain barked orders at the soldiers, and Julia knew it was about to be her turn. With her elbow, she drove the door lock home and leaped for the driver's seat.

One of the soldiers standing near the captain saw what she was doing and rushed to stop her. But instead of shooting her, he reached inside the vehicle and grabbed hold of her clothing.

Julia had removed a scalpel from her bag and slashed at him wildly. The man roared in pain and fell backward.

With his hold broken, Julia forced the car into gear, revved the engine, and released the brake.

Immediately, there was a deafening chorus of gunfire as the Nissan's tires were flattened and the chassis dropped onto the rims. Now, Julia was in real trouble.

She let go of the scalpel and held up both of her hands. With two soldiers covering him, the captain extricated her from the vehicle and slammed her up against its side.

She saw a flash of skin as the back of his hand came forward and cracked into the bone of her cheek just beneath her left eye.

The force of the blow caused Julia's vision to dim. Her knees shook and she felt she was about to lose consciousness.

The captain stepped away while his men

kept her pinned against the SUV.

As Julia's senses returned, she had the distinct impression that they were about to do something very bad. She felt certain that she was going to be raped. But these men had something much worse in mind.

The captain squatted and began slapping Sayed's face to bring him around. It took several minutes to revive him, but when he finally came to, the captain called over additional men to pick him up. They held him until he could stand on his own and then they stepped away.

Without saying a word, the captain drew his pistol from his holster and Julia's stomach dropped. She opened her mouth to plead for the interpreter's life, but as she did, a soldier drove his fist into her midsection and knocked the wind from her body.

As she gasped for air, she saw the captain place his weapon against the side of Sayed's head and watched in horror as he pulled the trigger.

CHAPTER 5

McLean, Virginia
Wednesday (Two days later)

The bright spring day stood in sharp contrast to the new president's mood. Robert Alden had suggested a walk outside as a way to allow things to cool down between himself and the woman he was with. So far, it wasn't working.

"You and I both know," said the president's guest, "that the CIA is so risk-averse that even if you showed them where their asses were, they'd be afraid to grab on with both hands."

Stephanie Gallo was perhaps one of the biggest reasons forty-eight-year-old Robert Alden now occupied the highest office in the world. Gallo had not only helped orchestrate the Alden campaign for president and been one of its biggest donors and best fundraisers, she had delivered the mainstream media to him on a silver platter.

She was an entertainment titan who, upon the death of her husband in the early 1970s, had spun a "midmarket newspaper and two shitty AM radio stations" into a series of conglomerates that owned newspapers, movie studios, and television stations around the world. She was the person who had convinced Alden not only to run for president, but that he would win.

Would. It was an interesting choice of words. She had not said *could* win, but *would* win. She was that confident. And she was right. The election had been a blowout. Alden's mild-mannered opponent never stood a chance.

To secure this incredible win, Gallo had insisted that her media strategy be at the very center of the campaign. It was the hub that everything else radiated out from. They had worked tirelessly and it had paid off with overwhelming dividends. Alden owed Gallo a tremendous debt, which made the discussion they were having that much more difficult.

"If we can't remain calm about this, Stephanie, there's no way we'll be able to think clearly."

"Remain calm?" Gallo shot back. "How calm would *you* be if it was your daughter

those animals had kidnapped?"

If Robert Alden hadn't already been married, he and Stephanie Gallo would have made a stunning couple. The new president was athletic and handsome. He stood six-foot-two with dark hair and hazel eyes and had a magnetic personality that drew people instantly to him.

At fifty-five, Stephanie Gallo was seven years his senior, but didn't look a day over forty. She was an incredibly attractive woman with auburn hair, blue eyes, and a large, sumptuous mouth. She was tall, five-foot-ten when not in heels, and had a very alluring physique.

An international celebrity in her own right, Gallo competed successfully in a largely male world and made no apologies for doing it as a woman. Women around the world adored her not only for her sense of style, which retained just a hint of sex appeal, but also for her frank belief that God had blessed women with curves and that any woman who tried to exercise her body into a replica of a teen-aged boy's was a fool.

But despite everything she had going for her, all of the notoriety, money, and power, right now she needed a man: this man. Only Robert Alden could effect her daughter's release, and Stephanie Gallo was determined to make that happen — no matter what it took.

Alden put his hand on her shoulder. "I understand how you must feel."

Gallo didn't like being patronized. "Really? Then why aren't you doing anything? We own that fucking country, for God's sake. Agree to the terms!"

And here they were again, back at the beginning of the argument. Alden tried to explain his position once more. "Stephanie, I agree with the CIA's assessment. These people kidnapped Julia for this very reason. They knew you would come to me and ask me to intervene.

"The terrorist imprisoned in Kabul, the one they want for Julia, is an al-Qaeda operative — a very bad one. Do you know how many high-level Afghan government officials he has helped kill? For the Afghan government, this is like capturing Lee Harvey Oswald, John Hinkley, and John Wilkes Booth all at once. We can't say that we want Afghanistan to obey the rule of law only when it serves our interests. Besides, I ran on a platform of being tough on terrorists and not repeating any of the mistakes of my predecessors."

"Screw your platform and screw your predecessors," snapped Gallo. "We're talking about Julia's life, for Christ's sake."

"I'm sorry, Stephanie. I —"

"What do you mean, you're *sorry*? Are you telling me that we can't convince the Afghans to give us this Mustafa Khan for twenty-four hours, forty-eight tops, so that we can get my daughter back?"

"And if we lose him?" asked Alden.

"Then flood the skies with Predators and retask all of our satellites over Afghanistan. I don't care. I just want her back."

"I know you do. I do too. I also care about what happens in Afghanistan. You've got to know that this is not easy for me."

Gallo scowled at the president. "This is your first chance to really exercise your power, and you're afraid to use it. That's what I think."

Alden could feel his blood pressure rising, and he fought to keep it under control. "I warned you both about this. Julia knew the risks when she took that job over there."

"That doesn't change anything."

"Stephanie, I've explained to you how this works. The Afghans take the lead in kidnapping investigations within their own country — even those of American citizens. The CIA, everyone at our embassy in Kabul, and our entire military apparatus in theater are doing everything they can to get

Julia back."

"Except giving her kidnappers the one thing they've asked for."

Alden shook his head sadly.

"You're the president of the United States. You're telling me you can't tell the Afghans that Khan is part of a larger investigation we are running and that we need to interrogate him in our facility at Bagram? Once we trade him for Julia and get her back, we can hunt him down ourselves. If the Afghans caught Khan once, we should be able to catch him a second time with no problem."

"First of all, the Afghans got lucky because someone tipped them off. Second, what you're asking me to do is dishonest, and that's not how I operate."

Gallo stared at Alden and let the president's statement hover between them like a lit stick of dynamite.

It didn't take Alden long to get uncomfortable. His guest didn't have to say a word. He knew what she was thinking. "Listen, Stephanie, we're going to get Julia back. I promise."

"I'm sorry, but your promise is not good enough. You need to start doing more. A *lot* more."

"Or what?"

Gallo's eyes bore right into Alden's. "Or

your presidency is going to be one of the shortest in U.S. history."

"Are you threatening me?" he asked.

"You're damn right I'm threatening you. We've lost two days. It's time for you to get her back."

"And if I don't?"

"Then," said Gallo, choosing her next words carefully, "the world is going to quickly find out that the new American president was not only an accessory to the deaths of four innocent people, but actively conspired to cover it up."

Fifteen yards away, in the thick blanket of trees that bordered Stephanie Gallo's equestrian estate, a young Secret Service agent froze dead in her tracks.

CHAPTER 6

Rockwood, Maine
Thursday

Scot Harvath pounded down the abandoned logging road with his enormous white Caucasian Ovcharka right by his side.

A former Navy SEAL who, until recently, had been the nation's top counterterrorism operative, Harvath was in his late thirties, five-foot-ten, with a handsome, rugged face, sandy brown hair, and bright blue eyes.

His dog, Bullet, stood nearly forty inches at the shoulder and weighed almost two hundred pounds. Caucasian Ovcharkas, or Caucasian Sheepdogs, as their name translates to, had been the breed of choice for the Russian military and the former East German border patrol. They were exceedingly fast, fiercely loyal, and absolutely vicious when it came to guarding their territory and those closest to them. If ever a dog and its owner resembled each other, it was these two.

Harvath and his girlfriend, Tracy, had spent their winter in Maine this year. Tracy's grandfather, a former Navy man himself, had a winterized cottage on Moosehead Lake and was glad to see it used.

The peace and quiet had agreed with both of them. The snowshoeing, skiing, hunting, and chopping wood had taken Harvath to an entirely new level of physical fitness. He couldn't remember the last time he had felt this good.

Now, spring had come early and summer appeared to be right on its heels. The snow and ice disappeared almost overnight and the temperature for two weeks straight had been downright balmy.

Harvath had been torn about the upcoming summer. On the one hand, he was excited to be getting back to work. The new president had been very aggressive with his first hundred days. Campaigning on a platform of "change," he had done just that the minute he stepped into the Oval Office — and not necessarily for the better. Robert Alden had singlehandedly eviscerated the nation's intelligence apparatus.

Granted, much of it, especially at the CIA, needed to be ripped out and rebuilt, but for every smart move the man made, he made two more that were downright dangerous for the nation's security. The elimination of the top-secret program where Harvath had been working under the previous administration was a prime example.

Dubbed the "Apex Project," it was buried in a little-known branch of DHS called the Office of International Investigative Assistance, or OIIA for short. The OIIA's overt mission was to assist foreign police, military, and intelligence agencies in helping to prevent terrorist attacks. In that sense, Harvath's mission was in step with the official OIIA mandate. In reality, he was a very secretive dog of war enlisted post 9/11 to be unleashed by the president upon the enemies of the United States anywhere, any time, and with anything he needed to get the job done.

His sole mandate had been to help protect Americans and American interests at home and abroad by leveling the playing field with the world's terrorists. And since they chose not to play by any rules, Harvath wasn't expected to either.

He took the tactics from his enemies that worked and turned those tactics right back on them. He had also invented several of his own along the way. Harvath took no pleasure in the killing he was required to do for his country, but he understood that to keep

America from harm, violent men often had to be met with violence. The men Harvath killed were beyond diplomacy; beyond being reasoned with. Violence was the only language they understood.

President Robert Alden, though, was of a different mind. The winds of change had blown him into office and because of that he believed he had been given a mandate. The hawks had flown high above the American political landscape for eight years; now the doves had taken flight. The American people had spoken. That was democracy and Harvath both understood and respected it, but America wouldn't make its enemies disappear just by putting someone new in the Oval Office. The republic would always need its sheepdogs, no matter which way the political winds blew.

Maybe Alden would get lucky and actually bring about true reform in the American intelligence community, but if what he had done so far was any indication of what was to come, things were not going to get any better any time soon.

Bureaucrats at the CIA and elsewhere were too risk-averse and too concerned with getting promoted to focus on beating America's enemies. The men and women in the field were not getting the resources they needed, nor were they getting even halfway decent management or leadership. The nation spent billions of dollars to find solutions to intelligence problems that shouldn't even exist. Americans slept soundly in their beds at night believing their country had countless James Bonds around the world infiltrating terrorist networks and rogue regimes in order to keep them safe and prevent the next attack. If they only knew the real truth, they'd be marching on D.C. with torches and pitchforks. How nineteen goatherds could do what they did on 9/11 to the most powerful nation on the face of the earth was still beyond Harvath. What puzzled him more was that heads had not rolled at the CIA over the attacks.

Accountability, as well as personal responsibility, had been chucked out the window of American government. It also had been abdicated by the American voter. As long as most Americans could have their McDonald's drive-throughs, listen to their iPods, and watch *American Idol,* they didn't seem to care how negligently the nation's national security apparatus was being run.

Bread and circuses. The Romans had it right. As long as people had food and fun, they didn't care much about the erosion of their nation.

That said, a small and growing number of Americans did care, and as their voices grew, Harvath hoped they would attract more attention to themselves and more attention to what needed to be done. Time was running out for the ineffective "business as usual" system in Washington. One day soon, the American citizenry was going to wake up. Harvath only hoped it wouldn't take another catastrophic attack to make that happen.

For his part, Harvath was glad to have cast off the bureaucratic shackles of Washington. As of June 1, he would start a new position in the private sector with a private intelligence-gathering company. Not only would he continue to use his full skill set in the service of his country, he'd also be increasing his income several times over. It looked like the perfect win-win situation, and no matter what Harvath did, he was always about winning.

He hit the seven-mile mark on his run and clicked the button on his Kobold chronograph to halt the stopwatch. He slowed to a walk and used the bottom of his shirt to wipe the sweat from his face. When he looked down at his dog, he noticed something was wrong. The hair on Bullet's back was standing straight up.

They were deep in moose territory and

there was always the possibility of an encounter with a black bear or a bobcat, but they tended to shy away from humans, unless they had young with them and you got too close.

Harvath stopped walking and tried to discern what was bothering Bullet. As he did, the dog began growling. They were less than fifty yards from where Harvath had left his SUV, and that was the direction Bullet's attention seemed drawn to.

Something told him he'd better get control of his dog, but when he reached for his collar, Bullet took off.

Harvath yelled for him to stop, but the dog kept going. For a fraction of a second, Harvath stood transfixed. It was like watching a lion charge across the savanna.

The beauty of the moment was short-lived. The dog was likely headed for danger, and Harvath took off after him.

He soon disappeared into the trees near where Harvath had parked his truck and began barking. It wasn't his normal bark, and Harvath was now certain that something was very wrong.

Running at a full-out sprint, he came around a stand of trees and noticed the front door of his Trailblazer was wide open, and parked right behind the SUV, blocking it in, with its engine still running, was a blacked-out Chevy Tahoe.

Bullet stood on his hind legs with his huge front paws pressed against the Tahoe's driver's-side window. He was barking even louder and more angrily than before, his long, sharp teeth gnashing together.

Harvath drew the Taurus TCP .380 he jogged with and approached the Tahoe. As he got closer, he saw that it had government plates. He didn't know what it was doing here, but he didn't like it.

Leaving Bullet to distract whoever was inside, Harvath kept his gun out of sight and approached the passenger-side window. Sitting in front were two men of medium build with short hair and dark suits. They looked like Feds, Secret Service or maybe FBI, but that still didn't explain what they were doing in the middle of nowhere parked behind *his* SUV and why one of his doors had been opened.

Harvath had always lived by the maxim *have a smile for everyone you meet and a plan to kill them.* It was what had kept him alive in his particularly dangerous line of work. The key was in striking the right balance between healthy suspicion and crippling paranoia; not an easy feat with the number of enemies Harvath had made over the years.

Part of the appeal of Maine had been that nobody knew him here and he could relax. It was a plan that had been working right up until just a few moments ago.

Tightening his grip on his weapon, Harvath tapped the glass with his free hand and caught the men inside by surprise.

The suit in the passenger seat lowered his window, but only partway. "Jesus Christ," he exclaimed. "Is that your dog?"

"And my truck," replied Harvath, nodding toward the SUV the men had blocked in.

"You want to call him off?"

After scanning the inside of the Tahoe, Harvath whistled. Bullet growled for a few seconds, then leaped down and came around to Harvath's side of the Tahoe.

"What's your name?" demanded the passenger.

Harvath didn't like the man's attitude. "William Howard Taft," he replied. "What's yours?"

Cutting off his less-than-affable partner, the driver answered, "I'm Benson. He's Wagner. We're United States Secret Service."

As if they had rehearsed this a million times, both men reached into their jackets in unison, ostensibly to remove their credentials.

"Whoa, whoa, whoa," said Harvath. "Let's

take it easy. Nobody needs to be in a hurry."

Benson motioned for Wagner to relax, and, using his left hand, he pulled back the left side of his suit jacket to show Harvath what he was doing. Slowly he slid his thumb and forefinger into his inside pocket and retrieved his credentials. He then opened his ID wallet and extended his arm toward Harvath. "We're from the Portland office."

"What were you doing in my truck?"

"It was unlocked," interjected Wagner.

Harvath ignored him and kept his eyes on Benson.

"We were looking to see if you'd left a map or some indication of which direction you were running," answered the driver.

"Why?"

"We needed to speak with you as soon as possible. Your girlfriend . . ." said Benson, his voice trailing off as he replaced his credentials and looked down at a notepad on his armrest for the name. "Tracy. She told us we could probably find you out here. She said this was where you normally run."

"She didn't mention that dog, though, did she?" added Wagner angrily. "That fucking thing almost bit me. It's like a goddamn polar bear. I'm lucky I got back into the car in one piece."

Harvath patted Bullet on the head and smiled. Benson seemed okay, but he didn't care much for this other guy, Wagner. "Good dog," he said to Bullet, and then, turning back to Benson, asked, "What do you want?"

"The president needs to see you," the man replied.

"Which one?"

"The new one. President Alden."

The name still took some getting used to for Harvath. *"Alden?"* he repeated. "Why does he want to see me?"

Benson shook his head. "No idea. We were told to find you and transport you to Greenville Municipal. There's an aircraft waiting there to take you to him."

Wagner looked out his window at Bullet, who began growling at him again.

"I don't think so," replied Harvath as he covertly tucked his weapon into his waistband, covered it with his shirt, and prepared to walk away.

"Mr. Harvath," insisted Benson, "we were told that whatever the president wants to discuss with you, it's very important and very time-sensitive. That's why we came all the way out here to find you."

Harvath had no idea what Alden could possibly want with him, but based on what he had seen of the man's judgment, it wasn't anything Harvath wanted to be involved with. If the new president was interested in him, he should have thought of that before he fired him and Harvath had found a new job. "Please tell the president that I respectfully declined. I don't work for Washington anymore."

"In that case," said Benson as he slowly reached for the glove compartment and opened it, "we were asked to give you this."

The agent withdrew a sat phone and handed it to his partner. Wagner, still wary of the dog, balanced it on the partly open window until Harvath took it.

"What's this?" he asked.

"A snowcone maker," said Wagner as he rolled his window back up. "You'd think a smart guy like William Howard Taft could figure that out."

Harvath took the window rolling up as a sign that their meeting was over and backed Bullet away from the Tahoe just as Benson put it into reverse.

Moments later the government SUV U-turned onto the deserted logging road and disappeared.

CHAPTER 7

The interior of the Super Puma EC225 helicopter was as elegant as any private jet Harvath had ever flown on. White hand-stitched
leather seating was complemented by black
Hermès pillows and polished chrome tables.

While it was a little cold for Harvath's
taste, he had to give the helicopter's owner,
whoever he was, points for style. When he
had been told that transportation was standing by, this was not at all what he had envisioned. President Alden had surprised him.
Whether that was a good thing had yet to be
seen. Harvath was reserving judgment until
he had actually met the man face-to-face.

He had returned home with the satellite
phone and set it upon the kitchen table while
he went upstairs to take a shower and change.
When he came down, Tracy was waiting for
him with two mugs of coffee. They had gone
back and forth about what to do, with Tracy

playing devil's advocate throughout. She knew that as much as Harvath was fully prepared to take on his new job, he still missed his old one. He was a patriot, and serving his country was his ultimate calling.

In the end, Harvath agreed that it couldn't hurt to talk. Blowing the new president off, even if he had eliminated the project Harvath had worked on, was probably not the best of ideas — especially with what he did for a living. At some point, he could very well need the president's help. The least he could do was to hear the man out.

Harvath went outside and activated the sole number that had been programmed into the satellite phone. On the second ring, the president himself answered.

Alden was polite, but brief. He was in Maine and wanted to see Harvath in person, hence the helicopter he had standing by. He was not at liberty to explain things over the phone and would fill Harvath in when they met. Though Harvath had not voted for Alden and questioned many of his policies, he still respected the office and agreed to go meet him. Within twenty minutes, Harvath was airborne, and within forty more he had arrived at Seal Harbor.

Seal Harbor was a very affluent New England enclave located on the southern end of Maine's Mount Desert Island. While the better-known town of Bar Harbor had been attracting celebrities, tourists, and politicians for generations, Seal Harbor was where the truly rich and powerful could enjoy the island's thick forests, gently sloping mountains, and jagged coastline without being bothered.

One such resident was a lifestyle and home-decorating maven with an immensely popular television series. With her primary residence in Manhattan and other homes in Connecticut, upstate New York, and Nantucket, her sixty-two-acre Seal Harbor estate was occupied only a fraction of the year. She often loaned out the twelve-bedroom, pink granite "summer" cottage, which had been built by a wealthy automobile family in the early 1900s, to friends and business associates. Invisible from the road and completely insulated from the public, the estate allowed its guests to get away from it all and relax in an intensely private setting. It was exactly this high degree of privacy that had attracted the estate's current guests.

The Super Puma's tires touched down on an impeccably manicured esplanade of grass. When the air-stairs were lowered, Harvath exited the helicopter and was met by a pair of Secret Service agents, who led him to the main house.

They walked up a paved path and entered the kitchen via a breezeway. With its retro appliances and vintage furnishings, the room gave one the feeling of having stepped back in time.

After Harvath was screened for weapons, he was taken down a paneled hallway to a dramatic wooden staircase. Following its red and gold runner to the top of the stairs, he was met by another pair of Secret Service agents, who accompanied him down a long wainscoted hall to a pair of mahogany doors with shiny brass hardware.

Standing guard there was a lone, female Secret Service agent. Having been recruited to the former president's protective detail before being tasked to the Apex Project, Harvath still maintained a lot of contacts in the Service. He was aware of how Robert Alden had cleaned house and forced "improvements" there as well.

His intent had been to demonstrate more diversity in the agents who surrounded him. It was a noble endeavor, but like many other well-intentioned efforts Alden had undertaken, he had rushed through it like a bull in a china shop, more concerned with appearances than results.

As part of the president's mandate, many

exceptional agents were promoted to his detail, as were many less-than-exceptional agents. Some of the most experienced agents were then asked to step aside and take other assignments outside the White House in order to make room for the younger agents Alden wanted to pull up through the ranks. The president was not only gambling with his life, he was also gambling with the lives of all those sworn to protect him.

The Secret Service had tried to dissuade the president from such a drastic course of action, but no matter how many alternatives they offered him, Alden wanted the results he wanted and he wanted them immediately. His childish refrain of "I won" was often heard in the White House and was intended to end all discussions. It created much resentment and was beneath the dignity of the office, but the president didn't seem to care. Such was the depth of his insecurity.

Looking at the fresh-faced, blond-haired, blue-eyed agent on the door, Harvath wondered if she was one of those who had been recently rocketed to the top of the Secret Service ticket. Over his career, he had known a lot of extremely qualified female agents, all of whom had been serious ass-kickers. They had also all paid their dues and earned their stripes. Promoting anyone in this job based on anything other than talent, experience, training, and commitment was a potentially tragic mistake.

Harvath tried to push the thought from his mind. Alden had made his bed and he would have to lie in it. The president's policies, as well as the makeup of his protective detail, were not Harvath's problems.

Smiling at the agent, Harvath waited as she knocked and then opened the door for him. Once he had stepped inside, she closed the door and resumed her post in the hall.

The room looked like a study in a British manor house, with soaring ceilings, exposed beams, and tall leaded-glass windows. The walls were covered in silk and exhibited a hodgepodge of oil paintings hung salon style. At the end of the room, near a fireplace large enough for a hockey faceoff, were two couches. Sitting upon the couches were two people Harvath had never met, but whom he recognized instantly.

The first was President Robert Alden. The second, whose presence made no sense to him, was one of the president's biggest donors and supporters, media mogul Stephanie Gallo.

Both stood and greeted Harvath as he crossed to the sitting area.

"Thank you for coming," said the president, as he shook Harvath's hand. "Scot Harvath. I'd like to introduce you to Mrs. Stephanie Gallo."

"I'm pleased to meet you, Mr. Harvath," said Gallo.

"Likewise," replied Harvath as he accepted the woman's hand. He had seen her on television and in countless magazines, but she was even more stunning in person.

"I hope your flight in was comfortable."

Harvath smiled. "It was very comfortable, but I'm confused."

Gallo arched her perfectly tweezed eyebrows. "About what?"

"When the president promised to bring change to Washington, I didn't expect it to include his Marine Corps helicopters."

Alden chuckled. "You can thank Mrs. Gallo for your transportation, Mr. Harvath. That was her helicopter you flew here on."

"Thank you."

"You're welcome," responded Gallo, not certain whether the man was trying to be charming or if he was being a smartass. She didn't like people she couldn't read. They tended to be difficult to control, which made them difficult to work with.

"Why don't we take a seat?" suggested Alden as he motioned Harvath to one of the couches. On a low table was a silver coffee service. "May I offer you some coffee?"

"Thank you," said Harvath.

Alden filled three cups and once they were all seated with their coffee, the president got down to business. "Mr. Harvath, I've asked you here today on a very sensitive matter. Are you familiar with a man named Mustafa Khan?"

Harvath shook his head. "No. I'm not."

The president opened a dossier and read. "Mustafa Jamal Khan. Dual British/Pakistani citizen, age thirty-six. One of Osama bin Laden's junior lieutenants, Khan was born in the U.K. to Pakistani parents. He attended university in Britain, as well as al-Qaeda training camps in Afghanistan and Pakistan. He has a degree in finance and worked in insurance, international banking, and at the London stock exchange before giving everything up and moving to Karachi and committing himself to al-Qaeda full-time. He was said to have been moving back and forth between Afghanistan and Pakistan's Northwest Frontier Province, where he helped plan a series of deadly terrorist attacks, including the assassinations of several high-ranking Afghan government officials. No one had ever been able to pinpoint his exact location until the Afghan National Army captured him just over a week ago.

They now have him awaiting trial in Kabul and plan to make an example of him."

Closing the folder and handing it to Harvath, Alden then said, "Three days ago, Mrs. Gallo's daughter, Julia, was kidnapped in Afghanistan."

"I'm so sorry about that," said Harvath as he accepted the folder and opened it.

The president continued. "The people holding her have agreed to let her go in exchange for Mustafa Khan."

At that, Harvath looked up from the file. "Do we know who has her?"

"Based on our intelligence, we believe we're dealing with Taliban militants aligned with al-Qaeda."

"Do we think Mullah Omar has a hand in this?"

"Him or someone close to him," replied the president.

"What about the Afghan government?" asked Harvath. "What's their position on this?"

"When the ANA tracked Khan down, he was being protected by a cadre of more than fifteen al-Qaeda bodyguards. The Afghans suffered heavy losses. More than thirty-five of their soldiers died."

"And considering the Afghan government wants to put Khan on trial, I'm guessing they're not exactly amenable to handing him over to us so we can trade him for Mrs. Gallo's daughter?"

Alden gave Stephanie Gallo a glance as if to say, *See? I told you this man knows what he's doing,* and then replied, "No, they're not. And unfortunately, we can't force the Afghans to cooperate."

Harvath sensed that they were beginning to close in on the reason he had been invited to this meeting. "Even though we're talking about an American citizen, the kidnapping happened in Afghanistan, so that means that the Afghans have authority over this."

"Correct," replied Alden.

"I assume CIA, FBI, DIA, State, and all of our military assets in the region are at the disposal of the investigation?"

The president nodded.

Harvath had been down this delicate road before and knew how to read between the lines. "I'm guessing you want to make sure no options go unexplored, is that correct?"

"Exactly," stated Gallo.

Alden held up his hand to quiet her. "Mr. Harvath, I did my homework before asking you here. While I regret having to close the project you were working on under the previous administration, it was by no means a comment on your exceptional abilities or exemplary service to our nation."

Harvath had never been comfortable with fulsome praise and was doubly suspicious when it came from politicians. "Should I assume that the reason I'm here is to assist in the recovery of Mrs. Gallo's daughter?"

"In a manner of speaking," said Alden.

There was something the man wasn't telling him.

The president took a deep breath, his cheeks filling with air, and exhaled slowly before responding. "The Afghans have not made an acceptable amount of progress on Julia's kidnapping. In all fairness, I believe the government in Kabul means well, but they . . ." Alden trailed off as he tried to find the right words.

Gallo had no trouble coming up with them. "The entire government in that shithole of a country is inept and they don't have control over anything. They can't even move around Kabul without heavily armored convoys. The Taliban and al-Qaeda, on the other hand, go wherever they like whenever they like. We've put billions of dollars and countless lives into that country and what do we have to show for it? Not nearly enough, that's for damn sure."

She had hit the nail on the head and all three of them knew it. Harvath looked at the president, who replied, "Mrs. Gallo is a good friend of mine, and I want to do everything possible to get her daughter back."

Harvath looked back down at the file. "It says here that Mrs. Gallo offered a sizable ransom, but it was turned down."

"Ten million dollars," stated the media titan.

It was an incredible amount of money.

"They've made it very clear," said Alden, "that they're interested in one thing and one thing only — the release of Mustafa Khan."

"So what is it exactly you want me to do?" asked Harvath.

"Give him to them," replied Gallo.

Harvath looked up at her. "Excuse me?"

"You heard me," she said. "We want you to travel to Afghanistan, snatch Mustafa Khan out of that prison in Kabul, and exchange him for my daughter."

CHAPTER 8

"This is a pretty dangerous operation we're talking about," said Harvath.

"And from what I understand," replied Gallo, "you're not exactly allergic to getting your hands dirty."

"Pardon me?" he said, not sure he was hearing this woman correctly.

"Are you having a problem understanding me, Mr. Harvath?"

"I think I might be."

Gallo looked at the president and rolled her eyes.

Harvath was growing increasingly displeased with what he sensed was going on here. Friend and major donor or not, it was completely out of bounds for the president to have read a civilian in on his background.

Alden recognized what was happening and tried to clear the air. "Mrs. Gallo was part of my transition team. She has top-secret clearance. To the degree I felt was necessary, she has been filled in on your background."

"Mr. Harvath," continued Gallo. "I'm not looking to hire a clown to make balloon animals at a child's birthday party. I need an experienced operator who can and will do everything necessary to bring my daughter back alive."

Harvath marveled at the irony of it all. Gallo had rallied the media behind Alden's candidacy. She and others like her in the "news" industry were anti-U.S. military, anti-extreme interrogation tactics, anti-Gitmo, and pro-terrorist rights on a daily basis. Now she not only needed, but wanted the help of exactly the kind of person she vilified in her papers and on her television stations. Even more ironic was that she had sought out the help of a president who had run on scaling back his nation's "overaggressive" military and who didn't know the first thing about the military, intelligence, or foreign policy.

But the icing on the cake was that they both appeared to want Harvath to reprise his previous job, the one Alden had just eliminated. It was everything Harvath could do not to laugh out loud. None of the sheep ever wanted a sheepdog around until one of them spotted a wolf. By then, it was often too late.

Even though he had never met Julia Gallo, he felt sorry for her. From what he could tell of her file, she was a good person, dedicated to serving others, who had gone to Afghanistan to make a difference. Harvath knew the Taliban all too well and what they did to their prisoners. For her sake, he hoped that she actually could be rescued.

Harvath looked at the president. He already knew what the answer to his next question would be, but he had to ask it anyway. "If I do accept this assignment, what kind of support can I expect from the White House?"

Alden paused before replying. "Unfortunately, none."

Harvath had figured as much.

"The United States government," continued the president, "cannot be tied to this, or to you, in any way. At this point, you're a private contractor who has been employed by a private American citizen, Mrs. Gallo. That would be the extent of it."

Harvath was quiet. He had spent the better part of his adult life hunting down and killing terrorists, not breaking them out of prisons. It flew in the face of almost everything he stood for. Even so, he knew that Julia Gallo shouldn't be made to suffer just because he disliked the terms of her release.

Gallo sensed hesitancy and tried to pinpoint where it was coming from. "According to what I've been told, you've operated in Afghanistan before, correct?"

"I have," answered Harvath.

"And you've got contacts there."

"A few."

"Enough to get my daughter back?"

"Nothing's ever a slam dunk," replied Harvath. "A lot will depend on the situation on the ground."

Stephanie Gallo placed her cup and saucer on the table. "Let's talk money."

Harvath was uncomfortable with the idea of haggling over the value of saving an American citizen's life. That said, he did know he was being asked to do a very dangerous job that few were as qualified as he to carry out.

He also knew that putting together the kind of team he'd need in Afghanistan wouldn't be cheap.

"It's going to be expensive," he stated as he tried to come up with a rough number in his head.

"What are we talking about?" the media maven asked.

"The right people, weapons, vehicles, intel? It'll run into the six figures very quickly."

Without blinking an eye, Gallo replied. "I'll give you five hundred thousand dollars up front and another five hundred thousand when you get my daughter back. As far as expenses are concerned, I'll have two million dollars wired to a bank of your choosing within the hour. Do we have a deal?"

Harvath looked at the file in his lap and studied the photos of Julia Gallo and her slain interpreter once more. Closing the folder's cover, his eyes met Gallo's and he gave her his answer.

Half an hour later, after sorting out as many of the details as possible, Harvath climbed back aboard the Super Puma helicopter and lifted off. On the other side of the estate, Elise Campbell, the young Secret Service agent who'd been standing post outside the door to the study, had just finished her shift.

As she watched the helicopter rise above the trees and recede into the distance, she wrestled with what she was about to do. Making sure no one was within earshot, she punched a number into her cell phone and raised it to her ear. When the call connected, she thought seriously about hanging up, but instead said, "It's Elise Campbell. We need to talk."

CHAPTER 9

Kabul, Afghanistan
Friday

Stephanie Gallo removed the first hurdles to Harvath's assignment with nothing more than a handful of phone calls. Via a relationship with the board of the international aid organization her daughter worked for, she arranged for Harvath to be listed as a new volunteer and paved the way for an expedited visa for him from the Afghan embassy in D.C.

When Gallo returned Harvath's passport, it was accompanied by a large amount of American currency, which he sewed into the bottoms of his two suitcases.

Gallo arranged to fly him on her Dassault Falcon 7X long-range jet from D.C. to Dubai, and though the aircraft could have easily taken him on to Kabul, he declined. He wanted to attract as little attention to himself as possible when he arrived in Afghanistan. He had even dressed down. In addition to jeans and a long-sleeved Under Armour shirt, he wore a pair of Asolo hiking boots and a low-key Blackhawk Warrior Wear jacket system.

He boarded his Kam Air flight for Kabul in Dubai, and as he passed the cockpit, he picked up the unmistakable odor of "Russian aftershave." The former Soviet pilots who made the hop from the UAE to Afghanistan were notorious for their drinking problems. Harvath hoped the man's drinking wouldn't impair his ability to fly the plane.

He spent an extra couple hundred bucks for first class, which meant that his armrests were held together with blue duct tape instead of gray and that five out of a possible twenty screws bolted his seat to the floor instead of the three the poor folks back in coach had.

Harvath wisely declined the in-flight meal and instead snacked on food he had bought in the duty-free shop before leaving Dubai.

He had spent a good amount of the flight over to the UAE sleeping. He wanted to get adjusted to the nine-and-a-half-hour time difference between Afghanistan and D.C. as quickly as possible. Even though Stephanie Gallo's jet was extremely comfortable, his body still felt tired and stiff.

Had he had the time, he would have preferred a couple of days in Dubai to allow his body to unkink and his internal clock to reset. Going into a place like Afghanistan jetlagged and off his game was a good way to get killed.

Harvath stared out the window and tried to relax his mind as some of the most godforsaken territory on the planet slipped beneath the belly of the aging Kam Air 737.

When they finally came over the jagged mountain peaks just outside Kabul, the sky was a bright blue and Harvath saw that snow remained on many of the mountaintops. It must have still been cold at night, as a thin haze hung over the city from the diesel stoves known as *bukharis* that Afghans used to heat their homes.

As the plane made its steep descent and came in on approach, they flew over Kabul's notorious Policharki prison, where Mustafa Khan was being kept. From above, it looked like a giant wagon wheel surrounded by four very high walls.

Harvath compared the prison and the area around it to the satellite imagery he had seen before leaving the United States. As he did, his thoughts were interrupted by a slight concern. Though the plane was quickly descending, Harvath had never felt the landing gear lowered.

Within seconds, the plane reached one thousand feet and there was a blaring siren from the cockpit as the gear horn announced the pilots' potentially fatal error.

Harvath gripped his duct-taped armrests as the pilots transferred power to the aircraft's large engines and tried to abort the landing.

The Kam Air plane barely missed the rooftops of houses near the end of the runway as it climbed back up, dropped its gear, and came back in for a second attempt.

Safely on the ground, Harvath peeked inside the cockpit at the Russian pilot on his way off the plane. The man was so covered in sweat he looked as if he'd been thrown in a shower fully clothed. *So much for a quiet arrival,* thought Harvath. The landing-gear incident was not a good omen.

Stepping onto the tarmac, Harvath took a deep breath. He'd been on airplanes and inside stale terminal buildings for over twenty-four hours, and though it wasn't the freshest air in the world, it was still better than the recycled stuff he'd been forced to endure.

Kabul International Airport was exactly how he remembered it — bland, boring, and indistinguishable from any number of Third-

World airports he had passed through over his career. The two-story terminal was constructed of concrete covered with opaque, white plaster and blue trim. Though the temperature was somewhere in the forties, airport employees shuffled slowly across the tarmac as if it were three times that. Antennas bristled from every rooftop and a smattering of old planes, many of them Russian, sat off to one side waiting for someone to haul them to the scrap heap.

Adjacent to the commercial portion of the airport was the international military airfield. It was ringed with razor wire and armed checkpoints. Sleek new jets and helicopters stood in marked contrast to the aircraft Harvath had just disembarked from, and it seemed a fitting metaphor for what side of the fence he was now on in his professional life.

Making his way across the tarmac, he entered the terminal building and waited for his suitcases. Once he had them, he proceeded to customs, where the Afghan inspectors were even less interested in him than the Emiratis had been. Muslim nations were not exactly known for being bastions of activity and intellectual curiosity. Nevertheless, had he run into a problem in either country, he carried an envelope of currency in his breast pocket that would have smoothed everything over. *Baksheesh* — the Arabic equivalent for *bribe* — was the universal lubricant that drove the engine of commerce everywhere, but especially in the Islamic world. Having operated all over it, he had watched Baksheesh work miracles.

After filling out an entry card and passing through passport control, Harvath stepped into the bustling main terminal area. Though his demeanor never would have suggested it, he was completely switched on. Afghanistan was incredibly dangerous, especially for foreigners — both military and nonmilitary. And not having had the time to grow a beard or to take other steps to blunt his Western appearance, he looked every bit the outsider.

His eyes scanned the terminal as he made his way toward the front doors. Outside, people waiting to get in stood in line to have their belongings searched and to undergo a pat-down. Watching the absence of skill exhibited by the male and female Afghan National Police officers conducting the physical searches, Harvath guessed it would only be a matter of time before a suicide bomber got inside and detonated near the ticket counter or some other densely packed spot within the airport. As he pushed through the doors, he was glad to leave the building behind.

The muddy parking lot was a mass of people dodging dingy minibuses, soiled SUVs, and derelict sedans. Off to the right, on the edge of the parking lot, was a pair of heavily armored Suburbans surrounded by a group of equally well-armed and -armored men whose appearance screamed "private security contractor." The locals referred to the American contractors as "the Gunmen of Kabul" and the Afghan president had been working hard to get as many of the companies closed down as possible.

He claimed that many of the contracting companies were corrupt and had been using their guns and power to commit murders, smuggle drugs, deal drugs, rob banks, and conduct extortion.

While a handful of contractors had most likely gone rogue and deserved the contempt of both the government and their peers, the majority were honorable, professional outfits that believed in their mission in Afghanistan. They also believed that the Afghan president was on a bogus witch hunt and charged contracting firms exorbitant licensing fees. There were also rumors that the firms being hounded the hardest were those who neglected to pay off the right government bureaucrats in return for administrative protection. The net effect was that the smaller contractors had to get very creative in order to make ends meet, especially with license fees now north of seventy thousand dollars.

On the other side of the lot, leaning against a dented Toyota Land Cruiser, reading a paperback, was one such contractor.

Greg Gallagher, or Baba G, as the Afghans had nicknamed him, which meant Grandfather G, was a fifty-year-old Force Reconnaissance Marine. He and Harvath had been assigned to the same Amphibious Ready Group in the Persian Gulf early in Harvath's career as a SEAL. They had been good friends ever since.

Gallagher had come to Afghanistan four years ago after taking early retirement from the Corps. Most assumed he had come in search of adventure and easy money, and very few people knew the real reason he was there.

Force Recon Marines were similar to SEALs in that they conducted deep reconnaissance operations, carried out strikes and other small-scale offensive actions in hostile or politically sensitive environments, captured and destroyed enemy targets, and engaged in the sophisticated world of direct action. In short, they were the special operations forces of the U.S. Marine Corps and Greg Gallagher was one of their best operators. At least he had been until he shot a young child whose father had charged a roadblock in Iraq.

It was a textbook example of how when everything can go wrong it does. Gallagher and his men were augmenting a checkpoint during a time of heightened violence in Iraq. There was intelligence stating that four different vehicle-borne explosive devices, or VBEDs, were going to attempt to infiltrate downtown Karbala, which was sixty miles southwest of Baghdad and considered by Shia Islam as the second-holiest city after Mecca.

One of Karbala's most popular attractions was the tomb of the prophet Mohammed's grandson, Husayn ibn Ali. Known as the Masjid Al-Husayn, the tomb was believed to be one of the gates to paradise and was a popular Shia pilgrimage location. According to U.S. military intelligence, it was also the bombers' primary target.

The vehicle that Gallagher had fired upon was a white Chevy Caprice. It had swung out from behind the line of cars waiting to be inspected and rushed the checkpoint despite repeated commands to halt. Not even warning shots had deterred its driver. Based upon his rules of engagement, and fearing for the safety of his Marines and the civilians clustered near the checkpoint, Gallagher engaged the vehicle and painted a racing stripe up the center of the hood and right through the windshield of the car.

When the vehicle skidded to a stop just before the checkpoint, everyone braced for impact. Within seconds, the driver leaped from his vehicle and pulled his bloody child from the backseat. He sat down on the road cradling his little boy and wailing in Arabic. When he had ascertained that the car posed no threat, Gallagher — an accomplished medic — personally attended to the boy while the team's interpreter translated for the father.

The boy was very sick and the father had been trying to get him to the hospital. He had no idea there was a checkpoint, and when he had seen the long line of vehicles, he feared his son wouldn't survive the wait, so he had decided to risk coming up the shoulder to ask the Americans if he and his son could be granted permission to pass.

Gallagher called in a helicopter for transport, but it arrived too late. The little Iraqi boy bled out in his father's arms.

Though the father was clearly to blame, Gallagher didn't see it that way. He had pulled the trigger and his bullets had killed that little boy. It made no difference to him that the investigation had absolved him of any wrongdoing and that the vehicle could very well have been carrying an explosive device instead of a sick child.

Tactically, he had done the right thing, but Gallagher couldn't get beyond the fact that he had killed a little boy. Finally, he had left the Corps.

At six-foot-four and 225 pounds, Baba G was a big bear of a man and still looked every inch the Marine. He had an intense pair of dark eyes, a full head of gray hair kept at an acceptable length, and a short, wispy beard that, no matter how hard he tried, refused to come in fuller.

He was wearing jeans and hiking boots, along with a denim shirt and a black Duluth Trading Company carpenter's jacket.

As Harvath neared the truck, Gallagher tossed his book onto the front seat and smiled. "Mister. Mister," he shouted, mimicking the swarm of Afghan cabbies that had been dogging Harvath since he had come out of the terminal. "You need ride?"

"No thanks," replied Harvath as he drew alongside Baba G's Land Cruiser and dropped his bags. "I was told to wait here for a big, handsome Marine. You haven't seen one, have you?"

Gallagher looked over both shoulders.

"There was one here a few minutes ago, but he heard some squid was in town and ran home to lock up his goats."

"Those Marines," chuckled Harvath, "always so protective of their women."

Gallagher pretended to go for his gun, but then stopped and extended his hand. Harvath grasped it and Baba G pulled him in for a hug. "It's good to see you, brother."

"You too," replied Harvath.

Breaking off the hug, Gallagher bent and grabbed Harvath's suitcases. "You're just in time for rush hour," he said as he opened the back of his truck and tossed the bags inside. "Depending on how fast the donkey carts are moving, it could take us at least fifteen minutes to get to the compound."

"I hate Friday traffic in Kabul."

"You and me both," Gallagher replied with a smile as he pointed Harvath around to the passenger side of the Land Cruiser.

Climbing inside, Harvath looked down at the book the Marine had been reading. "Jackie Collins?" he asked as Gallagher climbed into the driver's seat and shut his door.

"The infidel section of the Kabul library is somewhat limited, my friend," Baba G replied, as he slid the gearshift, which was surrounded by expired air fresheners, into first. "But we do what we can. TIA, right?"

85

TIA was an acronym that stood for *This Is Afghanistan.* It was a catchall phrase that unburdened them of the need for long, drawn-out explanations of things. Both men had come to appreciate that Afghanistan was a country and culture unique unto itself. Here, certain things happened certain ways for certain reasons. To try to explain or understand them in a Western frame of mind was a waste of time. Hence, TIA.

Before letting out the clutch, Gallagher reached behind his seat and withdrew a small, insulated cooler bag. "A little something to help you adjust," he said as he handed it to Harvath. "Courtesy of the local Welcome Wagon."

Harvath unzipped the lid and saw that it contained a cold six-pack of sugar-free Red Bull and a 9mm Glock 19. "I feel at home already," he said as he removed the pistol, checked to make sure a round was chambered, and then tucked it into his waistband before popping the tab on a Red Bull.

"Don't get too comfortable," replied Gallagher. "There've been a couple of developments since we last spoke and I don't think you're going to like what I have to report."

CHAPTER 10

They splashed through the streets past drab Soviet-era buildings, mud-walled compounds, and stores fronted by pushcarts and wheelbarrows filled with cheap merchandise from Pakistan.

Afghan men squatted in groups alongside the road or shuffled slowly through the cold air that still clung to the six-thousand-foot-high city, their hands clasped behind their backs in the Afghan fashion while women in cornflower-blue burkas filled ratty shopping bags with their marketing or carried large plastic jugs of water. Children ran everywhere.

The late-morning traffic was thick and was accompanied by a cacophony of car horns. The only person who wasn't honking was Baba G, who was busy answering Harvath's questions.

"You're absolutely sure?" asked Harvath one more time.

Baba G nodded as he downshifted and maneuvered his Land Cruiser around one of Kabul's many traffic circles. At the top of the circle were two trucks filled with Afghan National Army soldiers, all of them armed with heavy weapons, as well as 7.62mm machine guns mounted to the roll bars of their vehicles.

Harvath didn't know what he liked less, the close proximity of so many cars — any number of which could be carrying al-Qaeda or Taliban militants — or the fact that Mustafa Khan was no longer being kept at Policharki Prison. "Why'd they move him?"

Gallagher smiled and rubbed his left thumb and forefinger together. "For the same reason we thought we'd be able to get him out."

"Baksheesh."

"Welcome to Afghanistan."

Harvath was familiar with the ancient adage that "you can't buy an Afghan, you can only rent one," and Policharki wasn't immune from this long-standing Afghan tradition of trading money for favors. In fact, Policharki was infamous for being able to hold anyone but a rich man. Bribe the right guard, the right family of a guard, or the right elders of the village the guard was from and anyone could be sprung from Policharki.

Harvath hadn't expected freeing Khan to be a walk in the park. He and Gallagher had assumed that the al-Qaeda operative would have been kept away from the general population and that it was going to take big money not only to get the two of them inside, but also to get back out again with Khan in their custody.

What had bothered Harvath from the start, though, was that if he was thinking this way, then al-Qaeda had to be as well. They would be willing to spend a lot of money to get him back, and this must have been exactly what the Afghan government was worried about. They had come to the conclusion that Policharki couldn't hold him, so they had moved him. The question was, *where?*

"So how do we find him?" asked Harvath.

"I've got some feelers out," said Gallagher as they passed another heavily armed Afghan National Army checkpoint.

Harvath watched the picture recede in his side-view mirror. "I don't remember seeing so many soldiers the last time I was here."

"The government is trying to exert more control over Kabul. Attacks and suicide bombings have been going through the roof. Everybody's all keyed up."

Harvath was aware of the fact that the situation in Afghanistan had deteriorated, but seeing how severely Kabul, which once had a modicum of security, had been affected didn't do much for his mood. "Tell me about the feelers you've got out."

"The Afghans are big-time gossips. Nobody talks more than they do. I've got a guy in the Afghan National Police who has a couple of cousins in Afghan intelligence. I've fed him some information in the past. Nothing stellar, pretty low-hanging fruit, but it made him look good at work and so we've got a happy relationship. We're meeting him this afternoon. *Insha'Allah,* he'll have something worthwhile for us."

Harvath laughed at Baba G's use of the popular Muslim phrase for *Allah willing.* "You haven't gone native on me, have you?"

"When in Rome," answered Gallagher, applying his turn signal as they approached a narrow, dead-end street. Three-quarters of the way down on the left-hand side was Baba G's Kabul compound. His company owned, or more appropriately "managed," another in Jalalabad, which was where Gallagher was normally based.

As in all the other compounds in Afghanistan, there were no windows facing the street. The main entrance consisted of a pair of thick, nine-foot-high steel doors, painted green, with a normal-sized door cut into the steel to make it easier for people to come and go.

Gallagher pulled a U-turn, brought his truck to a stop outside the gates, and turned off the ignition. "Welcome to the Plaza," he said as he opened his door and hopped out.

Harvath picked up the cooler bag, met him at the rear of the Land Cruiser, and grabbed his suitcases. Gallagher walked up to the door and rang the buzzer. Moments later, it was opened by Gallagher's business partner, Tom Hoyt.

Hoyt was a chain smoker from Miami who stood about five-foot-eight and had a thick head of salt-and-pepper hair. He was in his early fifties, spoke fluent Arabic, and could have passed for the brother of movie actor Robert Mitchum.

As ex-U.S. Army intelligence, Hoyt was the logistical mind behind the company he and Gallagher had named International Security Solutions, or ISS.

"Hey! The circus must be in town," said Hoyt as he looked past Gallagher and saw Harvath standing in the street. "There's a SEAL outside."

"Neek hallack," Harvath replied in Arabic, suggesting his friend go perform an anatomically impossible act.

"Wow. And he's got quite a mouth on him too."

Once they were inside, Hoyt bolted the door and gave Harvath a slap on the back. "It's good to see you again. Have you gained weight? You SEALs just go right to shit the minute the Navy kicks you loose."

Harvath smiled. Hoyt loved to play up interservice rivalries, and so did Gallagher. Both could be merciless — especially when they were drinking.

Harvath tapped Hoyt's burgeoning mid-section and said, "Married life seems to agree with you, doesn't it?"

Tom threw his hand up in the air and almost lost his cigarette. "I bought her a color TV *and* a satellite dish, but all she still wants is sex, sex, sex. I'm a man. Not an animal, for Chrissake."

Hoyt was referring to his younger and much more attractive wife, Mei. She was a Chinese national who had come to Kabul to start a restaurant to serve its growing Chinese population, many of whom worked in the "massage industry."

It had been love at first sight for Hoyt, and he had almost bankrupted himself eating every meal in Mei's restaurant. She was twenty-five years his junior and made him feel like he was eighteen years old again. In addition to being incredibly sexy, she was smart as hell — smarter than Hoyt, which was something he hadn't come across that often in life. More important, she understood him and even appreciated his off-color sense of humor.

Within six months Mei had sold her restaurant and had moved into the compound with Hoyt. She was in charge of day-to-day operations and did all of the cooking — breakfast, lunch, and dinner. Harvath had visited the compound on two different trips to Afghanistan, and no matter where they went out to eat, the food was never as good as Mei's.

"Speaking of which," said Harvath. "Where's your better half?"

"The Dragon Lady?" replied Hoyt with his characteristic feigned disrespect for his wife. "She's off playing mahjong somewhere."

Harvath shook his head.

"What?"

"I don't know why you talk about her like that."

Hoyt looked at Gallagher and shrugged his shoulders. "She left an hour ago to play mahjong, right?"

"That's what she said," replied Gallagher.

Harvath was about to make a crack about Hoyt's marital skills when the compound's majordomo stepped out of the main building. He was a chubby, thirty-year-old Afghan with slicked-back hair and a pointy goatee. He was the youngest of eight children, and his parents had given him the Urdu name for pine flower. Hoyt had found that hysterical, and since the name was too hard to pronounce, everyone just called him Flower.

Flower recognized Harvath immediately and walked right over. The two men gave each other the customary Afghan greeting and embraced.

"It's good to see you, Flower," said Harvath. "How is your family?"

Flower smiled and replied, "Good, Mr. Scot. Good. I have two more boys now."

"*Two?* How many does that make total?"

"Four boys. One girl," beamed Flower.

"And his wife's pregnant again," replied Gallagher.

"Flower," quipped Hoyt. "Maybe I should give your wife Mei's TV set."

Harvath laughed. "That's great. When is she due?"

"Any time," said Flower as he pulled his cell phone from his pocket and held it up, indicating he was on call.

"Congratulations."

Flower bent and picked up Harvath's bags.

"I'll take you to your room."

While Mei managed the compound, Flower was in charge of the heavy lifting. When the municipal power went out, which happened daily all over Afghanistan, the call went out for Flower to fire up the auxiliary generator. If someone needed a ride, they called Flower. If you needed anything from the market — Flower. And even though he couldn't shoot to save his life, he knew how to point a sawed-off shotgun in the right direction and look imposing, so Gallagher and Hoyt even took him on operations from time to time.

Flower had a bedroom at the compound, which not coincidentally was the closest to the gate, so he was also the de facto porter. Harvath had no idea when the man ever had time to see his wife and children, much less make more. Flower took his job very seriously and worked harder than most people Harvath had met.

The single-story compound was laid out in a rough U shape. In the center was a long courtyard and next to it a small parking pad big enough to hold three vehicles if you parked them bumper to bumper. Right now it was empty except for ISS's sole armored vehicle — a Toyota pickup.

There were seven bedrooms, each with a

tiny bathroom and handheld shower. Every bedroom had its own entrance and one window that faced onto the courtyard. There was a kitchen and a long communal room that functioned as the compound's bar, dining room, and entertainment center. Detached from the main building was a small structure that housed ISS's communications and strategic operations center. On the roof were a series of satellite dishes and antennas.

Flower walked Harvath to his room, set the bags inside, and turned the heater on via a small remote. "Very cold at night," he offered.

There was a small wardrobe, a desk, and a single bed with one thin blanket on it. Harvath knew the weak wall heater and his current bedding weren't going to cut it.

Reaching into his pocket, he withdrew a handful of Afghanis and peeled off several large notes. "The store on the corner has those thick wool blankets hanging outside. Can you go down and buy me a couple, please?"

Flower nodded. "Anything else?"

Harvath rattled off a short list and once the man had gone, he closed the door and unpacked his bags.

Tearing up the lining in each suitcase, he removed the stacks of currency and placed them in a small backpack along with his laptop. He fished another Red Bull out of the cooler bag and then took it, along with his pack, down to Hoyt's room.

He knocked on the glass and when he heard Tom's grunt he opened the door and stepped inside. The room reeked of cigarette smoke. Hoyt had one going in the ashtray at his desk next to his computer and another in his hand. "Everything okay with your room?" he asked. "I upgraded you to the one with the biggest bathroom mirror we have. I know how you SEALs are about looking at yourselves."

"Very funny," replied Harvath. "You know, as a returning guest I would have appreciated an ocean view or at least the club floor."

"Pay off your bar bill and I'll talk to my manager. Speaking of which," said Hoyt as he leaned over and flipped open the door of a small refrigerator next to his desk. "How about a beer?"

Harvath held up his hand. "Maybe later. Greg and I have to meet an Afghan contact of his for tea. I don't want to smell like a brewery."

"Probably a good idea." Hoyt flipped the fridge shut.

"I came to see you about a safety deposit box."

"What do you need to store?"

Harvath held up his pack.

"Close the door," said Hoyt.

Even though Harvath disliked being trapped inside the room with all that smoke and no fresh air, he did as he was told.

Hoyt stood up, placed his cigarette in his mouth, and crossed to a small closet. When he opened the door, it was obvious that most of the clothing belonged to Mei. "The lion, the bitch, and her wardrobe," he muttered through the cigarette as he removed everything.

Next, he took down the rod and pulled out the shelves. Then, he pried a panel off the back of the closet and revealed a Cannon-brand gun safe that had been set into the concrete wall.

"Where'd you get that?" Harvath asked.

"Mei had it at the restaurant."

"Where'd *she* get it?"

"I've got no idea. Knowing Mei, she probably stole it," replied Hoyt as he punched in his code.

Harvath doubted that and was about to say as much when Hoyt swung open the safe's door. Inside was a rather thin weapons cache, especially for men who were supposed to be in the private security business. All Harvath saw was a single AK-47, a pistol-grip Mossberg twelve-gauge shotgun, another Glock

19, and a few boxes of ammunition.

"What happened to all of your gear?" asked Harvath.

"Ever since one of the sons of Afghanistan's illustrious president got into the private security business, owning weapons has become very expensive."

"But you guys had a *ton* of stuff."

"Still do. We just don't keep it here."

Harvath looked at him. "Why? Have they outlawed them?"

"All but," said Hoyt. "You're supposed to pay per man, per gun, and per contract that your company is working under. It's a big pain in the ass. The Afghan bureaucrats not only get rich off the bribes, they *still* paperwork us to death. I go through the trouble of keeping a few of our weps on the up and up, but as far as the rest are concerned, the Afghans can go fuck themselves."

"So as long as your papers and payments are up to date," said Harvath, "you can have whatever you want?"

"It's complicated. *If* you cross all your t's and *if* you dot all your i's you can legally carry a pistol and a long gun. That said, contractors in Kabul still get stopped on a regular basis and have their perfectly registered weapons confiscated. The Afghans do it to Afghan contractors as well as ex-pats.

It's totally fucked up.

"Now, if you get caught with a crew-serve weapon like a PKM, you're going straight to the big house. Same for grenades and RPGs. Plus P and hollow point ammo are also big no-nos. Even so, everybody's got that stuff, especially if they plan on traveling outside Kabul. Let's face it, this isn't the Caymans, it's Afghanistan."

"True."

"Basically, the number-one rule Greg and I have is to just keep everything below the window line and out of sight."

"What a scam," replied Harvath.

"TIA," said Hoyt as he motioned for Harvath to hand him his bag.

Removing his laptop, Harvath handed Hoyt the pack. "I'm going to need a receipt for that," he joked.

"You can talk to our accountant when she gets back from mahjong. Anything else?"

"You wouldn't happen to have a holster for the 19 I'm carrying, would you?"

Hoyt riffled through a few items stacked on one of the shelves in the safe and came up with a Blackhawk Check Six conceal-able leather holster. He tossed it to Harvath, closed the door, and put the wardrobe back together.

Harvath pulled the Glock from his waistband and set it on the bed. After he had slid the holster onto his belt he replaced his weapon and looked in the bathroom mirror to see if he was printing. Confident no one could see the weapon beneath his untucked shirt, he turned back to Hoyt. "I also need a secure link for email."

"I've got one and Greg's got one. If that jarhead's not watching war porn, you can probably get online in his room."

"Thanks," said Harvath.

Hoyt waved at him with his cigarette as he went back to whatever it was he'd been doing on his computer.

Gallagher's room was two doors down and the door was ajar. Harvath knocked, but there was no answer. Pushing the door open, he stepped inside.

Scanning a room when he entered was second nature for Harvath. Years of training had wired him to take a quick and detailed mental picture of what he saw.

For all intents and purposes, Gallagher's room looked like it belonged to a very neat, very well-organized person. The bed was perfectly made. Papers were stacked neatly on his desk next to his computer. The items on his shelves were in perfect order and precisely spaced. Harvath guessed that a drill instructor could have bounced a quarter off

Gallagher's bed, taken a ruler to the spacing of the items on his shelves, and run a white glove over the door frame and come away with nothing to fault.

The room reflected a picture-perfect Marine — a man who had his act entirely together. That's what made the last thing Harvath noticed that much more unsettling. In Gallagher's wastebasket were eleven empty beer bottles. Unless Baba G had been hosting a party last night, it looked like he might have been hitting the booze pretty good. Harvath hoped the man wasn't being haunted by any demons from his past.

With Khan having been moved, this assignment had already taken one bad turn. It would probably take several more before it was over. That was just the nature of this business. But the last thing Harvath needed to worry about was if Greg Gallagher was going to be able to perform at 100 percent.

He was going to have to keep an eye on him. One screw-up, and good people could be killed.

CHAPTER 11

Alexandria, Virginia

"I really appreciate your seeing me so late," Elise Campbell said as she stepped inside the small Pitt Street town house. "We've been on the road a couple of days and I had some paperwork to catch up on after my shift ended tonight."

"Don't worry about it," replied Carolyn Leonard as she took Campbell's coat and hung it on a peg near the door. "I remember the hours. How about some coffee?"

"Do you have anything stronger?"

"I do," said Leonard with a smile. "Come on in."

Carolyn Leonard was a fit and attractive woman, ten years older than Elise Campbell. She had red hair and a quiet, yet powerful presence. Leonard was one of those people you might not notice the moment you walked into a room, but once you did, you couldn't help but be impressed by the confidence she exuded. It was a trait that, in her personal life, seemed to intimidate most of the men she met. The only ones able to get beyond who she was and what she had done for a living were other law enforcement officers. The fact that she had been the head U.S. Secret Service agent for the previous president of the United States simply freaked a lot of guys out.

"We're not going to wake the children up, are we?" asked Campbell as she took a seat on a stool in the kitchen.

"They're not here," said Leonard of her twins. "They're visiting my mother."

Campbell knew well enough not to inquire after Leonard's ex. He'd left her with two young kids and a mountain of credit card debt at the high point of her career. She was the first woman to ever head a presidential protection detail and the insecure excuse for a man she'd married had not only left her, he'd slashed and burned everything in his path on his way out of the relationship.

As devastating as the experience had been, Leonard had continued, right until the day after the inauguration. She was one of the high profile refuseniks who declined to remain with the Secret Service in the new administration and who had elected to leave,

104

rather than comply with what they felt were dangerous choices being made by the new president. The defections created a lot of bad feelings in an organization that already had significant morale problems.

While many exceptional Secret Service agents still wholeheartedly believed in the mission, there were those who were dead tired of the dearth of leadership and the crushing layers of exceedingly poor management. The newly elected president's desire to turn his protective detail into a 1980s style Benetton ad, rather than promote, hire, and train on ability, was the tipping point for agents like Leonard.

Despite the bad feelings swirling throughout the Service, agents who knew Carolyn Leonard still respected her. Those who remained behind were indeed sorry to see her go, but few of them held her decision against her, especially not Elise Campbell.

Leonard knew better than anyone how hard it was to be a woman in the Service. She had taken Campbell under her wing early on and had been her mentor as best she could. Being head of the president's detail and a single mother of two little ones never seemed to leave enough time. Leonard had always felt that she hadn't done enough for Campbell.

Campbell, on the other hand, had soaked up every piece of advice and had hung on every word of Carolyn's as if she had been sitting at the feet of a master, which in a way, she had. Leonard was a legend in the Service and Campbell felt honored by their time together, no matter how limited it was.

"Is Chardonnay okay?" asked Carolyn as she pulled a bottle of Toasted Head from the refrigerator.

"That's great," replied Campbell.

Carolyn set the bottle down along with two glasses and fished her wine key out of her junk drawer. When the bottle was open, she poured a glass for each of them and then sat down on one of the stools. "Cheers."

Campbell raised her glass and they toasted. Carolyn studied the younger agent's face. She hadn't changed much in the years since she had left the Virginia Beach Police Department to join the Secret Service. She still looked young and was still very pretty.

While times had changed since Carolyn had joined the Service, she knew it hadn't changed that much and that it was still difficult for women, especially attractive ones like Elise. The long hours, the days and weeks away from family, the lonely hotel rooms — it all came together to create some less than professional situations if people weren't vigilant.

Carolyn took a sip of wine and then set the glass down. Raising her eyebrows, she asked, "So what did you need to talk about?"

Elise took a drink before responding. "The president."

Call it intuition, but Carolyn instantly had a bad feeling about where this might be going. Fairly or unfairly, President Robert Alden had a reputation as being a bit of a womanizer — this, despite the fact that his wife, Terry, was a very good-looking woman. Many said the rumors about Alden were untrue and were due only to his good looks and the fact that so many women found him so desirable. In Carolyn's experience, though, where there was smoke, there was usually fire, and the idea of the president coming on to one of the agents sworn to protect him, though incredibly unprofessional, was not beyond the realm of possibility.

"What about him?" replied Leonard.

Campbell took another sip from her glass and stared past her mentor to the calendar on the woman's refrigerator. "When you were on presidential detail, did you ever hear anything you weren't supposed to hear?"

Carolyn studied her young protégée. "All the time. But it's your job to ignore it and forget it."

"What if I can't?"

"Then you need to find another job."

"C'mon, Carolyn," stated Campbell as she turned her eyes to her. "You know some things aren't that easy."

"Nothing about the Secret Service is easy," replied Leonard, "especially protecting the president. If you want easy, become a politician. Other than that, either you can do your job as an agent or you can't. There's no gray." Pausing, Carolyn then added, "Did the president say or do something to you that made you uncomfortable?"

"No. Absolutely not."

"Did he say something to someone else about you or what he wanted to do to you?"

"Carolyn, my God. No. Is that why you think I'm here? You think I'm upset because the president came on to me?"

"He wouldn't be the first."

"Well, nothing happened," Campbell replied flatly.

"So then, what are we talking about?"

Campbell eyed the bottle of wine and before she could ask, Leonard topped off her glass.

Elise held the stem near the base and slowly moved it in a circle. "What do you know about Nikki Hale?"

"Alden's campaign staffer? The one who died?"

Campbell nodded and took another sip of wine.

"Not much more than what I heard from the agents working Alden's detail during the campaign. She was young, twenty-five or twenty-six I believe. She was also very pretty. If I remember correctly, she had something to do with the campaign website; director of new media or something like that.

"A lot of people on the campaign didn't like her. They thought she was a little too young and a little too inexperienced for such an important position. She rode the campaign bus and was on the plane everywhere Alden went. Everyone wanted to have that kind of access and I guess a lot of folks were jealous of her."

"Do you remember how she died?"

Carolyn thought about it for a minute. "It was the end of last summer, just before the general elections, I think. Head-on collision in the Hamptons, right?"

Campbell nodded. "Fourth of July weekend. Alden had been out there for a big fundraiser."

"From what I heard, Nikki Hale was quite the partier, and that night was no exception.

Her blood alcohol level was double the legal limit. She crossed into oncoming traffic and killed herself along with a family of four in the opposite lane."

"I think President Alden had something to do with it."

Carolyn looked at her. "You what?"

"I overheard him talking with Stephanie Gallo."

"Elise, your job is not to listen in on the president's private conversations. Besides, do you think the man would be so dumb as to admit to something like that in front of one of his Secret Service agents?"

"I was in the woods on Gallo's estate. I don't think either of them knew I was even there. As far as I could tell, they thought they were completely alone."

"Wait a second. Why come to me with this?" asked Carolyn.

"Because I don't know what to do. I need advice."

Leonard set her wineglass down on the counter. "You want my advice? Forget the entire thing. You heard a snippet of a conversation and have taken it out of context. Your job is to protect the president, period. You start getting distracted, trying to make sense of what you're hearing, and you'll not only get the president killed, you'll get yourself killed as well."

"But what if he was involved in Nikki Hale's death somehow?"

"If you think he might have been involved, tell your supervisor at the Service."

"What if I'm wrong?" asked Campbell.

"Then you won't have to worry about overhearing any more of the president's private conversations because you'll be bounced so hard you'll need the space shuttle to deliver your final paycheck."

Campbell was silent for a moment. "What if I told you Gallo knows all about it and she's blackmailing the president?"

"I'd say that's his problem."

Elise shook her head. "You've made no secret about not being a fan of President Alden's."

"Well that's the beauty of being a private citizen," answered Leonard. "I can do that because I no longer work for the Secret Service."

"Well, I believe in him. I *voted* for him."

"You're behind the curtain now, Elise. Be prepared to be disillusioned. There aren't many honest men or women in Washington anymore. Politicians get where they are by the sheer force of their egos, not their convictions. And you know what? It's our fault as voters. We don't demand better candidates, so we end up getting what we deserve — on both sides of the aisle."

"I agree with you. The majority of them are crooked and we should consider them all guilty until proven innocent," said Campbell. "But I thought Alden was different. I still do."

Leonard poured a little more wine into her glass. "For the sake of argument, let's say you're right about what you overheard. How can someone blackmail an honest man?"

Campbell didn't have a response.

"What exactly," asked Leonard, "did Stephanie Gallo say to the president?"

"She said that if he didn't give her what she wanted, she was going to expose his involvement in the deaths of four innocent people and his would be one of the shortest administrations in U.S. history."

"How do you know this had to do with Nikki Hale's death?"

"Because after that threat," answered Campbell, "they walked off arguing about the night she died."

"Did you hear anything more specific?" asked Carolyn.

"Not really. Not from where I was standing."

"What possible role could the president have had in Hale's death? Did he get her loaded and hand her a set of car keys?"

"I wasn't there. I don't know, but Gallo was very insistent about his complicity and the president was very bothered by the whole thing."

"So what was it Gallo was pressing him for?" said Leonard, switching to a more jovial tone. "Has she changed her mind about wanting a cabinet position?"

Elise didn't think now was an appropriate time to be making jokes. *"No,"* she replied harshly. "Actually, her daughter was just kidnapped in Afghanistan and she wants the president's help."

"I'm sorry," replied Leonard. "I wasn't aware of that."

Elise brushed it off. "It's okay. No one knows. They're keeping it very quiet. Gallo's daughter is a doctor who was working for some NGO over there. Apparently, the kidnappers want to trade her for some high-ranking al-Qaeda operative that the Afghans are holding for trial."

"And Alden is going to arrange the trade?"

"Not exactly," said Campbell.

"What do you mean, *not exactly?*"

"He doesn't think it's right to force the Afghans to give the AQ operative up. He's a terrorist who has been involved with the killing of multiple Afghan government officials. President Alden supports the Afghans in establishing the rule of law and thinks they should prosecute the guy in full."

"And Stephanie Gallo isn't pleased with that position, is she?"

"You've got two children," replied Campbell. "How would you feel if one of them was being held hostage and the person you'd helped get elected to the most powerful office in the world wouldn't get your child back for you?"

"I'd be angry, very angry."

"As is she, apparently."

"Hence the blackmail," stated Carolyn.

Campbell nodded.

"Kidnapping a United States citizen is serious business. For all intents and purposes, we *own* Afghanistan. I've got to imagine that we're throwing everything we have at this. There's no way we're leaving any rocks unturned over there. Short of forcing the Afghans to give us the al-Qaeda operative to trade out for Mrs. Gallo's daughter, I don't know what more the president could do, which makes me think either he's prepared to call her bluff or there's actually nothing there for him to be blackmailed over."

"There's something else," stated Campbell.

Carolyn raised her eyebrows again and waited.

"The trip we just wrapped up was official business — all except for one leg."

"What was the leg?" asked Carolyn.

"We flew to Maine so the president could see Stephanie Gallo."

Leonard pursed her lips and exhaled. She had heard that the first lady was no fan of Stephanie Gallo's. Terry Alden's contempt for the woman was thinly veiled at best. It made no difference how much Gallo had aided her husband's campaign. The first lady didn't see Gallo as an ally, she saw her as a rival for her husband's time, interest, and affection. In fact, it had been widely rumored that it was because of Mrs. Alden's strong protestations that Stephanie Gallo did not stay on past the transition period and move into a permanent position within Robert Alden's administration.

Considering the kidnapping, though, the trip should not have automatically been suspect.

"They met at an estate in Seal Harbor owned by some television personality Mrs. Gallo knows," continued Campbell.

"I'm not surprised. He's a hands-on guy.

Her daughter was kidnapped and he's keeping her in the loop. At this point, nothing would surprise me about his meeting with her."

"I'm not saying the meeting was remarkable, but you might think who they met with was. Are you familiar with a former Secret Service agent named Scot Harvath?"

"Harvath?" Leonard said, somewhat surprised. "What was he doing there? On second thought, don't tell me. I probably don't want to know. Are you sure it was him?"

"I asked one of the agents who cleared him. They confirmed it and told me a little about who he was. So you're familiar with him?"

"Very, but Harvath doesn't work for the government anymore. Whatever he was doing for the previous administration was shut down. He left for the private sector. In fact, when I announced that I was leaving the Secret Service, he emailed me and put me in touch with the group he's supposed to start working with."

"Well, as of that meeting in Maine, he's now working for President Alden, or more specifically, Stephanie Gallo, as she's apparently the one who is paying him."

"Probably a smart move. Harvath is an exceptional operator. He was a SEAL before joining the Secret Service and coming to the White House. He's a good person to have consulting on this."

"Based on what I heard, I think he's doing a lot more than consulting," replied Elise. "I think the president brought him in to snatch that al-Qaeda operative from prison in Kabul and trade him for Gallo's daughter."

"Are you serious?"

Campbell nodded. "Which now brings us back to the president and the night Nikki Hale died."

CHAPTER 12

Afghanistan

Julia Gallo knew the Pashtu word for whore. She'd heard it muttered behind her back and under people's breath in countless villages throughout Afghanistan. This time, though, it was different.

The four boys standing above her in her small, mud cell were repeating it in an effort to build up their courage. For what, she had no idea, but she knew that it wouldn't be good. She was being held by the Taliban, that much she had ascertained, and Taliban children were raised on extremist videos. They were subjected from ages as young as three years old to videos of suicide bombings, beheadings, torture, and rape. It was a diet of unadulterated horror that served to desensitize them to violence and inoculate them against having any pity whatsoever for their enemies. Gallo had no illusions about how they viewed her. She *was* their enemy.

In less than a week of captivity, she had become an emotional and physical wreck. They kept her in a room twelve feet long by eight feet wide. The room had one window, which had been nailed shut and covered over on the outside by a piece of canvas. Her only connection with the world outside was a small ventilation hole the circumference of a Coke can cut into the bottom of one of the walls near the floor. Through it she could make out a small tree of some sort in the foreground and a narrow mountain valley beyond.

Lying on her stomach studying the tree and the small sliver of valley was the only thing that kept her from losing her mind.

Using the tree, she marked the passage of the hours based on the shadows cast by its slim trunk and twiglike branches. She counted its buds and wondered if she would still be here, still be alive, when the tree bloomed. She marveled at how despite being a doctor and understanding the science of life, she had never really stopped to appreciate it. There was a bitter irony in coming to finally value and understand it only to be on the verge of losing it.

Gallo subsisted on the meager amount of food she was given once a day — short, ropy pieces of beef, scraps of nan bread, or almonds, washed down with lukewarm tea. For her bodily functions, there was a hole in the floor on the opposite side of the room.

A narrow wooden bed with a thin blanket was the only furniture she enjoyed, and at night the temperatures fell so low, Gallo wondered if she was more likely to die from hypothermia than at the hands of the Taliban.

She knew why she had been taken. Sayed had been right. The Taliban were going to make an example of her. She had pushed her luck too far and it had finally run out.

The Taliban had interrogated her mercilessly upon her arrival. They had called her a spy and had threatened to execute her. Why they had not yet done so was a mystery, but she had read enough accounts of kidnappings in Afghanistan to know that it could take time before they finally dealt with her. That was the way things worked here. They could be incredibly cruel, like cats that had caught a mouse. They delighted in seeing their captives suffer.

Julia had been required to take a security preparedness class in the United States before leaving for CARE's mission in Afghanistan. She learned about what to do and what not to do and that kidnappers could keep better control of you if they kept you frightened and off balance. She tried not only to remember the training she had received about how to handle being a kidnap victim, but also why she had come to this country in the first place.

Julia had come to Afghanistan because she wanted to help its people. She now realized that she had also come in search of adventure, even danger. The longer she had been in-country, the bolder she had become, and in becoming bolder she had taken up an extremely provocative cause. Though she deeply believed in what she was encouraging Afghan women to do, she now had time to truly examine her motives. Would she have been as passionate if her trips into the countryside didn't serve to heighten her sense of danger?

Looking death in the eye, she could no longer delude herself. She had been addicted to the danger. She justified the risk by focusing on the people she claimed to be helping. She reveled in the awe her peers back in Kabul showered upon her for traveling so far outside the relative safety of an already unsafe city. She was a smart woman and should have known much better.

Life in Afghanistan was an extremely dangerous gamble. She hadn't needed to go looking for trouble. Working at the CARE hospital in Kabul was dangerous enough. Afghanistan wasn't some drive-through safari park where as long as you kept the windows rolled up and the doors locked you'd come out unscathed.

She had pushed her luck farther than she should have, and the crushing isolation she had since been subjected to, and the promise of a very unpleasant fate, only drove the point home. But of course, now Sayed was dead and it was too late.

Julia wondered if her mother knew what had happened. Certainly, the CARE International doctors were aware that she and Sayed had gone out and had not returned. The question, though, was whether they even knew where to begin searching for her. By Gallo's calculations, they were at least three, maybe four hours away from where she and Sayed had been ambushed. A bag had been placed over her head and her watch had been taken away, so she had no idea how long they had traveled before reaching wherever they now were.

The door to her cell had been repeatedly kicked open, both day and night. She never knew when anyone was going to materialize in its frame and she tried to keep her headscarf wrapped around her head at all times. When the men did enter, she kept her eyes cast down toward the floor. Her heart palpitated and she had trouble taking deep breaths. It was like living through one prolonged panic attack.

Intermingled with the feelings of terror and loneliness were the sorrow and guilt over Sayed's murder. While she tried to push the image of him from her mind, it always found a way back in. They had killed him in cold blood and she knew they were capable of that and worse toward her.

The chanting of the young boys increased in intensity. Gallo steeled herself for what was going to happen. Being in captivity, she had not taken her birth control pills recently and then almost laughed out loud at herself for the concern. Getting pregnant was the least of her problems at this moment.

She looked at the young boys and recalled the high level of homosexual activity among the Taliban. There was an old fable that said that birds flew over Taliban territory with only one wing because they needed the other to guard their rectums.

One of the boys reached his hand out to touch her breast. Reflexively, Gallo slapped it away. The other boys laughed, and the first boy's face flushed red. Julia couldn't be sure whether it was embarrassment or anger.

The boy, who couldn't be more than sixteen, drew his hand back and struck her hard across the mouth. Julia tasted blood. The other boys laughed and the chanting began again in earnest. When the boy reached out to touch her breast again, Julia didn't stop him.

When he made contact his hand crushed down like a vise. Julia winced and bit down on her lip to keep from crying out. His grasp was amazingly strong.

She almost felt that she deserved this — that this was the price she must pay for having gotten Sayed killed.

As the boy's other hand clamped down on her opposite breast, Julia willed her mind to leave her body. She wanted to travel as far away as possible.

She had made it to a small village in the south of France where she had vacationed after graduating medical school when the sound of the door being kicked open pulled her back to her tiny cell.

Standing in the doorway was the mentally challenged man who had been feeding her. In his hands he held the cardboard box he always carried. Slung over his shoulder was a rifle, its barrel covered with tape. On his feet was a pair of new basketball shoes.

Upon seeing the boys in the room, the man

set down his box and unslung his rifle.

He pointed it at the boys, but it had no effect. They weren't scared.

The man repeated a Pashtu phrase Julia was familiar with. *"Lar sha. Lar sha!"* Go away.

The boy gripping Julia's breasts called the man over to the bed. He approached slowly and looked confused.

The boy let go of one of Julia's breasts and motioned for the man to put his hand in its place. The man shuffled forward and Julia resigned herself to the fact that what was about to happen might turn out to be worse than she had imagined. Fighting back the nausea rising in her throat, she prepared her mind to return to the south of France.

The man studied the situation as the boy and the others behind him egged him on. The chant of *whore, whore, whore* in Pashtu was taken up again, and he looked at Julia with an emotion she couldn't quite decipher. Then he lowered his rifle, and she closed her eyes for what would happen next.

But it didn't happen. With amazing force, the man snapped his rifle straight up. There was a crack as the butt of the weapon connected with the boy's jaw.

Spinning, the man raised the weapon as high as he could and began beating the other boys. They shouted curses at him and he shouted right back, but none of them raised a hand to strike him.

He hit them repeatedly against their backs and shoulders as they dragged their dazed friend from the room and ran.

Once they had gone, the man slung his rifle, reached down, and helped Julia up. He was incredibly strong for his small size. He helped her to the bed and took her chin in one of his rough hands.

He turned her face from side to side, examining her split lip, and then let her go.

Returning to his cardboard box, he unpacked her paltry meal and muttered to himself repeatedly the Pashtu word for *bad.*

Julia had never spoken to the man. Each time he had entered to bring her food, she had kept her eyes cast toward the floor. She had remained quiet, her goal to appear meek and unthreatening. The last thing she wanted was to draw the ire of her kidnappers.

But now that the local boys had made their intentions clear, she needed to make sure she was protected from them.

While far from the stereotypical knight in shining armor, the mentally challenged man had come to her rescue once. Would he do so again?

The man appeared to take his job very seriously — unceremoniously kicking her door in at all hours in some form of surprise inspection. She had no idea if the kicking was necessitated by a sticking door or if it was designed to keep her on edge. If it was the latter, it was working. Every time the door crashed open, Julia's heart raced into the red zone. She never had any idea who was on the other side or what their intentions were. Were they coming to kill her? Beat her? Rape her? The not knowing had frayed the nerves of the normally cool and collected doctor right to their bitter ends.

"*Stan a shukria,*" she said. *Thank you.*

The man in the basketball shoes acted as if he didn't hear her.

"*Sta noom tse dai?*" she asked. *What's your name?* "My name is Julia," she said. "I'm a doctor."

Doctors were revered in Afghanistan and she hoped that if her kidnappers could see her as someone who could provide value to them, they might think twice about killing her. Though her Pashtu was limited, it was passable.

But despite her attempt to communicate, the man continued to mutter to himself.

After laying everything out, he gathered up his box, tucked it under his arm, and headed for the door.

"*Stan a shukria,*" Julia repeated.

As he reached the door, the man stopped. He then spun so quickly that he startled Julia, and she shrank into the corner.

He stepped quickly, almost violently across the room and shoved his hand into his pocket.

When he pulled it out, he held two Afghan sweets known as *dashlama* in his upturned palm. Suddenly very timid, like a little boy feeding an animal at a petting zoo, he offered them to Julia.

Slowly, she crept forward and reached her hand out to take the sweets.

The man watched and then motioned with his fingers to place them in her mouth.

Julia placed one of the candies on her tongue. The man smiled, but as soon as the smile appeared it was replaced by a frown.

He returned to muttering the Pashtu word for *bad* and left the room, slamming the door on the way out.

CHAPTER 13

Kabul

Baba G's Afghan National Police contact, Inspector Ahmad Rashid, had picked a small restaurant in an obscure part of the city that rarely, if ever, saw any white people.

Based on how violent things had become in Kabul, Gallagher advised that they go native. They wore the *salwar kameez* — the baggy cotton trousers and loose-fitting tunics — as well as the *pakol* hats upon their heads and *patoo* blankets over their shoulders to combat the intense cold that would build in the late afternoon as soon as the sun started to dip behind the mountains.

After changing into his Afghan clothes, Harvath stopped in Hoyt's room to access his "safety deposit box" and then stepped out into the courtyard. Gallagher looked him up and down and reminded him to leave his sunglasses behind. Few things in

Afghanistan screamed, "I'm a Westerner, shoot me," louder than a pair of shades, and that went double if they were Oakleys.

"Thanks, Greg," said Harvath. "But this isn't my first rodeo."

Gallagher laughed. "I'm so used to carting civilians around that it just becomes second nature to tick off all the boxes. Let me see your walk."

"My Afghan walk?"

Baba G nodded.

"Then what? A bathing suit contest and the talent portion of the show?" remarked Harvath. "I've got it. Don't worry about it."

Gallagher wasn't giving in. "We're not driving into downtown Detroit, buddy. TIA, remember?"

Harvath shook his head. He was as detail-minded as the next guy, but Gallagher took things to a whole new level. He had learned long ago not to argue with him. They'd get on the road a lot faster if he simply gave the man what he wanted.

Harvath tucked his hands behind his back beneath the *patoo,* leaned forward, and began the slow, shambling Afghan walk. At the edge of the small courtyard, he turned and came back. "Are we good?"

"I'll make sure to park as close to the restaurant as possible," he replied.

"Up yours," said Harvath.

Once they were in the Land Cruiser and Baba G had it started, Harvath cracked another can of Red Bull and cranked the heater up as far as it would go. His jet lag had made him extra susceptible to the cold.

"You can monkey with that all you want," admonished Gallagher. "It won't do any good until the engine heats up."

"Really?" Harvath replied as he took another sip of Red Bull.

Baba G was about to explain when he realized that Harvath was being facetious. For a moment, he had forgotten who he was with. Harvath had used humor to deal with good situations and bad for as long as he had known him. He decided to change the subject. "How's Tracy doing?"

Harvath had been so exhausted, he honestly hadn't thought much about her since he'd landed in Kabul. He'd learned a long time ago that one of the keys to being successful and staying alive in his line of work was the ability to compartmentalize. If you couldn't put the rest of your life in a box and keep a lid on it while you were in the field, this wasn't the career for you.

Gallagher was an old friend, though, and the question wasn't out of bounds. Still, the relationship with Tracy was complicated. "She's good," he replied.

"Are her headaches any better?"

This was where things got complicated. Tracy had been shot almost two years ago by someone with a very serious vendetta against Harvath. She had survived and recovered, but not 100 percent. The doctors had advised her to avoid stress as much as possible. There had been little to no stress in Maine. In fact, they had joked that it had been like spending the winter inside a snow globe. But the net effect on Tracy's headaches had been negligible. She still got them and when she did, she had to pop some pretty strong medication to beat them back. Tracy was tough and she refused to give up. She also, however, refused to move forward.

An ex-Navy Explosive Ordnance Disposal technician, she had seen danger up close and had even had an IED she was defusing detonate prematurely and take one of her eyes. The doctors had matched it perfectly and you had to look very closely to notice any of the scarring her face had suffered. Lesser people would have given up, but not Tracy, and Scot admired the hell out of her for that.

Where she refused to move forward was in their relationship. Harvath wanted to get married and Tracy didn't. She knew how badly Scot wanted children and she just didn't think she could handle the headaches and kids. They were engaged in a quiet stalemate and had been most of the winter.

On the job front, Harvath couldn't have hoped for a person more understanding or supportive of his career. Tracy was content keeping the home fires burning for as long as his assignments took him wherever they took him. She appreciated both the danger and the fact that this work was what he was born to do. She would never make him decide between being with her or pursuing his career. Tracy allowed him both. What she asked in return was to accept their relationship as it was and to not ask her to make any changes.

It sounded reasonable, but the longer he and Tracy were together, the more he realized what a great mother she would be — even with the headaches. Harvath wanted kids and he wanted to have them with her. He still held out hope, as dim as he knew it was, that Tracy might change her mind and come around.

"The headaches are still the same," said Harvath. "Regularly irregular and when they come they're pretty tough."

"Have you guys seen any specialists?"

"Tons," replied Harvath as he took another

sip of Red Bull.

"That sucks," said Gallagher.

Harvath attempted to change the subject. "How long have you known this police inspector we're going to see?"

"Ahmad?" asked Gallagher as he did the math in his head. "About three years now."

"And you trust him?"

Baba G laughed. "If I didn't, we wouldn't be going to Kabul's version of South Central LA for this meeting. Don't worry. He's good people."

Don't worry. It was a funny piece of advice coming from the man who had insisted upon seeing Harvath's "Afghan walk."

"Normally, we just meet to gossip. Sometimes, we trade pieces of intelligence. This is the first time I'm going to offer him money for something."

Harvath looked at him. "Any reason to believe that might change things between you?"

"If anything, it'll probably make me more valuable to him and technically, I'm not giving him any money, you are. Ahmad and I are just facilitators, or *fixers,* as they say. I'm hooking you up with him and then hopefully he'll hook you up with some information."

"Hopefully," repeated Harvath.

"Don't worry," Gallagher said yet again.

As they drove toward their rendezvous, the streets were as crowded as they had been before. Men rode three and sometimes even four to a motorbike. Yellow and white taxis were everywhere, as were donkey carts and bicycles. Cars were parked halfway on sidewalks and men stood in the road every fifteen feet selling prepaid phone cards. Baba G had the Land Cruiser's radio tuned to an Afghan station with music that sounded like a Bollywood sound track.

They passed the normally anemic Kabul River, which was swollen with spring runoff, and had to stop for two men who were driving a flock of dirty sheep out of a muddy alley and across the road. All the while, Harvath kept his eyes alert for trouble. His local garb might help in not drawing attention to himself, but he had no doubt that he still looked every bit the American and that he was one big target.

He pressed the Glock hidden beneath his tunic for reassurance, and when he looked over at Baba G, he saw that he was not only watching the traffic, but scanning the sidewalks and parked cars for danger as well. Kabul was like a Wild West town surrounded by Indian country. There wasn't one single place where you could let your guard down.

When they reached the restaurant, there

weren't any parking spaces available in front and Baba G had to park about a block down. "Don't leave any valuables in the car," he cautioned.

Harvath tapped his side and replied, "Don't worry."

The restaurant was housed in a two-story concrete structure with a dark green corrugated metal awning hanging over the sidewalk. On the ground floor was a small shop selling household odds and ends like the one Harvath had sent Flower to for extra blankets. Next to the shop was a door that opened onto a staircase leading to the building's second floor. Harvath tried to make out the writing on the door as they approached.

"Private club," offered Gallagher. "Pashtuns only."

"Seriously?" asked Harvath.

"Not really, but the sign is written only in Pashtu, not Dari, so the message is pretty clear. If you're not Pashtun, find someplace else to eat."

Harvath was well aware of how the hierarchies operated here. Afghan identity followed a clear trajectory of loyalty. Family came first, then clan, village, tribe, and finally, at the bottom of the list, was national identity as a citizen of Afghanistan.

Afghan tribalism was pervasive throughout the country and was a big reason why it was so fractured. Pashtuns, who accounted for roughly 45 percent of the population, hated the Tajiks, and Tajiks, who made up 25 percent of the population, hated the Pashtuns. Together, the Pashtuns and Tajiks both hated the 10 percent minority Hazaras, and the tribalism continued right down the ladder to include the lowly Uzbeks, Turkmen, Baluchi, Nuristanis, and all the other minority groups.

The only time the tribes worked together was when they united to repel an outside invader. After the invader was sent packing, the tribes went back to waging war against each other. In essence, Afghanistan was both its own best ally and its own worst enemy.

If you wanted to develop contacts with the most powerful people in the Afghan government, the Pashtuns were the ones to be in bed with. From the president of Afghanistan on down, the Pashtuns occupied the most important posts. Though the government was working hard to desegregate its infrastructure, it still had a long way to go and Baba G had been wise to align himself with a highly placed Pashtun police inspector. Harvath just hoped the man would have the information they needed.

CHAPTER 14

Gallagher and Harvath climbed the dank stairs to the restaurant and were shown to a private room near the back. Its floor was covered with a variety of faded Afghan carpets and several brightly colored cushions. A pair of mismatched curtains had been drawn across the windows. Sitting in the corner, near a small propane heater, was Ahmad Rashid. A round man in his late forties, he rose to greet his guests.

After Rashid and Gallagher had touched hearts and completed their embrace, Baba G introduced Harvath.

"I'm pleased to make your acquaintance," said Rashid as they shook hands. His English was excellent. As Harvath and Gallagher had walked from the truck to the restaurant, Baba G had explained that Rashid had been a university student before two of his brothers had been killed by the Taliban. After aiding his family in hunting down those responsible, Rashid had become a police officer. He had a very sharp mind coupled with a keen eye for opportunity and had risen quickly through the ranks of the ANP. The man was adept at trading favors and Gallagher claimed that while Rashid never technically broke the law, he often bent it in exceptionally creative ways.

The inspector was in plain clothes, wearing a gray sweater over a blue tunic and a vest popular with Afghans that resembled the vests photographers or people on safari often wore. Harvath didn't know if the man was on duty or not, but considering that cops were prime Taliban and al-Qaeda targets, going plainclothes was probably a very good idea.

Beneath his traditional *pakol,* Rashid's hair poked out over his forehead in loose black curls. The sides, like his jet-black beard, were neatly trimmed.

He motioned for Harvath and Gallagher to join him and they each picked a cushion and sat down.

Rashid articulated instructions to the waiter and once he was gone, he and Gallagher engaged in the customary Afghan preamble regarding each other's health, families, and various local goings-on.

When the waiter returned, he rolled a

green plastic mat out along the floor and upon it set glasses, a pot of tea, and dishes filled with several things to eat. The police inspector poured the steaming hot green tea known as *chai sabz* for each of them. It had been seasoned with cardamom, and the scent quickly filled the air. Despite the heater and having three bodies in the small room, it was still so cold you could almost see your breath.

Rashid explained to Harvath what all the dishes were and encouraged him to help himself. Harvath hadn't eaten since his arrival and hadn't realized how hungry he had been. He tore off a large piece of freshly baked Afghan bread known as *nan* and then served himself some rice. He added a few chunks of cooked lamb and then covered everything with yogurt sauce. In order to protect his stomach, he avoided the salad and took a serving of fried vegetables, known as *borani.*

Harvath had always enjoyed the cuisine in Afghanistan and laughed at Westerners who arrived expecting to lose weight only to return home having added several pounds.

There was a dish of sugar cubes on the mat, and Rashid, who like most Afghans had a sweet tooth, picked up three and dropped them into his short glass of tea.

Soon, he and Gallagher began talking shop.

"The city is surrounded by the Taliban," said Rashid. "All four highways, even the road to the Shomali plains, are now under their control."

"I heard fuel truck drivers are being offered ten thousand dollars to make the run down to Kandahar," replied Gallagher.

The inspector nodded and dropped another sugar cube into his tea. "It's an 800 percent increase over what Afghans are paid for carrying anything else. The only problem is that the Taliban forbade transporting fuel to foreign troops."

Gallagher looked at Harvath and said, "A contractor asked one of Flower's brothers if he wanted to make the run, and the man wisely declined. But another man from their village agreed. The Taliban stopped him on the road and chopped his head off."

Harvath grimaced in disgust.

"Commercial aircraft can no longer refuel at the airport in Kandahar and most military bases are being forced to ration, even the Americans," said Rashid. "The greater problem, though, is that the Taliban once again control most of Afghanistan. As they did in their rise to power in the 1990s, they're promoting themselves as the best

and most reliable force for stability throughout the country."

"Which is only bolstered by the fact that
the Afghan government cannot project any
power outside of Kabul," added Gallagher.

Rashid looked at Harvath. "Your country
has invested significantly in us, but unfortunately the U.S. does not have much to show
for it. I'm afraid we are all losing ground."

Harvath didn't disagree. The situation in
Afghanistan was deteriorating daily. The
mujahideen had defeated the Soviets, and
while Harvath still held out hope, he had to
admit that if the United States did not dras-
tically change its strategy, there was a very
good chance that the Taliban, along with
al-Qaeda, were going to be the winners. An
outcome like that would be devastating not
only for Afghanistan, but for America and
the rest of the world. It was an all too real
possibility that Harvath didn't like thinking
about.

He nodded as Rashid continued. "I know
many Afghans who will not go back to life
under the Taliban again. These people are
beginning to plan their exit strategies."

"The United States will turn things
around," stated Harvath.

The inspector smiled. "That's exactly what
the Soviets said before they pulled their

troops out."

"We'll see," said Harvath. "The Afghan people deserve better than the Taliban. They deserve a government that can protect them and provide an environment that will allow them to succeed."

Rashid raised his glass. "I agree."

Gallagher and Harvath raised their glasses and they all took a sip. When they had been lowered, Gallagher quietly got to the heart of the meeting. "Does the Amniyat have anything new on the American doctor's kidnapping?"

Amniyat was a local term for the National Directorate of Security, Afghanistan's domestic intelligence agency, also known as the NDS.

"No. Nothing. They questioned the people of the last village she and her interpreter had been in and no one knows anything. As you know, her organization's vehicle and the body of the interpreter were found a couple of kilometers away, and village elders within thirty kilometers have all been questioned, but still nothing," said Rashid, who then turned to Harvath. "I understand that is why you are here."

Harvath nodded.

"Ahmad," Gallagher replied, "my friend represents Dr. Gallo's family. As I explained to you, he is a man of much experience and is highly regarded by the government of the United States. He has a deeply ingrained dislike for both the Taliban and al-Qaeda, as well as much experience dealing with them. I am hoping you will be able to help him."

"By finding Mustafa Khan, correct?" asked Rashid.

Gallagher nodded.

"My government will not be very happy if Khan does not stand trial for his crimes."

"And you?" asked Harvath. "How would you feel about it?"

"As a police officer, I would be professionally disappointed, of course. But as a Pashtun, I know that justice will eventually be served. Several of Khan's victims have been Pashtun. Their families know who he is and he won't be able to hide forever. Now, whether tribal justice should trump the national rule of law in Afghanistan is another debate entirely."

"The rule of law notwithstanding, can we assume you may be willing to help?" asked Harvath.

Rashid smiled. "Have you ever heard of the Red Mullah, Mr. Harvath?"

Harvath shook his head.

"Mullah Sorkh Naqaib, or as he is more commonly known, the Red Mullah," continued the inspector, "is a high-ranking Taliban commander from Helmand Province who specializes in attacks on British troops. Over the last three years, he has been arrested and released three times. Each time he purchased his release through bribery.

"The last time was just this past summer when he was being held in NDS custody at Policharki prison. He had a visitor smuggle in fifteen thousand dollars and a half hour later he was free. An investigation wasn't begun until Naqaib bragged to the British press about how easy it is to get out of jail in Afghanistan."

"So what you are saying," stated Harvath, "is that with money all things are possible."

Rashid clicked his tongue against the roof of his mouth. "No. What I am saying is that the Afghan government is tired of being embarrassed. These are not stupid men who run our country. Many of them are corrupt, but they realize that they must at least appear to be trying to do their jobs if Afghanistan hopes to enjoy continued international support. These men fatten their bank accounts from the aid money that flows into the country, and rivers run downhill not up."

"Meaning?"

"Meaning, prison guards are not sending a portion of the bribes they receive back to

Kabul. The men in power don't profit when prisoners escape. In fact, it jeopardizes their positions, so they have taken measures to crack down on it. This is why Mustafa Khan was moved."

"Do you know where he was moved to?"

Rashid nodded, but remained silent.

Gallagher looked at Harvath and gave an almost imperceptible nod. Harvath slid his hand beneath his *patoo* and discreetly withdrew an envelope filled with cash. He was well aware that no senior Afghan liked to be passed money directly, so he tucked the envelope beneath one of the cushions between him and Rashid. "Dr. Gallo's family and I appreciate any support you can give us," Harvath said as he reached for his tea and took another sip.

The inspector scooped up some rice with his nan and looked at it as he chose his next words. "There are many men like me who still believe in Afghanistan's future, but only a foolish man would ignore the possibility that our future may not be that bright. The Taliban might return to power, and we have our families to think of. As you may know, mine is not very popular with the Taliban. There is much bad blood between us."

Once, Harvath had been put in a position of having to choose between protecting his family or his country. It was a decision he never should have been asked to make, but he hadn't hesitated. He had chosen his family. In that respect, part of him understood where Ahmad Rashid was coming from. There was also part of him that didn't. The man was apparently willing to undermine his own government in order to finance his personal escape plan.

Maybe if Harvath had experienced everything Rashid had experienced over the last thirty-some-odd years he would see things differently. He honestly couldn't say. Nevertheless, he replied, "I understand."

Looking at Baba G, Rashid asked, "Do you know the abandoned Soviet military base on the Darulaman Road?"

Gallagher nodded.

"Beneath the barracks, there is an old detention facility. After the current government was installed, our president reopened the facility. It's his own private prison. That's where they've moved Mustafa Khan."

"You're absolutely sure?"

The inspector nodded.

"What's the security like?" asked Gallagher.

"Afghan Special Forces. All handpicked by the defense minister, all Pashtuns loyal to the president."

"How many?" asked Harvath.

"I don't know, but I may be able to find out," said Rashid.

Harvath's mind moved in multiple directions as he made a list of the specific intelligence they'd need to mount their operation. "We'll also need schematics, drawings."

"I'm not sure if any professional drawings exist."

"I'd prefer professional drawings, but I'll settle for unprofessional as long as they're accurate."

"The Soviet base is directly across the Darulaman Road from the CARE hospital," said Gallagher.

"Correct," replied Rashid.

It took Harvath a second to realize the irony. "Isn't that where Julia Gallo's NGO, CARE International, is based?"

"Yes."

They had been keeping their voices low, but Gallagher lowered his even more as he said, "This might work to our advantage."

"How?" asked Harvath.

"Way before CARE International came along, it was a Soviet hospital. In fact, the Soviets built it."

"So?"

"So, the Soviets did *a lot* of construction in that area, including the building of their embassy. Many of the structures are rumored to be connected to the base by underground tunnels. The hospital was one of the closest buildings to the base. If they were going to build an escape tunnel that would have been one of the easiest places to do it."

Harvath turned to Rashid. "Do you know anything about these tunnels?"

"I've heard about them, yes," he replied.

"But have you ever seen them yourself?"

"No, but I may know someone who has. If there's a tunnel between the hospital and the base, he'll know about it."

"How soon can you get hold of him?" asked Harvath.

The inspector looked at his watch. "I will call you in two hours."

Harvath wrote down the number for the prepaid mobile phone Flower had purchased for him and then made a list of gear he would need Rashid to procure. "Can you get these things for me?"

As the inspector read the items on the list, he raised his eyebrows. "This is quite an unusual list."

"This is going to be quite an unusual job. Can you get them?"

"I'll make some calls."

"Okay," said Harvath, anxious to get back to Baba G's and make some calls of his own.

"We'll talk again in two hours."

Inspector Rashid stood and offered Harvath his hand. "If you need anything else in the meantime, Mr. Gallagher knows how to get hold of me."

As Harvath and Baba G turned to leave, the police officer added, "Please be careful. Kabul is a very dangerous place."

Chapter 15

There was gunfire on the way back to the ISS compound, but it wasn't directed at Baba G's Land Cruiser. It was small-arms fire, referred to in military parlance as *saf,* and as best they could tell it had come from a block or two away. Too close for comfort and even more unsettling when Gallagher explained that saf, RPG, and suicide bombing attacks were on the upswing in the Afghan capital.

Back at the compound, Harvath grabbed a bottle of water from the kitchen and then commandeered Baba G's room so that he could send secure emails and make a few phone calls. As he waited for his laptop to power up, he noticed that Gallagher's trash can had been emptied and that the bottles from the night before had been removed.

While his browser connected with the Internet, Harvath took a long slug of water, glanced at his watch, and did the math. It was nearing 5:00 P.M. in Kabul, which meant it was almost 8:30 A.M. back in D.C. He forced the jet lag from his mind and focused on the work he needed to get done.

Pulling out his encrypted BlackBerry, he texted a colleague based in D.C. with the message "Need help. Can u talk?"

Three minutes later he received a response. "Life/death? In a meeting."

Harvath shook his head. CIA was obsessed with meetings. If their management showed even half as much interest in supporting the excellent people it had in the field and green-lighting operations to nail bad guys, America would be a much safer place. Harvath texted back a one-word response — "Yes." He was fairly certain the free world would continue to survive if his contact stepped out of a meeting for a few minutes.

Less than sixty seconds later, his Black-Berry rang. Activating the call, Harvath raised the phone to his ear and said, "Nine-one-one, what's your emergency?"

"I think the CIA is trying to kill me," replied a voice from Northern Virginia.

Harvath laughed. "Death by Power-Point?"

"Worse," said the voice. "Mandatory sensitivity training. They're killing us with kindness."

Only CIA, thought Harvath, *would waste*

time and money putting its paramilitary opera-tives through sensitivity training. If it wasn't so sad, it might actually have been funny. "My tax dollars at work."

"Look at it this way," the voice stated. "When I eventually kill bin Laden, I'll be able to do it while embracing all of the differences between our cultures that make us both unique and special."

"Not if I get to him first."

This time, it was Aydin Ozbek's turn to laugh. Harvath's CIA contact was a part of the Agency's Special Activities Division, which was responsible for counterterrorism activities. He and Harvath had gotten to know each other the previous summer when cases they were working on intersected.

Harvath had a lot of respect for Ozbek, who refused to let the CIA tie him up in bureaucratic knots. If management wouldn't cooperate, the man wasn't afraid to do what needed to be done, even if it meant coloring outside the lines. Ozbek represented not only what was right about CIA, but what direction it needed to take to go from being a Cold War era relic that many referred to as the "Failure Factory" to a modern terrorism-fighting machine.

It went without saying that Ozbek's style didn't exactly endear him to his superiors.

The only reason he still had a job at the CIA after breaking multiple laws in pursuit of a nest of Islamic radicals operating on American soil last summer was that Harvath had asked the president to intervene on his behalf. Now that the CIA had a bean counter with no intelligence experience in charge and a president in the Oval Office who knew even less about the intel community, Ozbek needed to tread carefully.

Harvath and Ozbek were similar in many ways, in particular the love they held for their country and the animosity they possessed toward its enemies, especially Islamic fundamentalists.

Even if Harvath hadn't saved Ozbek's job, the two would have been good friends. The job-saving part of the relationship did, however, mean that Harvath had a lot of bonus points on his side of the board.

"There's a bit of a delay on the line," said Ozbek. "Where are you?"

"Kabul," replied Harvath. "How'd you get out of your sensitivity training so fast?"

"I told my supervisor you were a North Korean arms source I was developing and that I needed to take your call. You should have seen the look on the guy's face."

"Knowing you, his BS detector was probably pegging into the red."

"On the contrary," said Ozbek. "I could hear the gears grinding away in his mind as he tried to figure out how to work it into his next report and take credit for it. So what are you doing in Kabul, or shouldn't I ask?"

"I'm looking for something."

"Something or *someone*?"

"Both," said Harvath, "but I need the *something* before I can get my hands on the *someone*."

Ozbek understood Harvath's need to watch what he said over the phone and didn't press him any further. "How can I help?"

"How deep is the talent on your Afghan desk?"

"Pretty deep."

"Any people there from the Soviet days?" asked Harvath.

Ozbek thought about it a moment. "I think they've hired one or two of the retired guys back as private contractors."

"Can you get to a computer in the next few minutes?"

"I'm going to miss out on the trust fall, but if I have to, I have to."

"I'll drop something in the box," said Harvath.

"Roger that. How soon to do you need a reply?"

"ASAP."

"All right," said Ozbek. "I'm on it."

Harvath thanked him and disconnected the call. He then opened the web-based email account he and Oz used to communicate and left a note for him in the draft folder.

What he wanted to know was what kind of intel the CIA had developed on the old Soviet military base where Mustafa Khan was being held, as well as the hospital across the road. Hopefully the CIA had turned the Soviet embassy inside out as the last of the Russians were rolling out of Kabul and maybe, just maybe, they had come up with something that he could use.

The next thing Harvath had to do was prepare a report for Stephanie Gallo. She had no background in intelligence or national security and Harvath had to assume that no matter how badly she wanted her daughter back, any correspondence he exchanged with her could end up being compromised.

Before leaving, he had explained that his communications would be purposefully vague and that there would be periods when he would not be able to send her any reports at all. He wasn't in Afghanistan to trade emails with her, he was there to rescue her daughter.

Harvath knew, though, that despite her tough exterior, Stephanie Gallo was still a mother, and like any parent, she was undoubtedly agonizing over her daughter's situation. When Harvath thought of Stephanie Gallo, it was her role as parent that he tried to picture.

Drawing from the code words they had developed, he dashed off a quick message.

Have arrived. Rug dealer has moved. Working on new location. Will be in touch when I know more.

He debated adding an assurance that he felt good about the prospects of getting Gallo's daughter back alive, but he decided against it. He hadn't been hired to hold her hand. He had been hired to get results. In the end, that's all anyone would care about.

Logging out of that email account, Harvath switched over to gmail and found a message waiting from Tracy. In it was a picture she had taken of Bullet lying by the front door of the cottage.

Who needs a deadbolt? Hope you had a good flight. Stay safe. See you when you get back.

Harvath smiled. Tracy was a wonderful woman. He sent her a reply, logged out of the account, and opened Google Earth to see what kind of open-source imagery was available for their target locations.

The imagery was somewhere between one to three years old yet fairly detailed. All the same, Harvath wasn't happy with what it showed him. At least three of the buildings, and possibly more, had brand-new roofs and displayed other signs of having been upgraded. It was very possible that the base was being used as more than just the Afghan president's private detention complex.

Before they did anything, they were going to need to get a look at those facilities. And the closer, the better.

CHAPTER 16

Washington, D.C.

Thirty-two-year-old Elise Campbell lived in a tiny apartment on Massachusetts Avenue between Sixth and Seventh. It was a "junior" one-bedroom with an efficiency kitchen, a narrow bathroom, and a living/sleeping space separated by a sleek divider that only went three-quarters of the way to the ceiling.

Lining the walls were black and white reprints of famous French photographs. Stainless-steel shelving held an assortment of hip periodicals, as well as a commemorative coffee-table book about the New York Yankees, and a small entertainment center housed a flatscreen TV, a DVD player, and an iPod docking station.

All told, the apartment looked more like a trendy hotel suite than a space someone actually called home. It was obvious that Elise

Campbell didn't spend much time there. The only personal touch was a collection of framed photos of friends and family along the windowsill.

She had grown up in the eastern portion of the Commonwealth of Virginia often referred to as the Tidewater region. Her father had been a Virginia Beach police officer and had risen through the ranks to become a detective, as had his father, and his grandfather. Even Elise's great-great grandfather had been a law enforcement officer in the Tidewater area. She was the fifth generation of Campbells to continue the tradition, which was significant not only because she was the first Campbell woman to join the VBPD, but because both of her brothers had chosen careers in the corporate world. One had become a banker and the other a stockbroker.

Many believed Elise had followed the distinguished Campbell tradition to please her father and grandfather, but the answer was more simple than that. For Elise, as it had been for the Campbells who had come before her, law enforcement was a calling. She believed in justice and fair play. She believed in protecting those who were too weak to protect themselves, and she also knew that no matter how hard the police worked, they would never rid the world completely of evil. There would always be a need for cops because evil would always need to be kept at bay.

Elise also believed that she would touch more lives, and affect them for the better, than either of her brothers would in their chosen fields. She didn't see that as a knock on them and what they had chosen to do. Their careers were their callings and she respected them for having the guts to break with what the family had expected them to do.

Though she would never make the kind of money her brothers did, her compensation wasn't measured by a paycheck. It was measured by the sense of satisfaction and fulfillment she got from performing her job well and from the distinguished men and women she served alongside.

Her decision to switch to the Secret Service hadn't been easy, but it was one of the smartest career moves she had ever made. While she loved her colleagues and her job with the Virginia Beach PD, she never felt she'd make a good detective like the Campbells before her, and the pressure from her father and grandfather to follow their career track was just too intense.

Though she didn't see herself as a detective and wanted to get away from the pressure from Dad and "Pop" to be one, she also didn't want to entirely give up a career in law enforcement. Simply put, she loved being a cop. Oddly enough, it was her chief, Jack Jarett, who had encouraged her to consider a career in federal law enforcement.

Jarett had an uncanny ability to read people, and he had seen early on that regardless of generations of Campbell service to the VBPD, Elise wasn't going to stay in Virginia Beach forever. It was obvious that she wanted to do more and see more than just the Tidewater.

As a graduate of the FBI's NEIA program and a member of the Major City Chiefs organization, Chief Jarett had a lot of contacts in D.C. Though he practically had to threaten to fire Elise Campbell to get her to pursue the leads he had set up for her, she interviewed with the FBI, the DEA, and the Secret Service.

All three organizations invited her back for follow-up interviews and all three subsequently offered her positions, but it was the Secret Service that appealed to her the most.

While Pop had been supportive of her career move, her father couldn't hide his disappointment. And though he might have considered Elise's decision abandonment, her brothers congratulated her for following her own desires.

She knew they were full of it. With her gone from the Virginia Beach PD, they could both feel better about having bucked the family tradition as well. It made no difference that she was still in law enforcement. As far as they were concerned, she was on their side now and their father could not use her as a wedge anymore. She became a means for her brothers to magnify their independence from their father, and he blamed her for everything he felt had gone wrong with their family, including its geographical breakdown, with one brother in New York, another in Chicago, and her even in nearby D.C.

Campbell didn't care for being the family's emotional football, and even though she loved them, she had grown somewhat estranged over the past couple of years. With all of the travel and long hours in the Service, it was easy to put any semblance of a personal life on hold. It didn't mean she didn't want to have one, it just seemed as though there wasn't time for anything more than casual relationships.

She knew that also bothered her father. Not that he was aware of the kind of casual relationships she was having, but she wasn't married and neither were her brothers. Her father saw it as yet another example of the unraveling of America and indicative of how the nation was committing cultural suicide.

Elise wanted to have a family. It was just a matter of meeting the right man. But as capable as she was as a law enforcement officer, she was incredibly shy when it came to meeting men. It was an odd juxtaposition that her friends constantly teased her about. Some were fond of saying that if she ever met the right man, it better be while he was in the process of committing a crime, or she was very likely to let him escape.

She doubted that was how it would play out. She was simply old-fashioned. She believed that when she met the right man, they both would know it and that would be it. Plain and simple.

And as far as remaining desirable until that someone special came along, Elise had nothing to worry about, as the Service required that she remain in top physical condition.

To that end, and even though she had been at Carolyn Leonard's so late the night before and had allowed herself to sleep in because she had several days in a row off, she'd still gone for a five-mile run once she was up.

After returning to her apartment, she took

a long, hot shower and continued to think about everything she and Carolyn had discussed.

Leonard was right. The final decision about what to do rested with her. She had also laid out a million different ways that pursuing the president's alleged involvement in Nikki Hale's death could blow up in Elise's face and end her career.

The upside, if there was one, was minimal compared with what the downside very likely would be. That said, Leonard had admitted that if she was in Elise's shoes, she would have had trouble dropping the matter as well.

Campbell didn't need the added encouragement, but she appreciated her mentor's admission. In fact, Elise's mind had been made up from the beginning. She just hadn't realized it. No matter how small the upside, or how great the downside, she couldn't sit back and do nothing.

While she'd remained neutral on-duty during the primaries and through the general election, off-duty she had been an ardent Alden supporter. Many of her friends had said she was in serious need of a twelve-step program in order to kick the Alden Kool-Aid habit. Those same friends would be stunned if they saw her questioning him now. In all fairness, she herself was stunned. A week ago, if anyone had suggested President Alden could have been involved in anything untoward, much less a cover-up around the death of Nikki Hale, she would have told them they were out of their minds. Yet here she was, ready to begin her own quiet, and highly illegal, investigation of the newly elected president of the United States.

Pouring a cup of coffee, Elise grabbed her cordless phone off the counter and headed back into the living room. Scrolling through her BlackBerry, she found the number she was looking for, plugged it into the cordless, and then leaned back onto the couch and took a quick sip from her mug.

The call was answered by a woman with a heavy Bronx accent. "East Hampton Town Police. Detective Klees."

"Hi, Rita. It's Elise."

"Hey there," responded a voice deepened from years of smoking. "How ya doing?"

"I'm good. I'm good," said Campbell.

"You been watching the Yankees? They're off to a good start."

Elise laughed. You could take the girl out of the Bronx, but you couldn't take the Bronx out of the girl. Rita Klees was a rabid Yankees fan.

"Are you surprised?" asked Campbell.

"Look how well they did in the Grapefruit League this year. They're going all the way."

"From your lips to God's ears," replied Klees. "I've still got my reservations about Girardi, but he's very good-looking, and he's starting to grow on me."

"Rita, the man's married," Campbell teased.

"So was Alex Rodriguez until he met Madonna. Listen, as long as Mrs. Girardi keeps Mr. Girardi out of East Hampton, he'll be fine. But if he happens to come to town and just happens to bump into this particular material girl, I can't be responsible for what Cupid does to the poor guy."

Elise laughed again. She had no doubt that if Girardi, or any other New York Yankee, showed up in her jurisdiction, Rita would personally put them under twenty-four-hour surveillance. Not only that, but she would probably find a way to introduce herself and end up inviting them out to her favorite tavern to drink them under the table. She was one of those people you couldn't help but enjoy being around. She had an infectious laugh and a larger-than-life personality. She was an irresistible force that immediately became the center of gravity in every room she ever walked into.

An attractive woman in her late forties

with dark hair and bright blue eyes, Klees had a pair of breasts almost as big as her personality. She was fond of saying that her boobs did for her what Columbo's wrinkled raincoat had done for the clever television detective. Most men, and more than a few women, believed that breast size and intelligence were inversely proportional. That patently asinine line of reasoning was fine by Klees. She was smarter and better at her job than any four men put together. The NYPD had known it and had promoted her accordingly. She'd earned her gold shield faster than any woman in the history of the force.

But after losing two close friends on 9/11, she'd decided she'd had it with New York City. She traded in the stress, the crime, the hassles, and a not insignificant portion of her paycheck for life in the Hamptons. And while she didn't live like a rock star or a hotel heiress, she was happy. Rita made friends wherever she went and East Hampton was no exception.

Though she was several years removed from Manhattan, she still maintained excellent contacts back at the NYPD and with many of the federal law enforcement agencies. When organizations like the Secret Service came to East Hampton, it was a no-brainer for Rita's chief to assign her as the liaison. That was how she and Elise Campbell had become friends.

Due to the number of threats he had received, Robert Alden had been assigned Secret Service protection very early on in the primary campaign, and Elise had been one of the agents tasked to his detail. Part of her responsibility was doing advance work and interfacing with local law enforcement wherever the senator traveled. Though Elise wasn't working the trip on which Nikki Hale was killed, she had made several visits to East Hampton with Alden and had gotten to know Rita Klees very well. Their mutual love of the Yankees vaulted Campbell's standing in the East Hampton detective's eyes, and on multiple evenings off, Rita dragged Elise to some of her favorite watering holes. And even though Campbell had not returned to East Hampton since the Hale incident, she and Rita still kept in touch via email — which technically meant that she was on the daily receiving end of humorous emails forwarded by the East Hampton detective.

"So, you coming to town or did you call just to talk baseball?" asked Klees.

"No to both, unfortunately."

"What's up?"

"I need some help with something," said Campbell. "Do you remember the Nikki

Hale case?"

"The wasted senior staffer who plowed her car into that minivan head-on last summer? Yeah, I remember it. Why?"

"I need to see the file."

"What for?" asked Klees.

"Off the record?"

"Sure. Off the record."

"There's a concern that someone may not have been completely truthful in their witness statement."

There was a pause and Elise thought she could hear her friend taking a puff on a cigarette, though she doubted even the larger-than-life Rita Klees would be allowed to smoke in the East Hampton Town PD headquarters.

When Rita finally answered, her tone had changed. She was a lot less jovial and a lot more businesslike. "Which witness are we talking about?" she asked. "And who exactly is concerned?"

"I can't say," replied Elise.

"*Can't say* to which question?"

"Both."

"No offense, Elise, but you were just one of Alden's advance people and you weren't even out here during the whole Hale thing. Why am I getting this call from you?"

"Because we're friends."

Klees was silent again. Elise strained to discern if it was because Rita was taking another drag, but she couldn't tell. She assumed it was because Klees was deciding how to respond.

"Are you in some sort of trouble?" asked the detective.

"No. Of course not," she replied. "Why would you think that?"

"Because you're not being straight with me."

Whether it was because she'd been a cop, or because she was a native New Yorker, Rita had an exceptional bullshit detector.

In all fairness, Elise did too, and she knew better than to try to lie her way through this. "I can't go into the specifics."

"Why not?"

"I told you. I can't say."

Again, Rita was silent.

"Listen," continued Elise. "I could be completely off-base here. That's why I need to see the file. And that's why I'm asking you."

"So this isn't an official Secret Service request, then," stated Klees.

"No," replied Campbell. "It's just cop to cop."

"Well, cop to cop, there's no way in hell I'm sending you a copy of this file."

Rita's retort stung, and it took Campbell a few seconds to reply. "I'm not asking for my own permanent copy."

"Elise, I've seen people lose their careers over stuff like this. I like where I am and I'd like to stay here. I also like my captain, even if he is a Mets fan. He'd be in a hell of a lot of trouble if this thing went sideways."

"I don't want to get you or anyone in your department in trouble, Rita. Listen, like I said, I don't know if there's anything to this or not."

"So what exactly are you looking for?"

"I won't know until I see the file."

Rita was silent yet again as she thought it over and then replied, "I can't send you a copy of the file, but I can let you see the one we have here. On one condition."

"Shoot."

"You come completely clean and tell me what you're looking for. And if I think, even for a second, that you're not being totally honest, cop to cop or friend to friend, it won't matter. Our deal will not only be off, but I'll get your boss on the phone and find out what the hell is going on, even if I have to reopen this case and make it official."

CHAPTER 17

Northeastern Afghanistan

A trip to Nangarhar Hospital in Jalalabad confirmed what Elam Badar already suspected — his son's jaw was broken. Though it was difficult for the boy to speak, Elam Badar had coaxed from Asadoulah what had happened. When the boy explained that Mullah Massoud's retarded brother, Zwak, had attacked him without provocation, the father was incensed.

He had always thought it ridiculous that the elders of Massoud's village allowed Zwak, the halfwit, to run around with a rifle, even if the barrel was taped at the end. The man should have been kept indoors. Allowing him to roam the streets of his village accusing visitors of being spies or having come to poison the village well was asking for trouble. And now trouble had come.

Asadoulah told his father how he had

made the hour trek to the neighboring village to visit friends. While there, the boys told him about the American that Massoud's men had taken hostage. Like many Afghan boys, Asadoulah had never seen an American woman before. His friends offered to show her to him.

Asadoulah told his father that Zwak must have been on the other side of the hut they were using to hold the woman because no sooner had he begun peering through a crack in the wooden door than the retarded man appeared, called Asadoulah a spy, and clubbed the boy in the jaw with the butt of his rifle.

Elam Badar knew that Zwak had a difficult time remembering the faces of those from even neighboring villages. He himself had been called a spy many times by Massoud's brother and had been prevented from even walking past their well on more than one occasion. Zwak took his mock duties seriously, but in this case he had gone entirely too far. And so had his brother.

If the Taliban commander *was* holding an American woman hostage, that was bad enough, but to put Zwak in charge of guarding her seemed downright foolish. The halfwit was incapable of responding appropriately. The fact that he had countered a bunch of boys peering through a crack in a door with violence proved what a danger he was. His attack on Asadoulah couldn't be ignored. Zwak and his antics had been tolerated for far too long. Now a boy's jaw had been broken. Enough was enough.

Elam Badar parked his truck on the edge of the village and walked toward its center. He was not a particularly big man, nor was he particularly brave, and he did not relish the idea of having to deal with a Taliban commander like Mullah Massoud. But this was about honor, and the Pashtun code was very clear about how such things must be handled, specifically when it came to an assault on a family member.

In the center of the village, built into a small copse of trees, was an elevated wooden structure with a wide veranda. It was here that the council of village elders, or *shura,* conducted all of the affairs for the village. Elam Badar mounted the structure's stairs and removed his shoes before stepping inside.

One of the villagers sitting on the floor inside recognized him and stood to greet him. They touched hearts and embraced. "It is good to see you, brother," said the villager.

"And you," replied Elam Badar, who, though anxious to speak with the village elders, quieted the anger in his heart and chatted with the man for several minutes before requesting to be seen.

"What has happened?" asked the man.

Elam Badar forced a smile. He knew all too well how quickly gossip spread, and he didn't want Mullah Massoud or his halfwit brother to have time to concoct a story to explain away the attack. He wanted to take them completely by surprise, and so said, "Nothing of great importance. I have a small matter that concerns both of our villages that I need to discuss."

He was shown to a small room off to the side where the village elders had just finished a meeting with a handful of men on another subject. After the greetings, the village elders ushered the other men out and invited Elam Badar to take tea with them.

As he had done with the villager at the door, Elam Badar kept his anger in check and adhered to Pashtun etiquette. They talked about several different subjects of mutual interest before arriving at the true reason Elam Badar had come.

"I understand you have an American visitor," he said. "A woman."

Of the four elders in the room, it was customary for only one to speak. The man who did was in his sixties with an ash-colored beard and a stern disposition. He had a thick scar that began at the bridge of his nose and traveled downward across the left side of his face to just beneath his ear. Elam Badar knew that the scar was a souvenir from one of the many battles the elder had fought against the Soviets. His name was Baseer.

"Our village is often blessed with visitors," replied the chief elder with a motion of his hand that indicated he considered Elam Badar's visit a blessing.

Elam Badar nodded politely and kept going. "She must be very important if she is being kept guarded."

An uncomfortable silence descended upon the small room. Elam Badar allowed it to linger for several seconds before continuing. "Are you aware that while he was guarding her, Zwak assaulted my son?"

It was obvious from the look on Baseer's face that this piece of information took him by surprise. Elam Badar allowed his eyes to shift to the faces of the other three elders and he saw that they were equally shocked. Feeling the wind at his back, he removed from his pocket the paperwork that the young doctor at the hospital in Jalalabad had given him. Carefully unfolding them, he handed the pages to the elder. "With the butt of his rifle," Elam Badar, asserted, "Zwak *broke* my son's jaw."

The elder studied the paperwork and then handed it to his colleagues to read. "You have four boys, correct?"

"Yes," replied Elam Badar.

"Which one are we talking about?"

"My oldest. Asadoulah."

"I am sorry for his jaw being broken and for your family's trouble in this matter," said Baseer.

"Thank you," Elam Badar responded.

The elder stroked his beard as his mind processed what he had heard. "Zwak is a simple man, we all know this, but he has never before been violent."

Elam Badar's eyes widened. "He accuses everyone who enters your village of being a spy and prevents those he doesn't recognize or cannot remember from walking anywhere near your well."

Baseer shrugged and raised his palms. "Yet still, he has never harmed anyone. Let me ask you. Your son can speak?"

Elam Badar nodded.

"What did he tell you happened?"

"He said that he had come to your village to visit friends. They told him about the American woman and asked if he wanted to see her. He agreed and they took him to where she was being held. While he was trying to see her through a crack in the door, Zwak came from the other side of the building and struck him in the jaw with the butt of his rifle."

Once again the elder was silent. Elam Badar watched him as he stroked his beard and wondered if they truly grasped the seriousness of the situation. The Pashtun code was on his side in such a matter. No longer able to contain his anger over this situation having even been allowed to develop in the first place, Elam Badar opened his mouth and his ill-chosen words burst forth. "I know the American woman is not a guest in your village. She is a hostage, and you know it too. Have you any idea how dangerous this is for us? It's not just your village that will suffer repercussions for this. If word gets out, we'll all suffer because of what Mullah Massoud has done."

Baseer held up his hand. This man was getting away from himself very quickly. The other village was nearly five kilometers away. Whatever Mullah Massoud had done, it wouldn't affect them.

That said, Baseer was not happy that word had spread about the American woman. He had warned Massoud against bringing her back to the village. He had suggested they find someplace else to keep her, but Massoud had insisted. No doubt his decision came in part at the behest of the Russian, the one they called Bakht Rawan.

The Russians had never had the Afghans' best interests at heart, and the elder doubted that much had changed since their "departure" from Afghanistan. The elder had seen far too many of them in recent years to believe they had given up wanting a stake in his country.

But as much as the elder didn't trust Bakht Rawan and the rest of his countrymen, the matter before him had to do with Mullah Massoud.

It sounded as if the Taliban commander had placed too much confidence in his brother and though the elder had not yet heard Zwak's side of the story, so far it was a very unpleasant situation that had the potential to get much worse. Elam Badar's son had had more than his pride wounded. Something needed to be done. Villages had gone to war against each other over less, and while Massoud could summon hundreds of battle-hardened soldiers, Elam Badar's village possessed guns and experienced mujahideen as well.

"We will speak with Mullah Massoud," said Baseer.

"But he was not there to see what happened to my son," protested Elam Badar.

The elder held his hand up again. "We will also speak with Zwak," he added.

Once more, Elam Badar's passion flared. "There can be no excuse for what happened to my son."

Smiling, Baseer signaled that the meeting was over. As Elam Badar embraced him, the elder held on for a little longer than normal. "We will make this right. I promise you. Your family and your village are important to us."

Elam Badar felt indignant, but he tried to push the emotion back down into the pit of his stomach where it had begun. "Thank you," he replied.

The other elders embraced Elam Badar and summoned the villager he was friendly with to walk with him back to his truck.

When they stepped outside, the sun was already slipping behind the mountain peaks that surrounded the village and the temperature had begun to drop.

Baseer watched Elam Badar descend the wooden stairs and disappear from sight beyond the copse of trees. Beneath his breath, he silently cursed Mullah Massoud. He and all of his Taliban brothers were going to be the death of Afghanistan.

CHAPTER 18

Kabul

When Mei began sending out buckets of beer and enormous plates of food from the kitchen, Gallagher turned off the TV and rang the dinner bell.

As people selected seats around the table, Mei ditched her husband and grabbed the chair next to Harvath. Flirtatiously, she tucked her arm through his and glancing heavenward said, "Finally, a *real* man. My prayers have been answered."

"Mine too," replied Hoyt as he grabbed a large bowl of fried rice and scooped a portion onto his plate. "I haven't had a decent night's sleep in months."

Everyone laughed. In addition to Harvath, Mei, Hoyt, and Gallagher, there were three of Mei's Chinese girlfriends and two of ISS's other employees seated at the table for dinner. Mark Midland was a twenty-six-year-old American communications expert who functioned as Tom Hoyt's right-hand man and helped run the ISS ops center. He was tall and thin, with strawberry blond hair, pale skin, and a face full of freckles.

Across from him was a thirty-four-year-old Canadian, Daniel Fontaine. He was a former member of Canada's storied counterterrorism unit, Joint Task Force 2. While he claimed he had left JTF2 to get into the private security world in order to make enough money to pay for a ranch he had his eye on back home, Harvath had never believed him. There were plenty of other outfits that paid a lot more than Hoyt and Gallagher.

The Canadians were a smart bunch when it came to gathering their intel. Harvath's guess was that Fontaine worked for the Canadian Intelligence Security Service and was in Afghanistan to gather intel for the Canadian military operating within the country under NATO command. His ISS job was just a cover.

Fontaine was a handsome, six-foot-one man with dark hair who was used to commanding most of the attention from Mei's girlfriends, as well as any other female visitors who came to the ISS compound.

If Fontaine wasn't working protection on

one of the ISS security contracts, he spent most of his evenings out partying with the Western ex-pat community. And what Gallagher and Hoyt referred to as "partying," Harvath saw as most likely developing relationships with non-Canadian nationals and gathering intel.

But no matter what Fontaine's true marching orders were, both Gallagher and Hoyt praised him as being an exceptionally talented operator. He was also an immediately likable guy, and though he and Harvath had only met once before, they had gotten along very well.

The sticky part for Harvath was whether Fontaine could be brought into what Hoyt comically referred to as their "circle of trust." Both Gallagher and Hoyt not only knew that Harvath was in Afghanistan to spring Khan, they were being paid to help him do it.

While Fontaine might be a good guy to involve in their operation, if he was what Harvath suspected him to be, he'd feed all of their plans straight back to Canada. So, as much as Harvath liked him, he decided to keep him out of the loop on Khan. As far as Fontaine was concerned, Harvath was in-country to drum up leads and help consult on the Gallo kidnapping.

As the meal continued, everyone was drinking except for Harvath. His jet lag weighed on him and he decided to stick with caffeine. They also had yet to hear from Rashid, and Harvath wanted to keep a clear head until they had a better angle on what was going on. That went for Gallagher too.

When Harvath saw him reaching for his third bottle of beer, he shot him a look. Baba G was Harvath's right arm while he was in-country, and he needed to stay sharp. He was getting paid a lot of money to be on call twenty-four hours. He wouldn't be good to anyone drunk.

After Rashid had missed the two-hour call window by an hour, Harvath gave up looking at his watch. *TIA,* he reminded himself. He was on Afghan time now, and a promise from an Afghan to get back to someone in two hours didn't necessarily mean he would get back to you in two hours. *You have watches, but we have time,* the Afghans were fond of saying.

When the cell phone in his pocket did begin to vibrate, it took Harvath by surprise. He fished it out, only to realize it wasn't his Afghan phone ringing, but his U.S. BlackBerry.

Standing up from the table, he excused

himself and stepped outside into the cold night air. A fire was going in the courtyard's fire pit and Harvath walked toward it as he activated the call and held the device up to his ear. "This is Harvath."

"Scot, it's Oz," replied his pal back at CIA.

Harvath was glad to hear from him. He hoped the man had good news. "Were you able to speak with anyone from the Afghan desk?"

"I talked to two of them as well as an agent who'd been senior on the Soviet desk when the Russians pulled out."

"And?"

"You were right about one thing," said Ozbek. "The agency did have operatives there taking advantage of the troop withdrawal in 1988, as well as the collapse of Afghanistan's Kremlin-backed government in 1992 when the Russians shuttered their embassy."

"How about the hard intel I need?"

"According to these guys, not much was left behind. And what the Russians did leave was pretty well sanitized."

"So no drawings, no blueprints, nothing about the old Soviet base?"

"I'm sorry."

Harvath filled his lungs and exhaled,

watching his breath float upward. "All right," he said. "Thanks for trying."

Disconnecting the call, he slid the Black-Berry back into his pocket and stood for a moment warming his hands over the fire. From inside the dining room, he heard more laughter. In the ever-worsening hell that was Afghanistan, it was good that they could relax long enough to laugh.

That made him wonder what Julia Gallo was experiencing at the moment. She was undoubtedly cold, hungry, and very scared. She also probably had no idea whether she was going to live or die. Kidnapping was one of the cruelest tortures a person could be forced to endure. Every time the jailer's key turned inside the lock, every bump or shuffle outside your cell door made you wonder, *Is this it? Are they finally coming for me? Is this the moment I die?*

He picked up a piece of brittle scrap wood and dropped it into the fire. Somewhere behind him, he heard the door to the dining room open.

Turning, he saw Baba G with his jacket on and his cell phone in his hand. "Rashid just called," he said. "He's got something for us and wants to meet."

Harvath wasn't surprised that the man had reached out to Gallagher. They were the ones with the relationship. He was a stranger. He just hoped that trusting Rashid wouldn't turn out to be a mistake.

CHAPTER 19

Within five minutes, they had gathered their gear and were ready to roll. Flower, who had returned from eating dinner with his family, was outside waiting for them behind the wheel of Gallagher's Land Cruiser.

Baba G got in front to ride shotgun while Harvath hopped in back. As Flower put the truck in gear and pulled away from the curb, Harvath pulled a Red Bull from the backpack at his feet and prayed that their meeting would be a short one. While being forced to stay awake was one way to get acclimated to local time, doing so while rolling through Kabul after dark had a considerable downside.

Traffic was light as most Afghans huddled at home, trying to keep warm. The people who were out were Westerners, patronizing the many restaurants and clubs that catered to them across the city.

As they exited a traffic circle onto a smaller

side street, Harvath took a mental snapshot to help him keep track of their route, just in case the unthinkable happened and he had to make his way home alone.

Following Gallagher's instructions, Flower performed a series of surveillance detection routes, or SDRs, and when the trio was satisfied they weren't being followed, they headed toward their rendezvous.

Inspector Rashid had provided Gallagher with a specific route, which Flower now followed.

He threaded the Land Cruiser through quiet streets and neighborhoods, some of which Baba G had never been through himself.

They had just turned out of a narrow side street when Harvath noticed Gallagher's posture change. "What's up?" he asked from the backseat.

Flower answered before his boss. "Checkpoint."

"Double-check your weapons," said Gallagher. "Make sure *everything* is out of sight. Have your ID available and remember to smile and be friendly. We're just a couple of NGO workers out for dinner."

As Harvath did as Gallagher suggested, he asked, "Have you ever seen a checkpoint here before?"

"No, but they move around all the time."

"It doesn't bother you that we've got a lot of money with us and right in the middle of the route that Rashid sent us on there's a roadblock?"

"Of course it bothers me," replied Gallagher, "but this could just be a checkpoint. With all the attacks, the Afghans are on heightened alert. Just stay calm and we'll be okay."

Harvath didn't believe in coincidences and adjusted the position of his holster so he could access his Glock quickly if he needed to.

Ahead of them were several green Ford pickup trucks with the Afghan National Army emblem on the side. Flower brought the Land Cruiser to a halt and rolled down his window. Gallagher and Harvath did the same with theirs.

The soldiers looked cold and bored. Harvath took that as a good sign this wasn't a holdup. If it was, the men at the checkpoint would be nervous and switched on.

He smiled as he'd been instructed and holding his hand over his heart bade the soldier outside his window, *"Salaam alaikum."*

The soldier had both hands on his AK-47, but he nodded and returned Harvath's greeting.

Gallagher bantered with his soldier in broken Dari, while Flower spoke in calm, quick sentences. When Harvath heard the soldier laugh, he started to relax. Seconds later, the soldiers bade them all a good evening and waved them through the checkpoint.

"See? Nothing to worry about," stated Gallagher as he powered his window back up and they drove on.

Ten minutes later, when they were within two blocks of their destination, Gallagher pulled out his mobile and called Inspector Rashid. The gates were open and waiting for them when they arrived.

Flower drove into the narrow courtyard and killed his lights. "I'll wait here," he said.

"You sure you don't want to come inside?" asked Gallagher.

He shook his head and, removing a pack of cigarettes from his heavy winter coat, pointed to a small guard shack where the men who had shut the gates behind them had gone and said, "I'll be over there."

Gallagher climbed out of the Land Cruiser and Harvath followed, his backpack slung over his shoulder.

A sentry outside the house they were using for the rendezvous stuck his hand out and asked for something in Dari. Harvath looked at Gallagher, who translated for him. "Take the batteries out of your cell phones. We'll get them back when we leave."

The Afghans harbored a paranoia regarding cell phones, especially their ability to act as beacons for American missile strikes. Warring factions had been known to toss compromised phones over the walls of each other's homes in the hopes that they could draw an American military response.

The Taliban were so afraid of mobile phones, they made cell providers in many parts of the country shut down their networks at night so they couldn't be tracked.

Harvath found it ironic that other than batteries, they hadn't been asked to surrender anything else. They didn't look into Harvath's bag, nor were he or Gallagher frisked. They were free to walk into the meeting armed, as long as it wasn't with a functioning cell phone.

The men slipped off their boots and were met inside by Inspector Rashid, who embraced them both. They touched hearts in greeting with the police officer and were shown into a large living area where two bearded men were already seated. The men rose and Rashid introduced them as Marjan and Pamir — his cousins who worked for the National Directorate of Security.

Once the group had said their traditional hellos and had shaken hands, Harvath and Gallagher removed their coats and sat down upon thin cushions on a green-carpeted floor.

Though the room was surrounded with windows, the panes of glass had been carefully covered over with paper. A small chandelier cast a yellow glow over the otherwise barren room.

Dishes of candy and sweets sat on the floor along with a silver pitcher and several glasses.

"Unfortunately," Rashid said with a smile as he reached for the pitcher and began pouring for everyone, "we only have American tea this evening."

"My favorite," replied Gallagher.

The instant his was poured, Harvath recognized what "American tea" was a euphemism for — *whiskey.*

Harvath sipped his drink slowly. Gallagher, on the other hand, made short work of his first round and wasn't shy about accepting a second. Cultural sensitivity notwithstanding, Harvath was concerned that Baba G needed to watch his intake. While he was all for male bonding, especially with foreign intelligence assets, this wasn't boys' night out. The whiskey was a preamble to a negotiation for which he and Gallagher needed to remain sharp.

After forty-five minutes of chit-chat, during which, Harvath noted thankfully, Baba G ignored his third round, they got down to the reason they were sitting in an NDS safe house in Kabul on a Friday night — snatching Mustafa Khan.

Rashid's cousin, Pamir, had the best news Harvath had heard yet. He not only knew of the underground tunnels radiating out from the old Soviet military base, he had been through many of them and could get his hands on any maps Harvath wanted.

Marjan had been tasked to the base's secret interrogation facility at one point and could provide any intel needed.

Inspector Rashid had certainly delivered, but Harvath was wary that it was all just a little too convenient. Undoubtedly they saw him as a walking ATM machine. Suckers were born every minute, but rarely did they roll through Afghanistan with the kind of money that Harvath was carrying.

He'd been leery about giving Rashid so much up front, but Gallagher had insisted, and Harvath trusted his knowledge of the marketplace to know the right amount to get Rashid's attention.

Well, they had apparently gotten the police inspector's attention. The question was, could they rely on what they were purchasing?

As if reading Harvath's mind, Inspector Rashid got to his feet and asked his guests to follow him. Harvath and Gallagher obeyed, with Marjan and Pamir right behind.

At the end of the hall, Rashid removed a key from his pocket and opened the door to a bedroom. Arrayed along two single beds were almost all of the items Harvath had requested.

Entering the room, he began going through the gear and inspecting it. Gallagher stepped in and took a look at it as well.

Once he had finished the inspection, Harvath asked Rashid, "What about the munitions?"

"The munitions you asked for are not easy to get."

"We can't do this without them."

The inspector smiled. "You requested something highly specialized."

Gallagher looked at Harvath and rubbed his thumb and forefinger together.

"How much to get the munitions?" asked Harvath.

"Let's have some more tea," replied Rashid.

Harvath turned toward the door and said

to Gallagher, "We obviously made a mistake. Let's go."

Rashid put his hands up and inserted himself into the doorway. "Please, my friends," he said. "I am here to help you."

"Then I suggest you help us find those munitions."

"Of course, of course. Anything is possible."

"With the right amount of money, right?" replied Harvath.

"As I said, this particular item is not so easy to get."

"But it is possible."

"If he cannot locate any of the items on your list, we can," stated Pamir.

Rashid smiled as if that settled everything and directed his guests back into the living room. Reluctantly, Harvath acquiesced.

After twenty more minutes of "tea," they discussed terms. While the prices weren't unreasonable, Harvath knew the Afghans expected to haggle and he was an exceptional negotiator. When they were finished, the cost had not been dramatically reduced, but Harvath had locked in a key insurance policy — Marjan and Pamir would join their team to help snatch Mustafa Khan.

Of course, the NDS operatives were not crazy about this idea at first, but the promise of a bonus of several times what each man made in a year sealed the deal.

They spent another hour talking, with Rashid, Marjan, and Pamir drinking the majority of the American tea in the pitcher.

When they said good-bye, the two Americans received long, whiskey-soaked hugs from their Afghan hosts.

Harvath removed several thick stacks of cash from his backpack and placed them under one of the cushions in the living room.

Out in the courtyard, Marjan and Pamir's men loaded the equipment into the back of the Land Cruiser and covered it over with a couple of blankets.

Sliding his cell phone back into his pocket, Rashid walked over to the truck and gave Flower a new set of directions, which would allow them to avoid the most recently positioned mobile checkpoints.

After pulling into the road, Gallagher looked over his shoulder. As he watched the gates to the NDS safe house close behind them, he asked, "So what do you think?"

In the darkness of the backseat, Harvath remained silent. Rashid had turned out to be better than he had expected, and Marjan and Pamir looked poised to pick up where the police inspector's expertise had left off, but in all honesty, Harvath knew they were still a long way from where they needed to be.

Their preoperational planning had been tossed out the window when Mustafa Khan had been moved from Policharki. They were starting from scratch now and Harvath didn't like that. Nevertheless, they were moving forward. He only hoped that they were moving fast enough.

CHAPTER 20

East Hampton, New York

Elise Campbell stepped off her train and onto the East Hampton platform. The evening air was chilly and damp.

The Secret Service agent had caught a high-speed Acela Express from Washington to Penn Station and from there the Long Island Railroad via Jamaica Station out to the easternmost town on the South Shore of Long Island. Standing beneath the portico was Detective Rita Klees.

"Whatever you do," said Rita as she greeted Elise with a hug and took her bag, "please tell me you didn't eat any train food."

"Rita, I've been on trains and in stations for over seven hours. So sue me, I broke down and had a sandwich."

Klees made a face. "I refuse to eat that garbage they serve." Nodding toward her car she said, "C'mon. We'll get you a real dinner. *And* a drink."

The detective threw Campbell's overnight bag into the cargo area of her Mini Cooper and then slid into the driver's seat. After starting the car, she picked up a pack of cigarettes and asked, "Do you mind?"

The car already smelled like an ashtray. "Go ahead," said Campbell as she rolled down her window.

They chatted about Elise's trip up from D.C. as Rita drove to a small restaurant called Thackers and parked her car. She grabbed her briefcase from the backseat and the two women made their way inside.

It was obvious by the attention Klees received from the hostess, as well as the piano player segueing out of the song he had been playing and launching into the Sinatra classic that closed every Yankee game, "New York, New York," that she was a bit of a regular.

Rita waved and said hello to other patrons she knew as they were shown to a quiet leather booth in the corner. When the hostess presented the menus, Klees declined and asked Elise, "You're a meat eater, right? Do you like short ribs?"

"I love short ribs," replied Campbell.

"These are the best you'll ever have," she said and then looked back at the hostess.

"Two orders of the short ribs, then, and I'll have a Johnnie Green on the rocks."

Elise ordered a glass of red wine and the hostess disappeared. Reaching into her briefcase, Rita removed a thick folder and set it on the table.

"Is that it?" asked Campbell.

Klees nodded.

Elise had spent the trip up from D.C. trying to figure out what to say to her friend. She knew she couldn't lie to her, which left her with only one option — the truth. *But how much of the truth should she reveal?* "I need your word that none of what I'm about to tell you will go any further."

"If we're talking about a crime being committed —" began Klees, who stopped when a waiter appeared with their drinks.

Once he had gone, Elise said, "I don't know for sure if a crime has been committed. That's why I'm here. But, if I'm wrong and there's nothing to this, then my career's over."

"So this has to do with the president?"

Campbell nodded.

"Can I assume he's the one you were referring to when you said maybe somebody wasn't completely truthful in their witness statement?"

Again, Campbell nodded.

"Okay. Did he have something to do with the accident?"

Elise looked at her friend. "I hope not."

"Then where's all of this coming from?"

"I may have overheard a conversation."

Rita stirred the ice cubes in her drink. "Now I understand."

"This puts me and the Secret Service in a very difficult position," said Campbell. "If he didn't do anything wrong and it gets out that I told people about the conversation, then the entire Secret Service not only looks bad, presidents will forever distance themselves from us, which will make it even harder to protect them."

"But if he did do something, then he's an idiot to have mentioned it in front of you."

"He didn't exactly know I was there."

"What are you talking about?"

"I was standing guard in a wooded area. He couldn't see me. He stopped within earshot and I heard his conversation."

"Who was he talking with?"

"Do I have your word that this will stay just between us?" asked Elise.

Rita nodded.

"He was talking with Stephanie Gallo."

"That's who was having the fund-raiser for him here."

"I know," said Campbell.

"That's also whose *house* he was staying at."

"I know."

"It's *also* where Nikki Hale had been before she left and had her accident."

Campbell reached for her wine and took a long sip.

"Were Gallo and the president having this conversation in person or was he on the phone?" asked Klees as she glanced around the room to make sure no one was eavesdropping on their conversation.

"They were together, taking a walk on her horse farm just outside D.C."

"What exactly did they say?"

Elise filled Rita in on the kidnapping of Julia Gallo, the ransom demand, and Stephanie Gallo's threat to expose the president's involvement in the death of Nikki Hale unless the president got her daughter back. When she was finished, she lifted her wineglass, sat back, and tried to dissolve into the booth.

"I'm stunned," said Klees.

"You and me both."

"He doesn't seem like that type of guy."

"I know," replied Campbell.

"So what exactly are the specifics of his involvement or this alleged cover-up around Nikki Hale's death?"

"That, I don't know. He and Gallo walked off before I could hear the rest of the conversation."

"Then you do have a problem. A *big* one."

"But if he wasn't really guilty, why would Gallo threaten to expose him and ruin his presidency?"

"Good point," said Klees as she stood up with her drink and left the file sitting on the table between them. "I'll have to think about that. I'm going to go have a cigarette. When the waitress comes back, order me another cocktail, okay?"

The East Hampton detective stood outside long enough to smoke two cigarettes and polish off her drink before returning. She was tempted to have a third cigarette, but worried it would be obvious that she was avoiding going back in and having to face Campbell. She steeled herself with the knowledge that as a detective, especially one in whose jurisdiction the crime in question took place, she had every right to do what she had done to Elise. It was time to face the music.

Walking back into the restaurant, she found a fresh Johnnie Green at the table and Campbell on her second glass of wine. The file was back where she had left it and their dinners had arrived. As she had expected, Elise was not happy.

"You told me you were going to let me see the entire file."

"That is the entire file," replied Klees as she took a sip of her new drink.

"It can't be."

Rita set down her cocktail and said, "East Hampton PD conducted the investigation as well as the on-scene accident reconstruction. The vehicles in question were impounded to our motor pool, where each underwent a full safety inspection by our mechanics.

"The bodies of the deceased were removed from the scene to the Suffolk County medical examiner's office in Hauppauge. Per the attached report, their portion of the investigation was to detail the cause of death for each fatality and to run toxicology tests to determine the intoxication and/or presence of any other substance or substances in the drivers' bodies that would have impaired them. As you can see from the report, Nikki Hale was the only one who was impaired. Case closed."

"*Case closed?*" replied Campbell as she reached over and shook the file. "You've got photographs, diagrams of the crash scene, everything but witness statements."

"That's because there were no eyewitnesses to the crash. One of our patrol officers was the first person on the scene."

"But what about the people back at Stephanie Gallo's estate? What about them? What about putting together what led to Nikki Hale's intoxication? Who was drinking with her? Who saw her last and so forth?"

Klees understood where Campbell was going. "You were a patrol officer when you were with the Virginia Beach PD, not a detective, right?"

"What do you mean by that?" she asked, a bit defensively.

Rita put up her hands. "I'm just trying to explain the way these things work. As a patrol officer, you take eyewitness statements at the scene. Anything above and beyond that is normally handled by detectives.

"If Nikki Hale had survived the accident, then the investigation would have definitely been more in-depth. We would have wanted to know what happened at the fund-raiser, how much she had had to drink, etcetera, because she'd be facing criminal charges. But since she's dead, there's no one to charge with a crime. Hence, case closed."

"So you let me come all the way out here knowing there were no witness statements for me to go over?" asked Campbell.

"You said you wanted to see the file. You didn't say you only wanted to see witness statements."

"Which I *assumed* were in there."

"And which you could have specifically asked about," replied Rita.

Elise shook her head in frustration. "I feel like you lied to me."

"I never lied to you. You held back from me, and I'll admit I wasn't 100 percent forthcoming with you, but what you were suggesting over the phone was that there might be adjunct criminal activity to Nikki Hale's death. I could have kicked it up the chain of command and made it official, or I could do it this way. I love you, Elise, but cop to cop, there wasn't a third option."

Campbell lifted her fork and stabbed at her food. "Without any witness statements, I can't even begin to piece together what happened that night and what the president's involvement in all of this might be."

"Wouldn't the Secret Service have written up a report of some sort?" asked Klees.

"I'm sure they did, but that's not something I have access to."

"Maybe not," replied Rita, as an idea began to form in her mind, "but you could get access to the agents who were on duty the night Hale was killed."

Elise thought about it. "Theoretically, but I don't have any authority."

"Maybe you could. Sort of."

"What do you mean?"

"If a civil suit had been filed, everyone, including then senator and now president Alden, would have been subpoenaed."

"But a civil suit never was filed, was it?"

Klees shook her head. "No. With Charlie and Sheryl Coleman and their two children dead, the only surviving relatives were Charlie Coleman's parents. They decided not to sue."

"Sheryl Coleman didn't have any family?"

"None."

"At the risk of sounding callous," said Campbell, "everyone sues today at the drop of a hat, but in this case it might have been justified. I'm no lawyer, but I would think that the Coleman parents could have named both Gallo and President Alden as defendants. They would have been prime targets."

"From what I heard," replied Rita, "they were."

"You mean Charlie Coleman's parents did want to sue?"

Klees nodded.

"So what happened?"

"The Hamptons' rumor mill has it that

209

Stephanie Gallo bought them off."

"Are you serious?" asked Elise.

"If you believe the gossip," replied Klees.

"And do you?"

"I saw Charlie Coleman's parents not long after the accident. His mother was beside herself and his father was mad as hell. I also gathered that he was not a big fan of Senator Alden's.

"He lawyered up pretty quick and hired a big firm out of Manhattan. They wasted no time in getting a lawsuit rolling. They were a couple of months into everything when all of a sudden the firm was discharged."

"Because Gallo bought them off?"

"Makes sense," said Klees "The one thing Gallo has in greater supply than anything else is money. I have a feeling that if she wanted to avoid a messy trial and save her candidate the embarrassment and bad press, she could pull it off."

"That's something else that's bothering me," remarked Campbell. "How did this story never make national news? Something this scandalous, especially during an election, is pretty juicy, doubly so by today's journalistic standards."

"I'm sure President Alden can thank Gallo for that as well. She's a very powerful woman. Probably insisted on some sort of a gag order from the get-go."

"And if the Colemans reached a settlement with her, she probably would have had them sign a bunch of nondisclosure agreements. They'd be gagged so tight their lips would turn blue."

"Agreed."

"So without any other relatives, that's it," said Campbell. "They're the only ones who could bring a civil action to get to the bottom of what happened."

"Not necessarily," replied Klees. "There may be someone else who still has legal grounds for a suit."

"So? How would that give me any leverage with the agents who were posted to Gallo's home that night?"

"It depends on how far you're willing to go to get to the bottom of this."

Campbell drained the last sip of wine from her glass, held it up to get the waiter's attention, and then replied, "I'm still sitting here, aren't I?"

CHAPTER 21

Afghanistan
Saturday

Mullah Massoud arrived back at his compound along with Sergei Simonov and the small security contingent they had taken with them. They had visited a village called Surobi, halfway between Jalalabad and Kabul. As it was safer for Massoud to travel at night, they had conducted the entire trip in two cars under the cover of darkness.

Per standard practice, none of the Taliban commanders attending the meeting had known its exact location until shortly before the meeting was scheduled to take place. They had many things to discuss, but the most important was their spring offensive.

The Taliban had successfully placed a noose around Kabul, and the readiness status of their forces was excellent, but their infrastructure and the condition of their military equipment was quite poor. The Russians and several other countries covertly supported their cause, but were only willing to supply so much. If they flooded Afghanistan with hardware and other things that could be traced back to them, they risked the wrath of the United States government and its allies.

Most of the commanders were pessimistic about what they were going to be able to do with the limited resources they had at hand. Opium eradication in Afghanistan had been stepped up dramatically, and that meant their main source of revenue had been just as dramatically stepped down. If they were to have any long-term success, they needed more money to buy more equipment and to train more fighters. Without a major infusion of cash, all their achievements of the last several years would be for naught.

None of this was news to Massoud. In fact, he'd been one of the first commanders to see it coming, but the other commanders wouldn't listen to him. The poppy crops had produced so much money for so long and the Americans had been so halfhearted in their attempts to stem the flow that they thought they had a license to print money that would never expire.

As their circumstances started to erode, so

did their blind faith in Mullah Omar. His empty promises and unwise alliance with bin Laden and his Arab al-Qaeda would be his ultimate undoing.

Massoud knew something that no one else in the room but Simonov did. Soon things were going to change. While the other commanders complained and worried about the progress of the spring offensive, Massoud had looked beyond it. He had seen a new future for Afghanistan and he was quietly confident in the resurgence the Taliban was going to achieve under his command.

His optimistic mood, though, did not last long. During a break in the meeting, Massoud and Simonov learned that Mustafa Khan was no longer a resident of Policharki. The talk was that he had been moved to another, more secure facility.

The two men were well aware of how the Afghan grapevine worked. Every piece of information was normally inflated as each person in the chain exaggerated his involvement or knowledge of the topic to make himself look more important and better informed. The Taliban commander and his Russian colleague would have been considerably more heartened if the "news" had been of a full blown escape rather than a transfer. If the Afghan government had indeed moved

Khan to a more secure facility, it would mean the Americans would have a much tougher job on their hands.

While Massoud didn't particularly care how difficult the task was for them, he was dependent upon their success. Mustafa Khan was the key not only to the Taliban's ridding itself of al-Qaeda, but also to its being able to drive the American and other international troops out of the country so they could retake complete and final control of Afghanistan.

When they returned to Massoud's compound it was shortly before sunrise. Most of the men were already saying their dawn prayers.

To help him stay both warm and awake in Surobi, the Taliban commander had consumed large quantities of tea. Though he had urinated before leaving, he had refused to allow any stops on the way back, even for himself. Combined with the hour at which the meeting had finally ended he was not only late for prayers, he also needed to urinate again most urgently.

Stepping out of the vehicle, Mullah Massoud shooed away one of his lieutenants eager to speak with him and headed for the compound's rudimentary toilet facilities.

After relieving himself, the Taliban commander performed his ablutions and then hurried to his quarters for his prayer rug. Upon opening the door to the main room, he was quite surprised to find his brother, Zwak, leading the four village elders in prayer. His pride was quite apparent, as the volume of his voice was much louder than it should have been.

Massoud removed his shoes and stepped quietly inside. After retrieving his prayer rug, he respectfully laid it on the floor and prostrated himself toward Mecca.

He followed the prayers until their completion and then greeted the elders and his brother. Stepping away for a moment, he opened his door and found his lieutenant waiting for him. The man's message was no longer urgent now that the commander had discovered the village elders waiting for him.

Massoud sent the lieutenant for tea and stepped back inside. The room was colder than it should have been and Massoud realized that in his excitement over the visit from the elders, Zwak had forgotten to turn on the heat. Approaching the propane heater in the corner, the Taliban commander took down a box of matches and got it going.

He was tired and not much in the mood to deal with village politics, but he had no choice. Undoubtedly, the elders needed something important from him and had appeared at such an early hour in the hopes that their request would magically jump to the top of his list.

Though he was annoyed to see them, he knew his place. He might be the most powerful man in the village, but it was necessary that he respect the elders. They provided him and his men with cover and that was very valuable. The quality of his life was directly proportional to how content the elders were.

Though Massoud had tried a long time ago to force communication to go through his lieutenants, the elders hadn't gone for it. They would deal with no one but him and him directly. It could be an incredible distraction at times, but it was also a sign of great respect, and respect was a two-way street.

The men made small talk about the weather, how deep the snows had been, and the relatively strong grip the cold still held on their valley, especially at night. Once the tea came, Zwak played host and made sure everyone was well taken care of before he saw to himself.

When they had been served, Baseer, the chief elder, explained why they had come.

Upon mention of the American woman, Zwak's mouth spread into a broad smile, revealing several of his missing teeth. "Doktar. Doktar," he sang as he brought his hands together.

Massoud motioned for him to be quiet. Baseer waited until Zwak had calmed down before continuing. "Zwak," he said, addressing him directly. "Did you strike someone with your rifle yesterday?"

The man's smile faded and a confused expression fell across his face. He looked around the room for his rifle like a child suddenly gripped by the fear that a cherished blanket or stuffed animal had disappeared.

Spotting his rifle, Zwak visibly relaxed and turned back to face the elder. As the man was about to repeat the question, Mullah Massoud stepped in and came to his brother's defense. "What are you talking about?"

Baseer recounted his meeting with Elam Badar from the previous evening and how his son Asadoulah's jaw had allegedly been broken.

"Why did he not come to discuss this with me?" demanded Massoud.

"You are a Taliban commander," replied the elder. "Elam Badar is a farmer. It is understandable that he came to speak to us first."

The Taliban commander shook his head. "This should have been settled between us like fathers, but he did not have the courage to come to me. What else did he say?"

Baseer shrugged. "This was his primary concern."

Massoud laughed. "He spoke of *nothing* else? He attempted to build no further case against my brother?"

Seconds passed before the elder spoke. "He did raise concern over Zwak's behavior in the past."

"What kind of behavior?"

"His aggressive behavior."

"*Aggressive behavior?* That is ridiculous," scoffed the commander.

Baseer fixed him with a hard stare. "Massoud, you yourself encourage this behavior. You have given him a rifle —"

"Which you know has been specially modified for him."

"Be that as it may, you are well aware of how he acts toward people from outside our village. He accuses them of spying or trying to poison our water."

The commander looked at his brother and smiled. "Because of his hard work, our water is pure and we have not had one spy in our village."

Zwak, who had grown more agitated as

the conversation grew more intense, stared nervously at his brother. "No spies," he said. "Clean water. Safe water."

"Do you feel that your brother was the best choice to guard the woman?" asked Baseer.

"In conjunction with the lock upon the door, yes I do," said Massoud. "He is very attentive and has watched prisoners for us before."

The elders had all known Zwak since he was a boy. He was just as much a member of their family as he was of Massoud's. "Zwak is a very important member of our village, and in respect to the well and chasing away spies, he has done a very good job," offered the elder, careful not to demean Zwak or his powerful brother.

"And he has never harmed anyone," added Massoud. "Not once. If his behavior frightens people, Elam Badar is the only one complaining. If he is so delicate, maybe he should stay home and tend his children while his wife tends his affairs."

The commander had paid Elam Badar a very egregious *shkanza* and the elder was glad the man was not present to have heard the insult uttered. "Maybe we should ask Zwak what happened," stated Baseer.

Massoud turned to his brother. "Zwak, do you know the boy we are taking about,

Asadoulah?"

Zwak nodded and repeated the words, "Bad boy, bad boy," several times.

"Did you see him yesterday?"

Zwak was frightened and his eyes darted from side to side. Slowly, he nodded.

"Did he come to where you were watching over the American woman?"

"Protecting," said Zwak, correcting his brother.

It was an odd choice of words, but Massoud had learned long ago that it was easier to communicate with his brother using the words he chose. "Did he come to where you were *protecting* the American woman?"

Zwak nodded and began repeating the words "bad boy, bad boy," again.

"Did he make you angry?"

Zwak began to rock back and forth as he nodded.

"What did he do?"

Zwak didn't want to answer and put his arms around himself as he continued to rock.

Massoud repeated the question. "Zwak, what did he do to make you angry?"

He still wouldn't answer, and Massoud pushed him by raising his voice.

The mentally challenged man began to cry as his brother pressed the question. "Tell me what happened," he demanded.

Unable to take it any longer, his eyes filled with tears, Zwak yelled at the top of his lungs, "Unclean! Unclean! Unclean!" and wouldn't stop.

The commotion brought people running to Massoud's door, and he ordered them to go away. Standing up, he walked over to the door, bolted it, then came back and put his arm around his brother's shoulder.

It took more than five minutes for Zwak to calm down and to stop trembling. The only sound in the room came from the hiss of the propane heater and the short, quick gasps of air Zwak took as he tried to stop crying.

"Elam Badar is concerned that someone could inform the authorities about the American woman and that it would be bad for our villages," Baseer interjected into the relative silence.

Massoud looked up from comforting his brother. "I suspected there was more said during your meeting. It sounds like Elam Badar is threatening us, and it wouldn't be the first time he has caused trouble. He does not care for the Taliban."

The elder locked eyes with the commander. "Be that as it may, on this point, his concern may be justified."

Massoud was getting angrier by the second and fought to keep himself under control. "Elam Badar is a fool. He has no idea what he is talking about."

"So, we're wrong to be concerned then? The woman's presence is no danger to us at all?"

The Taliban commander did not care for the elder's facetiousness. "If Elam Badar keeps his mouth shut there is no danger, especially to Elam Badar and his village."

"And if he doesn't?"

Massoud spoke slowly and clearly so that the elder would understand that the topic was no longer open for discussion. "I will worry about Elam Badar. And as far as the woman is concerned, her presence, at least for the time being, is necessary and will also benefit our cause."

"So you have said, but what exactly is our cause, Massoud?"

It was all the commander could do not to reach out and slap this arrogant old man. Silently, he vowed that he would make Elam Badar pay for his interference. "You know full well what our cause is."

"I do," replied Baseer, "but I remain confused about why our cause needs to be intertwined with the Russians."

"You know why."

"I know only what you have told me. But

regardless, right now we must focus on making compensation to Elam Badar and his family."

"Compensation," exclaimed Massoud. "For what?"

"For his son's broken jaw," snapped the elder.

"We still don't even know what happened."

"We know enough," replied Baseer, as he rose to his feet and was joined by his three silent colleagues. "I will let you decide what is appropriate, but I want it done quickly. If his grievance is left too long, Elam Badar could become a very serious problem for us — and by *us* I mean our entire village.

"I am counting on you to do the sensible thing. And I expect you to see that no harm comes to him or his family."

Massoud embraced the elders, but as soon as they had left the compound he crossed the courtyard to Simonov's room and pounded on the door.

When the Russian answered, it was obvious he had been sleeping. "What is it?"

"I need you to do something for me," replied the Taliban commander, "and I need it to look like an accident."

CHAPTER 22

Though Harvath had slept fitfully, he'd gotten a better night's sleep than he had expected. He took a hot shower in his meat locker of a bathroom and shaved. After getting dressed, he walked across the courtyard to the dining room.

Opening the door, he bumped into Daniel Fontaine, who had just finished eating and was on his way to see a client. They were in the midst of exchanging greetings when Gallagher yelled, "In or out!" and demanded that the door be shut.

Harvath stepped inside and closed the door behind him. Hoyt and Gallagher were sitting at the table reading the *Kabul Daily,* which was a stack of pages they had printed off different news, sports, and entertainment websites and stapled together. Both men were wearing reading glasses.

Mei was scrambling eggs in the kitchen and the dining room smelled fantastic. Judging from the tray of fresh croissants on the table, Flower had already been out to the best bakery in Kabul. It was run by an Iranian whom Harvath, Gallagher, and Hoyt were convinced was a spy for Iran.

The bakery was a superb front, as it offered every kind of Western-style baked good, including pizza, as well as such other Western products as Gatorade, Doritos, and Hershey's chocolate. Westerners based in Kabul flocked to the Iranian by the carload. Harvath could only imagine the kinds of relationships the man was building and the level of intel he was gathering from his unsuspecting customers.

Harvath poured himself a mug of coffee and sat down at the table. "I distinctly remember when I checked in," he said to no one in particular, "requesting a morning paper."

Gallagher didn't bother looking up from his reading material. "It wasn't outside your door this morning?"

"Nope," replied Harvath as he took a sip of his coffee.

"Damn paperboy. If it's not in the bushes, it's up on the roof. Take Hoyt's."

Hoyt held up his middle finger in response and kept reading.

"You want an omelet?" asked Mei as she

stuck her head out of the kitchen and pointed a spatula at Harvath.

"Yes, please."

"He no eat omelet," Hoyt shouted back at his wife, mimicking her Chinese accent. "He on Continental breakfast plan. One cup coffee. One Iranian bagel. One swift kick in ass out door."

Mei swore at her husband in Chinese and vanished back into the kitchen.

"If that woman had any sense, she'd leave you," said Harvath.

"If that woman had any sense," clarified Gallagher, "she never would have married him in the first place."

"I heard that," said Mei as she reemerged from the kitchen carrying a heaping plate of food.

"You all in trouble now," added Hoyt, continuing to mimic his wife's accent.

As she passed him, she snatched the pages from his hand and delivered them, along with the food, to Harvath.

"Hey," exclaimed Hoyt. "That's my paper *and* my breakfast. I've been waiting longer than he has."

"The kitchen is now closed," stated Mei.

"What do you mean *closed?*"

Returning to where her husband was sitting, Mei bent down and grabbed one of his love handles. "I married an old man. Okay. But not a fat old man. Your new diet starts today."

Hoyt lunged to kiss her, but Mei evaded his grasp and with a shriek ran back to the kitchen. "And stop making fun of my accent," she admonished him. "Or you won't get dinner either."

"That's okay," replied Hoyt, "I'm getting sick of eating dog anyway."

Hoyt's remark was met with another string of invective in Chinese.

Harvath kept his eyes on his food, but couldn't help laughing.

"You think that's funny?" demanded Hoyt. "I'll show you funny. The *dining room* is now closed. Hand over that breakfast, sailor."

Harvath put down his fork, raised his shirt, and flashed his Glock, then went back to eating.

Hoyt swore and reached for another croissant just as Mei reappeared to clear the tray.

Gallagher slid his glasses atop his head and set his paper down. "What's on the agenda for today?" he asked as he slid his coffee mug over to Hoyt and motioned for his partner to pour.

Hoyt leaned back and grabbed the pot. After he had poured for Gallagher, he held it up to inquire if Harvath wanted more. When Harvath nodded, Hoyt smiled and put it back, out of Harvath's reach.

"I want to pay a visit to the CARE International Hospital," said Harvath as he took his plate with him and walked over to the coffee pot to top off his mug.

"Are we doing recon on the Soviet base or background on Julia Gallo?"

"Both," said Harvath as he sat back down. "How soon can we leave?"

Gallagher looked at his watch. "I've got a squash game in a half hour. Then there's my Rotary Club meeting."

"Don't forget the Kabul Junior League luncheon," added Hoyt.

"I almost did forget," replied Gallagher as he ticked off his "appointments" on his fingers. "I'm sorry, but it looks like I'm booked solid all day."

Harvath picked up his fork and, scooping up a large bite of omelet, replied, "I'll see you out front in fifteen minutes."

"So much for our bake sale."

When Harvath exited the compound, he found Gallagher sitting in the Land Cruiser with his Jackie Collins book. About seven or eight wisecracks raced through Harvath's mind, but he kept them to himself and just shook his head as he hopped in the passenger seat and closed the door.

"Don't start with me," Gallagher warned.

Harvath shook his head again and reached over to turn up the heater. It seemed to be twice as cold today as yesterday.

Gallagher pulled to the end of the short street and then turned left onto the main road. When he turned the radio on to his Afghan Bollywood station, Harvath was ready for him. Removing a CD he'd burned on his laptop, he slid it into the player.

As "Apache" by the Sugarhill Gang began to play, Harvath settled back into his seat and smiled.

"What the hell are we listening to?" Gallagher demanded.

"Classic American funk music."

"I want my radio back on."

"You've been in-country too long. You've gone native."

"I'm going to go medieval if you don't turn that crap off," he threatened.

"Sorry, brother," replied Harvath. "This is an intervention. It's for your own good. After we work on your musical taste, we're going to cowboy you up in the reading department."

Five songs and a litany of curses from Gallagher later, they arrived at the CARE hospital on Darulaman Road. It was fronted by blast barriers and an eight-foot-high stone wall that ran the length of the road.

Unauthorized vehicles were not allowed inside the main gate, so Harvath and Gallagher parked near the perimeter wall. They were given a cursory pat-down by a male guard, who failed to notice that both men were carrying pistols, and were waved inside. Harvath could only hope that the man's sole job was to discourage suicide bombers. If it entailed anything else, CARE had some big problems on its hands.

The hospital was a narrow, whitewashed two-story building with single-story wings sprouting off it. The grounds were typical Third World — hard-packed brown earth with little to no vegetation. The only hint of color came from the occasional woman who decided to wear a blue burka rather than the ever-popular black. Cultural sensitivity be damned, it was a practice Harvath found demeaning to Muslim women. Walking around with a bag over your head was walking around with a bag over your head. It made no difference how apologists for Islam tried to bullshit it as liberating and empowering for women. No matter where he encountered them, they reminded him of aliens that had just climbed off a spaceship from some strange planet far, far away.

He and Gallagher walked up the drive to the main entrance and stepped inside. Though there were some women right behind them, Harvath knew the laws of polite Western society didn't always translate well in Muslim nations.

His instinct was to hold the door for them, but doing so would not only have confused them, it could have drawn the ire of any of the men they were most likely traveling with. While he thought it was stupid and didn't like acting that way, Harvath knew it was often best to pretend the women weren't there at all.

In the corner of the lobby was a registration desk. Harvath greeted the young man sitting behind it and gave him the name of the doctor he had come to see. The man picked up his phone and, as he dialed, handed Harvath a pen and asked him to sign the log book.

With Gallagher standing next to him, Harvath printed the names Samuel Colt and Jack E. Collins. Though he couldn't be sure, he thought he heard Gallagher sling the F word at him under his breath.

After hanging up the phone, the young man pointed to the waiting area and said, "Please, five minutes."

"Tashakor," Harvath replied. He and Gal-

lagher grabbed seats along the wall and sat down. The waiting area was packed, especially for a Saturday.

"Best medical care in Afghanistan," said Gallagher. "Lots of volunteer docs from the West. This is a first-rate hospital."

Harvath looked around. Everything was clean and there was a faint odor of antiseptic. It was better than most of the hell-hole medical centers he'd seen across the Third World. Even so, it still wasn't someplace he'd want to have to undergo a procedure.

The waiting area was filled with families. All of their women were shrouded in burkas, so the only adult faces he could see belonged to the men.

Afghanistan was a hard place to live, and that was reflected in their countenances. They looked drawn and haggard, their faces as weather-beaten and craggy as the jagged mountains that surrounded their country. Dark, solemn eyes stared off in different directions. The only vitality in the room came from the children, who were running and laughing.

Sitting near Harvath and Gallagher was a family of adults who did not speak. An older man peeled an orange and silently offered slices to the other men sitting near him. Harvath couldn't tell if they were waiting to go in or waiting for someone to come out.

His question was soon answered when a young Afghan doctor in a white lab coat entered the waiting area and asked the man at the reception desk a question. The man leaned forward and pointed in Harvath's direction.

Harvath gave Gallagher a jab with his elbow and nodded at the approaching doctor. While he wasn't the American medical director they had come to see, Harvath assumed the young doctor had been sent to collect them.

As he neared, Harvath began to stand, but then noticed the doctor's eyes were not on him, but on the family sitting next to them.

Easing himself back into his chair, Harvath watched him. He could tell by the young man's face and his body language that he wasn't bringing good news.

When the family saw the doctor, the men quietly rose, their faces masks of apprehension.

As the young Afghan spoke to them in Pashtu, Baba G translated as best he could. The patient — a woman — had died. Several of the men seemed to have expected this. One of the men, though, became angry.

As the doctor tried to calm him down, Gallagher told Harvath that he was the woman's husband.

The doctor explained that the hospital had done everything it could for her, but that she had arrived with injuries that were beyond treatable.

Gallagher translated the words "comfortable" and "no pain." Despite the doctor's reassurances, the husband flew into a rage.

Everything in the waiting room came to a complete stop as the husband raged at the doctor. Every pair of eyes, even those of the staff, was watching the commotion unfold.

The husband was well over six feet tall and quite broad-shouldered. Standing behind him were two more relatives, who were equally broad and almost as tall. Harvath's instincts, as well as his Secret Service training, told him that this situation had the potential to go bad very quickly.

Nevertheless, it wasn't his problem. There was no need for him to get involved.

To the young doctor's credit, he kept calm, even with the husband right in his face. Everyone could see, though, that he was slowly losing control over the situation. The highly agitated husband's anger, along with the volume of his voice, continued to rise.

Someone at the registration desk must have made a phone call because a hospital security guard armed with an AK-47 suddenly appeared.

Approaching calmly, the guard politely asked the husband to relax and lower his voice. In response, the husband shoved him backward.

Harvath was tempted to do something, but reminded himself that this wasn't his fight. The doctor now had backup, and together with the security guard, the two of them could take care of themselves. He watched as the husband continued screaming at the doctor for letting his wife die.

Showing exceptional restraint, the guard once more stepped in and politely asked the husband to calm down. This time, though, the husband did more than just shove. In the blink of an eye, he had snatched away the guard's AK-47. Harvath had just become part of this fight.

Launching out of his chair, he came in on the edge of the husband's peripheral vision. He struck hard and fast. Grabbing the weapon with his left hand, he pointed the muzzle in a safe direction while he popped the giant Afghan behind his left ear with his right.

It was a simple yet effective move that completely short-circuited the Afghan's brain and dropped him onto the floor.

Harvath spun to engage the two large

relatives, but discovered that Baba G already had it taken care of. Even though he could have said several things to them in Pashtu, the look on the Marine's face was all that was necessary. The Afghans wisely decided not to tangle with the two Americans.

Instead, they bent down, picked the giant up off the floor, and helped carry him out the door. When they were gone, Harvath handed the AK-47 back to the poorly trained security guard.

The shaken young doctor looked at him and said, "Thank you," before turning his attention back to the remaining family members and carrying on with his duties.

"Well, I think that certainly calls for a Red Bull," Baba G joked as he and Harvath retook their seats. "There's a canteen outside and I'm buying. What do you say?"

"I think my heart rate's high enough," said Harvath with a laugh. "That's probably about the last thing I need right now."

Gallagher smiled and put his hand on his friend's shoulder. "You could have really put the boot to that guy and no one in this room would have blamed you."

Harvath imagined the husband's grief, and while grabbing the guard's weapon had been a stupid thing to do, he didn't deserve to have the shit kicked out of him on top of everything else.

"You were right there ready to mix it up," Harvath said, shifting the focus off him. "I'm glad to see you've still got it."

"We all think we've still got it," replied Gallagher. "The key is in knowing how much is really left."

He was right. One of the secrets of survival in this business was knowing your limitations.

Harvath nodded, and as he did, an American doctor in his early fifties appeared in the waiting room and began heading in their direction.

"It looks like we're up."

CHAPTER 23

Dr. Kevin Boyle, Medical Director for the CARE Kabul hospital, was an amiable, balding, five-foot-ten general surgeon from Omaha, Nebraska. He had been in Afghanistan since 2005 when the Afghan Ministry of Public Health asked CARE, a not-for-profit organization dedicated to transforming the lives of sick, wounded, and disabled children and their families throughout the developing world, to take over the former Soviet one-hundred-bed hospital and health clinic.

After getting the rundown on what had happened in the waiting area, Boyle thanked Harvath and Gallagher and then took them on a tour of the facility. As they walked, he told stories about not having any heat when they started out, as well as how badly ravaged the buildings had been from years of war and neglect. He pointed out burn marks on the floors in the hallways where the Taliban had set up campfires during their siege of Kabul.

Harvath asked Boyle to detail the training their doctors received before leaving for Afghanistan, especially as it related to kidnappings. And though it wasn't as thorough as Harvath would have liked, it was considerably more than most organizations offered their staff. If Julia Gallo could remember to do what she had been taught, she had a much better chance of staying alive.

Boyle led them up a flight of stairs, past a seated Afghan security guard, and through an iron gate to the main building's second floor. Here, he explained, were all of the hospital's administrative offices and lecture rooms.

In the middle of the corridor was a door marked *Surgeons,* which he unlocked and held open for his guests.

The surgeons' office was a large square room with windows on the far side that looked out toward the main gate and the old Soviet military base across the road. There was a metal desk in each corner with extra chairs in front. Only two of the desks had computers.

Stuffed bookcases and mismatched file cabinets lined the perimeter of the room. There was a small door that led to a private bathroom. Upon it was a single hook overloaded with white coats.

Boyle introduced the only other person in the room, an Afghan surgeon named Dr. Hamid, who was busy at one of the computers. After shaking hands, Boyle led his guests to a couple of chairs in front of a desk on the other side of the room. He disappeared into the bathroom and returned with three clean coffee cups, which he filled with hot water from a dispenser next to one of the file cabinets.

Dropping a tea bag into each one, he then set the mugs down on the desk, pulled up a chair, and said, "Thank you again for what you did downstairs."

Harvath was about to respond when the young Afghan doctor from the waiting room entered with a thick stack of folders tucked beneath his arm. Boyle waved him over and introduced him as Dr. Atash, one of their family medicine residents. He still looked shaken by what had happened.

He shook hands with Harvath and Gallagher, then excused himself to discuss his charts with Dr. Hamid.

When Atash had walked away, Gallagher turned to Dr. Boyle and said, "You should think about hiring additional security. Next time, you may not be so lucky."

"True," he replied, "but unfortunately,

we need a new ultrasound machine more than we need additional security. But that's not important. We're here to talk about Dr. Gallo."

"We are," said Harvath. "And as Mrs. Gallo explained to you in her email, Mr. Gallagher and I have been brought in to help secure Julia's release."

"Well, the hospital is ready to help in any way we can."

"That's good. So let me ask you, when Dr. Gallo came to work here, did you know who she was, or more important, who her mother was?"

"I did. Julia's mother is friendly with one of our board members, but she wanted to be treated like every other doctor we have, not like the daughter of Stephanie Gallo."

"In other words, no special treatment."

Dr. Boyle nodded as he took his tea bag out of his cup and dropped it in the wastebasket. "She also didn't like talking about her mother or her family much. She was real tight-lipped about it."

"But did people know who she was?" asked Harvath as he tossed his tea bag too.

"If you'll pardon the graveyard humor, doctors like to say that the only way three people in a hospital can keep a secret is if two of them are dead and the other is in a coma."

Harvath had read copies of all the reports dealing with Julia Gallo's kidnapping. He knew that all of her colleagues at the hospital had been thoroughly questioned. Unfortunately, hospitals weren't the only places with thriving gossip mills; so were ex-pat communities. Add in the fact that gossiping was the Afghan national pastime, and Julia Gallo was all but guaranteed to have caught the attention of the Taliban. It was just a matter of time.

"She didn't trade on the family name," continued Boyle. "That was for sure. She didn't need to. She was a damn good doctor and really cared about the Afghans she treated. Maybe even cared too much."

"What do you mean by *too much?*" asked Harvath.

Boyle showed him an official reprimand that had been placed in Julia's file. Proselytizing, whether it was religious or political, was strictly against CARE's rules, especially in Afghanistan. They expected their doctors to lead by example, not by persuasion.

The medical director detailed their rural medicine program and how Julia had jumped at the chance to travel to remote villages outside Kabul. It was dangerous work, made even more so by allegations that she was encouraging women to do things like go to school, report abusive husbands and fathers, and refuse to enter into forced marriages.

Looking back, Boyle realized he should have forbidden her from making any more trips outside the hospital, but because of her family's VIP standing within the organization, he had looked the other way. Instead, he had written up the reprimand, provided Julia with a copy, and put the original in her file. He had hoped it would show her how serious what she was doing was, but it didn't seem to have worked.

Kevin Boyle was a good person, and Harvath could see that. He believed in what he was doing for the people of Afghanistan and he cared very much for his staff. He felt guilty about what had happened to Julia Gallo, but what he didn't know was that her kidnapping had nothing to do with what she was encouraging the women of Afghanistan to do. It had everything to do with her mother and her mother's close ties with the new president of the United States.

If the Taliban hadn't been able to snatch her in the countryside, they might eventually come to the hospital to grab her. And if that had happened, Harvath knew that it would have been much worse than what had transpired in the waiting room that morning.

He asked Boyle to fill in several blanks from the reports he'd read about the kidnapping and then asked a few additional questions about hospital security. Gallagher also asked one or two of his own.

When they were finished, the men stood and shook hands. As if it was an afterthought, Harvath said, "I heard you're a Navy man?"

"I am," replied Boyle with a smile. "They're the ones who sent me to medical school. How about you?"

"I was in the Teams."

The medical director was impressed. "Well, I can understand why Mrs. Gallo wanted you on board."

"If I had known there was another Navy man in Kabul, I wouldn't have had to bring a Marine on the team," Harvath said, pointing his thumb over his shoulder at Gallagher, who rolled his eyes.

Removing his Afghan cell phone and opening up the address book, Harvath added. "If I need to call you, where can I get hold of you?"

The medical director dictated a number he said was good day or night, and Harvath entered it into his phone.

Boyle accompanied the men to the bottom of the stairs, where they all shook hands one more time, and after Harvath assured the surgeon they could find their own way out, said good-bye.

Despite having seen most of the small hospital on their tour, Harvath wanted to poke around a little bit more before they left. He was particularly interested in locating the mechanical room and any other below-grade facilities. As they looked around, he took a mental inventory of everything he saw.

A half hour later, they were nearing the double doors that led into the waiting area when a voice from down the hallway called for them to stop.

The men turned to see Dr. Atash jogging in their direction.

"I need to speak to you, please," he said, slightly out of breath.

"If this is about what happened earlier," replied Harvath as the young doctor drew closer, "it's okay. You don't need to say anything."

"No. This is about something that happened in Nangarhar."

"Nangarhar?"

"Yes," he said. "At the Nangarhar Hospital in Jalalabad."

As Jalalabad was home to the other ISS compound and had been his stomping ground the majority of time he'd been in

Afghanistan, Gallagher was interested immediately. "What happened?" he asked.

"I had been working there for the last month as part of my residency program. I was taking care of a boy, a teenager actually, who had been struck in a fight. His jaw was fractured. As I came into the exam room, I overheard his father talking with him in Pashtu about a woman, an American, who had been kidnapped."

"Were they from Jalalabad? Which neighborhood?" asked Gallagher.

Dr. Atash shook his head. "No, they were from a village in Khogyani."

"Did they mention her by name? Did you overhear a description or anything that could prove they were talking about Dr. Gallo?" asked Harvath.

"No they didn't."

"Did you tell anybody about this?"

Atash shook his head once more.

"Why not? Why keep this to yourself?"

"I assumed it was another aid worker. These things happen all the time. The organization they work for pays the ransom and the worker is returned. It's not my job to get involved in these things. I could put the entire hospital at risk."

"So why are you telling us?"

"I apologize for not saying something upstairs, but it wasn't until I finished reviewing my charts with Dr. Hamid that he told me who you were. He didn't know that I hadn't heard about the kidnapping."

"Did you know Dr. Gallo?"

"Not well. She taught obstetrics here to my class. But she's my colleague and I want to help her. Besides, I'm also Pashtun and it's my duty to repay you for what you did for me this morning."

Ten minutes later, Harvath and Baba G walked out of the CARE hospital and headed for the main gates.

"How do you want to play this?" asked Gallagher. "Should we get the military involved?"

"We don't even know if Dr. Gallo is being held in that village."

"If we can roll up this Elam Badar and his son Asadoulah, it might not matter. Get to them, and we may just get to Julia Gallo."

"We could also end up spooking whoever has her."

"That's a possibility, but at the very least," responded Gallagher, "somebody has got to get eyes on that village."

"I agree," said Harvath. "I think we ought to take a drive to —"

Gallagher cut Harvath off as he pulled his

vibrating cell phone out of his pocket and, looking at the caller ID, said, "It's Rashid."

Baba G raised the phone to his ear and listened. After a short conversation, he flipped it shut. Looking at Harvath, he said, "We've got bad news."

"What is it?"

"Rashid just heard from his cousins. The Afghans are going to move Khan again. They say that if we're going to grab him, we have to do it tonight. They want to meet with us in half an hour."

CHAPTER 24

Gallagher made the drive from the CARE hospital to Kabul's famed "Chicken Street" in just under twenty minutes. As it was one of the city's most popular shopping districts, it wasn't unusual to see foreigners walking up and down the street, and as it was only a block away from the headquarters of the Afghan National Police, it also wasn't unusual to see high-ranking ANP and even NDS officials doing their shopping here. It was therefore an excellent location to hold a clandestine meeting.

The small shops of Chicken Street's rug merchants sat cheek by jowl with antique dealers and jewelry shops. Anything could be had on Chicken Street, from traditional Afghan carpets, vintage rifles, and ivory-handled knives, to gold necklaces, silver earrings, or bracelets studded with one of Afghanistan's most prized gemstones, the intensely blue lapis lazuli.

Gallagher parked a block away and paid a group of street kids, who materialized out of nowhere, a buck apiece to keep an eye on the Land Cruiser.

As Harvath stepped out of the truck, he was accosted by a new group of children, who shouted, "Mister, mister. I'm your bodyguard, okay?"

Gallagher had warned him about this, as well as the burka-clad women who trolled Chicken Street with phony prescriptions, begging naïve Westerners to give them money to buy medicine for their "sick" children. Kids who begged to be bodyguards were harmless, in his opinion, and even respectable, as they were actually willing to work for their money, but the women with the bogus prescriptions were simply scam artists.

Harvath looked at the bright faces of all the kids gathered around him. "*Yak* dollar, mister. Only *yak* dollar," they said, *yak* being the Dari word for "one."

"Okay, *yak* dollar," Harvath relented, and the children all cheered. The gaggle of boys tagged along until they reached a nondescript rug shop, where Harvath gave them each a dollar and the shop's owner shooed them away.

After the kids had disappeared, the owner showed the two Americans into the back of his shop, where he pulled a trap door down from the ceiling and extended an aging wooden staircase that led to the second floor. The men mounted the narrow steps single file and emerged in a warehouse space that smelled faintly of tobacco and damp carpets.

Sitting on a large rug at the opposite end were Inspector Rashid and his two cousins, Marjan and Pamir. In the middle was a pot of tea. Judging from the steam coming from their cups, it appeared to be Afghan and not American.

The shop owner retreated to the first floor, telescoped the stairs back into their hiding place, and closed the trap door to give the men their privacy.

After conducting the customary greetings, the three Afghans invited their American counterparts to sit down and take tea. Harvath wanted to get straight to business, but he knew you never said no to tea, so he sat down and accepted a cup. Fortunately, the Afghans were in no mood for chit-chat. Once the tea was poured, they got right to the point.

Marjan was the first to speak. "Our president is so determined that Mustafa Khan stand trial for his crimes that he wants to watch over him personally."

"What do you mean *personally?*" asked Harvath.

"He is going to have Khan moved to the presidential palace."

"Where are they going to put him? In a guest room?"

Marjan shook his head. "Of course not. There are two cells beneath the palace."

"When are they going to move him?"

"As early as tomorrow," replied Pamir.

"Which is why," interjected Rashid, "we must do this tonight."

They were right. Grabbing Khan at the old Soviet base made more sense than trying to launch an assault on the presidential palace, but they still didn't have everything they needed.

"What about a map of the tunnels?" asked Harvath.

Pamir reached into a small shoulder bag that was sitting on the floor behind him and pulled out a medium-sized tube. "Right here."

Harvath looked at Marjan. "You can sketch the base layout, as well as the interrogation facility?"

The NDS operative nodded.

"Then the only thing we're missing . . ." Harvath began to say, but his voice trailed off as Inspector Rashid stood and disappeared behind a pile of carpets.

He returned carrying a watertight, high-density, plastic Storm case and said, "Are the munitions."

Gallagher looked at Harvath and smiled. "I told you he was good."

"I never doubted it for a second," lied Harvath.

The room was warm and he removed his jacket and set it on the floor behind him. Rolling up his sleeves, he looked at the Afghans as Rashid retook his seat and said, "Now we need a plan."

They spent the next six hours evaluating their objective and assessing their options. The shopkeeper downstairs kept the tea coming and sent his son out twice for food.

One of the biggest things bothering Harvath about the operation was the satellite imagery he'd seen. According to Marjan, the Afghans had reconstructed several of the base buildings to use as barracks. The NDS operative's assurance that the barracks were only used when training exercises were being conducted did little to stem Harvath's concern, especially considering that the interrogation facility was located beneath one of them.

Not knowing how many Afghan Special

Forces soldiers were guarding Khan was one thing, but they also had no way of gauging how many soldiers would be in the barracks above, or how many would be on the base in general. The fact that his team could easily be outnumbered and overwhelmed weighed heavily on Harvath's mind, as did the fact that if that happened, there would be no cavalry he could call for help.

He and Gallagher drilled Rashid, Pamir, and Marjan relentlessly. Looking at his watch, Harvath decided they all needed a break. There were only a couple of hours of daylight left and he wanted to drive the perimeter of the base, as well as visit the ruins of the old palace at the end of Darulaman Road to see what kind of vantage point it might provide.

The men agreed to reassemble at midnight, and Harvath warned them all one last time not to talk to anyone, especially Rashid, who had repeatedly offered to reach out to a few more contacts to see if he could nail down the exact troop strength at the base. It was more important that they maintain the element of surprise. Besides, based on Harvath's plan, it didn't matter if the Afghans had five men there or five hundred. Either it was going to work or it wasn't.

Harvath wrapped the Storm case in a plastic garbage bag and waited while Gallagher brought the Land Cruiser around. Once it was loaded, the two Americans drove down Chicken Street and headed for the Darulaman Road.

Baba G was uncharacteristically silent.

"You can still back out," said Harvath.

"What makes you think I want to back out?"

"Nothing. I'm just saying."

"I don't like rush jobs."

Harvath nodded. "Nobody does, but when the window of opportunity opens, you move or it closes."

"We can still bring Fontaine with us."

Harvath understood Gallagher's apprehension, and the idea of bringing someone as qualified as the Canadian was tempting. Though he and Baba G had both the right kind of training and the experience for an operation like this, Pamir and Marjan were a different story. At best, the two Afghans were window dressing. If the *fit* hit the *shan,* there was no way of knowing how they'd react. Having Fontaine along would dramatically improve their odds, but he had the potential to be a political liability. Harvath couldn't allow the president or the United States to be implicated in what he was going to do. "We're not taking him," he finally said.

Gallagher understood and changed the subject. "So you're sure Boyle will let us stage at the hospital?"

"It depends on how much he trusts us. This whole thing could end up being a big problem for him. If we spring Khan and the Afghans figure out he helped, it'll be very bad for him and the hospital. We have to do it in a way that provides cover for him."

"And how do we do that?"

"I'm still working that one out," said Harvath.

"Well, you'd better hurry up," replied Baba G. "Without Boyle's cooperation, there's absolutely no way this thing is going to work."

CHAPTER 25

East Hampton, New York

Elise Campbell and Rita Klees were leaning against the detective's Mini Cooper, finishing their Starbucks coffees as Christine De Palma pulled into the gravel parking lot of the Cobblestone Nursery at 7:30 A.M. on the dot.

"Thank you for meeting us this morning," said Rita as De Palma climbed out of her Mercedes SUV and came over to greet them.

She was an attractive, petite woman in her late forties. Her medium-length brown hair was pulled back in a bun and her face bore only a hint of makeup. She wore a green Barbour jacket, a gray cashmere sweater, tan jodhpurs, and a pair of green Wellington boots. "Of course. You said this had to do with Sheryl and Charlie's accident?"

"It does," replied Klees as she introduced

Elise. "I'd like you to meet Elise Campbell of the United States Secret Service."

Campbell stepped forward and the two women shook hands.

"Is it okay if we speak inside?"

"Certainly," replied De Palma. "Follow me."

Pulling a large brass ring from her pocket, De Palma found the correct key, slid it into the lock, and opened the front door. She flipped on the lights and deactivated the alarm. The room was cold and smelled of damp earth. After locking the front door behind them, she led the women through another door and across a small landscaped court to a vintage greenhouse.

Inside, the temperature was much more agreeable. The air smelled of flowers and other fresh greenery. De Palma flipped a series of switches and somewhere a fountain began to bubble. In the center of the greenhouse was a cast-iron table with matching chairs.

De Palma pulled one out and motioned for the ladies to sit. "The greenhouse beats meeting in my cramped office any day of the week."

"Mine too," replied Klees.

"So what can I do for you?"

"First of all," stated Elise, "I want you to

know that this is all completely off the record and has nothing to do with the East Hampton Police Department. I asked Rita if she knew you and she offered to introduce us."

"Okay," said De Palma, drawing the word out.

"As Sheryl Coleman's business partner," Elise continued, "you could have had grounds to bring a wrongful death claim. Why didn't you?"

De Palma was a bit taken aback. "Am I suspected of having done something?"

Campbell smiled and shook her head. "No. Not at all. I'm just curious."

"What does this have to do with Sheryl and Charlie's death?"

"Mr. Coleman's parents began a civil action, but then dropped it. Supposedly, there was some sort of settlement."

"There was nothing *supposed* about it," replied De Palma. "Stephanie Gallo had been trying to get them to drop that suit from day one, but Charlie's father wouldn't quit. He hated Alden and he said no amount of money in the world could get him to back down."

"He told you that?"

De Palma nodded. "He probably shouldn't have, but we're like family, even more so after Charlie and Sheryl and the kids were killed."

"So what happened to change their minds?"

"Apparently, they had just gotten through the first set of questions they wanted the defendants to answer —"

"Interrogatories?" asked Elise.

"That's right," she replied. "Gallo and Alden's attorneys kept trying to outmaneuver the Colemans with continuances and that kind of garbage and I think Herb and Janet realized just how many years they could be in court over it. The suit definitely wasn't going to keep Alden from getting elected, which is something I think Herb secretly wanted. Finally, Gallo made the Colemans an offer they couldn't refuse."

"May I ask how much?"

"That, I don't know. All I know is that they had turned down multiple offers from Gallo up to that point. According to Herb, she handed them a blank check and told them to fill in any amount they wanted."

"Seriously?"

De Palma nodded.

"How about you? Were you ever offered a settlement?"

"I don't think I was ever even a lawsuit contender in anyone's eyes. When Sheryl was killed, along with Charlie and the kids, I inherited her full share of the business. I didn't have a reason to sue."

"So Stephanie Gallo never approached you? You never heard from any of her people?"

"No, why? Are you trying to tell me I should sue?"

Campbell put up her hands. "No not at all. That's not why I'm here."

"Then I'm confused. Why *are* you here?"

It was a good question and one Elise had spent the night on Rita Klees' pull-out sofa bed trying to find an answer to. "What if there is more to this story than any of us know?"

"Like what?"

"What if someone that night did do something that led to the accident?"

De Palma placed her elbows on the table and leaned forward. "Agent Campbell, do you have any evidence to support that?"

Elise took a deep breath and blew it out. "I'm not sure."

"You're not sure? Now I'm really confused. Why are you even talking to me? Why aren't the East Hampton police following this up?"

"It's complicated," offered Rita.

De Palma looked at her. "We're not only

talking about the death of my business partner, we're also talking about the death of my best friend. Those children were my godchildren. We were family, so if you know something, I want to hear it."

Klees took her time and explained the limitations of pursuing a criminal investigation exactly as she had for Elise the night before.

"So if there is some sort of evidence from that night that's being suppressed," stated De Palma, "I'm the only one who can bring a civil suit to punish the person or persons responsible?"

"If there is such evidence," said Campbell, "then that's correct."

Christine De Palma sat back in her chair and was silent for several moments. "I always thought Gallo offered Charlie's parents the money to avoid the embarrassment of a trial. I never took it as an admission of guilt."

"We don't really know what her motivation was," cautioned Elise.

"But you believe there's something more to what happened that night or you wouldn't have come all the way out here to talk to me."

"That's correct."

"So what exactly do you think happened?"

"I think someone made a very big mistake

and has tried to cover it up. But to find out who it was and how big a mistake they made, I need your help."

"This could be all smoke and no fire, though. You want me to go through all the hassles and the risks of mounting a lawsuit against not only Stephanie Gallo, but also the president of the United States just because you have a suspicion that something may have happened?"

Elise shook her head. "You don't have to mount anything. All I need to do is to say that you're considering a lawsuit."

"That's all?"

"That's all. If my suspicion is wrong, you're not out anything. But if I'm right, you get your friends and your godchildren the kind of justice they deserve."

For several moments, there was only the sound of the fountain. Finally, De Palma spoke. "Tell me what you need me to do."

CHAPTER 26

Afghanistan

Sergei Simonov didn't take any pleasure in having to kill Elam Badar, but he wouldn't lose sleep over it either. The Afghan peasant had picked a fight with the wrong man. His veiled threats to the *shura* of Mullah Massoud's village had earned him an early ticket to paradise.

Massoud had debated taking out the son, Asadoulah, as well, but the Russian had advised against it. Killing two people at the same time and making it look like an accident was very difficult unless they were a bomb-making team.

Once Massoud had acquiesced, the Russian discussed the best way to handle the situation. They agreed that the sooner the problem was taken care of, the better. And though it posed considerable risk, they further agreed that it should happen in broad daylight, or as much daylight as possible, which would make it very hard for people to believe that what had transpired was anything but a tragic accident.

The winding footpath the Russian now hid near was just as Massoud had described it. In all his years among the Afghans, their intimate knowledge of the terrain never ceased to amaze him.

The bleating of the injured sheep on the rocky ledge below had continued unabated for nearly a half hour. While he waited, Simonov pictured his son, Sasha, in his mind's eye. Soon, they would not only be together, inseparable, but he would have the money to care for him properly. He would be able to afford the best surgeons, not just those idiots the state hospitals had provided in Russia.

He could take Sasha anywhere in the world for treatment, America even. He would spare no expense and would go to any lengths to help his boy regain as much of a normal life as possible. They only had each other and needed to stick together. Together, anything was possible. Together, he would prove to his boy how much he loved him and how sorry he was for what had happened to him.

As the bleating of the sheep started to deaden Simonov's hearing, he suddenly noticed another sound; the sound of feet shambling up the rocky path. He began to slow his breathing. The moment was almost here.

Elam Badar was close enough to hear the bleating of his animal now and his pace quickened.

Simonov marveled at how the world worked. Both he and the Afghan had been drawn to this moment by the same thing — a deep and abiding love of their sons, as well as a misfortune that needed to be set right.

The Russian ignored the fact that he had the benefit of surprise, strength, and experience on his side, and instead believed that he would succeed in killing Elam Badar simply because he loved his son more. They were championing two separate causes, and in Simonov's mind, his was more worthy.

When Elam Badar appeared on the path and peered over the jagged outcropping for his injured sheep, the blue-eyed Russian took a final breath and sprang from behind the rocks.

At the sound of movement, the Afghan spun, but it was too late. Simonov was already on him.

Elam Badar should never have underestimated Mullah Massoud.

To the broken neck, the Russian added a very badly broken arm and then rolled the body off the path and watched as it landed with a thud only feet from the wounded animal.

His job complete, Simonov stepped back and disappeared into the landscape.

But as he retraced his steps back up and over the top of the mountain, his heart rate quickened as he suddenly realized he was being followed.

CHAPTER 27

Two hours later

When the door was kicked open, Dr. Julia Gallo was caught in a significant state of undress. The outside temperature that afternoon had been quite mild, which meant that inside the small, poorly ventilated mud brick room where she was being kept, the temperature had been stifling.

She had been lying on the floor trying to stay cool while staring out the small hole in the base of the wall. She wore only a damp T-shirt and trousers, both of which clung provocatively to her body, and her long, red hair hung loose about her shoulders.

Her overseer had returned. The mentally challenged man had not been there that morning to feed her. In fact, no one had come by her cell at all that day, and she had been battling a terrible fear that she had been forgotten or worse still, purposely left to die.

Julia was ravenous, and as the man set the tray down, she noticed that there was more food on it than usual. Whether it was an attempt to make up for his tardiness or an additional apology, like the candies he had given her yesterday, she could not say. She also didn't much care. Whoever these people were, they were not feeding her enough. A meal this size, as paltry as it still was, was the least they should have been feeding a prisoner. She had no idea how much weight she had lost since Sayed had been murdered and she had been taken into captivity, but she had to imagine it was significant and she hadn't had that much extra weight to lose to begin with.

Julia collected her clothes and quickly dressed. Affixing her hijab, she looked down and noticed her guard's new basketball shoes were gone, and in their place he wore a pair of battered boots too big for his feet. When she looked up, she saw that his eyes were red and puffy.

Something had happened to him, and intuitively she knew it had to do with the boys who had come to rape her the day before. Pointing at his feet, she spoke quietly the Pashtu word for shoes, *"Botaan?"*

The man's eyes welled with tears and he

rubbed his sleeve across his face to try to hold them back. He began stammering and gesturing at his feet. Julia couldn't understand what he was saying, but it sounded like his shoes were gone and that it had something to do with his brother.

He had been very attached to his shoes and she found it horrible that his own brother would take them away. The Taliban were absolute bastards. Stealing from a mentally challenged man was reprehensible. But if al-Qaeda had no problem using the intellectually disabled as suicide bombers, then she shouldn't find it difficult to believe that the Taliban would prey on them as well.

Her body was desperate for nourishment, but Gallo poured some tea and held the metal cup out to her guard.

He didn't know what to do. His captive was offering him tea? Having been steeped in the Pashtunwali his entire life, he understood that he was obliged to accept and so took the cup.

"*Sta noom tse dai?*" asked Julia. *What is your name?*

He drank the warm tea in one long swallow and wiped his lips with the back of his hand. "*Zema num Zwak dai,*" he replied. His sadness over his shoes temporarily forgotten, Zwak's broad face broke into a wide smile.

Whether it was his size, his beard, or the pointy sweatshirt hood he always wore, the man reminded Julia of a gnome. *"Zema num —"* she began, but Zwak interrupted her.

"Doktar," he said proudly.

Julia smiled back at him. He had heard and understood her yesterday. "Hoo," she replied. "Doktar Julia."

"Doktar. Doktar," Zwak repeated, even prouder of himself.

They were communicating. That was good. If she could bond with him, maybe she could convince him to let her go. She had learned a long time ago that the fastest way to build a bond with someone was to ask them to do you a favor.

"Sarraoh nan shpa," tonight cold, she attempted in her broken Pashtu. *"Sheta brresten? Lutfan."* Do you have any blanket? "Please."

"Doktar. Doktar," Zwak repeated. *"Soor wextu."*

Julia smiled and nodded. *"Hoo, soor wextu."* Yes, red hair. *"Sheta brresten?"* Any blankets? she asked once more.

Zwak looked at the blanket on Julia's bed and then back at her. Then without another word, he set down the metal cup and walked out of the room, slamming and locking the door behind him.

He was a strange little man. She wondered if she had offended him. Resigning herself to the fact that there was nothing she could do about it now, she sat down on her bed, tore off a piece of nan bread, and used it to scoop food into her mouth.

She poured more tea and savored the rest of her food. When she was finished, she discovered that Zwak had hidden two more pieces of *dashlama,* just like the candies he had given her yesterday, under her plate. Julia put one in her mouth and tried to enjoy it. *Stay positive,* she repeated to herself, but it was so hard.

She wasn't living day to day. She wasn't even living hour to hour. It was minute by minute, and she was slowly losing her mind, as well as her will to live. She chastised herself for being so weak. She needed to snap out of it. She had to focus on something worthwhile that she could live for.

She searched herself, but couldn't come up with much. The one significant person in her life was her mother, and their relationship wasn't exactly storybook material. Julia had spent a good part of her adulthood trying to find her own sliver of sunshine beyond the mammoth shadow her mother cast. It was that search that had brought her to Afghanistan and, ultimately, to the cell in which she now sat.

If the Taliban killed her today, she felt she wouldn't have left much of a mark on the world.

A voice deep inside told her she was being too hard on herself, but she refused to listen to it. She didn't want to be told she was a good person and that her life had value. She had gotten Sayed killed, and who knew how many other Afghan women who had been naïve enough to follow her political advice had been brutalized or killed because of it. *Rise up. Take control of your lives. Embrace your rights,* she had told them. It was all easy enough for an American woman to say, especially one who could go home to her First World country any time she wanted.

What an idiot I have been, Gallo thought as she broke down.

The tears were flowing down her face when the door to her cell was kicked open. It took her by surprise, as it always did, and her heart leaped into her throat. Looking up, she expected to see Zwak, but instead she saw several of the men who had killed Sayed.

They moved quickly. Two of them jerked her up off the bed while a third approached with a light blue burka and other items.

Once her wrists were bound, her eyes blindfolded, and the burka had been pulled down over her head, she was shoved outside.

She heard several vehicles come to a skidding halt only feet away and she was thrown roughly inside the nearest one.

As it lurched away, she could feel the presence of another person near her. As he began to cry, she knew in an instant that it was Zwak and that wherever they were taking her, it was so they could kill her.

CHAPTER 28

Kabul

Harvath knew enough about surgeons to know they weren't night owls, and that went double for missionary doctors. He also knew that the best time to get someone to do what you wanted was when they were running for the fence.

In the case of Dr. Kevin Boyle, his fence was sleep, and Harvath waited until just after ten o'clock at night to call him. He had come to the conclusion that the less Boyle knew about what was going on, the better.

He dialed the number the medical director had given him and woke the man out of a sound sleep. Having seen the call schedule while they were walking through the hospital, Harvath knew the resident on duty that night was none other than Dr. Atash. Explaining that he was leaving to follow up a lead in Kandahar Province in the morning and needed to speak with Atash once more before he left, Harvath asked Boyle to call the security team at the hospital and clear him and Baba G as well as their vehicle through the main gate.

Boyle grumbled his assent and hung up the phone without saying good-bye or asking if Harvath needed anything else. He doubted Boyle would bother to try to track down Atash and tell him to expect visitors. Even if he had, it wouldn't have been a problem. Harvath didn't say when he would be at the hospital. Based upon how exhausted the surgeon sounded, he was pretty confident that he'd fall back asleep within sixty seconds of placing the call to the guards at the front gate.

From their reconnaissance of the old Soviet military base, Harvath and Gallagher had identified two alternative evacuation points where they would station Flower and Inspector Rashid in two different vehicles. Tom Hoyt would monitor the operation from the ops center back at the compound. And just to make sure he wouldn't be disturbed, Mei and her girlfriends had taken Fontaine and Mark Midland out drinking and dancing courtesy of a stack of bills Harvath had slipped her. Everything, so far, was right on track.

As the main threat to the CARE hospital was a suicide bomber or an active shooter who tried to walk or drive onto the property, the primary security focus was the front of the property along Darulaman Road. The rear, while secured by a high, gated fence, wasn't patrolled as heavily, and even less so at night. Electricity was not only expensive, but also unreliable, so the rear of the property wasn't even lit. This was where Harvath had decided Marjan and Pamir would enter.

When it was time for the operation to begin, Flower led the way in the Land Cruiser while Harvath and Gallagher brought up the rear in a van purchased specifically for the job.

Three blocks later, Flower slowed down as Inspector Rashid pulled out from a side street and took the lead. His job was to navigate them around any checkpoints and make sure Harvath and Gallagher arrived at the hospital without being stopped.

When they reached the Darulaman Road and could see that traffic was moving without any impediments, Harvath grabbed his cooler bag from behind his seat and pulled out another Red Bull. "You want one?" he asked Baba G.

"You got any beer in there?"

"Sure, you want it in a bottle or draft?"

"Forget it," said Gallagher as he reached behind his seat and withdrew a bottle of water. Unscrewing the cap, he took a long sip, and then put the bottle back.

"When this is all over, I'll buy you as much beer as you can drink."

"I want that in writing."

Baba G might have worn an outward air of confidence and nonchalance, but underneath he was obsessively cautious. He had not only triple-checked all of their gear, he had quadruple-checked it and had made Harvath run through the plan so many more times than was necessary that Hoyt eventually turned on the television back at the ISS compound to drown him out.

Harvath reminded himself of how Gallagher had performed in the hospital waiting area that morning and the way he'd been in the Marines. The man had excellent instincts. He'd have Harvath's back. The ones he really needed to worry about were Marjan and Pamir.

The NDS operatives appeared professional enough, but there was no telling how they would act under pressure. Even though they were going in as a four-man team, Harvath had designed the entire assault around him and Gallagher doing all of the heavy lifting.

As they neared the CARE International

Hospital, Gallagher slowed, applied his blinker, and slapped his warmest American grin to his face as he turned into the main drive. Harvath handed over his ID, which Gallagher added to his own as he rolled down the window.

A bored sentry with an AK-47 slung casually around his neck stepped out of the heated guard shack, checked their IDs, then opened the gate and waved them through.

They drove the van to the main entrance and parked. With its sliding door on the driver's side, the guard down at the gate couldn't have seen what Harvath and Gallagher were doing without walking all the way up to the hospital.

After a quick check inside to make sure the coast was clear, the two men unloaded their gear onto a small hand truck and pushed it inside.

Entering the building, Harvath's Afghan cell phone began to vibrate. Removing it from his pocket, he read the text message out loud to Gallagher. "Flower just handed off the money to Rashid."

"Which means we ought to be seeing Marjan and Pamir momentarily."

Harvath nodded as he slipped the phone back into his pocket and continued. Unlike American hospitals, the CARE hospital was very poorly staffed at night. In addition to Dr. Atash, Harvath doubted there were more than two other employees in the building, both of them Western nurses, who were probably either off sleeping or surfing the net in the nurses' lounge.

The men came to a stop before a doorway marked *No Admittance* in English, Dari, and Pashtu, which led to the hospital's mechanical room. Harvath and Gallagher had discovered it on the unguided portion of their tour earlier and now opened the door and pushed the hand truck inside.

As Gallagher unloaded the gear and moved it down the two flights of stairs to the mechanical room, Harvath took off his coat, grabbed his empty backpack out of one of the containers they had brought in, and stepped back out into the hallway.

After rechecking to make sure no one was about, he headed for the operating theater and a small door off to the side that led to the surgeons' changing room. Inside, he scrounged four white lab coats. He donned one himself, then put the others in his pack.

The theater was composed of three small operating rooms around a central hub where the surgeons scrubbed in. In operating room B, Harvath found a small gurney with a folded blanket atop it. He wheeled it back into the locker room and left it near the door.

Slinging his pack, he stepped into the hallway and walked to the exit door at the very end. When he opened it, Marjan and Pamir were already waiting for him. He handed each of them a lab coat and once they had put them on, they followed him.

They retrieved the stretcher from the surgeons' locker room and navigated it back down the hallway to the stairwell where he had left Gallagher.

After helping move the rest of the gear down into the mechanical room, Pamir began searching for the access point to the tunnel. In less than two minutes, he had found it.

Harvath had overestimated Soviet ingenuity. The entrance wasn't hidden behind a false wall or some elaborate blast door, but rather was behind an oversized cast-iron air grate now partially hidden from view by a stack of boxes. It was obvious the hospital's engineer had no idea what the grate was for or where it led.

As Marjan and Pamir cleared a path to it, Gallagher began laying out the gear. Harvath watched as Pamir produced a rather crude set of picks and went to work on the old Chinese tri-C padlock on the grate. The operative worked quickly and was actually able to get the lock off in a respectable amount of time. The only problem was that even with the lock removed, the grate refused to budge.

Harvath's first thought was that it had rusted shut. He knew how hard cast iron was to cut. The proper way to do it was with a plasma torch, but he doubted they were going to find that kind of torch in Kabul, especially in the middle of the night. The grate was set in the thick cement wall, so somehow working it free wasn't an option either. There was the possibility of trying to saw the grate or to blow it out with plastique, but making that much noise was out of the question.

Harvath was about out of ideas when he saw Pamir place his flashlight in his mouth and insert a dental mirror on an expandable wand between the bars of the grate. Ten seconds later, he held his thumb up in the air and handed the flashlight and mirror to Marjan, who held them for him as he went to work on the padlock he had found on the other side.

When Pamir had the second and final lock removed, he held on to the grate while Marjan searched for oil to lubricate the hinges. When they were good and soaked, Pamir slowly pushed the grate in toward the tunnel. It moved without making a sound. Pulling it back toward the mechanical room, Pamir put it back in place and then he and Marjan joined their American counterparts near the gear and began getting ready.

Harvath and Baba G struggled with both their boots and their uniforms, which were a bit on the small side, but would have to do. Next came armor. Rashid had provided four sets of chest rig plate carriers used by the Afghan Special Forces along with the plates. As an added precaution, Tom Hoyt had lent Harvath some Point Blank brand soft body armor which he wore beneath his uniform. Gallagher was doing the same with his.

Hung from the chest rigs were numerous pouches loaded down with everything they saw themselves needing. Baba G then handed out the encrypted Motorola radios and bone mics that would allow them to communicate, albeit only if necessary and only with each other, as the radio signal would not pierce the heavy concrete of the subterranean passage. They did a radio check and then Gallagher handed Marjan and Pamir each an AK-47.

Harvath removed Hoyt's twelve-gauge Mossberg shotgun and laid it on the table next to Gallagher's. Both had been outfitted with Blackhawk Breachersgrip-style pistol grips that cut recoil in half and even allowed for the weapon to be fired one-handed.

Opening the Storm case Rashid had presented him with above the rug store, Harvath loaded both weapons and secured six extra rounds of the highly specialized munitions in the sidesaddle of each shotgun.

After divvying up the rest of the equipment, Gallagher slipped into the stairwell to exchange final situation reports via text with Hoyt back at the ISS ops center.

Three minutes later Gallagher returned and flashed the thumbs-up. They were good to go.

Rolling his balaclava down over his face, Harvath picked up his weapon, pulled open the grate, and gave his team the signal to move out.

CHAPTER 29

The tunnel was pitch-black and Gallagher only had two pairs of night vision goggles, also known as Night Observation Devices or NODs. As he and Harvath were the designated hitters for the operation, the night vision devices and their IR illuminators went to them. This meant that Marjan and Pamir would be quite literally left in the dark.

Going through Gallagher's gear, Harvath had found two Streamlight Sidewinder flashlights and remembered something a buddy of his had been teaching to high-end tactical units back in the States. For nighttime and low-light operations, the flashlight could be set to emit green light and clipped to an operator's belt. With the articulating head pointed toward the ground, the Streamlights would throw out just enough illumination to allow the NDS operatives to see where they were going, without alerting anyone farther down the tunnel that they were coming.

The team lined up in a formation known as a "stack," with Harvath in front, followed by Pamir and Marjan, and then Gallagher in back carrying a small backpack loaded with extra equipment.

The tunnel was wide enough to drive a jeep through. It was constructed entirely of concrete and its walls were covered with peeling paint and faded Cyrillic writing. Harvath hated it. Tunnels were deathtraps that funneled gunfire and improved the hit rate of even the poorest of shooters. There was no cover or concealment anywhere. If they got into a firefight down here, they were going to be in deep trouble.

Harvath tried not to think about it as he kept a watchful eye for booby traps, as well as any monitoring systems that might tip the Afghan Special Forces off that they were coming.

Pamir had assured Harvath that very few Afghans actually knew of the tunnels, much less exactly where they ran and how they connected.

Knowing that the gossip-loving Afghans had invented viral marketing, Harvath found that hard to believe. Nevertheless, Pamir had insisted that while there were rumors about the tunnels, only a handful inside the NDS actually knew of them and that was only because the information had been passed to them by their counterparts in Soviet Intelligence. He was very confident that the Special Forces soldiers guarding Mustafa Khan hadn't been read in on them.

To bolster his point, Pamir pointed to how Marjan had worked in the interrogation facility, but didn't know anything specific about the tunnels.

Though Harvath wouldn't bet the farm on it, it wasn't impossible either. The NDS was highly compartmentalized. In fact, it was about the only organization in Afghanistan that *could* keep a secret. Their units didn't even have names, just numbers like fifteen or twenty-six; they were that secretive. Harvath just hoped that Pamir was right. If the Afghan Special Forces were watching the tunnels, he didn't like their odds of being able to snatch Mustafa Khan, much less get out of this operation alive.

As per their target, the aging interrogation facility was built beneath the old Soviet officers' quarters. Based upon the open-source satellite imagery Harvath had pulled, the distance from the hospital to the officers' building was about 350 yards. When they were planning everything out it hadn't seemed very far, but now that they were underground, in the dark, and taking pains to watch out for trip wires, electronic sensors, or anything else, the distance felt a lot longer.

According to Pamir, the tunnel ended at another mechanical room, beyond which was the interrogation facility. From what they had been able to gather, the base was empty right now except for the Special Forces soldiers guarding Khan. Active Afghan National Army units were out doing training exercises in the mountains, prepping for the Taliban's impending annual spring offensive.

Marjan anticipated a squad of eight to fourteen soldiers at the most, and knowing what he did about them, he didn't expect more than two to be down in the interrogation facility actually watching over Khan. And the only reason there'd be two and not one was that the last thing the Afghan president would want was for the al-Qaeda operative to be able to strike a one-on-one deal with one of his guards to help free him from captivity. Having two men on him at all times would, he hoped, keep the soldiers honest.

The rest of the Special Forces soldiers would be upstairs in the barracks, with a couple of men keeping watch outside.

As the end of the tunnel came into view,

Harvath signaled for everyone to stop. Gallagher moved up to the front of the column and Harvath crept forward to sweep the rest of the tunnel and make sure it was clear.

Their entry point was another cast-iron air grate, just like the one back at the hospital. He tried to peer inside the base mechanical room, but boxes or crates of some sort on the other side made it impossible to see.

Retracing his steps, he came back, briefed the others, and then had them follow him forward.

At the grate, Harvath and Gallagher provided cover as Marjan and Pamir unclipped the Streamlights from their belts and went to work.

First they lubricated the hinges and then Pamir worked the locks. He got the first one off without difficulty, but the second was a problem. The crates in the mechanical room were jammed right up against it. No matter how hard he tried to jostle the lock, he couldn't manipulate it to an angle where he could insert his picks and get it open.

When Harvath moved closer to see what was taking so long, Pamir showed him. Night vision goggles were not very good for up-close work, so he flipped his up and took a look. The crates in the mechanical room were wedged so tightly against the lock no one could get at it.

Flipping up his goggles, Gallagher came over to examine the situation. After Harvath gave the crate another firm push, Gallagher held his hand up and offered to help. The only problem was that they had no idea how solidly the crates were stacked. With Harvath and Gallagher both pushing, they might succeed in creating enough space for Pamir to work in, but they might also tip the stack over and sink the entire operation.

Harvath shook his head at Gallagher and pantomimed his concern over the crates. Gallagher pulled his goggles back down, stepped back, and watched as Harvath came up with another idea.

He had packed very lightly for his trip to Afghanistan, but one of the things he had brought with him was his favorite fixed-blade knife. It had been produced by Benchmade to commemorate Marc Lee, the first Navy SEAL killed in the Iraq war. If the Terminator carried a knife, this would be it. It was one of the most radical designs Harvath had ever seen and it could take any punishment thrown at it.

As Harvath had done with knives throughout his career, he had demonstrated his sense of humor by placing a short piece of tape on the sheath with the words *Plan B.* It always gave people a good laugh.

He removed the knife now, and guiding Marjan to where he wanted him to hold the Streamlight, he went to work.

He slid the blade between two slats of wood on the crate blocking the inside padlock and began to pry them away. He rocked the knife back and forth, until the slat started to splinter and then finally came free with a sharp *crack.*

Inside the tunnel, the noise sounded as loud as thunder. The team froze in place for several minutes as they waited to see if it had drawn any attention to their presence.

When Harvath was confident that it was safe to proceed, he pried off two more boards and peered inside the crate, which was packed with loose belts of 7.62 ammunition.

He worked quickly, pulling out belt after belt and stacking them neatly on the floor. As soon as he'd made a big enough dent, he stood back and let Pamir tackle the other lock.

Once it was off, Pamir motioned for Harvath to help him. Together, they slowly pulled back on the cast iron. The minute it began to groan, they stopped. Marjan appeared with the oil and nodded for them to continue as he applied extra doses to the hinges.

The groan abated and Harvath and Pamir opened it the rest of the way. Now, the only thing standing between them and the mechanical room were the crates.

Flipping his goggles back down, Harvath stood guard as the other men carefully began removing the crates and stacking them in the tunnel.

It took over twenty minutes before they had cleared enough space to crawl inside.

When it was ready, Harvath hoisted his shotgun and reminded Marjan and Pamir one last time of their number-one rule of engagement. The Afghan Special Forces soldiers were not their enemy. None of them were to be killed.

CHAPTER 30

Harvath and Gallagher entered the mechanical room first. It was nearly identical to the one back at the hospital. Once they had it cleared, Gallagher signaled for the Afghans to join them.

As Gallagher helped them crawl across the crates and made sure they didn't make any noise, Harvath tracked down the electrical panel.

Power outages were a daily fact of life in Afghanistan, but Harvath doubted the Special Forces soldiers were equipped with NODs. Plunging them into darkness would give his plan a major advantage.

Marjan was positioned at the electrical panel while Harvath, Gallagher, and Pamir assembled near the door of the mechanical room. Harvath flipped up his goggles and Gallagher followed suit. He allowed his eyes to get accustomed to the green light radiating from Pamir's Streamlight and then signaled for it to be turned off. Harvath then cracked the mechanical room door and peered into the hallway.

As Harvath's eyes adjusted still further, he saw that straight across from their position, exactly as Marjan had said it would be, there was a heavy metal door that led to the stairwell to the officers' barracks. That meant that just around the corner, and outside his line of sight, was the interrogation facility.

Harvath listened for sounds of a sentry or anyone in the stairwell. There was nothing.

He nodded to Gallagher, who opened his pack and removed a lock and a length of chain.

Counting down from three on his fingers, Harvath then eased the door the rest of the way open and slipped silently across the hallway.

With his weapon up and at the ready, he entered the stairwell and checked to make sure it was completely empty. When he exited, Gallagher was waiting for him. Quietly, they closed the door and chained it shut.

Harvath did a quick peek around the corner. Pulling his head back, he gave the all clear and then signaled Pamir, who turned and flashed his Streamlight to Marjan inside the mechanical room to begin the countdown.

With the clock ticking down, Harvath took one more look around the corner and then he and Gallagher got moving.

They crept down the hallway and stopped just before the door to the interrogation facility. Voices spilled out from inside, which was the good news. The facility was being used. The bad news was that it sounded like much more than two guards.

Taking a deep breath, Harvath adjusted his weapon and waited. Behind him, Gallagher did the same.

It was only sixty seconds, but sitting there, exposed in the hall, it felt like an eternity. All of Harvath's senses were on fire. His entire body was coiled, ready to spring. As he let the air out of his lungs, Marjan threw the switch and the entire basement level went dark.

Flipping down his NODs, Harvath applied pressure to the trigger of his shotgun and spun into the room.

It was about thirty feet long by fifteen feet wide, and along the opposite wall were three cell doors, two of which were open.

Four Afghan Special Forces soldiers sat on rugs in the middle of the room chatting as if nothing had happened. None of them had even bothered to turn on a flashlight, so certain were they that their auxiliary generator would kick in at any moment. Their weapons sat on the floor next to or in front of them, while two more soldiers were sound asleep in the open cells on either side of Mustafa Khan. Harvath fired his first round before even fully entering the room.

The TASER XREP, which stood for Extended Range Electro-Muscular Projectile, was a self-contained, fully functional TASER circuit payload housed inside a twelve-gauge shotgun shell that could take down targets at up to a hundred yards and had recently been issued to the Afghan National Army and the Afghan National Police in order to deal with riots and civil insurrection.

As the XREPs were totally self-contained, they had the benefit of allowing the shooter to engage a separate target with each pull of the trigger. But with no wires leading back to the shotgun, the suspect could only be given one hit from the projectile's battery. Once the effect wore off, no further electricity could be introduced unless the subject was reengaged with another round. This meant the shooter had to act fast.

The rounds were incredibly quiet and there was only a hushed thump as Harvath's first XREP left the barrel of his shotgun and ripped down the length of the room, catching his target in the upper chest. The man's body stiffened and he roared as the voltage coursed through his body and incapacitated his neuromuscular system.

Entering the room right behind Harvath, Gallagher pulled his trigger and nailed his first target dead-on. Both men then moved to engage their second targets, but while Harvath caught his soldier square in the center of the chest, Gallagher's shot went wide.

Suddenly, a soldier who had been sleeping on the bunk inside one of the open cells appeared with his AK-47.

"Check the cells!" Harvath yelled.

Gallagher engaged the soldier in the open cell and fired while Harvath took out the remaining soldier sitting on the floor.

Gallagher's shot was perfect, and the soldier's weapon clattered to the ground as his muscles seized and he fell like a tree trunk.

But just as suddenly as the first soldier had appeared, another sprang from the cell at the far end of the room bobbling a flashlight and his weapon. Harvath didn't have a good angle, but he turned his weapon in the man's direction and pulled the trigger anyway.

The XREP raced from the barrel of his Mossberg, only to clank off the cell door as the man let loose with a burst of fire from his barely level rifle.

As the room erupted in strobes of muzzle flash and a deafening barrage of rifle fire, the rounds ricocheted off the concrete walls.

There was a loud slap when one of them slammed into Harvath's back as he dove to the ground.

It felt as if someone had walked up behind him and cracked him with a heavy metal shovel. And while the air hadn't been completely knocked out of his lungs, it had come real close.

Rolling onto his side, Harvath ignored the pain and jacked his final XREP into the chamber. He brought his Mossberg up to fire, but stopped as Gallagher, who had closed on the soldier, bravely stepped around the cell door and fired.

Harvath couldn't tell if it was one of the dumbest or most courageous things he had ever seen, and he didn't have time to figure it out. Even though in general the XREPs packed a lot more punch than the conventional, pistol-style TASER and subjects tended to remain out of it for a lot longer, there were always exceptions where the effect could be short-lived.

He sucked in a deep breath and pushed himself up off the floor. Everything still worked, which meant he wasn't paralyzed, and as best he could tell, he wasn't bleeding

— all good signs.

Gallagher had seen Harvath get hit and wanted to check the extent of the damage. Harvath waved him off. They had too much work to do.

The center cell door was locked up tight, and after they had divested the soldiers of their weapons, hogtied them with EZ cuffs, and covered their mouths with duct tape, they searched for the keys.

When Harvath found them, he opened Khan's cell. Despite everything that had just taken place in the room, the al-Qaeda operative sat smugly on the edge of his bed in the dark as if he had expected this all along. Harvath hated the arrogance of the Muslim fanatics, and laying eyes on this one in the eerie green of his night vision goggles, he immediately despised him.

"Stand up and turn around," Harvath ordered.

"Who are you?" demanded Khan.

"The Tooth Fairy," replied Harvath as he drew back his hand and struck Khan in the face. "Now get up."

Harvath had to yank the man to his feet. Once he was up, Harvath spun him around, secured his hands behind his back, and slapped a piece of duct tape over his mouth.

Gallagher had reloaded both of the shotguns, and he handed Harvath's to him as he exited the cell guiding Khan.

They moved quickly to the hallway where already they could hear the sound of pounding coming from the other side of the stairwell doorway. Harvath knew it wouldn't be long before the Special Forces soldiers retreated upstairs and dropped a grenade down in an effort to blow the door open. He didn't want to be anywhere near when that happened.

Once they were all in the mechanical room, Harvath sent Pamir and Marjan up and over the crates while Gallagher used his second chain to secure the door. When that was done, he scrambled over the crates and waited on the other side to assist Khan.

After Harvath climbed into the tunnel and snapped the locks shut behind him, he could see Pamir and Marjan standing in the green glow of their Streamlights. Reassuming control of the prisoner, he told Gallagher to take point and for Marjan and Pamir to follow. Harvath and Khan would bring up the rear.

"Are you okay?" Gallagher asked.

"I'll be okay," replied Harvath. "Go."

Gallagher nodded, and as he and the NDS operatives disappeared into the darkness, Harvath nudged Khan forward. The man refused to move.

Harvath's back was throbbing and he was in no mood to play around with this asshole. He slid his arm underneath Khan's, grabbed his trapezius muscle in a vise grip, and lifted up on Khan's arms.

Pain shot through the terrorist's body and he stutter-stepped forward to get away from it. Reluctantly, he began walking.

The hardest part of Harvath's assignment was almost complete. He had Khan. Now all he had to do was get him someplace safe and then coordinate the exchange for Julia Gallo.

His injury notwithstanding, he should have felt much better than he did. But having laid eyes on Khan, Harvath knew that he wouldn't be able to trade him for Julia Gallo. He couldn't let an animal like this just return to terrorism. He was going to have to come up with another way, and that meant this thing wasn't over, not by a long shot.

CHAPTER 31

Harvath peeled off his soft armor and dropped it to the bathroom floor. Pulling up his T-shirt, he turned and looked into the mirror at the softball-sized bruise growing on his lower back. The ricochet had missed his plate entirely and had slammed right into his soft armor. Though the bullet had been flattened out and its impact had been somewhat blunted from having skipped off the wall, his injury still hurt like hell.

Opening up Gallagher's med kit, he fished out a one-thousand-milligram horse-pill-sized Motrin, affectionately referred to by SEALs as *Vitamin M,* and chased it down with a long swig from the can of Red Bull he'd brought into the bathroom with him.

Transporting Khan, from the hospital to the safe house Gallagher had arranged for them, had gone exactly as they had planned. After donning their white doctors' coats, they wrapped the terrorist's head with gauze, strapped him to the gurney, threw the blanket over him, and wheeled him right out the front doors to their van. Pamir and Marjan had followed, pushing the hand truck loaded down with all the gear. After helping load Khan and the equipment into the back of the van, they had left the grounds the same way they had come in. The hospital had remained quiet the entire time. Never once did they see another soul.

The safe house was in Kabul's Shahr-e Naw district — home to many of Afghanistan's opium kingpins and corrupt politicians. The neighborhood was full of newly constructed mansions, impressive even by American standards. Many of Shahr-e Naw's dubious landowners had built more than one residence and made sizable, not to mention quasi-legitimate flows of income by renting out their additional homes to Westerners. It was exactly such a property that Gallagher had secured for them.

Taking Khan back to ISS's Kabul compound was out of the question. Not only was it not set up to hold a prisoner, there were too many people who would ask too many questions. Here, nobody asked any questions and the neighbors kept to themselves. Even better, the cops had been paid off by the opium lords to stay out of the neighborhood and anyone who could afford to live here had private security, which meant it wasn't unusual to see men with guns coming and going at all hours of the day and night.

Only four people knew about the safe house — Flower, Harvath, Hoyt, and Gallagher. Inspector Rashid had offered to act as an escort on their way back, just in case there were any checkpoints, but Harvath had turned him down. Instead, once they were free of the hospital, he had Flower sit with Rashid and monitor his radio. Flower knew the route Gallagher and Harvath were driving and could warn them in time of any potential problems. As it was, things went off without a hitch.

Harvath and Gallagher stashed Khan in a cleverly constructed panic room the safe house's owner had constructed in his basement. The room was perfect for holding their prisoner. There was a hole in the floor that functioned as a Turkish-style toilet, there were no windows, and the walls and ceilings were solid concrete. Mustafa Khan could make as much noise as he wanted and no one would ever hear him.

Gathering up his gear, Harvath stepped out of the bathroom and walked down the marble-floored hallway into the living room. Gallagher was sitting on one of the leather sofas with a bottle of Heineken in his hand, watching the large plasma TV. "Want one?" he asked, holding it up.

"Why not?" replied Harvath as he sat down on the couch.

Gallagher walked into the kitchen and returned with another beer for himself and one for Harvath. "How's your back feeling?" he asked as he handed over one of the bottles.

"I'll live."

Gallagher was silent for a moment. "Listen," he finally said. "About missing my second target —"

Harvath stopped him. "Those XREPs take some getting used to. The important thing is that you popped that last guy before he could get off a second burst."

Gallagher nodded and after a lengthy sip of beer asked, "So now what?"

It was exactly the question Harvath had been wrestling with. Technically, he shouldn't have had any misgivings. His assignment was very straightforward — find Mustafa Khan and trade him for Julia Gallo.

For simply agreeing to undertake the operation, Harvath had already been paid five hundred thousand dollars. Bringing Julia back alive would net him another five hundred thousand dollars. He'd be an idiot to screw that up. All he had left to do at this point was to conduct the exchange and the assignment would be over.

The problem, though, was that Harvath had decided not to let Khan go. The man was a terrorist, and that's exactly what he would go back to being. There was no reforming these assholes. You had to either lock them up or kill them. Setting Khan free was an option Harvath was not willing to entertain. Not when it meant more people who didn't deserve to die would die. There was also the possibility that a man with Khan's background could be behind the next 9/11 or 7/7 attacks. Knowing he had had him and had released him back into the wild if something like that ever happened was not something Harvath could live with. And the more he thought about it, the more he realized he might not have to.

Looking at Gallagher, he asked, "How long do you think it will be before word gets out that the Afghans have lost Khan?"

Baba G rolled the bottom of his Heineken on the armrest, leaving a chain of wet circles. "I don't know. This is going to be pretty embarrassing for the government. The Afghan president has made a big deal out of how Afghanistan is a nation of laws and how he intended to see that Khan was put on trial. My guess is that they're going to keep it secret for as long as they can."

"How long until the Taliban and al-Qaeda know he's been snatched?"

"With the moles they've got everywhere? I'd say twenty-four to forty-eight hours tops."

Harvath looked at his watch and calculated the time difference with D.C. He owed Stephanie Gallo an updated report. He also needed her to do something for him.

"Do you think we can get Hoyt and Mark Midland to help babysit?" he asked.

Gallagher nodded. "If the price is right."

Putting down his beer, Harvath pulled out his cell phone. "Good. Call them and tell them to get over here." Then he added, "And I need to have a powwow with Fontaine."

"*Fontaine?* Why?"

"Because now that the Khan part of the operation is over, he's going to help us get Julia Gallo back."

CHAPTER 32

Town Tavern, Washington, D.C.

"So, you want to tell me what we're doing here?" asked Max Holland as he set his drink down on the table and looked Elise Campbell in the eye.

Holland, a twenty-five-year veteran Secret Service operative, had short gray hair, blue eyes, and hands the size of catchers' mitts. He had been Robert Alden's lead protective agent during the campaign and had been promoted to head of his detail when Alden was elected president. At fifty-three, he was the oldest agent protecting the president — something his smartass colleagues were more than happy to point out at all hours of the day and night. In fact, they liked to joke that Holland could never stand too near the military officer who carried the nuclear football for fear that his "I've fallen and I can't get up" Life Alert necklace might trigger an accidental launch.

The Secret Service agent took it all in stride. With the flood of young and relatively inexperienced agents that had been transfused into the White House, Holland was their senior in more ways than one. He knew their jokes were only good-natured ribbing. The most important thing was that they respect him, and they did. While Holland would have preferred that the president be surrounded by more experienced agents, there had been such a mass exodus after the election, he could do nothing more than make sure the people that the president did have were the absolute best that the Secret Service could provide.

Quietly, Holland resented the hell out of his colleagues who had taken early retirement rather than serve under President Alden. As far as he was concerned, they were a disgrace to the Secret Service. No matter how much they didn't care for the new POTUS, they should have still been able to carry out their commitment to protecting the person who held the office. The exodus had destroyed many friendships and poisoned many more to the point that they were as good as ruined.

Looking across the table, Holland wondered what personal problem Campbell was going to unload on him. One of the drawbacks of being the most senior man on the team was that a lot of the agents saw him as a father figure and continually wanted to unburden themselves to him.

The best reason he always held these meetings at the Town Tavern in Adams Morgan was that it was the unofficial home of Chicago sports fans in D.C., and while Campbell droned on about her credit card debt, boyfriend problems, or how she felt her parents didn't really understand her, Holland, a native Chicagoan who had been married and divorced twice, could keep one eye glued to the Cubs game on the TV behind the bar.

"Do you remember Nikki Hale?" the young agent asked after their food had arrived.

"Sort of," he said as he took a bite of his bacon cheeseburger. "Why?"

"I heard she was pretty out of it the night she died."

"That's what they say," replied Holland as he held up his empty glass and got a nod from the bartender.

"Did you see her that night?"

"Elise, why the sudden interest in Nikki Hale?"

The great thing about train rides was that they gave you plenty of time to think, and

Elise Campbell had done just that as she made her way back from East Hampton. She understood the path she had chosen and she knew it wasn't going to be easy. That was why she had decided to start with Holland. "I think there's more to what went on that night than people know."

"Like what?"

"Like —" began Campbell, before she was interrupted by the bartender, who set a new draft in front of Holland and asked her if she wanted another Diet Coke. Declining, she turned her attention back to Holland. "Like whom she'd been partying with before she sped off."

"Like maybe the president?" offered Holland as he clamped down once more on his cheeseburger and tore off another bite.

"If they were actually *together,* then yes."

"Leave it alone, Elise."

"Why? What if the president actually had something to do with what happened that night?"

Holland chewed his food slowly and then took a long swallow of his Bud Light. "I'm going to eat my dinner and forget that we ever had this conversation."

"What are you talking about?"

"Elise, why are you so interested in Nikki Hale's death?"

Campbell knew from being a cop that when someone answered a question with a question, he was usually avoiding telling you something.

Prepared for the fact that her next question could very well end her career with the Secret Service, she took a deep breath and let it fly. "You were working Alden's detail the night Nikki Hale died. I want to know if the president had anything to do with it."

Slowly, Holland put down his cheeseburger and pushed his plate away. Picking up his napkin, he wiped the grease from his fingers. "In sixty seconds, I'm standing up and walking out of here."

"Why?"

"Fifty-nine seconds," he replied as he raised his glass to his mouth and knocked back half of his beer.

Campbell waited for him to put the glass back down and then said, "You're going to be subpoenaed over what happened."

"What are you talking about?"

"There's going to be a new investigation."

Holland couldn't tell if the woman was telling the truth or not. "How would you know?" he asked.

"Trust me, I know."

Holland laughed, removed two twenties from his wallet, and dropped them on the bar. "See you around."

Elise put her hand on his arm as he rose from his stool. "I'm doing you a favor, Max," she said, and then corrected herself. "Actually, I'm doing the Secret Service a favor, a big one, but I can only do it if you help me."

The elder Secret Service agent closed his eyes, pinched the bridge of his nose with his thumb and forefinger, and sat back down. "What is this all about, Elise?"

"It's about a new lawsuit against the president for his involvement in Hale's death."

"Who says he had anything to do with it?"

"Stephanie Gallo."

"Gallo? What are you talking about? Did she tell you this?"

"Not directly, no."

Holland stared at her for a moment before it hit him. "Jesus, Elise. You overheard the president and Gallo talking about something, didn't you?"

"This isn't about me."

"For the first time tonight, you're right. It isn't about you. It's about the Secret Service and our ability to protect the president. How the hell are we supposed to do that if he won't let us get close enough to him because he's worried we're eavesdropping on him?"

When Elise tried to reply, Holland interrupted her. "If you hate the guy so much, why don't you just resign like the others did? Why do this?"

"I don't hate the president. I *voted* for him. But that doesn't mean we should look the other way if a crime has been committed. We're law enforcement officers."

"Whose job it is to protect the president," replied Holland, "not to solve crimes. We're in *protection,* not detection."

"Max, listen —" she began.

"No, Elise, you listen. Nikki Hale got drunk, she got behind the wheel, and she caused a horrible accident. She took four other people along with her. It was tragic, but it's over. Don't pick at the scab."

"Max, I can help head this thing off and save us all a lot of trouble and embarrassment, but I can't do that if you won't cooperate."

"Hale's dead, Elise. *She's* the one responsible for what happened. Case closed."

"You're wrong about that."

"How do you know?" Holland asked. "How do you know there are going to be subpoenas? Who's behind all this?"

"Are you going to help me or not?"

"That depends. You've got to give me something first."

Elise reached for the remnants of her Diet Coke and weighed what to tell him. "The family Hale plowed into and killed —"

"The Colemans."

She nodded. "Their only living relatives were Charlie Coleman's parents. They started a lawsuit, but eventually agreed to an out of court settlement, supposedly paid for by Stephanie Gallo."

"Big deal. Gallo's free to do what she wants with her money. And why wouldn't she want to make the lawsuit disappear? She had a lot invested in Alden's campaign, and the drinking that night happened at her fundraiser, on *her* property. With a bank account like hers, I would have done the same. Plus, with Nikki Hale dead, there's no one to charge with a crime. And when the elder Colemans folded their tents and went home, that was the end of any civil suits too."

"Not necessarily. There's someone else who can bring a suit for what happened that night."

"Who?"

"Sheryl Coleman's business partner."

"I don't understand how you know all of this," said Holland.

"I was invited to talk to her."

"Invited by whom?"

"It doesn't matter."

"The hell it doesn't. This smells like a political hatchet job. Who's putting you up to this?"

Elise resented the insinuation. "Nobody's putting me up to this."

"Then why are you doing it?"

"Because it's my job."

"No it isn't. Let it go, Elise."

"What are you so worried about?"

Holland drained the last of his beer and then held the empty glass up to get the bartender's attention again. "What I'm worried about," he said as he set it back onto the bar, "is how the Secret Service could be made to look in all of this."

"Why should that matter? Has the Secret Service done something wrong?"

Holland waited until the bartender had set down his new Bud Light and walked away before responding. "You said you could do the Secret Service a favor. How?"

"I might be able to convince Sheryl Coleman's business partner not to pursue the lawsuit."

"So might Stephanie Gallo and her mighty checkbook."

"Not this woman," said Elise. "I've met her. This isn't about money."

"You know," he said as he raised his glass, but stopped just before it reached his mouth, "it's funny how you just happened to over-hear something between the president and Gallo and now all of a sudden this woman wants to bring a lawsuit. I'd think long and hard about what you're doing, Elise."

"I have, Max. Believe me. So about that night?"

Holland took another long sip of beer and set the glass back on the bar. "Are you sure about this?"

Elise nodded.

"Yes, after the dinner that night, the president was with Nikki Hale."

"What were they doing?"

"I wouldn't know. Unlike some agents, I don't eavesdrop on the president."

Elise let the remark slide. "What do you think was going on?"

"I'm not going to speculate."

"There was a lot of talk that they might have been having an affair."

"Is that a question?" asked Holland.

"Yes, it's a question."

"You worked his detail. What do you think?"

"I was an advance person for most of the campaign. If there was anything between them, I didn't notice it."

"Like I said," replied Holland. "I'm not going to speculate."

"Fine. How long were they together after the party that night?"

"About forty-five minutes."

"Were they drinking? Do you think Alden could be held liable for her condition that night?"

"First of all," said Holland as he raised his beer to take another swig, "I'm not an attorney. And second, I think Nikki Hale bears the ultimate responsibility for her condition. You remember what her reputation was."

Elise looked at him. "I do, and I also know what people have said about Alden. I need to know you're not covering for him, that this isn't some wink-wink, boys-will-be-boys sort of thing."

"The man's personal life is his business. You can say what you want about Kennedy and Marilyn Monroe, but we all know how Clinton's affair blew up in his face. We also know how the Service came away from that with black eyes. Morale is at an all-time low. We don't need a scandal and we don't need agents having to testify about what they saw or didn't see.

"I'll tell you this, though. I don't care how many Americans love this new president, his administration has gotten off to a very rocky start. A mistress would be bad for his image, but a dead one would be fatal."

Elise thought about that remark for a moment before asking, "Did you see Nikki Hale leave that night?"

"I saw her and the president part company. I didn't see her leave the estate."

"Had they been in his bedroom?"

"No, Gallo's library study."

"Were they alone?"

Holland nodded.

"What about the drinking?"

"You already asked me that," he replied.

"And you didn't answer. Had they been drinking?"

"Maybe."

Elise studied him. *Maybe?*

"I wasn't in the room."

"Max, her blood alcohol content was off the charts. You're telling me she wasn't bombed when she left?"

"Maybe she had been drinking with him and it just hadn't hit her yet. All I know is that she didn't look pie-eyed to me when she left."

Elise was confused. "Then what happened?"

"She made another stop before leaving the estate that evening."

"She did? Where?" asked Elise.

"That, you're going to have to figure out for yourself," replied Holland as he stood up from the bar and polished off the rest of his beer.

"Hold on a second, Max. You can't just leave it like that. If I've got to go around asking every agent who was on duty that night what they saw or might have seen, word's going to get out."

Holland hadn't thought of that. Reluctantly, he threw her a bone. "Talk to Hutch."

"*Hutchinson?* But he was on Mrs. Alden's detail that night."

Reaching over, Holland collected his forty dollars off the bar. "Thanks for dinner. If you want to chat about this some more, I'll expect to see a process server on my doorstep."

As he disappeared into the crowd and exited the Town Tavern, Elise thought about what he had said. *A mistress would be very bad for the president's image, and a dead mistress would be fatal.*

CHAPTER 33

Spinghar Mountains, Afghanistan
Sunday

The cluster of mud brick buildings abutted a summer grazing pasture not far from the Tora Bora cave complex. Even when the roads were clear it was an extremely rough ride. Now, with snow and ice still on the ground at this altitude, it took Mullah Massoud an extra hour to get there, which didn't do much to improve his mood.

Yelling for his men to get out of the room, he slammed his AK-47 down on the table and let loose on his Russian counterpart, who was sitting on the floor having tea. "I told you to make it look like an accident, you idiot!"

"Calm down," said Simonov.

"How dare you tell me to calm down!" roared the Taliban commander.

The Russian lifted the kettle and poured

another cup. "We'll have tea and we will talk."

Massoud took two steps onto the rug and kicked the teacups across the floor. His face was flushed and his eyes were bulging. Simonov had never seen him like this before.

"My village will have to go to war now because of you!"

Quietly, Simonov stood, retrieved the cups, and brought them back to the rug.

The Taliban commander was furious.

"You and I have seen too many battles together to have our friendship end this way, Massoud," said the Russian. "I am inviting you one more time to sit and have tea with me."

Removing his boots, Massoud sat down on the rug. As the Russian refilled the cups, he spoke. "Your brother is not wearing the shoes I gave him. Why not?"

"Because I took them from him," snapped the Taliban commander. "It was to be his contribution to the debt paid for breaking Asadoulah Badar's jaw."

"Well, you can give them back to him."

Massoud snorted. "I might as well. Shoes will no longer cover the debt."

"No. That's not the reason," said Simonov. "Your brother caught Asadoulah fondling the American woman. Zwak warned him

323

repeatedly but he wouldn't stop. He was protecting her."

"How do you know this?" demanded Massoud.

"The woman told me herself."

"Why? What were you doing even speaking to her?"

"I received an email from the mother. Four questions asking for proof of life. I needed the answers to prove that we still had her alive."

"Elam Badar's son lied," said the Taliban commander as it all sank in.

"It would appear so."

"And we killed him."

"Correction," said the Russian. "I killed him, but as far as his village is concerned it is the same thing."

"You also killed two other men. Tell me what happened."

Simonov explained how he had carried out Elam Badar's killing exactly as they had planned, but that he had been seen by two other men from his village and had been forced to kill them as well.

"How did you kill them?" asked Massoud.

"One round each to the head."

"That was very rash."

"I had no choice," said the Russian. "I had

to act quickly."

The Taliban commander shook his head. "And the bodies?" he asked.

"They won't stay hidden forever."

Massoud signaled for Simonov to continue. The Russian explained how he had returned to Massoud's village as quickly as possible, but when he discovered that the Taliban commander was not there, he decided to act.

Gathering several of Massoud's best men, he loaded gear and equipment into three trucks, collected Zwak and the American woman, whom he disguised in burkas to make it look as if they were traveling with two women instead of just one, and then headed for their fallback location. If Elam Badar's family or anyone in his village tried to retaliate by alerting the American military or Afghan forces, it would do little good at this point.

It was a small consolation, and the Taliban commander massaged his temples with the heels of his hands. "Now that two other men from his village have been killed, Elam Badar's death will no longer be viewed as an accident."

"I agree."

"And all you want to do is to sit here and have tea?" demanded Massoud, his anger rising again.

"Have tea *and* discuss my plan," said Simonov.

"Will your plan prevent my village from going to war?"

The Russian smiled. "No. But it will prevent Elam Badar's."

CHAPTER 34

Butkhak, Afghanistan

Twenty kilometers east of Kabul on the Jalalabad Road was the village of Butkhak. Of the several small NGOs working in this village, only a handful could afford security. One such group was Clean Water International. Though they weren't one of Gallagher's richest clients, they were one of the steadiest, and that meant a lot to ISS's bottom line.

Baba G liked to joke that instead of referring to themselves as CWI, a more appropriate acronym for their organization would have been PSH, short for pot-smoking hippies.

Afghanistan was awash in vacant real estate, and Gallagher had seen an opportunity for ISS in being able to provide not only physical security for NGOs in the form of armed manpower, but also safe places for them to be housed.

Most Afghans didn't know the first thing about marketing to the Westerners who were flooding into their country. All they knew was that if they could land even the smallest of fishes, they could make big money.

Through one of Gallagher's many Afghan contacts, he'd been offered a sizable, walled property in Butkhak. The area was booming with reconstruction projects, and he knew it was only a matter of time before he found a tenant. The main house also had something he'd never seen before in Afghanistan — a Jacuzzi. Gallagher had agreed to represent it on the spot.

What had sold him on the compound had also sold the pot-smoking hippies. From the moment they had seen the Jacuzzi, they were hooked. It was only later that he realized that the property also included a dilapidated greenhouse, which the hippies gladly repaired out of funds from their own pockets. Though the rent and security package Gallagher had sold them was likely a tad more than their office somewhere in Europe had budgeted, the money always arrived on time in Gallagher's account every month.

There were several structures on the property, one of which Baba G had excluded from the hippies' lease. It was here, inside a long, stone, garagelike structure, that he and Hoyt kept their most important investment.

Gallagher referred to it as the "Golden Conex," and as he unlocked the twenty-foot-long shipping container he quoted a line from Willie Wonka, "A small step for mankind, but a giant step for us."

Harvath let out a whistle. The ISS team had put together quite an impressive collection of small arms. In addition to crates of fragmentation grenades and RPGs, there were neatly stacked rows of battle rifles, submachine guns, and shotguns. Along one wall a pegboard had been mounted and from it hung a myriad of pistols. There were belt-fed weapons along the back, crates of ammunition, boxes of spare magazines, as well as an armorer's bench. It was like stumbling into Santa's workshop.

Leaning right up front was a pink M-16 covered in Hello Kitty stickers. "Who does this belong to?" he asked.

"Oh, that?" replied Gallagher. "That's Hoyt's."

"Come on."

"It's a surprise for Mei's birthday."

"He better hope she loves it," said Harvath with a shake of his head as he picked up a considerably more manly LaRue Tactical Stealth OSR — Optimized Sniper

Rifle. It had a SureFire suppressor, Magpul Precision Rifle Stock, Harris bipod, and a Leuopold Scope.

"I'm running a special on that one today," said Gallagher.

"Oh, yeah?" replied Harvath as he got comfortable with the weapon in his hands. "How much?"

"For you, mister, *yak* dollar."

"Sold," said Harvath, setting it aside. "How about these?" he asked, pointing to several Heckler & Koch MP5 submachine guns.

"Those are particularly fun. They scare the shit out of the Afghans, especially when you attach the suppressors."

"Why?"

"Most of them haven't seen that kind of weapon before. Plus, I don't have to tell you how good they are for CQB work."

No, he didn't. Harvath had done a lot of close quarters battle with the MP5 and knew it was an exceptional weapon. "I'll take it," he said.

"Take two," joked Baba G with a wave of his hand. "They're small."

"I think one will be fine."

As they decided on the rest of the gear they would need, there was the sound of tires crunching on gravel outside. Harvath looked at his watch. Daniel Fontaine was right on time.

He stepped outside and greeted the former Canadian counterterrorism operative as he climbed out of his truck. "Did you get everything?" he asked.

"You owe me two hundred dollars," said Fontaine as he shook Harvath's hand.

Harvath looked at him. "On top of the stack of cash I gave you in Kabul?"

"I got stopped at a checkpoint on the way out of town," said the Canadian with a shrug. "It was either one hundred bucks and they take half of the stuff, or two hundred and we call it even. I decided to call it even."

"Good choice," replied Harvath as he followed him around to the back of his SUV.

Fontaine lifted the tailgate and threw back the blanket covering the cargo area. Underneath were several cases of beer and hard liquor.

"And Hoyt said all your late nights in Kabul would never amount to anything," stated Harvath.

"Obviously, he was wrong," replied Fontaine.

"Obviously."

"But wait," said the Canadian as he stepped away from the tailgate and over to the rear passenger-side door, "there's more."

Harvath joined him as he opened the door and flung back another blanket, revealing a case of sugar-free Red Bull on the backseat. Looking at it, Harvath said, "There's one missing."

"Fine," replied Fontaine. "Take five bucks off what you owe me." But after thinking about it for a second, stated, "Better yet. Fuck you. That's what you get for waking me up at three in the morning."

Harvath laughed, peeled two hundred bucks from a wad of bills in his pocket, and handed it to him. Though Afghanistan was an Islamic country, there was still alcohol to be found. Getting this much of it, especially on such short notice, was a considerable feat. Fontaine had done well.

Still plagued by jet lag and not having had much sleep, Harvath appreciated the gesture and helped himself to a can of the energy drink.

"Tough night?" asked Fontaine as he watched Harvath pop another one-thousand-milligram Motrin in his mouth and wash it down with a swig of Red Bull.

"Just an underground party," said Harvath as he slid a couple of cans into his pockets and closed the door. "You didn't miss much."

"Where's Baba G?"

"Santa's in his workshop," said Harvath, pointing toward the structure, "checking off items on my Christmas list."

Fontaine smiled, and after covering up the booze with the blanket, closed the tailgate. Following Harvath toward the building, he said, "I've got first dibs on the Hello Kitty rifle. The Taliban hate Hello Kitty."

CHAPTER 35

Only a fool or a heavily armored military column went anywhere in rural Afghanistan uninvited. To enter the village of Asadoulah Badar, the young man Dr. Atash had treated for a broken jaw, Harvath, Gallagher, and Fontaine would have to be invited.

The best way, especially for Westerners, to secure such an invitation was to offer the village *shura* something they needed. Based on Gallagher's relationship with his tenants in Butkhak, he came up with what he thought was the perfect offer.

In exchange for half the booze in the back of Fontaine's SUV, Clean Water International's project leader agreed to allow the trio to pose as a scouting team. They were given a brief overview of CWI's mission and how they conducted project assessments. More important, the project leader contacted a resourceful "fixer" and interpreter they used in Khogyani who was adept at getting the most difficult jobs done, as long as the money was right. They asked him to reach out to the village *shura* to see if they would consent to being considered for a clean water project.

After agreeing to a price, the interpreter explained that he would call back in a few hours once he had been to the village and had met with its elders. Harvath gave the CWI leader an alias as well as his Afghan cell number for the interpreter to call back on.

They loaded the cargo area of Gallagher's Land Cruiser with all of the weapons except for their pistols, threw a blanket over them, then loaded the alcohol on top and covered that with another blanket. If they were stopped along the Kabul to Jalalabad Road, they could plead to the lesser offense, give up the booze, and keep going. That was simply the price of doing business in Afghanistan. Once they got off the main road and headed for Khogyani, though, they weren't likely to run into many official checkpoints. At that point, they were going to make sure they had the bulk of their firepower very close at hand.

CWI's Afghan houseboy cooked them lunch, and then, after changing into their baggy *salwar kameez,* or "man-jammies," as

Harvath like to call them, the trio hit the road.

Gallagher drove while Fontaine rode shotgun and Harvath sat in back and tried to catch up on his sleep. The narrow, two-lane highway took them through snow-capped mountain passes and tunnels carved by hand out of solid rock. Garishly decorated, hand-painted Pakistani trucks, known as *jingas,* often found themselves stuck inside the tunnels or losing significant portions of their cargo, which were stacked Beverly Hillbillies-style, higher than common sense would ever allow.

They were halfway to Jalalabad when Baba G told Harvath to wake up. "All hands on deck," he said.

Harvath's hand moved to the butt of his Glock before his eyes were even fully focused. "What's up?"

"We're coming up on Surobi," replied Fontaine.

"What's in Surobi?"

"Nothing good," responded Gallagher.

"It's known to have a very heavy Taliban presence," said Fontaine. "Lots of the hits on convoys have supposedly been orchestrated out of this village. They also run bullshit checkpoints at night, shaking down anyone dumb enough to be out driving this way."

They were in the Kabul River Valley and would be following the water the rest of the way to Jalalabad. Gallagher slowed his vehicle as they entered the outskirts of Surobi, took off his seatbelt, and made sure his door was unlocked. Fontaine and Harvath followed suit.

With traditional Afghan clothing hiding their body armor, and driving a slightly beat-up, unarmored Toyota, the hope was that the men would not draw too much attention to themselves.

As Gallagher and Fontaine spent a lot of their time bouncing back and forth between Kabul and Jalalabad, they both knew the Jalalabad Road quite well. "You want to stop for tea?" Gallagher asked Harvath as they rolled into the village itself. "There's a nice little tea house here."

"I think I'll pass," said Harvath as he made eye contact with a man walking along the side of the road wearing a black turban, the symbol of the Taliban. The look the Afghan shot back was pure hate. Some people called it the evil eye, though Baba G liked to refer to it as the "death stare," or the "hairy eyeball." Whatever the case, the man obviously wasn't fooled by Harvath's local costume. He was an outsider and therefore didn't belong.

"I've actually got the tea thing down to a science," continued Gallagher. "From the moment they first realize you're in town, you've got twenty minutes, give or take, until they start pulling the trigger."

Harvath turned away from the window and met Baba G's eye in the rearview mirror. "Why do they wait twenty minutes?"

"The lookout who sees you has to call his handler. The handler then has to call the higher-ups. The higher-ups then have to decide how much they think you're worth. Once they have a price they're willing to pay, they call the handler, who then argues with the lookout over how much he'll get paid for popping you. Of course the lookout thinks he's getting ripped off because the handler is taking too much off the top, which he is, so they argue back and forth for a little while longer until the handler relents and agrees to pay a little bit more. That's why I say it takes about twenty minutes, *give or take.*"

"The day they go to a straight rate card," Harvath said with a laugh, "you're in big trouble."

"That would make too much sense. TIA."

"TIA," repeated Harvath as he turned his eyes back to the window.

Surobi, like most of Afghanistan, was

nothing more than a collection of mud brick buildings. The only color at all came from the produce or mass-produced consumer goods being sold from drab roadside shops and stalls.

Harvath spotted three more men, all of whom were wearing black turbans and had AK-47s slung over their shoulders. The fact that they not only carried weapons, but so openly and brazenly displayed their allegiance to the Taliban, said a lot about Surobi. If only all of the Taliban and the rest of world's Islamic fundamentalists had the courage to so openly identify themselves. Instead, they hid behind women and children and used mentally challenged people to carry out suicide attacks. For all their talk about being brave warriors, they were the biggest cowards on the planet.

If the world could see these assholes for the animals they really were, maybe there wouldn't be such a hue and cry from the fools who wanted to afford them all of the protections due signers of the Geneva and Hague conventions. Forget the fact that idiots like the Taliban weren't signers of either Geneva or Hague, refused to appear on the battlefield wearing even so much as an armband to identify themselves as honorable combatants, and wreaked untold misery upon civilian populations — the major group the conventions were designed to protect.

Harvath just couldn't understand the liberal mindset. He was convinced that they believed deeply in what they said and what they did; his only problem was that it so often flew in the face of reality. They continually focused their rage on their protectors rather than their enemy. They denigrated their country, believing it was the source of all evil in the world. The truth was, when it came to Islam, it had been violent since its inception. Its clearly stated goal was worldwide conquest. It was a mandate handed down in all of its religious texts. And while Harvath believed there were peaceful and moderate Muslims, he knew from studying the religion that there was no such thing as peaceful and moderate Islam.

The entire religion was a mess and needed a complete gut-rehab. And though he had a good feeling his country's new president would probably not agree with him, he also knew that until the politically correct crowd stopped making excuses for them and undercutting any motivation to reform their religion themselves, the majority of Muslims wouldn't do anything. Their religion forbade them from even changing one word of the Qur'an. Islam had been Islam for fourteen hundred years and what it had been was violent. As far as Harvath was concerned, they could have the rest of the world, but they couldn't have his country.

Harvath was content to go door to door and eliminate as many trouble-making members of the "religion of peace" as was necessary. He didn't need, nor did he expect, so much as a thank-you for it. He knew it was the right thing to do and he would continue to do it for as long as he was able to squeeze a throat or a trigger. It was what he was trained to do and it was an oath he had taken. That he was no longer in the direct employ of his nation did not mean that he felt any less responsible to see to its protection. There was nothing he held more sacred than his duty to his nation.

Seeing a roadside vendor up ahead advertising Coca-Cola, Harvath told Gallagher to pull the truck over.

"Are you serious?" he asked.

"Of course. I want to be able to say I stopped for a drink in Surobi."

Baba G looked at Fontaine.

"Fine by me," replied the Canadian.

Gallagher navigated the truck to the side of the road and came to a stop in front of the small shop. "I'll wait here," he said.

"Chickenshit," replied Harvath as he

opened the door and hopped out.

Walking into the tiny store, he found a toothless old man sitting behind a worn table that functioned as the shop's makeshift counter, with a faded cookie tin that acted as its cash register. The old man smiled as Harvath entered. Covering his heart and bowing slightly, he wished Harvath peace. *"Wa alaikum salaam,"* Harvath replied.

The old man's smile remained as he waited to serve his customer.

"Coca-Cola?" asked Harvath.

Smiling more widely, the man removed one of the many plastic bags hung on the arm of his chair and shuffled across the dirt floor to a small cooler. *"Dua?"* the man asked holding up two fingers.

Harvath couldn't tell if he was the world's greatest salesman, or if he was trying to figure out how many people Harvath was traveling with to maybe relay the information up the road to a waiting sniper. It was an inhospitable way to think, especially as the old man seemed very nice, but it was the kind of viewpoint that kept people like Harvath alive.

Harvath held up four fingers and the old man beamed. He was making his day. As the man selected four Cokes and placed them in the bag, Harvath looked around the little shop. Not knowing when they might be eating again, he bought a can of nuts, some chocolate, and a tube of Pakistani Pringles.

The old man followed Harvath, carefully placing each item in the bag. Harvath was about ready to pay when he noticed a small, dusty row of books along the floor in the corner. The man had one or two books in German, Swedish, French, Italian, Dutch, and English — something for almost every potential NGO worker who might have once stopped at his place of business before Surobi became so dangerous.

Harvath looked through the titles in English. One in particular caught his eye. Picking it up, he smiled.

Done with his shopping, he followed the old man to the counter and paid him.

Handing the bag across the table to his customer, the old man said, "U.K.?"

"No, U.S.A."

"Ah, America. America good."

Harvath nodded and replied, "Afghanistan good, too."

Glancing toward the door to make sure they were still alone, the old man's toothless smile faded as he stated, "Taliban bad."

"Yes, " Harvath said as he picked up his bag. "Taliban very bad. But Afghanistan good."

The smile returned to the old man's face

and he watched his American customer leave the shop.

Outside, Harvath climbed back into the waiting Land Cruiser, pulled out the tattered Jackie Collins novel, and tossed it into the front seat.

"What took you so long?" asked Gallagher as he looked at the book. "I thought you were just buying a drink."

"I was making a new friend," replied Harvath. "You'd like him. Same taste in literature. You two could start your own book club."

"I don't think so," said Baba G as he put the truck in gear and pulled out onto the road. "You just couldn't pay me to sit around with a bunch of Taliban deconstructing *Lady Boss*."

"How about having a lady boss who pays you to deconstruct a bunch of Taliban who are just sitting around?" asked Harvath as he settled back into his seat.

Gallagher laughed. "Throw in a cooler of cold beer at the end and that would be my kind of job. But by the same token, I learned a long time ago that you should be very careful what you wish for."

CHAPTER 36

In Bagrami, on the outskirts of Jalalabad, Gallagher turned down the driveway of the largest walled compound Harvath had seen outside of Kabul. It sat in the middle of about eight acres and was surrounded by nothing but flat, rock-strewn, dusty ground. Tactically, it was a brilliant location. You could not only see trouble coming from any direction, you could also engage it and mow it down before it even got close to your front door.

"The realtors around J-bad will talk your ear off all day long about location, location, location," stated Baba G as they approached. "But for me, it's all about the interlocking fields of fire."

The compound had been constructed by a local Afghan contractor at the behest of the United Nations. It was built to exacting U.N. standards and was composed of two buildings with seventeen en suite bedrooms, a full basement with workout facility and safe room/bomb shelter, a large communal dining room and kitchen, an expansive garden, swimming pool, and tiki bar.

When the U.N. fled Bagrami on the heels of the overhyped Mohammed cartoon riots, Gallagher had heard about the property and drove down from Kabul to check it out. He and Hoyt had been wanting to expand their operations farther into eastern Afghanistan. NGOs were doing more work there and would need security. Gallagher also saw the compound as a great money-making opportunity and turned it into a guesthouse, complete with free WiFi access, and dubbed it the Shangri-La. Its garden tiki bar was the only international bar in the region and did a hell of a Thursday night business. In the summer months, Baba G sold memberships to the pool, where Westerners could swim and sun themselves without offending Afghan sensibilities. The man was always alert to opportunity.

There was a guardhouse outside the main gates, and as Gallagher's guards saw him driving up, they opened the large iron gates for him. He parked near the main building, and when Harvath stepped out of the vehicle, the first thing he noticed was how much warmer it was. The air was thick and humid.

The sky was clear and azure blue.

"Pretty nice, huh?" asked Baba G. "You've come down over four thousand feet in elevation."

"Very nice," replied Harvath as he unwrapped the *patoo* from around his shoulders and took the *pakol* off his head. It was at least twenty degrees warmer.

"It can get pretty cold at night, though," added Gallagher as two members of the house staff appeared. He directed them to grab the liquor out of the back of the truck and take it inside along with Harvath's bag.

Fontaine already knew his way around the Shangri-La and told his colleagues that he'd see them shortly for lunch.

Baba G gave Harvath a quick tour of the property, then put him in the biggest room he had available and told him he'd see him in the dining room in fifteen minutes.

Harvath drew back the drapes and opened the large French windows. The fresh air felt good.

Setting up his laptop, he logged on to the Internet and checked the email account he had established for communicating with Stephanie Gallo. There was a message waiting. The subject line read POL, short for *Proof of Life.*

Opening the email, Harvath read Gallo's update:

Wonderful news! All questions answered correctly! When will you get hold of the rug dealer?

Harvath didn't like stringing Stephanie Gallo along, but it was going to be necessary for a little while longer. He was way off the reservation, running an operation that she had not sanctioned. He dashed off a response telling her that they expected to move on the rug dealer in the next forty-eight hours. It was as far as he felt comfortable pushing things. If he couldn't locate Julia Gallo in the next two days, he'd have no choice but to set up the exchange with her captors. Waiting any longer than that was just asking for them to get desperate. The last thing he wanted was for them to start slicing off body parts, one of the Taliban's favorite attention-getters, and dropping them off in front of the American embassy in Kabul.

Pulling out his Afghan phone, Harvath dialed Hoyt at the Shahr-e Naw safe house. "How's our guest?" he asked when Hoyt answered.

"Who? Hannibal Fucking Lecter?"

Harvath sat up straighter in his chair.

"What happened?"

"After he soiled himself, Midland went in to try to clean him up and —"

"Wait a second," interrupted Harvath. "Why did Midland go in and not you?"

"Because rock beats scissors, that's why. Besides, I'm management and he's labor."

"Do you think he soiled himself on purpose?" asked Harvath.

"You're damn right he did."

"You should have left him like that."

"I didn't have a choice. Flower was raising holy hell. He thought maybe the guy was sick or something. Since he's our prisoner, it's our duty to see to his comfort. You know, all that Pashtunwali crap. Blah, blah, blah."

Harvath knew what Pashtunwali was and he had a lot of respect for it. It was far from crap. The rest of "modern" civilization could benefit from adhering to such a code of honor. "So what happened?"

"Midland and Flower went in to deal with the guy while I covered them. As Midland was removing Khan's pants, the shitbag bent over and tore a chunk out of his ear with his teeth."

"Jesus. Is he going to be okay?"

"Flower drove him over to the CARE hospital to get his ear sewn back on."

"*CARE?*" replied Harvath.

"Relax," said Hoyt. "He doesn't know anything about where we got Khan from. Besides, CARE is the best place for plastics."

Plastic surgeons or no plastic surgeons, Harvath didn't like it. "You should have gone with him. If he talks, this whole operation could be blown."

"Don't worry, he's not stupid. He won't talk. And as far as me going to the hospital with him, I figured you'd rather I stay here and watch our guest. If I'm wrong, I can call a cab right now."

Harvath put his elbow on the desk and rested his forehead in the palm of his hand. "No, you did the right thing. I'm glad you stayed there. Tell Mark I'll cover all his medical bills."

"I already told him that," replied Hoyt. "By the way, did you know the biter speaks English?"

"Yeah, he grew up in the U.K."

"Well he's one creepy son of a bitch. He keeps threatening us every time we open the door to his cage and I'm not talking run-of-the-mill, macho, I'm-going-to-kick-your-ass kind of stuff. He's one sick motherfucker."

"Don't let him get to you," said Harvath. "Do you guys need anything?"

"I need a couple more boxes of those XREPs."

"Please don't tell me you —"

"Yeah," said Hoyt. "We fired all of them. And you know what? They work even better when you put the motherfucker's feet in a bucket of water."

"Damn it, Hoyt!" snapped Harvath. "That's way out of line —"

"Relax," replied Hoyt. "We haven't done anything to him."

"Not even when he tore into Midland?"

"All right, we messed him up once."

"How bad?" asked Harvath.

"Flower beat the crap out of him. Midland and I had to pull him off. So much for Pashtunwali, eh?" said Hoyt with a chuckle.

"I told you the guy was dangerous. The only reason he got Mark's ear was that he was probably aiming for his throat and missed. I don't want you going into that room unless you absolutely have to. And if you do, and he moves, TASE him. That's an order. Understand?"

"You got it, boss."

"Good," replied Harvath. "Let me know if Mark has any problems at the hospital. By the way, what's he going to say anyway when the doctor asks him how it happened?"

"They're picking up Mei along the way. They're going to say it was rough sex."

Harvath couldn't believe his ears. "Now

you've got Mei involved in this?"

"I'm just kidding," said Hoyt. "Relax. Midland will say he tore his ear on a piece of sheet metal."

"You keep screwing with me," cautioned Harvath, "and I'm going to tear you on a piece of sheet metal."

"I'm shaking in my saddle shoes here, Aquaman. Get back to work and find our doctor. We've got everything covered on this end."

"If anything else happens with Khan, I want to know about it. Okay?"

"Roger that," replied Hoyt.

Harvath disconnected the call and stood up from the desk. Closing the windows, he stepped into the hall, locked the door behind him, and headed toward the dining room. Gallagher and Fontaine were already seated at the table when he got there.

"What's our status?" asked Gallagher as Harvath walked in.

Harvath couldn't talk about Khan in front of Fontaine, so he stuck strictly to Julia Gallo. "We've got positive proof of life."

Fontaine grabbed a large orange from the bowl in the center of the table and began peeling it. "So we're a go for Khogyani?"

"Yup."

"Let's assume we get a meeting with the

shura," said Gallagher. "Then what?"

"The first thing I want is a tour of the village. We take as many pictures as we can and map as many GPS points as possible. We'll push to look at everything. If they hold anything back or say that something is off-limits, we mark it as a location of interest.

"I want each of us planning as we walk through that village how we would come back in at night, hit our objective, and get out again. Are there any dogs? Any livestock we would want to avoid disturbing? If we got pinned down, where would we want to hole up and fight from? Where's the nearest location we could use as an LZ if we had a helicopter brought in? If it has to be a hot extraction and we're taking fire, how would that work? How thick are their doors? How many armed men could they field and how quickly? If we get the chance to do a walk-through, I want to make sure we're making the most of it."

"What about this kid with the broken jaw?"

"Asadoulah Badar," said Harvath.

Baba G nodded.

"We obviously can't come right out and ask the *shura* about him. There's no reason a bunch of NGO workers would know his name. We'd be blown right from the get-go."

"So what do you suggest?" asked Fontaine.

"We need to figure out a way to get them to offer him to us."

"What do you mean by *offer*?"

Harvath pulled out another Motrin and reached for one of the bottles of water on the table.

"The way you're going through those things," interrupted Gallagher, "you should have a PEZ dispenser."

"Do you think I can get a Jackie Collins one?" asked Harvath as he popped the painkiller and took a sip of water.

"You're going to fry your liver *and* your kidneys if you keep knocking those things back like that."

"Can we get back to Badar and the *shura*, please?"

Gallagher put up his hands in surrender and Harvath continued. "If we tell them we want to involve the young men of the village in the project as well, we might be able to arrange a casting call.

"After tea, we'll do our tour, and while we're touring, the *shura* can have the young men rounded up for us. We'll then do a Q&A with the kids, ostensibly to select the best candidates. If one of them has a broken jaw, we'll know."

"And if they don't bring him to the casting call?" asked Gallagher.

"Then we'll ask the *shura* where the rest of the men in that age group are. We'll tell them that we selected their village based in part on the number of young men in that age group who could help maintain the wells and irrigation systems and carry that knowledge to other villages within their tribe. We'll call them water ambassadors or clean water warriors. I don't really care. The point is that the *shura* should be concerned we're going to pull the project because we'd expected more boys in that age group to be there. They'll pony him up, even with the broken jaw. Trust me."

"And then?" said Fontaine.

"And then," replied Harvath, "we'll divide them into teams and elect captains. Get the GPS devices out and act like they can actually seek out water. We'll ask the kids on that team to show us where each of them live and we'll tag Asadoulah's house, assess the hell out of it in the short time we have, and come back for him later tonight."

Gallagher sat back in his chair and smiled. "That's got NGO written all over it. Not bad."

Harvath was about to respond when his Afghan cell phone vibrated. Pulling it from his pocket, he activated the call. "Yes?"

A voice on the other end used the alias Harvath had given the CWI people. "Mr. Staley?" it asked.

"This is he," replied Harvath.

"I am Ghazan Daoud. Your interpreter in Khogyani."

"Yes, Mr. Daoud. Have you spoken with the village *shura*?"

"Mr. Staley, there is a big problem."

Harvath could tell by the man's voice that he was very upset. "First of all, calm down, Mr. Daoud. Tell me what the problem is."

"There are soldiers everywhere."

"Where?"

"Here in the village."

"What kind of soldiers?" asked Harvath. "Taliban?"

"No, sir. NATO soldiers. They have the entire village surrounded."

"Why? Why are they there?"

"I'm not sure," said Daoud, "but there are three dead bodies outside right now."

"Bodies of NATO soldiers?" asked Harvath.

"No. Afghans. Two of them were shot. I am afraid of what the NATO soldiers might do, Mr. Staley. I have tried to speak with them, but they will not listen to me. Are you near? Please say you are near."

"Don't worry, Mr. Daoud. We are on our way and will be there as soon as we can. Do you understand?"

"Yes, Mr. Staley," said the interpreter. "Please hurry."

Harvath disconnected the call and set the phone on the table.

"What was that all about?" asked Gallagher.

"A group of NATO troops just hit our village in Khogyani."

"Is it Julia Gallo?" asked Fontaine.

"I'm not sure," said Harvath, "but we're not going to sit here and wait to find out. Let's go."

CHAPTER 37

The drive from Jalalabad to Khogyani normally took an hour. Gallagher made it in twenty minutes.

They encountered their first roadblock a mile out along the single-lane road leading through the village. Two eight-wheeled LAV III armored personnel carriers were parked diagonally blocking all traffic in or out. Their 25mm Bushmaster chain guns, along with a complement of 7.62 and 5.56 machine guns, were ready for action.

"Coming up on the roadblock," said Gallagher.

Two more LAVs were blocking the road on the other side of the village.

"Anybody see any activity on the ground?" asked Harvath.

Baba G shook his head. "Looks like all they've done so far is set up a cordon."

"Which means they're either waiting for another element to show, or they're gearing up to go in themselves. We run this exactly the way we planned on the way down," stated Harvath.

"Actually," said Fontaine as they closed on the roadblock and he reached in his pocket for his military ID, "we might have just caught a break."

"What kind of break?" asked Harvath.

"We'll see in a moment," he replied.

Fontaine rolled his window down and told Gallagher to pull all the way up. They were waved to a stop by a Canadian soldier carrying a C-7 assault rifle.

"Good afternoon, sir," said the soldier as he studied Fontaine's Canadian military ID card.

"Corporal," said Fontaine as he retrieved his ID and slid it back into his pocket, "who are you and what the hell are you doing here?"

"Mechanized Quick Reaction Force, B Company, First Battalion," the man responded. "We were sent in to hold this village."

"Hold it for whom?"

"The Americans. They're sending a unit to go house-to-house."

"Do you know what they're looking for?" asked Fontaine.

"No, sir."

"What's their ETA?"

"I don't know, sir," said the corporal.

"Who's in charge here?" demanded Fontaine.

"Captain West, sir."

"Captain Chris West?"

"Yes, sir."

Fontaine opened his door and stepped out. "Get him on the radio for me right now," he said as he began walking toward one of the LAVs.

"Get the captain on the line," the corporal ordered one of the soldiers standing near the LAV.

"Who's raising Captain West for me?" asked Fontaine as the hatch was raised on the armored vehicle and he ducked inside.

"Right here," said a soldier, who offered up a handset.

Fontaine took the handset and spoke into it. "Chris? This is Dan Fontaine. You and your men have just walked into the middle of our operation. We need to talk right now."

Fontaine listened for a moment and then gave the handset back to the soldier. He waited for the soldier to finish speaking with his superior and then he stepped out of the LAV. As he did, the soldier stuck his head out of the back and informed his sergeant that Fontaine and the men in the Land Cruiser had been granted permission to pass.

"So far so good," said Fontaine as he hopped back in the truck and the Canadian soldiers directed them around their roadblock.

"Where to?" asked Gallagher as he steered around the LAVs and got back on the road.

"We're going to meet up with their captain at the roadblock on the other side of the village."

"What do you think the Americans want with this place?"

"Drugs, weapons, Taliban or al-Qaeda fighters," replied Fontaine. "You name it."

"Julia Gallo?" Harvath asked.

"That'd be one hell of a coincidence."

"I don't believe in them," continued Harvath from the backseat, more convinced than ever that Fontaine was CSIS. "By the way, you still carry an active military ID?"

"Expired," replied Fontaine. "Nobody ever checks the date. How about you? I'll bet you have some interesting items in your wallet."

Harvath doubted the Canadian's ID was expired. He also knew that while he had never told Fontaine what exactly he did for a living, it was quietly understood that he worked for the U.S. government. Based on Harvath's special operations experience, it wasn't a huge leap to assume he did something other than pushing paper. The suggestion of what might be in his wallet was a way of intimating that Fontaine had a good idea who Harvath really was too.

It was also probably a reminder that the pot shouldn't call the kettle black.

"You know this guy West well?" asked Harvath, changing the subject yet again.

"He and I served in the Pats together," replied Fontaine.

Harvath was familiar with Canada's highly decorated regiment, Princess Patricia's Canadian Light Infantry. "Do you think he'll help us out?"

"We always say 'Once a Patricia, always a Patricia.'"

"Well, no matter what happens and no matter what reason the Americans have for wanting to get in there and do a house-to-house," stated Harvath, "we *are* going into that village. If Julia Gallo is in there, the longer we wait, the greater the odds are that they'll figure out a way to slip that cordon and smuggle her out. And for all we know, they might have fled with her the minute they spotted these soldiers coming. I don't want to wait around to find out."

"Agreed," said Gallagher.

"You got us over one hurdle," Harvath said to Fontaine. "Now how do we get over the second and into the village?"

Staring at the armored vehicles up ahead, he replied, "By appealing to West's innate sense of Canadian patriotism."

Harvath looked at him. "I think I like my plan better."

"Don't worry," replied Fontaine. "It's still your plan."

"This is it," said Gallagher as they slowed to a stop before the two LAVs that formed the roadblock on the other side of the village. "You want us to wait in here?"

"You can come, but try to let me do the talking. Okay?"

"We'll try," said Harvath, opening his door.

The three men exited the Land Cruiser and were greeted by Captain West, a career military man in his late forties with dark hair and pale eyes.

"What's this about us walking into the middle of *your* operation?" asked West as he shook hands with Fontaine.

The former JTF2 man didn't bother introducing Harvath or Gallagher. Even among their allies, spooks often preferred to keep their identities private. "We've had this village under surveillance for two days."

"Why?" asked West.

Fontaine dropped his voice and moved the

captain off to the side, out of earshot of his men. Harvath and Gallagher followed.

"We believe that the village elders have been harboring an al-Qaeda asset. We've got one of our men inside who can ID him. We were about ready to pull the trigger when you guys showed up. Speaking of which, what are you and your men doing here?"

"NATO command got some sort of tip from one of its Taliban informants. They passed it on to the Americans, who, knowing we were in the area, asked us to come in and establish this cordon."

"Did they get anything in the air for you?" asked Harvath. "A Predator? Anything?"

West shook his head. "They've been tied up. They couldn't get any assets on target before we arrived."

"So we don't know if anyone slipped out as your cordon was being established."

"No, we don't," said West as he turned back to Fontaine and asked, "Is this al-Qaeda asset you're looking for the same reason the Americans are on their way?"

"No," replied Fontaine. "It isn't."

"You sound pretty sure."

"I am."

"Well," replied West, "my gut says I should put the brakes on everything until the Americans get here."

"Chris, we've been chasing the al-Qaeda operative in that village for almost a year. And now that we have him cornered, he's sitting in there wondering who gave him up. Pretty soon, if he hasn't already, he's going to zero in on my operative, a Canadian, I might add, who'll be as good as dead when that happens. I need to shut this thing down now."

"Dan, you and I go way back, but orders are orders," said West.

"And what happens if this guy slips your cordon? I'm sure your men are good, but it's not beyond the realm of possibility. If we let a Canadian operative get killed and an al-Qaeda bomb maker, who specializes in targeting Canadian troops, escape, it won't exactly be a blue-ribbon day, will it?"

Captain West was silent as he thought it over.

Sensing that the man was leaning in their direction, Fontaine pressed him. "All we need is thirty minutes to button this down."

West finally spoke. "Okay, here's what I am prepared to do. Based on one of our operatives' being in imminent danger inside the village, I'm going to go ahead and authorize you to extract him, but that's it. The bomb maker is secondary and you can sort him out with the Americans when they get here. Agreed?"

Fontaine shook hands with West. "We're good with that."

"How many of my men do you want to take with you?" the captain then asked.

"You maintain your cordon. We'll go in and link up with our operative and take things from there."

"You might want to rethink that. When we showed up, there were a lot of villagers moving around with guns."

"Which brings up something else," said Fontaine. "Our operative indicated that there are three dead Afghans in there, two of whom had been shot. What do you know about that? I'm assuming you've got snipers out."

"We do, but it wasn't us. There's been no gunfire since we arrived," replied West. "But that's not to say that it couldn't start at any moment. Those villagers were getting ready for something. You should take some of my guys with you."

"We'll be okay," stated Fontaine.

"How are you going to do this without stirring up the hornets' nest? Do you know which structure he's in?"

"He's got a relationship with the village elders. If they give their permission, we'll be able to walk in and get him."

West didn't look as if he put much faith in

Pashtunwali. "How are you set for comms?" he asked.

"We've got radios in the truck," answered Gallagher. "Give us your frequencies and we'll be good to go."

West nodded and called over one of his men to accompany Gallagher to the Land Cruiser and help set up the radios.

"I'd also like to know where your snipers are," added Fontaine.

West nodded and motioned Fontaine back to his LAV. "I'll show you on the map how we're set up."

Fifteen minutes later, Harvath, Gallagher, and Fontaine were ready to roll. Harvath pulled out his Afghan cell phone and dialed Clear Water International's Khogyani interpreter.

"Mr. Daoud?" Harvath said when the man answered. "This is Mr. Staley. We're at the village now. The soldiers have agreed to allow us to come in."

"What do they want?" asked Daoud. "No one understands why they are here."

"It's all going to be okay," Harvath reassured him. "Are you with the *shura* right now?"

"Yes."

"I have two other members of my team

with me. Do we have the *shura*'s permission to enter the village?"

Harvath waited while the interpreter spoke to someone in the background and then came back on the phone. "Yes. You and your colleagues have their permission."

After being given a description of the building they were in and how to find it, Harvath disconnected the call, tucked the phone back in his pocket, warned his team to be on their guard, and headed with them into the village.

CHAPTER 38

As the men made their way into the dusty village, it was like walking into a ghost town. Every house and compound was shuttered and not a single soul roamed the streets, not even children. Any soldier worth his salt knew that kids were a combat indicator. When they disappeared it meant that something very bad was about to happen.

Nevertheless, Harvath ignored the hair standing on end on the back of his neck and kept going. He also ignored the pain from the hidden MP5 banging against his bruised back. "Everybody stay sharp," he said.

All three made mental notes of the buildings they passed. Finally, they came to the structure where the *shura* was meeting. Just as Daoud had said, laid out in front were three bodies covered with sheets.

Harvath and Gallagher approached to examine them while Fontaine kept his eyes peeled for trouble.

"This one looks like a broken neck," said Gallagher as he inspected one of the corpses. "How about the other two?"

Harvath looked under the first sheet and then the second. "Bullet wounds to the foreheads. Very clean."

"And also very professional. That's not the way Afghans normally handle their problems."

"So who shot them?"

"No idea," said Gallagher as Harvath set the sheet down and the two men straightened up.

Motioning toward the door of the structure, Harvath said, "Let's see if we can get some answers inside."

None of them were prepared for what they discovered. Crammed inside were at least fifty heavily armed men from the village. They all eyed Harvath and his tall, well-built compatriots warily. Harvath, Gallagher, and Fontaine all placed their hands over their hearts, bowed ever so slightly, and wished the men peace. A handful of men returned the gesture; most of them did not.

Daoud stepped forward and introduced himself. He was a short man in his late thirties dressed in traditional Afghan clothing, with a neatly trimmed beard and a checked *kaffiyeh* hung loosely around his neck.

After Harvath and his team had removed their boots, the interpreter led them into an inner room where the *shura* was waiting. As they were introduced, the men repeated the customary greeting to the elders of the village, who politely greeted them back.

The interpreter invited the men to sit down upon the floor, which they did. Harvath noticed very quickly that the *shura* had no intention of serving tea.

"Tell the *shura*," Harvath said to Daoud, "that we have come for the American woman."

The interpreter was confused, but based on the stern faces and powerful physiques of the three men, surmised they probably weren't NGO workers here to conduct a project assessment. "I don't think I understand —" he began.

Harvath held up his hand. "They'll know what we're talking about. Tell them."

Daoud turned to the *shura* and repeated what Harvath had said. He waited for their response and then translated. "They say they don't know anything about an American woman."

"Ask them why they have three bodies outside."

The interpreter posed the question, and

while the elders exchanged hushed remarks among themselves he tried to ask Harvath a question of his own, but Harvath silenced him. He was intent on studying the old men's faces and listening to the cadence of their voices. It was obvious they were very upset about something.

After extensive deliberation, the chief elder, a man named Fayaz, spoke and Daoud translated. "They say it is a private matter."

"Private?" repeated Harvath. "Please inform the *shura* that with their village surrounded, they no longer have privacy. In fact, if they don't turn over the woman immediately, I'm going to call in an airstrike."

The interpreter delivered Harvath's ultimatum and then asked a question on behalf of the elders. "The *shura* wants to know if this means there isn't going to be a clean water project for their village."

Are these people trying to horse trade with us? Harvath wondered to himself. It didn't make any sense. Not only had he just threatened them with an airstrike, but their village was surrounded. Soldiers were poised to come kick in every door, flip over every bed, and turn every one of their buildings inside out. What could they possibly have to bargain with?

"Tell them," said Harvath, "that I didn't

come here to negotiate. I want the woman, now."

Harvath waited for the interpreter to respond. When he did, his face reflected considerable shock. "The woman is not here," he said.

So these fuckers did know where Gallo was. It was all Harvath could do not to string the village elder up by his ankles and beat the shit out of him. "Where is she?" he demanded.

"First," Daoud translated, "we must reach terms."

Harvath was stunned by the audacity of these people. No matter how weak their hand, the Afghans never missed an opportunity to haggle. Harvath removed his radio so they could see he was serious about calling in a strike. "I'm giving you sixty more seconds and then I'm going to have your village turned into one big grease spot."

As the interpreter relayed the message to the *shura,* the elders began yelling *"Na! Na!" No, No,* together in Pashtu.

Daoud looked at Harvath and said, "They say they are not the ones who kidnapped the American woman."

"Tell them I don't believe them."

The interpreter relayed the statement and the *shura* broke into a barrage of heated crosstalk. After a moment, Fayaz, the chief elder, spoke and Daoud translated. "The *shura* says that their village is the victim here. The bodies of the men you see outside, they were killed by the man who took the American woman."

Harvath still didn't believe them. "Why are so many of your men armed right now? Obviously, you have been expecting trouble. Why shouldn't I believe it was because this village was involved with Doctor Gallo's kidnapping?"

When Daoud passed on Harvath's remarks, the elders erupted in another chorus of *"Na! Na!"* and the chief of the *shura* locked eyes with Harvath and began speaking as the interpreter translated. "We did not kidnap the American woman."

"Then who did?" demanded Harvath.

"Mullah Massoud Akhund. A local Taliban commander."

"And Massoud killed the men outside?"

"Na, na," said Fayaz. *No.*

"His Russian did," explained the interpreter.

"What Russian?" asked Harvath.

Daoud listened to the *shura* and then said, "Massoud's men call the Russian Bakht Rawan."

"How do you know it was this Russian

who killed the men?"

"He was seen by the son of one of the men."

"And where is he now?"

The interpreter conveyed Harvath's question to the *shura,* and the chief elder yelled toward the door. It opened and one of the armed villagers stuck his head inside.

Harvath didn't understand the entirety of the order Fayaz delivered, but he caught part of it and that was all he needed to hear. The elder had told the villager to fetch the young man they had been looking for, Asadoulah Badar.

CHAPTER 39

Because of his broken jaw, the young man was difficult to understand, and several times during their interrogation, the *shura* rebuked him for speaking too softly and ordered him to speak up.

The elders had already heard the story once, but they wanted the boy to tell it again for the benefit of the three men, the only things standing between their village and what they knew would be a crippling airstrike.

Asadoulah Badar, though distraught over the murder of his father, recounted the circumstances surrounding his death. He explained how one of their sheep had gone missing. Asadoulah and his father, along with his two cousins, Raham and Yama, who also tended the large family flock, had gone looking for the animal. They split in different directions, with Asadoulah taking one of the higher mountain trails on the opposite face. It was from that vantage point that he had seen the Russian dump his father's body so that it landed near the family's crippled sheep below.

As the Russian retreated up his side of the mountain, Asadoulah caught a glimpse of his cousins. They were still looking for the lost sheep, and he doubted they had any idea what was about to happen to them. Asadoulah tried to warn them, but they didn't hear. When he found their bodies, they were both dead, but unlike his father, who'd had his neck and arm broken by the Russian, his cousins had both been felled with single shots to the head.

Asadoulah finished his tale by explaining where he had seen the American woman. And though it shamed him to admit to his lies, he told the entire truth. He then explained how, based upon his lie, his father had met with the *shura* of Massoud's village and had chastised them for housing the American woman and had demanded redress for what had happened to his son. When he returned, he explained that he had called Massoud reckless and said that he posed a great danger to their villages.

In the face of such a despicable act of murder, the *shura* explained that the men of their village lusted for *badal* — revenge

— and the *badal* for killing was to kill. This was an affair they were not confident could be mediated with the *shura* of Massoud's village. Their men wanted blood, plain and simple. Vengeance was the cornerstone of Pashtun character. Had the soldiers outside not arrived when they did, the men would have had it. Fayaz shared his doubts about whether the bloodletting would have ended with the Russian and Mullah Massoud.

"I'm sure the men of your village are very capable warriors," said Harvath, "but Massoud is a Taliban commander, which means he has soldiers of his own, probably many more than you do. How did the men of your village expect to win?"

As the question was translated, the old man shook his head. "They were waiting for nightfall," said Daoud, translating the chief elder's remarks. "They had hoped to take Massoud and his men by surprise."

"Do you think they knew you were coming?" asked Harvath.

"The Taliban have their spies everywhere," replied Fayaz, "should Massoud be any different?"

Probably not, thought Harvath, who then asked, "Is there any reason, any reason at all that the Americans would take an interest in your village?"

Once the question had been translated, the chief elder put it to each of his colleagues on the *shura* in turn. Daoud translated as each elder replied. None of them could think of a single reason. Harvath could, though.

Massoud was Taliban and Chris West said that he and his men had been mobilized based upon a tip from a Taliban informant. The Russian had apparently intended for the death of Asadoulah's father to look like an accident. If that hadn't been the intent, he would have simply shot the man the same way he did Asadoulah's two cousins. Massoud now had a big problem on his hands.

It wouldn't take long for the family to find the bodies and to suspect that Massoud was behind the murders. Little did the Taliban commander know that there was actually a witness. Faced with the prospect that his neighboring village was going to be out for blood and would want to do as much damage to him as possible, he had to have envisioned that they might tip the authorities to the identity of their captive. That meant Massoud would have to deal with foes on two different fronts. What should he do? The answer seemed very apparent to Harvath and he was willing to bet he knew exactly why there was a cordon around the village and the Americans were on their way in. Massoud had set the two against each other.

Based on the description Asadoulah had given of the woman held captive in Massoud's village, he was convinced that it was Julia Gallo. What didn't make sense was that somehow the Russians, or at least *a* Russian, was mixed up in all of this. At this point, though, it didn't matter. What mattered was getting to Julia Gallo as quickly as possible and getting her back alive. And if Harvath was right about Massoud having tricked the NATO forces into surrounding Asadoulah's village, he'd have done it for one reason and one reason only — to buy himself time to get away.

Nevertheless, Harvath wanted to see Massoud's village for himself. The only question was *how*. Looking at Asadoulah, he began to get an idea.

Studying the elders, Harvath asked, "If I could provide an opportunity for you to prove that your village had nothing to do with the kidnapping would you act upon it?"

After the question was translated, Fayaz's response was simple and concise. *"Hoo,"* he said. *Yes.* "And if we help you," he continued through Daoud, "will you help get us the water project?"

The threat of the airstrike was one thing, but Harvath needed to earn the *shura*'s loyalty for what he was going to ask them to do next. In order for that to happen he had to give them something they needed, something that would make the *shura* look good to their village. Meeting Fayaz's gaze, Harvath replied, "*Hoo.* We will help you get the clean water project."

Excusing himself then to use the bathroom, Harvath took Fontaine and Gallagher with him so they could talk privately.

"I've got an encrypted sat phone back in the truck," said Harvath as he stood next to Fontaine outside the bathroom. "I need you to get hold of whoever you can, so that West will allow us to take some of these villagers out of here with us."

"Who do you expect me to call?" asked Fontaine.

"I'm sure you're well connected."

"Why not you? The only reason that Canadian cordon is there is that the Americans asked for it."

"I don't have that kind of pull," said Harvath.

Fontaine laughed. "Modesty, now that's an interesting character trait in an American."

He let the jab slide. "Listen Dan, I'm not even supposed to be here."

"Really? Okay, I'll bite. Where should you be then?"

"Back in Kabul," replied Harvath, "negotiating Julia Gallo's ransom."

"So you're telling me you're not authorized for this."

"That's exactly what I'm telling you."

"And you want me to pull strings for you so that you can take a bunch of villagers out of here to do God knows what."

"Not *God knows what*. We're going to take the *shura* out so they can meet with the *shura* from Massoud's village and mediate their dispute."

"You want to set up a *jirga*?" asked Fontaine, using the Pashtu word for a gathering orchestrated specifically to administer tribal justice.

"Yes."

"And how do you know that once the cordon is lifted here, the men of this village won't just march over that mountain and mow Massoud, his Russian counterpart, and the rest of his village right down?"

"Because I don't think Massoud, the Russian, or his men are even there anymore," replied Harvath.

"So what's the point?"

"The point is that we can gather some good intel there."

"You want to pull the NGO bit again?" asked Fontaine.

"I doubt it would work," said Harvath. "You can't draw a bucket of water from the well without the village elders' knowing about it. Any interest from an outside organization at this point, especially a Western one, is going to raise alarm bells."

"Then what's your plan?"

"The elders here have a legitimate reason to call for a *jirga* with the elders of Massoud's village. They could have one set up in less than an hour. Because of the violent nature of the dispute, the *shura* is going to travel with some muscle. We ride with the *shura* as far into the village as we can and then we bail out.

"We take Asadoulah with us and have him show us where they kept Julia Gallo."

"Kept? As in past tense? You're that convinced Massoud and company are long gone?"

"I don't know about long gone," said Harvath, "but I guarantee they've moved on. All we need to find out is where."

"And if we bump into some Taliban along the way?"

"Then we'll deal with them."

Fontaine looked at Gallagher and then back to Harvath. "Suppose I could make a phone call and get West and his men to look the other way for a few minutes, why would I want to?"

"Besides the fact that rescuing this woman is the right thing to do?"

"Besides that."

"I'll give you two reasons," said Harvath. "The first is that news of a Taliban commander working with a Russian operative would be very interesting to both of our governments."

Fontaine was listening. "And the second?"

"You can take credit for loosening up the cordon and arranging the *jirga*. The elders of this village seem like good people. You'd be doing them a favor and you know how highly the Pashtuns regard favors."

"Plus," Gallagher threw in, "with the cordon left in place after we leave, it will buy the two *shuras* time to reach an agreement. No matter how badly the men of this village are itching for a fight, they won't be able to leave. You'll also get points for helping to head off a war between their two villages."

Harvath agreed. "With all of the time you spend in this area," he said, "it wouldn't hurt to have these guys owe you one. Who knows how much intelligence they could mine for you?"

"That's assuming," said Fontaine, "I am even in the intelligence business."

"Of course," Harvath replied with a smile.

Fontaine was a smart guy and it didn't take him long to make up his mind. "If you can convince the elders to set up the *jirga,* I'll get West to turn his back long enough for us to get whomever we need out of town."

When they returned to the meeting room, the elders had laid out tea, and they invited the men to sit down with them and drink. Harvath, Gallagher, and Fontaine sat down, and as their cups were filled, Harvath spoke through Daoud and explained what he wanted to do.

Right off the bat, the elders expressed concern about Asadoulah's being part of the operation, but when Harvath explained why the boy's presence was necessary for more than just identifying the location where Doctor Gallo had been held captive, they began to relent. It was Baba G's unsolicited promise that he would personally guarantee the boy's safety that finally seemed to do the trick. Though Harvath couldn't have scripted a more perfectly timed response, Gallagher's spontaneous offering was seen by the *shura* as genuine and therefore trustworthy.

Once the details had been established and the limit to how far the elders would transport the team into the neighboring village was set, the men finished their tea and Harvath, Gallagher, and Fontaine walked back through the village to the Canadian cordon to put their plan into effect.

CHAPTER 40

Washington, D.C.

Todd Hutchinson was a classic, midforties narcissist incapable of recognizing that his better days were already behind him. A career B-team Secret Service agent, Hutchinson, or *Hutch* as he insisted on being called, had risen just about as high in the organization as he ever would. Though he was a thoroughly competent agent, simply by being "Hutch" the man had grated on the nerves of almost everyone who had ever worked with him, including the majority of the people he was charged with protecting.

One of the few exceptions was Theresa Alden. Through some opportune twist of fate, Hutch had been assigned to her detail during the primary campaign and he and the soon-to-be first lady had professionally clicked. She was a woman with multiple anxiety problems, which often kept her from sleeping. Some said that was why Hutch often worked night shifts on her detail, as he and the first lady liked to sit and talk. No one in the Service could understand what she saw in him, and when Hutch finally outlived all of the company pools for when Terry Alden would finally wake up and request his removal from her detail, they gave up on trying to figure it out.

The best physical description of him that Elise Campbell had ever heard was that he reminded people of five-foot-eight Burt Reynolds without the mustache. The female agents in the White House were in total agreement that there was no way there could be any sexual connection between him and the first lady. How she could enjoy being around him was anybody's guess, but Terry Alden did, and that was all that mattered. Therefore, Hutch had become a permanent fixture in the first lady's retinue.

Elise had arranged to meet Hutch for coffee after his overnight shift had finished. Until she could account for how Nikki Hale had spent her final hour and a half before driving away drunk and killing herself and four other people, she wouldn't be able to forget the conversation she'd overheard between the president and Stephanie Gallo.

She met Hutchinson at a Starbucks a few

blocks from the White House on Pennsylvania Avenue near Seventeenth Street.

"So what's with all the cloak and dagger?" he asked as they exited with their coffees and headed toward Lafayette Park. "We could have grabbed a table inside."

"I thought it would be nicer if we walked."

Todd Hutchinson looked up at the overcast sky and turned up the collar of his overcoat. "What did you want to talk with me about?"

Alone, and one-on-one like this, Campbell had expected the man to come on to her as he had in the past. Instead, his demeanor was surprisingly professional.

"I want to talk about the night Nikki Hale died."

Hutchinson's coffee cup was halfway to his lips when the question came, and instead of taking a sip, he lowered the cup and looked at Elise. "Why do you want to talk about that?"

"Call it professional curiosity."

"It was a sad night for everyone," he said, raising his coffee cup again and taking a sip.

"I understand you saw her shortly before she died."

"Who told you that?"

"Max Holland did," she replied.

"Why were you and Max talking about Nikki Hale?"

Campbell ignored his question and gently pushed forward with her own. "Do you think the president was sleeping with her?"

"Who?" responded Hutchinson. "Nikki? How would I know?"

"The night she died she had been alone with him for a while."

"Maybe they *were* sleeping together. Who cares?"

"Max says that after she left the president, she was still on the estate for a little bit before she finally climbed into her car to drive back to her hotel," stated Campbell.

"So?"

"So," she replied, "he also said while she might have had a drink or two with Alden, she didn't look drunk to him when she left."

"What does any of this have to do with me?" Hutchinson asked.

"I don't know. Why don't you tell me?"

As a Secret Service agent, Campbell had been trained in detecting microexpressions, small facial clues that indicated someone was either lying or trying to mask an intent to do harm. As she glanced at Hutchinson's face, she could clearly see the man was under stress and did not like answering her questions.

"Elise, listen," he said. "If Max knows where Nikki Hale went after leaving the president that night, he should tell you. If he doesn't want to, then that's between the two of you."

"Hutch, he did tell me. That's why I'm talking to you."

"It's unprofessional."

"Why?"

"Because by pointing you to me, he's casting aspersions on the first lady."

Campbell looked at him. "I don't get it."

"Listen, I know Holland doesn't care for me," said Hutch as they passed Blair House and entered the park. "There are plenty of senior agents just like him that I've either butted heads with or not gotten along with over the years. I don't want to lose my position. I like being on the first lady's detail."

"How are you going to lose your position by talking to me?"

"If I start telling tales out of school and the first lady hears about it, how long do you think it'll take for her to have me reassigned?"

Elise couldn't argue with him. It was the same fear she'd had, still had actually, about pursuing the conversation between the president and Stephanie Gallo. "So this is a job security issue for you."

"No," said Hutchinson, pointing to a nearby bench. "It's a loyalty issue. We're here to protect these people. That's our job. And their job is to let us, and that can't be easy for them. They aren't allowed many private, unguarded moments."

"Okay," said Elise as she sat down on the bench with him. "We all know that. It's drilled into us as agents, but —"

"No 'buts' for a second," said Hutchinson, interrupting her. "I want to know why you suddenly find Nikki Hale's death so interesting."

Elise had no intention of lying to Hutchinson. He had the same training she did and would be able to smell a lie a mile away. At the same time, she had no intention of being completely truthful with him either. "Someone is considering bringing a civil suit over her accident."

Hutchinson was clearly taken by surprise. "Who?" he asked.

"Christine De Palma. The business partner of Sheryl Coleman, who was killed that night."

"The wife of the man driving the minivan," Hutchinson said absentmindedly.

"Who also," added Elise, "was the mother

of the two children killed in that crash."

"Why now?"

"Maybe she wants justice."

"It was an accident. A lawsuit is not going to change anything. What grounds could this woman possibly bring a civil suit on?"

"Hale obviously had way too much to drink before she left the estate. I'm not an attorney, but from what I understand, if anyone contributed to Nikki's intoxication, and knowingly allowed her to drive drunk, they could be in some serious trouble."

Hutchinson balanced his coffee cup on his knee and stared across the park toward the statue of Andrew Jackson.

"How do you know about this lawsuit?" he asked.

"I'm friends with a detective in East Hampton."

"Do you think this De Palma woman is serious about the suit?"

"I don't know," Campbell replied. "But if she does go through with it, everyone who was there that night is going to get subpoenaed."

Hutchinson closed his eyes and shook his head. Exhaling a long breath, he opened them again and said, "The first lady is not fond of the women the president surrounds himself with. Stephanie Gallo and Nikki

Hale in particular. She resents the access Gallo has to her husband. It makes her feel like she has been cast aside. Wherever the president was on the campaign trail Gallo was always close by. In fact, she traveled with him more than Mrs. Alden did. Rumors of affairs have been rampant —"

"As have rumors of the first lady's drinking," interjected Campbell, wondering aloud about something many insiders had long suspected. "Some say that played a part in the president's not putting her out front as much as other candidates do with their spouses."

Hutchinson shrugged. "From what I saw, I'd say the stress was pretty hard on her."

"How does Nikki Hale fit into all of this? Was she with the first lady that night?"

Whether Hutchinson was resigned to the fact that the information was bound to come out at some point, or simply needed a colleague to unburden himself to, Elise couldn't tell. All she knew was that for some reason, Hutch had decided to come clean with her.

"Stephanie Gallo is a beautiful, powerful woman, but with all her money there is one thing she doesn't have — youth. That was something Nikki Hale had in abundance, and it was her that the first lady most suspected her husband might be having an affair with," he said.

"Did she have any proof?" asked Campbell.

"Not that I know of. I think she was going more on intuition than anything else. The president sure seemed to spend a lot of time alone with her."

Elise looked at him. "From what I understand, she was one of the primary architects of his web campaign. Considering how influential it was and how much money it raised, I'd say she was an important player."

"I'm not defending the first lady. I'm just telling you what I saw."

"Well, what did you see the night she died? Was she with the first lady?"

"Yes, she was," said Hutchinson as he turned away and looked off at the statue again.

"Why? What did the first lady want with her?"

"She had decided to confront her. She asked me to find Hale and bring her back to the guesthouse."

"Wait a minute," said Elise. "What was the first lady doing in the guesthouse?"

"She and the president had had an argument that evening over something. I wasn't there, so I don't know what it was about. All I know was that when I came on duty, he was still in the main house and she had moved to the guesthouse."

"Okay, so you tracked down Hale and brought her back there."

"No," said Hutchinson. "She was with the president at that time, so I left word with Max to send her to the guesthouse whenever they were finished."

"Then you went back and reported to the first lady."

"Correct."

"And how did Mrs. Alden take that piece of information?" asked Campbell.

"Not well," said Hutchinson. "She grabbed a glass and a bottle of wine and went upstairs."

"When did Nikki Hale get there?"

"About a half hour later."

"What happened then?"

"I brought her up to Mrs. Alden's room and left them alone."

"Were you the only agent posted to the guesthouse?"

"There were other agents on the grounds outside," said Hutchinson.

"But you were the only one inside," clarified Campbell.

"That's right."

"Did you hear anything or see anything after that?"

Hutchinson was slow to respond. "Mrs.

Alden asked if I would bring a glass upstairs for Ms. Hale."

Elise looked at him askance. "That's somewhat inappropriate, isn't it? You're there to protect her, not wait on her. Did you say no?"

"No, I didn't," said the man with a shake of his head.

"Why not?"

"Because it wasn't a big deal, all right?"

Elise couldn't help but feel that Todd Hutchinson had grown a bit too close to the first lady. Nevertheless, she let it slide. "So," she continued, "now Mrs. Alden and Nikki Hale were up there drinking together?"

"Apparently."

"Do you think the first lady was trying to get her drunk?"

"I think she was trying to get to the bottom of Hale's relationship with her husband. She probably thought the wine would help," replied Hutchinson. "You know what they say. In vino veritas."

"In wine there is truth."

Hutch nodded.

"Then let's suppose the first lady was trying to loosen Hale up to get at the truth," she said. "Did you hear any arguing? Anything like that?"

"Not at first."

"So they did argue."

"Yes."

"How long into their meeting was it?"

"I don't know," he said. "Twenty minutes, maybe a half hour."

"Did you overhear any of the specifics?"

"No, I was downstairs. It was just a lot of raised voices."

"Then what happened?" asked Elise.

"Hale came down the stairs and walked right out the front door. That was it."

"That was it? Didn't you think maybe you should try to stop her from leaving?"

"Why should I? I didn't have any way of knowing how much alcohol she had consumed. Besides, I'm not paid to conduct field sobriety tests. I'm paid to protect Mrs. Alden."

"And fetch wineglasses for her."

"Fuck you, Campbell."

"You couldn't have at least radioed one of the agents at the gate?" she asked.

"How the hell should I have known she was going to get in her car? She could have been going back into the main house to ask Stephanie Gallo to put her up for the night so she didn't have to drive back to wherever she was staying. Listen, from what I understand, Nikki Hale had a lot of experience holding her liquor. She didn't tumble down the stairs or weave on her way out the door. Could she have been drunk when she left? Sure. Was it my duty to know? Absolutely not."

"Does the president know all of this?"

"I would imagine the first lady filled him in," said Hutchinson.

Elise tried to think of something else to ask him, but her mind was blank. She was missing something, but she couldn't figure out what.

More confused than when she had started, she felt that she should wrap things up and let Hutchinson get home. She could think of only one other thing to ask him. "You said the president and the first lady had been fighting. Did he come to the guesthouse that night?"

"Yes," he said. "After Hale left."

There was something about his answer that bothered her. It came quickly — too quickly, and came off rehearsed. And as he was speaking, he turned back to look at the statue, and Elise thought she detected a telltale microexpression.

"So, what happened?" she asked. "Did they fight some more? Did they make up? What?"

"Nothing happened," Hutchinson replied, and there the microexpression was again.

This time she was certain of it. He was lying about something. That had to have been why he had looked away from her.

Elise watched his face closely and pressed her point. "What do you mean *nothing?* Something must have happened."

Hutch turned back and looked her square in the eyes. "By the time the president arrived, the first lady had passed out."

CHAPTER 41

Nangarhar Province, Afghanistan

Back at the cordon, Daniel Fontaine made two phone calls, and within fifteen minutes, Captain West had been given orders to allow the former JTF2 operative to leave the village with whomever he wanted. As his superiors failed to provide him with an excuse to give the inbound Americans if they happened to show up in the middle of this Canadian-sanctioned exodus, West encouraged Harvath and company to move quickly.

They compared the captain's maps with the one the *shura* had given them, which included the layout of the village and the location where Asadoulah had seen Julia Gallo. Convinced the information was reliable, Harvath gave the order for everyone to mount up. Including the elders' security detail, they numbered fifteen people.

Anticipating at least two checkpoints on

the way into Massoud's village, Fayaz, the chief elder, rode shotgun in Gallagher's Land Cruiser with one of his men at the wheel. Harvath, Gallagher, and Fontaine rode in back, their *patoos* pulled up high to help disguise their faces.

The rest of the men, including Asadoulah and Daoud the interpreter, who had agreed to come along for an additional fee, were divided between another SUV and a severely beaten-up pickup truck.

By the time the small convoy drove around the roadblock and out of the village, the sun had already disappeared from the sky. And as it did, the temperature began to drop.

As the *shura* had predicted, they encountered precisely two checkpoints on the way into Massoud's village. Before each of them, Harvath watched as Fayaz removed a special SIM card from his pocket and used it in his cell phone to make calls to notify the elders of the opposing *shura* that they were coming and should be allowed to pass through the checkpoints. He was a clever old man. Using different SIM cards clearly demonstrated that he wasn't as provincial as he looked and that he took his own operational security very seriously.

Thanks to the phone calls, at each checkpoint the speeding convoy was waved right through and not asked to stop. So far, so good.

Crumbling rock walls and the occasional abandoned mud brick building were the only signs that they were actually headed toward a populated settlement. Other than that, the landscape was completely desolate.

When they had driven as close as they dared with Harvath, Gallagher, and Fontaine, the convoy stopped. The three men hopped out of the Land Cruiser, quickly gathered the weapons and supplies they needed from the back, and with Daoud and Asadoulah in tow, signaled for the convoy to take off again. The drop had worked like clockwork, and the vehicles were moving again in less than sixty seconds.

Gallagher wasn't thrilled about relinquishing control of his SUV, but there was no other choice. It was now completely dark, and at the speed with which the vehicles had zoomed through the checkpoints, the men manning them never would have been able to count how many people were inside. All they would be able to report was that there was a total of three vehicles on their way into the village.

The other advantage to doing it this way was that though Harvath and his team would have to sneak into the village by foot, the Land Cruiser would be waiting for them when they got there.

According to Asadoulah, the structure where Julia Gallo had been held was less than a kilometer away, if you were walking straight through the center of the village. Wrapping their way around the outside of the village as they tried to avoid all human contact meant that their trip was going to take a little longer.

As they had been when they had gone after Mustafa Khan, Harvath and Gallagher were both wearing night vision goggles. Fontaine was wearing a pair he had brought as well, and to allow Daoud and Asadoulah to see where they were going without attracting any attention, Harvath had clipped the Streamlights Marjan and Pamir had used in the tunnel under Darulaman Road to each of their belts. He also made sure they both knew how to operate them in case they needed to be extinguished in a hurry.

Harvath, Fontaine, and Gallagher also had their bone mics in and carried their encrypted Motorola radios with them. Even though they had been switched to a new frequency, they had adopted call signs specific to this assignment. If anyone heard them, they intended to sound like a convoy of some sort. Harvath was "Convoy 1," Fontaine was

"Convoy 2," and Baba G was "Cover 6."

With the temperature dropping, they now donned Afghan-style coats with plenty of pockets to hold everything. Over their coats they wrapped their *patoos,* and they still wore the *pakols* on top of their heads.

Eyeballing the impressive array of weapons and equipment, Daoud and Asadoulah asked to be given firearms. Though Harvath knew most Afghans had experience with firearms, he didn't see any upside to these two carrying and turned them down. The men tried to argue with him, but Harvath shot them a look that quickly shut them up.

The village was built in a valley with a stream that ran right down through it. The terrain was rocky and steep. Though Harvath worried about his Afghan charges, of whom one was wearing sandals and the other was wearing the Afghan equivalent of penny loafers, his concern was misplaced. Even in the dark, with nothing but the small pool of light from their Streamlights, they steadily picked their way along like a couple of Afghan mountain goats. In fact, had they been leading instead of following, Harvath had a strong suspicion that he, Gallagher, and Fontaine would have been working very hard to keep up with them.

Fortunately, the village had no dogs and

very little livestock that could be disturbed. The men gave all of the dwellings a wide berth and reached a concealed area about two hundred meters away from their target without incident.

Gallagher removed his NODs and placed them over Asadoulah's eyes. Once the boy had become accustomed to seeing things through the goggles, Harvath illuminated the structure with an IR laser and they quietly asked if that was where Dr. Gallo had been held.

The boy studied it in relation to the other mud brick structures nearby and then whispered, *"Hoo."*

Before putting his plan together, Harvath had quizzed Asadoulah repeatedly not only on what Dr. Gallo looked like, but also on what circumstances she was being held under.

He found it hard to believe that Massoud's mentally challenged brother had been put in charge of guarding her, but Gallagher, Fontaine, and even Daoud explained that if the structure and lock on the door were considered secure enough, the Taliban often left their prisoners unguarded.

The village was quiet. After passing the second checkpoint, they hadn't seen any more armed men. Harvath's premise that

Massoud had called in the NATO troops on the neighboring village so he could slip away with Gallo unimpeded was looking more and more like a reality. Nevertheless, he didn't want to move too quickly.

The team lay in their concealed location and studied the small mud brick structure Dr. Gallo had been kept in. Nothing moved and no one appeared to be about.

Finally, Harvath gave the signal to get ready. Gallagher had already slid his NODs back on, and he continued to scan the area. He was responsible for staying back with Asadoulah and Daoud and providing sniper overwatch. Though he would have preferred being further up the mountain with better cover and concealment, the team had no choice. Gallagher would have to make do with conditions as they were.

As Harvath and Fontaine gave their weapons one last check, Harvath whispered, "In and out. Then we regroup and head for the secondary target."

Fontaine nodded, and after scanning the area once more for any signs of life, Harvath signaled that it was time to move.

With their silenced MP5s grasped beneath their *patoos,* the two men slipped soundlessly onto the road. They walked in the slow, shambling Afghan fashion, fully aware that from a distance they might look like the real deal, but anyone who got close enough to see their NODs would immediately raise the alarm.

They stayed close to cover, hugging walls and the sides of the few houses they passed, all the while making sure to avoid windows. Harvath could feel his heart pumping in his chest and the adrenaline coursing through his body. Even with Gallagher manning a rifle, they could be outgunned and overwhelmed very quickly. Harvath reminded himself to scan and breathe, scan and breathe.

When they reached the mud brick structure, Harvath flipped up his NODs and studied the door, while Fontaine kept watch. It was secured by a simple sliding bolt. After pressing his ear up against the door, he flipped his goggles back down and signaled the former JTF2 operator what he wanted him to do.

Both men then pulled their MP5s from underneath their *patoos,* and when Harvath nodded, Fontaine drew back the bolt and swung open the door.

Harvath entered first, followed by Fontaine. There was a small bed in the corner, but nothing else; no Julia Gallo. Harvath flipped up his NODs and motioned for Fontaine to close the door.

The tiny mud brick room was pitch-dark and smelled like damp earth and sweat. There was only one window, which had been covered with a cloth or a tarp of some kind from outside. Harvath removed the extra Streamlight he had grabbed from the "Golden Conex" and switched it on. Now came the moment of truth.

If Julia had remembered the security training CARE International provided its volunteers before they arrived in Afghanistan, Harvath would be able to tell very quickly if she had in fact been held in this makeshift cell.

While Fontaine kept guard, Harvath moved the bed and looked along the walls and floors behind it. *Nothing.* Next came the area above the door frame. *Still nothing.* Harvath examined both sides of each timber that ran across the mud ceiling and helped support the roof. Once again, he came up empty. It was the same story near the hole cut into the floor to be used as a toilet. Harvath was starting to lose hope. *Maybe Gallo hadn't been here at all.* Maybe it had been some other Western NGO worker the boy had seen. Or maybe Asadoulah was full of shit and leading them on a wild goose chase.

Harvath played his light along the base of the last wall until he came to a small ventilation hole about the diameter of a Coke can. Bending down, he focused his beam just to the left of it and found what he was looking for. Carved into the wall, about an inch above the floor, were the initials *JLG,* Julia Louise Gallo. She had done exactly what she had been taught to do. It was one of the key things taught to people operating in areas with a high likelihood of kidnappings: Whenever possible, wherever possible, *always* leave a trail.

Pulling his cell phone from his pocket, Harvath snapped a picture of Julia's initials and then stood.

"Our package was definitely here," Harvath said via his bone mic. "We've got confirmation."

"We've also got a problem," replied Gallagher from his position back with Daoud and Asadoulah. "You've got a truck full of bad guys headed right for you."

CHAPTER 42

"How many?" asked Harvath as he turned off his flashlight and flipped his night vision goggles back down.

"Four," said Gallagher. "Two in the bed and two in the cab."

"How far out?"

"A hundred twenty-five meters and closing."

"We're sure these are bad guys?" asked Fontaine over his mic.

"Unless the local 4H Club has started issuing RPGs, these are definitely bad guys. What do you want me to do?"

Harvath knew these were not simple villagers. Not with RPGs they weren't. These were Massoud's men, and he didn't need to think twice about what to do. "Take them out."

"Roger that," said Gallagher. "Hold your position."

It was a clear night with enough starlight

for a marksman like Gallagher to be able to engage his targets with the optics he had on his weapon. Flipping up his NODs, he settled his shoulder into the stock of his LaRue sniper rifle and calculated the lead on his moving target.

As the truck closed to within a hundred meters, Gallagher slowed his breathing and prepared to fire. Exhaling, he focused on his sight picture and gently applied pressure to the trigger.

There was a muffled *pop* as the round spat from the suppressed rifle and blistered through the air toward its target. Gallagher's lead had been perfect and the bullet took out the truck's right front tire.

The effect was instantaneous, and the driver immediately slowed the vehicle to a full stop. With no clue to what they could have hit to cause such a dramatic blowout, all of the men climbed out of the truck to survey the damage. Short of painting targets on themselves, the small party of Taliban soldiers could hardly have made it easier on Gallagher.

As they squatted in unison to investigate the shredded tire, Baba G whispered, "Clean-up in aisle five," and began applying pressure to his trigger.

The bullets ripped from the weapon, filling

the night air with a fine red mist as they tore into heads, throats, and even chests. There was a faint *tock, tock, tock* like the stamping of sheet metal as a handful of rounds either went slightly wide or passed directly through their victim's flesh and pinged into the body of the truck.

Gallagher had definitely oversaturated his targets, but it was one of those cases where if a little was good, a lot was better. He had absolutely no doubt that those four had climbed aboard the Seventy-two-Virgin Express and weren't going to pose a problem to anyone, anymore.

Flipping his NODs back down, Gallagher scanned the area as he inserted a fresh magazine into his weapon. "Convoy 1, you're all clear," said Gallagher over the radio. "Don't trip over the bodies on your way out."

"How close are they?" asked Harvath.

"Outside, up the road to your left. Within a hundred meters. And, by the way, you're welcome."

Turning to Fontaine, Harvath said, "If those are Massoud's men, there could be some worthwhile intel on them."

The former JTF2 operative illuminated his Suunto and checked the time. "I'll go," he said. "You need to get to that *jirga*, because as soon as those bodies are found,

413

their buddies are going turn this village upside down."

"That's assuming there are more of them," said Harvath.

"Trust me. They're like roaches. For every four Taliban you see, there are forty more hiding somewhere nearby."

"Unless Massoud took the rest with him."

"For all we know," cautioned Fontaine, "Massoud is still here. That's the mindset we need to operate under."

"Agreed," said Harvath. "Are you sure you're okay with checking out that truck?"

Fontaine nodded. "I'm sure."

"Thank you," replied Harvath as he made his way to the door. Hailing Gallagher, he said, "Convoy 2 is going to investigate the four downed tangos. Convoy 1 is returning to your position."

"Roger that," replied Gallagher. "Two out with a split. I'll cover you both as best as I can."

"Negative," said Harvath, who wanted to afford Fontaine as much protection as possible. "Keep your eyes on Convoy 2. Convoy 1 will come back on his own."

"Roger that."

Once they were ready, Harvath nodded and Fontaine pulled back the door. It was still quiet at their side of the village as the two men crept outside.

Harvath gave Fontaine the thumbs-up and the Canadian took off toward the four dead Taliban with the flat while Harvath retreated several feet, risked a flash photo of the structure with his camera phone, and then carefully made his way back to where Gallagher and the two Afghans were waiting.

Baba G didn't bother looking up at Harvath when he rejoined them. His eyes were focused on Fontaine. "We ready for phase two?" he asked.

"Yup," replied Harvath, who removed his Afghan cell phone and, handing it to Daoud, said, "It's time to make the call."

The interpreter took the phone and dialed Fayaz's cell phone. He spoke briefly to the elder, then disconnected the call and returned the phone to Harvath. "They are ready for us," he said.

Harvath nodded and, tucking the phone into his pocket, got on his radio and said, "Convoy 2, we're ready to roll to our next location."

"Copy that, Convoy 1. I'll meet you there. Convoy 2, out."

Using a tiny Cejay fingerlight to illuminate Fayaz's hand-drawn map of the village, Harvath and Gallagher went over the route they were about to take to the *jirga* one last time, but Asadoulah shook his head and suggested another route.

Harvath didn't like it. It was too direct and went straight through the center of the village. *"Na,"* he insisted, using the Pashtu word for *no,* and then retraced the route he intended them to take.

Grabbing Harvath's left index finger with the small aviator's light secured to it with Velcro, Asadoulah illuminated Harvath's proposed route once more and pointed to specific structures along the way. "Taliban, Taliban, Taliban, Massoud," he whispered with his broken jaw as he pointed to house after house after house.

Harvath looked at Gallagher. "What do you think?"

"Well, out of all of us," he replied, "this kid's the only one who's been to this village before. And I may not be crazy about walking right up Main Street, but he sure seems adamant about it."

"Fine," said Harvath as he turned off his fingerlight and tucked the map back into his pocket. "We'll do it his way, but that means no NODs. If even one person sees us and gets suspicious, we'll be blown before we ever make the *jirga.*"

CHAPTER 43

Though the moon wasn't full, it was entirely too bright for Harvath's liking, as were the stars. As the group moved deeper into the village, they threw long shadows across the ground and were silhouetted against every mud brick and stone building they passed.

They slipped from one property to the next, staying low and seeking out as many places of concealment as possible. There was no sound except for the wind, which had begun to pick up, and the river of snowmelt that rushed past the village as it made its way further down into the valley. The cold mountain air enveloping them was filled with the scent of wood smoke and roasting meats.

With his back against one of the many walled village compounds, Harvath was about to peek around the corner to make sure it was safe for them to proceed when he heard a noise. Immediately, he signaled for everyone to get down.

Straining his ears against the sound of the river, he tried to make out what he was hearing. As the noise got closer, he figured out what it was. *Footsteps.*

Contrary to what people saw in the movies, suppressed weapons were not completely silenced. Gallagher's taking shots from his suppressed weapon on the outskirts of the village was one thing, Harvath's trying to do so here among the densely packed houses was something else entirely. They couldn't risk it.

Waving everyone back, Harvath pulled his knife from its sheath. Letting his MP5 hang from its sling beneath his *patoo,* he readied himself to take out whoever was coming around the corner. With one hand poised to clamp down and cover the person's mouth so he couldn't scream out, and the other wielding the knife, which measured over a foot in length, Harvath prepared to attack.

The footsteps grew closer and as they did Harvath adjusted his grip on the weapon's notched handle. Slowing his breathing, he focused on the sound of the approaching figure. The person was less than a meter away at this point. Harvath inched closer to the edge of the building and got ready.

Closer the footsteps came. As they did,

Harvath took in a deep breath of air. Like a statue he stood perfectly still. As had been true in the raid on the interrogation facility beneath the Soviet military base in Kabul, and as was true in all such scenarios, the keys to success were speed, surprise, and overwhelming violence of action.

When the figure suddenly appeared, Harvath sprang.

Grabbing the person by the throat, Harvath yanked him off his feet, spun him around the edge of the building he was hiding behind, and slammed him up against the wall. The blackened-steel blade was up against the soft flesh of the person's throat in a fraction of a second. Harvath looked into the face of his victim and saw abject terror in his eyes. He also saw that his victim was a boy no older than fourteen.

Suddenly, Asadoulah had broken away from Gallagher and was at Harvath's arm imploring him in Pashtu, *"Na, na."* Then he spoke the first word Harvath had heard him say in English, "Friend."

Harvath looked at Asadoulah and then back at the teen he had pinned to the wall. Slowly, he lowered the boy back down to the ground.

He left the blade in place, just underneath the teen's chin, but removed his hand from around the boy's throat. As he did, Harvath raised his finger to his lips and instructed the teen to remain quiet.

The boy looked at Asadoulah and then back at Harvath and nodded. Harvath lowered the blade. The second he did, the boy tried to rabbit on him. Harvath, though, was ready. Grabbing hold of him, he once again lifted the teen off his feet by his throat and pinned him against the wall.

Harvath hissed for Gallagher and Daoud to come over, while Asadoulah tried to calm his friend down.

Daoud was at Harvath's side in a flash and Harvath instructed the interpreter about what he wanted to say to the boy. "Tell him we're not here to hurt him, but if he doesn't calm down I will."

Frightened by Harvath's intensity, Daoud hesitated. "Tell him," Harvath snapped.

The interpreter relayed Harvath's orders to the boy. "Now ask him how many Taliban are in the village right now."

Daoud obeyed, and despite Harvath's hand wrapped around his throat the boy was able to croak out an answer.

"At least twenty," the interpreter replied.

"Where?" asked Harvath.

The boy had no idea.

"What about Massoud?"

"Gone," Daoud translated.

"And the American woman?" Harvath asked.

Daoud listened and then said, "The boy says they took her with them."

Harvath lowered the teen back down to his feet, pointed at the ground, and told him to sit. Daoud was about to translate, but as the boy sat right down, he saw that Harvath had made himself perfectly clear.

"What are we going to do about him?" asked Gallagher. "We're not going to kill him."

"Of course we're not," said Harvath.

"We also can't let him go. If we do, he's going to raise the alarm and we're as good as dead. We'll not only have Massoud's men on us, we'll have every other member of this village gunning for us."

Gallagher was right. He remembered the story of a four-man SEAL team in Afghanistan that had been dispatched to capture or kill a high-ranking Taliban leader only to be discovered while doing their reconnaissance by a small group of goatherds. Hamstrung by politically correct rules of engagement and fearful of what their own government might do to them if they pursued the most logical option, the SEALs reluctantly and against their better judgment let the goatherds go.

Within an hour, the team was engaged in a firefight with over 150 Taliban. Three of the SEALs, as well as the sixteen-man rescue force sent in via a Chinook helicopter that was shot down, were killed. Only one of the SEALs survived, and even then just barely, to recount the horrific tale. It was a situation Harvath was not interested in repeating.

Looking at Asadoulah, Harvath said to Daoud, "Ask Asadoulah if this boy is one of the friends who accosted Dr. Gallo with him."

The interpreter put the question to Asadoulah, and the boy turned his face away in shame. That was answer enough for Harvath.

Staring back down at the teen he'd told to sit, Harvath said, "I want to know this boy's name."

The interpreter posed the question and the teen replied, "Usman."

"Repeat my promise to Usman that as long as he cooperates, no harm will come to him."

As the interpreter spoke to the boy, Harvath withdrew his map of the village and illuminated it with his fingerlight for the boy to see. "Tell him where we're going and ask him if he knows if there are any Taliban or any other villagers that he has seen out. In fact, I also want you to ask him why he is out."

Daoud put all the questions to the boy and then said, "His uncle's family has a stomach flu. His mother made dinner for them and he took the food to their house. He was on the way home when we found him."

"What about Taliban or other villagers?"

"He said he didn't see any other villagers. He saw a truck with four Taliban in it twenty minutes ago, but nothing since."

Harvath wondered if that was the same truck Baba G had taken care of. "Ask him where Massoud went."

Daoud asked, but the boy replied that he didn't know.

"How many of his men are still here?" Harvath asked.

The boy shrugged. "Only a few," he replied. "No more than ten."

"How do you know?"

"We have a small village. It is not easy for Taliban to hide here," said the boy.

Harvath didn't believe him. There was just something about this kid that he didn't like. Looking at Gallagher, Harvath asked, "Did you bring any restraints?"

Baba G reached into his pocket and handed a pair to Harvath, who ordered Usman to stand up and hold out his hands. Sliding his knife back into its sheath, Harvath locked the boy's wrists together with a pair of the EZ cuffs and then asked Daoud for his *kaffiyeh.*

Pantomiming what he wanted, Harvath waited for Usman to open his mouth and then used the long piece of checked cloth as a gag. He wrapped the remaining fabric around the boy's neck and the lower part of his face. It wasn't the world's best disguise, but it was better than nothing, and if the boy tried to yell for help, nobody was going to hear anything unless they were standing right next to him.

Harvath made Usman Daoud's problem and told the interpreter to keep hold of the boy's arm and make sure he didn't get away. Harvath then flashed his MP5 so Usman could see it, and had Daoud tell him that if he tried to run or made any noise whatsoever, he would shoot him. He told Asadoulah the same thing just in case.

Then, with the two teens in tow, Harvath gave the order to move out and prayed they wouldn't encounter any more trouble before they made it to the *jirga.*

CHAPTER 44

When the center of the village finally came into sight, Harvath instructed his group to stop while he pulled on his NODs and took a long, careful look around.

As Fayaz's map indicated, in the center of the village was an elevated wooden structure surrounded by a copse of trees. It looked like a tree house with a wide, wraparound porch. Lights burned inside, and over the tumble of the icy river as its water slushed down out of the mountains, Harvath could hear voices. The two *shuras* were still engaged in their *jirga*. It was time.

Harvath moved his three Afghan charges quickly through the open, over to the stand of trees, while Gallagher covered them. Once they were safely at the base of the structure, Gallagher traversed the open space and joined them.

"What do you want to do with him?" Baba G asked as he nodded toward Usman.

"Should we cut him loose?"

Harvath powered down his NODs and stuffed them into one of his coat pockets. "We'll let his elders decide what to do with him," he said as he pulled out his knife and sliced off the boy's plastic restraints. Daoud helped unwind the *kaffiyeh* from around his face and warned him to remain silent.

Putting Daoud in the lead, Harvath ordered his team up the stairs. At the door, the interpreter removed his loafers and stepped inside. Harvath and company immediately followed suit.

Inside there was a group of gnarled, weather-beaten men with automatic weapons. Some belonged to Fayaz and his *shura,* the others were local and immediately scrambled for their guns.

"Salaam alaikum. Salaam alaikum," Daoud repeated with his hand placed over his heart in an attempt to reassure the men that they meant no harm.

The locals weren't buying it. Harvath and Gallagher were Westerners and that could only mean one thing — trouble.

The men hurriedly leaped to their feet, the room filling with the metallic clicks of AK-47 safeties being flipped off.

"Salaam, salaam," Daoud continued to implore the men. *Peace, peace.*

Gallagher took a step to his right to better shield Asadoulah. One of the locals recognized Usman standing behind Harvath and began speaking to him.

"Tell them we're here to see the *shura,*" Harvath said to their interpreter.

Daoud relayed the message, but the man ignored him. Instead he kept speaking to Usman and was now cocking his head, beckoning the boy to step away from the strangers and join him on the other side of the room.

The interpreter once more repeated his request and the man swung his rifle barrel over and focused his sights right on the center of Daoud's face. Immediately, all of the color drained from his face.

It was a very aggressive move, and in unison Harvath and Gallagher pulled their weapons out from under their *patoos* and trained them on the handful of Afghans who were aiming at them from the other side of the room. It was a Mexican standoff, Afghanistan style.

Across the room, the man began raising his voice as he called for Usman to come to him. *"Na,"* Harvath said. *No.*

The man did not like that answer and was about to reply when a door on the other side of the room opened. In the doorway stood an older man with a long, gray beard, coal-black eyes, and a thick scar that ran from his nose to the bottom of his left ear. He appeared to be one of the village elders, and he was very angry.

He yelled at the villagers to put down their guns and, reluctantly, they did. He then turned his eyes upon the group of strangers.

Daoud bade the elder peace and, as they had not been invited into the village like Fayaz and his *shura* had been and were in effect trespassing, immediately requested *melmasthia* — protection and hospitality.

The elder studied the strangers and then slowly granted his approval. With that, Harvath and Gallagher lowered their weapons. As they did, Usman bolted for the elder and began yelling out what had happened to him.

The elder fixed the boy with a glare that stopped him in his tracks. He looked at Daoud for an explanation, which the interpreter quickly gave. The elder was obviously not happy with what he heard and he locked eyes with Harvath.

Harvath returned the man's stare and refused to look away. Finally, he held up his hand to silence Daoud and called for the strangers to follow him into the other room.

As they entered, Harvath, Gallagher, and Daoud politely greeted Fayaz and his *shura* as well as the members of the local *shura.* Their chief elder, who introduced himself as Baseer, asked the men their names and then invited them all to sit down and take tea. When the teenagers tried to join them, Baseer hissed through his teeth and dismissively waved them away to the back of the room, where he ordered them to remain standing.

The men sat down on a large blue rug. Baseer had more tea brought in, and small plates of food. Harvath knew that he had no choice in the matter. Taking tea was an ancient, time-honored tradition meant to show respect and secure good relations. Rejecting it would have been an incredible insult to his hosts. Nevertheless, Gallagher had taken out four Taliban soldiers on the edge of the village, and as Fontaine had said, where you see four Taliban there are always at least forty more nearby, or if one wanted to believe Usman, no more than ten. Whatever the number, Harvath felt like a sitting duck and wanted to be on his way as quickly as possible. To do that, though, he would have to convince Baseer and the other members of his *shura* that it was now in their best interest to work with him.

Daoud and Fayaz spoke briefly, and then the interpreter filled Harvath in on everything the two *shuras* had thus far discussed.

Waving Asadoulah over, Fayaz made the boy apologize to Baseer and the other members of his *shura* for how he had treated the American woman and for lying about his altercation with Zwak.

Usman was then summoned by Baseer, who severely chastised him and demanded the names of the other boys who had joined them in assaulting the American woman so that they could be dealt with. Once the boy complied, he and Asadoulah were dismissed from the room. It was now time to discuss the most serious issues.

Fayaz made it clear to Baseer and his *shura* that Harvath had the biggest stick in the room. He could call upon American and NATO militaries at will and they would do his bidding, including leveling this village with a massive airstrike.

As Daoud translated, Harvath was concerned that Fayaz might be laying it on a bit too thick, but if there was one thing the Afghans recognized and respected instantly, it was force. Watching the faces of Baseer and his fellow *shura* members, it was clear that Fayaz's words were sinking in.

Baseer looked at Harvath finally and said, "You have come for the woman?"

"Yes, we have," Harvath replied through Daoud.

"Mullah Massoud is one of the most powerful Taliban commanders in all of Afghanistan. If he had caught you here, he would have killed you."

"But he is not here, is he?"

"Na," replied Baseer. "He is not."

Harvath had been right, but there was little satisfaction in the knowledge. The important thing was getting Julia Gallo back safely. Removing his cell phone, Harvath showed Baseer the pictures he had taken and said, "We know the woman was held here and I have proof. I have sent these pictures to the American military commanders at Bagram. They know and I know that Mullah Massoud couldn't have kept Dr. Gallo here without your knowledge. Because of this, we make no distinction between you and the Taliban. If you do not cooperate with us, airstrikes will be launched immediately against your village. There will be nothing left here but dust."

Harvath was bluffing again, of course, but he'd dealt with enough village elders in his day to know that their primary obligation wasn't to a man like Massoud, but to the people of their village, whom the Taliban relentlessly manipulated, extorted, and hid behind.

"Give me the woman," added Harvath, "and we will go in peace."

Baseer shook his head. "I warned Massoud that taking her would be bad for our village."

"He should have listened to you."

"The only person he listens to is himself."

"And the Russian," offered one of the other elders.

Harvath's eyes studied the man as the interpreter translated his remark. "It sounds like this Russian has also caused much trouble for your village," said Harvath.

"Too much trouble —" continued the elder until Baseer held up his hand to quiet him.

"Did Massoud order him to kill Elam Badar?"

Baseer nodded. "Massoud was afraid that Elam Badar might tell the Americans about his prisoner."

"Who is the Russian? A mercenary?" asked Harvath.

Harvath studied the faces of the *shura* after his question had been translated, but none of them appeared anxious to answer it. Having already threatened to use his stick, he knew it was time to dangle a carrot.

"If you help me, I can help you," said Harvath. "I am in a position to be extremely generous."

"How generous?" asked Baseer.

"That all depends. What do you need?"

"We want a small hydroelectric dam built at the bottom of our valley. We also want new roads built."

Harvath thought about it. "These are both very important projects. Control over such projects would not only increase your village's wealth and power, but also the authority of your *shura*."

"And we want generators," said Baseer, "until we can generate enough power ourselves."

The elder certainly wasn't shy with his list of requests. "If you give me what I want," replied Harvath, "I will do everything I can to help you secure these things for your village."

Baseer listened to the interpreter's translation and then conversed briefly with his fellow elders. Turning back to Harvath, he said, "We only know the Russian by his Afghan name, Bakht Rawan. He is not a mercenary."

"What is he?"

"He is a Russian intelligence agent."

Harvath looked at Gallagher and then

back to the chief elder. "What's his connection with Massoud?"

"The Russians never really left Afghanistan," said the chief elder. "Not completely. Many supported and maintained intelligence networks throughout the country. Massoud was the Russian's student. He helped place Massoud in the NDS."

"Massoud was in the NDS?" replied Harvath.

"Hoo," said Baseer. "But he grew tired of it. He wanted to change Afghanistan, and for him, the Taliban was his answer."

"What about for you?"

"I have never believed in the Taliban," replied the elder.

Right answer, thought Harvath. Now let's see if he can keep them going. "And what does all of this have to do with kidnapping Dr. Gallo?"

Baseer looked at him and spoke slowly so Daoud could translate. "They offered to give you the woman back if you freed Mustafa Khan from prison, correct?"

Harvath nodded.

"What they didn't tell you was that the Russian was the one who helped the Afghan National Army locate and capture Khan in the first place."

"But that doesn't make any sense. Why

would they do that?"

The elder looked at Harvath and asked, "What do you know about the Lake of Broken Glass?"

CHAPTER 45

"I've never heard of any Lake of Broken Glass," replied Harvath.

"It is a story," said Baseer. "A fantasy."

"Then why are we talking about it?"

"Because the Russian was obsessed with it."

Harvath looked at Gallagher. "Have you ever heard of this lake?"

Baba G shook his head. "No, but I'm not exactly the resident expert on Afghan folklore."

Harvath turned back to the elder and through Daoud said, "How does this fit in with Dr. Gallo's kidnapping?"

"Afghanistan," the elder responded, "can seem like a puzzle. To understand it, you must put the pieces together correctly. Even if some of the pieces are only a fantasy. Through his network, the Russian became convinced that the Lake of Broken Glass was not a fantasy, but in fact a reality."

"So what is the Lake of Broken Glass?" Harvath asked.

"It is where Sheik Osama is said to have hidden all of his riches."

"Bin Laden?"

Baseer nodded. "Before his attacks on New York and Washington, he knew his money would not be safe in bank accounts. People say he took all of his money from these banks and used it to buy diamonds."

"I think I actually read something about that," said Gallagher.

"Me too," replied Harvath. "It's not a bad idea. Diamonds are easy to hide. They retain their value and they're virtually untraceable."

"They're also easily converted to cash and can be transported anywhere in the world without dogs being able to sniff them or setting off alarms."

"So how does this Lake of Broken Glass fit in?" Harvath asked.

"Sheik Osama was said to have hidden his diamonds in a cave somewhere in Afghanistan. To keep them from being stolen, he then had the cave flooded with water. Eventually, the wooden cases used to store the stones rotted away and the diamonds spilled out across the cave floor. The diamonds are said to sparkle so brightly that the flooded cave looks like a lake of broken glass."

The Afghans loved their tall tales, and while obviously the story had been embellished as it passed through the Afghan grapevine, Harvath couldn't help but wonder if there was something there. He remembered hearing testimony released after one of the first Gitmo trials that spoke of an Afghan man who had drowned with his pockets full of diamonds. He'd also heard of a DHS alert for dive shops to be on the lookout for Arab men wanting to purchase diving equipment which was born of confusion over SCUBA tanks discovered in a terrorist stronghold along the Afghan-Pakistan border. DHS believed al-Qaeda was training men to carry out attacks on bridges, cruise ships, and other water-related targets. Now, Harvath strongly suspected those two dots might connect in a way that no one had ever considered.

Whether there was fire behind all this smoke or not, Harvath had more questions he needed answered. "Explain to me why the Russian had Mustafa Khan arrested," he said.

"It is believed that Khan is the person who encouraged the sheik to remove his money from the banks and purchase the diamonds. People said that Khan also helped the sheik hide the diamonds. He was one of his most trusted lieutenants. When money was needed for an operation, it was Khan who went and fetched the diamonds from the lake."

"So if the Russian got hold of Khan," said Harvath, "he believed he could force him to reveal the location of the lake?"

The chief elder nodded.

"So why not just grab Khan himself? Why kidnap Dr. Gallo and go to all of this additional trouble?"

"From what Massoud said, the Russian was warned by his country not to betray their involvement. If the lake could be discovered, the diamonds were to be removed. Even though al-Qaeda has other sources of funding, they would be greatly weakened, and so would Taliban leader Mullah Omar. Always overly ambitious, the Russians intended to transfer the money to Massoud so that he could use it to unite the other Taliban commanders under his control, purchase more weapons, build his army, and wear down the American and other Western forces in Afghanistan exactly the way the mujahideen had done to the Soviet Union."

It was a bold plan and Harvath could see a lot of upside in it for the Russians. Al-Qaeda was the primary source of a lot of the radical Islamist trouble they were having in places like Chechnya. Also, if they succeeded and Massoud ending up running the country, the Russians would be able to ask for almost anything they wanted in return. Harvath's guess was that they would want to pick up on the abandoned pipeline project that had ground to a halt when America had bombed al-Qaeda terrorist training camps after the attacks on the U.S. embassies in Kenya and Tanzania.

Considering the way Russia actively bullied both Europe and its former Soviet republics, like the Ukraine, by regularly cutting off their natural gas supplies, Harvath could only imagine how much influence it would have if it controlled the only pipeline from central Asia straight through Afghanistan to ships waiting in the Arabian Sea. Russia would have a stranglehold on the entire region.

"The Russian chose the American woman carefully," said Baseer. "He knew about her mother's relationship with your president and he knew that your president would find a way to get Khan freed from prison."

"And then what was supposed to happen?" asked Harvath.

The elder held his hands up near his head and shook them as if to indicate that the Russian was crazy. "He expected the Americans to torture Khan until he told them the location of the Lake of Broken Glass. The Americans would then retrieve the diamonds and an exchange would be arranged for the girl. He would also insist on Khan's release so that Khan could return to Mullah Omar and Sheik Osama and blame the Americans for everything."

Harvath shook his head. It was an incredibly audacious plan. The downside for the Russians was next to nothing. Their man used his Afghan contacts to do everything. He used his Afghans to locate Khan. He then had them tip off the ANA to Khan's whereabouts, and then he most likely used Massoud's men to snatch Julia Gallo.

Then, if Khan was the real deal and there was indeed a cache of al-Qaeda gemstones somewhere in the country, the United States, or more specifically in this case, Harvath, would be forced to torture the information out of him to get the diamonds and trade them for Dr. Gallo's release.

If the Russian was smart, which Harvath believed he probably was, he would arrange for Khan to be released as far away from where the diamonds were being exchanged for Julia Gallo as possible. Probably on the other side of the country. At least that's how he would have done it, and then Khan would make his way back to bin Laden and Mullah Omar and fill them in. America would be the bad guy and no one would suspect the Russians or Mullah Massoud of having had any involvement whatsoever in the plot.

And if there were no diamonds, or Khan turned out not to be the right person to help locate them, Massoud and the Russian had a host of options to choose from. They could change their minds and accept the ten million Stephanie Gallo had offered for her daughter's safe return. They could let Gallo go. They could sell her into the lucrative white slavery market that operated throughout the Islamic world, or simply slash her throat and dump her body by the side of the road. In essence, it was all upside with very little on the down. Harvath had to give the men credit.

That said, they had made one significant mistake. Though keeping prisoners with them in their villages was a Taliban tradition, doing so in this case had been a bad idea. Massoud and the Russian would have been better off stashing Julia Gallo in a deep, dark hole somewhere where only they knew where she was. Because they hadn't, they had created a lot of problems for themselves, which Harvath hoped to add to.

"Do you know where Massoud and the

Russian are now?" he asked.

There was considerable discourse among the elders this time. Harvath sensed in all but Baseer a reluctance to cooperate and give up Massoud's location. Finally, the chief elder said, "We are not certain, but we think we may know where he is."

"How many men did he take with him?"

Baseer calculated in his head and then replied, "The Russian left first. We believe it was shortly after he killed Elam Badar. Massoud wasn't here. He was at a meeting with Taliban commanders in another province. The Russian took the woman, Massoud's brother, Zwak, and ten of Massoud's men. They left in three trucks.

"When Massoud returned to the village and heard that they had left, he organized about thirty men and divided them into six trucks. They left the village two trucks at a time to avoid drawing a Predator strike."

Massoud was smart. If they traveled in too big a group or drove too many people to the same place, they would attract a lot of attention to themselves. "How many of his men did he leave behind here?"

Baseer conversed with his colleagues. "At least sixty," he stated. "Maybe seventy-five."

Seventy-five? thought Harvath to himself.

That was a hell of a lot more than the "no more than ten" Usman had claimed. That kid either needed a remedial arithmetic class, or he was lying. Harvath felt pretty certain it was the latter. He also wondered if the boy had been lying about delivering food to his flu-stricken relatives. Whatever the case, Harvath was suddenly glad he had taken Asadoulah's advice and avoided the Taliban buildings that dotted his original route.

"You said you think you know where Massoud and the Russian may be," replied Harvath as he removed his map and spread it on the rug between himself and the elders. "Please show me."

Baseer studied the map and asked questions of the other members of the *shura* before responding. "Here," he said. "Here is where Massoud will be."

"What is it?" asked Harvath as he removed a pen and marked the location.

"It is a high summer pasture for animal grazing; very difficult to access, especially this time of year. There will still be much ice and snow there."

"Can you think of any place else Massoud might have gone?"

Baseer smiled and swept his hands wide. "He has many subcommanders and many allies throughout Afghanistan. He could have left for Pakistan, the Northwest Frontier Province, the Swat Valley."

Of course, the old man was right. Massoud could be anywhere. Harvath massaged his eyes as he drew his fingers in to pinch the bridge of his nose. His back was beginning to ache again, and he wished he'd brought more Motrin with him.

"But," said the chief elder, interrupting Harvath's thoughts, "we don't think Massoud went to any of those other places."

"Why not?" asked Harvath.

"Because of the Russian. There are very few places the Russian would be welcome without Massoud. The Russian also was running a very big risk by taking the woman. It was an act of desperation. He needed to go someplace close, someplace safe that he knew he could reach quickly. It would have been someplace he knew. That is why we believe he went to the pasture compound."

"I thought you said it was very difficult to access."

"Difficult," said Baseer, "but not impossible. If I was the Russian, it is where I would have gone."

Daoud leaned over the map and, after surveying it, pointed just below where the pasture was located and added, "If this is where they went, they would have passed through this village right here."

Harvath studied the map again. "Which means, someone there would have noticed all of those vehicles passing through."

The interpreter nodded. "I know this village. It's not very big. The people there definitely would have noticed."

For all Harvath knew, it could be a wild-goose chase, but he was inclined to trust the intuition of the village elders. What's more, their read of how the Russian would rationalize his moves made sense. It was also the best lead they had.

Harvath looked at Gallagher. "Do you have anything to add?"

"It'd be great if the elders' militia could escort us to where the cars are," said Baba G.

Daoud translated the request and Baseer was happy to oblige. The men stood, embraced, and wished one another peace. Harvath gave Baseer his Afghan cell phone number and asked him to please call if he thought of or heard anything else about Massoud, the Russian, or, most important, Julia Gallo.

When they stepped out of the meeting room, Fayaz's security detail snapped to their feet as they said good-bye and Baseer told some of his men to escort the party back to their vehicles. Harvath could tell that the man he'd locked eyes with earlier and who was calling for Usman to cross the room and come to him was not happy, but there was little he could do. He had his orders.

And though Harvath wanted to smirk, or toss him a wink, out of respect for the elders he kept his urge to be a smartass in check. It was only a fleeting thought anyway. His mind was already on where they were going and what he prayed they'd find there.

After putting their shoes on, the group descended from the wooden structure and readied to head off toward the vehicles. Gallagher placed Asadoulah close to his side. Harvath looked for Usman, but he was nowhere to be seen. Harvath figured that the kid had already run home to spin the story of being held at knifepoint into a saga of how he had singlehandedly fought off an entire battalion of bloodthirsty U.S. soldiers. After his father and brothers knocked the crap out of him for stretching the truth, they'd run out and tell their friends this story, but by then the American force would be upgraded to brigade strength at least. That was, of course, if the men in Usman's house didn't beat him unconscious for the shame he had brought upon them in accosting the American woman, who'd been, even as a prisoner, under Mullah Massoud's protection. However it happened, Harvath hoped the kid got a top-notch ass-kicking.

As they moved out of the copse of trees, Harvath pretended to be talking to Gallagher as he raised Fontaine over the radio. "Convoy 2, this is Convoy 1. Do you read me?"

"Loud and clear," said the Canadian.

"We're on our way down to the vehicles. What's your position?"

"I'm in a hide about thirty meters from the trucks. I already swept them. No bombs. They're clean."

"Anything we need to be on the lookout for?" asked Harvath.

"It's all quiet down here."

"Good. What about the Welcome Wagon crew we laid out?"

"I got some cell phones," said Fontaine. "That's it."

"No maps? No radios?"

"Nope. None of that. One of them had a couple of naughty pictures that looked like they were from an old *Playboy* magazine, though."

Harvath marveled at the hypocrisy. Ancient statues of the Buddha, *bad*. Pictures of Ms. April, not bad.

"I can see you guys coming now," said the

former JTF2 operative. "I'll hold here until everyone has mounted up. Don't go driving away without me."

"Don't worry," said Harvath.

The group entered the small clearing on the very edge of the village where Gallagher's Land Cruiser and the two other vehicles had been parked.

With no need to deal with checkpoints on the way out of the village, the vehicle assignments were changed. The battered pickup truck was the lead vehicle and carried a mixture of elders and their security. Fayaz and Asadoulah rode in the middle vehicle with the rest of the security team and Harvath, Fontaine, Gallagher, and Daoud in the rear position.

Once everyone was in their respective truck and the small column started moving, Harvath radioed Fontaine and told him to come out and hop in. As a precaution, Harvath stood next to the Land Cruiser with his weapon out and at the ready. Though he hadn't seen anyone, he'd felt eyes all over him since they had left the *jirga* and begun their walk down to the trucks. If someone was going to try something, now would be the time.

Fontaine appeared out of the darkness on the other side of the makeshift parking lot and made his way to the Land Cruiser.

"We all good?" he asked as he stood up on the running board and prepared to hop in back next to Daoud.

Harvath took one final look around and said, "I think so."

"Then let's roll."

Sliding into the front passenger seat, Harvath closed the door, but left it unlocked. Rolling his window down, he balanced the suppressor of his MP5 on the windowsill and tried to twist his body in such a way that the seat wouldn't be jabbing into his sore back.

"You're going to waste all of my heat," said Gallagher as he put the truck in gear and pressed on the gas to catch up with the vehicles in front of him.

"It's just until we clear the area."

"So," said Fontaine. "How was the party? Did they serve tea?"

For a moment, Harvath forgot about the throbbing in his lower back and the cold wind blowing through the window onto his face, and he laughed. "Yeah, they did. They also served up a nice juicy lead. I think we may know where Massoud and the Russian took Dr. Gallo."

"That's excellent news," replied Fontaine. "Are we going to go check it out, or do you want to hand this thing off to the higher-ups?"

Harvath turned around to look into the backseat. "That depends on Mr. Daoud. We'd need his help for a little bit longer."

Fontaine put his muscular arm around the pudgy Afghan. "What do you say? It could be fun."

"I most certainly disagree about it being fun," said the interpreter. "But that does not mean we cannot come to some sort of an arrangement."

"A diplomat and a capitalist," said Fontaine. "You ought to think about running for office."

Harvath smiled as he turned back around in his seat and thought about rolling up his window. Suddenly, he heard the distinct, pressurized sound of gas releasing as a rocket-propelled grenade was launched.

He had barely yelled the words, "RPG!" when everyone in the Land Cruiser saw the lead vehicle explode in a roiling fireball.

CHAPTER 46

The White House, Washington, D.C.

"I know it's hard for female agents to get dates, but please tell me that things haven't gotten so bad that you've resorted to seeing Hutch."

After her meeting with Hutchinson, Elise had walked over to the White House to check the Secret Service duty roster and see if she could arrange for a couple more days off. Right now, with so many unanswered questions, she didn't feel that she could rejoin the president's detail and do her job effectively.

Turning around to see who was talking to her, Elise Campbell discovered Matthew Porter, a forty-year-old agent on Terry Alden's detail. He was a decent guy with two kids and an attorney wife at the DOJ who processed FISA warrants.

"What are you talking about?" asked Elise.

"Don't bullshit me, Campbell," said Porter, as he smiled and shook his head. "It's written all over your face."

"I don't know what you're talking about."

"C'mon. I saw you two canoodling in Lafayette Park."

"Me and Hutch?" stated Elise. "You're crazy. Besides, who even uses the term *canoodling* anyway?"

"Whatever it was," said Porter. "It looked pretty serious to me."

"You've got an overactive imagination. It was nothing."

"Well, you're a big girl. You can make your own mistakes, but Hutch? You can do so much better than that. In fact, Claire and I've got at least a dozen guys we could set you up with."

Elise looked him right in the eyes so he'd know she was serious. "Matt, there's nothing going on between me and Hutch. We were talking shop."

"Sure," said Porter as he made quotation marks in the air with his fingers. "Talking *shop*. Without being crude, that guy'll nail anything that moves."

"News flash, Matt. That *was* crude."

Porter shrugged. "You know what? You're right. It's none of my business."

"Thank you."

"I just have to admit, I don't know what

women see in him. Especially girls like you."

"Girls like me," repeated Campbell. "What is that supposed to mean?"

"I mean women who are not only out of Hutch's league, but out of his planet system."

It was an interesting remark, and since Porter had brought it up, one that Elise felt worth pursuing. "Women like the first lady?"

Porter had a coffee cup in his hand and had made the mistake of just taking a sip. Though he tried to hold it in, he coughed the coffee back into his cup. "Are you fucking kidding me?" he laughed as he picked up a paper towel to wipe his mouth. "Hutch and Mrs. Alden? Now, that *would be* incredible."

Campbell looked around. At the moment, there was no one else in earshot. "So what did you mean then?" she asked.

"I meant very good-looking women, like you," Porter replied awkwardly. "Not that the first lady isn't attractive, she's just —"

Elise put up her hand to stop him. "Setting aside the first lady for the moment, what other women were you referring to when you alluded to *girls like me?*"

"I feel like I'm getting grilled by my wife."

"Don't change the subject, Porter."

"All right, all right. Wow, you don't have to be so touchy."

"I'm not touchy," replied Elise.

"I was just talking about some of the hot women Hutch has managed to land. I meant it as a compliment."

"Who are we talking about? Anyone I'd know?"

"What are we, girlfriends all of a sudden?" asked Porter. "I didn't come in here to gossip. I just want some coffee."

"Porter, you started this."

"Hey, you were the one in the park with the guy. And if you've got something going with him, that's cool. Just be careful."

"Careful?" said Elise.

Porter dumped his coffee out and reached for a new cup. "The last hot chick Hutch hooked up with ended up drinking herself into a stupor and slamming her car into oncoming traffic."

Campbell knew Hutchinson had been lying to her, but she still had trouble believing what she was hearing. "Are you talking about Nikki Hale?" she said, her voice barely above a whisper.

"Yeah, I am," said Porter, "and why are we whispering? Was she a friend of yours?"

Elise shook her head. "No, she wasn't."

"Good. For a second there I thought maybe I'd really put my foot in it."

"How do you know he hooked up with her?"

"Because I saw the two of them the night of the accident."

"Together?" asked Elise.

"No, they were down on the beach doing semaphore. Of course, *together*. Come on, Campbell."

Elise grabbed hold of Porter's lapel and led him further away from the other agents in the room. "I want you to tell me everything you saw. Right now."

"You know what?" said the agent as he removed his colleague's hand from his jacket. "I shouldn't have said anything. I actually feel for the guy. Short of turning a woman gay, I can't think of a worse thing that could happen. Let's just forget I said anything, okay? Hutch has been through enough."

"He hasn't even come close," replied Campbell. "Not yet. Not by a long shot."

Twenty minutes later, Elise Campbell had finished her conversation with Porter, left the White House, and was headed west on E Street, her BlackBerry pressed to her ear. "That's exactly why I called you," she said.

"Elise, you saw the whole file," replied

Rita Klees from her office in East Hampton. "Why would we screen a drunk driving victim to see if they had sex before they died? Especially with the budget cuts we've suffered. We don't do that. Not without a reason, and in this case there was no reason."

"So pull an inspection report out of one of your other files, or better yet, get me a blank one I can fill in myself."

"Okay, I'm hanging up now."

"Damn it, Rita. Help me out here."

"Elise, what you're asking me for is —" began the detective.

"Trust me," said Campbell. "I'll explain later. Just get that stuff for me. Please."

Before Klees could respond, Elise had already hung up. Though she hadn't yet figured out how she was going to navigate the minefield she was about to enter, something in the back of her mind told her that she might have made a decent detective after all.

CHAPTER 47

Nangarhar Province, Afghanistan

Bullets began slamming into the Land Cruiser before the lead vehicle that had been hit by the RPG had even come back to the ground.

Opening the driver's-side door, Gallagher grabbed his rifle and dumped out with Harvath right on his heels. Fontaine leaped out the rear passenger door, pulling the interpreter with him.

Harvath was trying to identify the firing positions of their attackers when all of a sudden Gallagher, who had been crouched behind the tire right next to him, yelled, "Cover me," over the din of heavy machine-gun fire and ran for the middle vehicle.

As soon as he took off, green tracer rounds began chewing up the dirt behind him. It was as if someone had a phosphorescent marker and was trying to draw a line to him.

Angry as hell at his friend, but left with no other choice, Harvath rolled out from behind the left front tire of the Land Cruiser and began firing.

Based on the tracer fire, Harvath could make out two distinct positions from which the belt-fed machine guns were being fired. When Gallagher had made it to the second vehicle, Harvath rolled back behind the tire, pulled out his NODs, and powered them up.

He could tell by where the rounds were hitting that their attackers knew they were hiding behind the tires on the opposite side of the Land Cruiser. But, because their attackers were higher up the hillside, all they could do was shoot down. They couldn't shoot through the tires or underneath the truck. Normally, Harvath would have seen that as a good thing. The only problem was that they had taken out the lead vehicle with an RPG. Two more and they could take out the middle vehicle as well as the Land Cruiser. The men had to do something, fast.

Sliding his NODs on, Harvath looked at Fontaine, who had already done the same, and nodded. In unison, both men rolled out from behind their tires and began firing at their attackers. This time Harvath had the advantage of his night vision goggles and

459

could see what they were up against.

In the green glow of his NODs the steep slope on the other side of the road looked like an anthill, swarming with fighters armed with Kalashnikovs. There were at least seventy of them; maybe even eighty. These had to be Massoud's men, and Baseer's count had been right on the money. Harvath also figured he knew who had tipped them off. If that little shitbird Usman suddenly stood up on the hillside and waved, it wouldn't have surprised Harvath at all.

Firing the last round in his magazine, he rolled back behind his tire. They were pinned down. They needed to get away from the vehicles to a more defensible position.

Harvath glanced over at Gallagher, who was pressed up against the rear of Fayaz's SUV with Asadoulah and the chief elder pressed up right behind him. As the two Afghans took advantage of the limited cover provided by the rear passenger tire of the SUV, Gallagher balanced his LaRue sniper rifle on the truck's back bumper and raked the hillside. As far as Harvath could tell, none of the other people in the vehicle had survived.

"We need to get the hell away from these trucks," Harvath yelled to Fontaine. "If they've got any more RPGs up there, we're going to get smoked."

Fontaine nodded. "What do you want to do?"

"About thirty meters down on this side of the road is an old mud hut. I saw it when we came in. It's not perfect, but it's a hell of a lot better than this."

"All right," said the Canadian as he readied the interpreter to run. "I'll stay here and provide cover fire."

"No," replied Harvath as he inserted a fresh magazine into his MP5. "You're not getting paid enough to bring up the rear."

"Then how about a raise?"

"The Afghan capitalist got the rest of my money. Now take him and get over to Gallagher's position. I'll cover you."

"Roger that," said Fontaine, who, after signaling to Gallagher what he was about to do, grabbed hold of the interpreter. "When I say go, I want you to stay low and run as fast as you can to that other truck over there. Do you understand?"

Daoud nodded.

"Okay. One. Two. Three. *Go!*"

As the two men took off running, Harvath rolled back out and began firing again. From Fayaz's SUV, Gallagher did the same thing, paying special attention to the two heavy machine-gun positions.

When he had once again exhausted his ammo, he rolled back behind the tire, ejected the spent magazine, and inserted a fresh one. It didn't take a military strategist to realize that even with very carefully placed shots, they were still going to need more ammo.

After checking to make sure Fontaine and Daoud had made it safely, Harvath moved to the Land Cruiser's rear passenger door and flung it open. Even on this side, it was riddled with the holes of bullets that had passed straight through from the other side.

The seats were shredded, their springs visible in many spots. Harvath pulled the release and tried to flip down the seat nearest him, but it wouldn't budge. Leaping back from the truck as another barrage of fire literally made it rock back and forth, Harvath hid behind the tire and questioned how much he was willing to risk to get that extra ammunition.

It wasn't a tough decision. Gallagher's truck was a bullet magnet. If he climbed in there again to reach over the seats to get what he needed, he'd be cut to ribbons.

And if the threat of another RPG hit wasn't bad enough, Harvath had just been given another very compelling reason to get the hell away from the Land Cruiser. The gas tank had been ruptured and he could now smell gasoline.

Moving up to the front tire, Harvath motioned to Gallagher and Fontaine that he was ready to roll.

With his MP5 slung over his shoulder, he waited for their signal, and when it came, Harvath sprinted out from behind the cover of Gallagher's SUV and ran faster than he had ever run before in his life.

Despite the cover fire being laid down for him, the dusty road exploded in a hail of enemy gunfire, throwing rock chips and clumps of dirt high into the air. As the bullets snapped and whistled around him, Harvath could almost feel the heat from the tracer rounds chasing him like a lit fuse.

As he skidded to a stop behind Fayaz's SUV, it sounded like the world's largest hornets' nest had been stirred. All of the enemy gunfire was now being focused on this one rapidly deteriorating piece of cover. Though Harvath was out of breath, he knew they needed to move, now.

He looked at Fayaz, Daoud, and Asadoulah and saw that they had stripped the dead security men in the SUV of their weapons and were now all armed. Three more guns in the fight. He hoped they were good shooters. With their limited supply of ammo, now was not the time to spray and pray. They were going to have to be dead-on tack-drivers.

Looking at Gallagher, Harvath said, "You and Fontaine take the Afghans and get moving for that hut."

"I don't think that's such a good idea," Gallagher said.

"Don't worry. I'm going to create a diversion," replied Harvath as he nodded toward Gallagher's chewed-up Land Cruiser. "I hope your insurance is all paid up."

"That's not what I'm talking about," said Gallagher, pointing at his leg. "I think you're going to have to leave me here."

Harvath flipped up his NODs and looked down. A bullet had torn through Gallagher's upper thigh and blood was pumping out of the wound. "I need a tourniquet!" Harvath yelled. "Now!"

"There's no time," said Gallagher.

"Bullshit there isn't," he replied. "Fontaine!"

"Right here," replied the Canadian, as he appeared with a length of seatbelt he had cut out of the SUV.

As they positioned Gallagher's leg to get the makeshift device in position, he leaned forward and Harvath noticed that he had also taken a round through the top of his left shoulder.

Gallagher must have seen the look on Harvath's face as he leaned him back against the truck's rear tire. "What is it?" he asked.

"Nothing. We need to get out of here."

Harvath pulled out a spent magazine, slid it through the seatbelt knot, and used it to tighten down the tourniquet. The old Marine grimaced in pain, but didn't make a sound. Within seconds the bleeding had stopped.

Harvath helped Gallagher lie down on his stomach for a superman carry. He placed Daoud between Baba G's legs to carry them like a wheelbarrow and then motioned Asadoulah and Fontaine to each of his outstretched arms. Fontaine took Gallagher's right arm because, as he would be required to hook his left arm under it to help carry the man, it would leave his right hand free for shooting.

Shouldering his MP5 so he could use Gallagher's LaRue, Harvath positioned himself against the SUV's back bumper and gave the *go* command.

In unison, the three men bent and picked up Gallagher, while Harvath began firing at Massoud's men on the hillside. With Fayaz in the lead, they began running toward the mud hut.

As they did, Harvath turned his attention

away from their attackers and onto the leaking Land Cruiser.

When the lucky round finally found its mark, the SUV exploded, sending a brilliant flash and a towering pillar of fire into the night.

CHAPTER 48

Whether Massoud's soldiers knew where they were headed or not, Harvath and his team were dogged the entire way by wildly fired shots, many of which came incredibly close. Winston Churchill's famous line notwithstanding, there was absolutely nothing exhilarating about being shot at, even if your enemy was missing.

The run-down mud brick hut the team finally took shelter in only had three pockmarked walls and was missing its roof, but it was definitely a step up in the cover it afforded. Next to a stack of water-filled jerry cans there was nothing better at blast attenuation in the middle of nowhere than a thick mud wall.

Making Gallagher as comfortable as possible, Harvath checked his wounds again. So far the tourniquet on his leg was working. It was the bullet through his shoulder he was most worried about. Gallagher's breathing had become labored and Harvath was concerned that he had dropped a lung. Even so, he sought to reassure his friend. "You're going to be okay," he said.

"In that case, why don't you get me a beer?"

"As soon as the waitress comes back with my onion rings."

Gallagher laughed and coughed up blood, confirming Harvath's worst fears. If the man didn't get medical attention soon, he wasn't going to make it.

Leaving him in the care of the Afghans, Harvath stepped over to Fontaine, who was keeping watch out of one of the crumbling windows. "They're going to be on us any minute," said the Canadian.

"I know," replied Harvath. "Let's get hold of West and have his combat controller call in some close air support."

"How are we going to mark our position?"

"I've got a couple of fireflies," said Harvath, removing an infrared marking beacon from his pocket. It was made by the same Cejay company as his fingerlight and looked like a small plastic ice cube. When snapped onto a nine-volt battery, it emitted an infrared strobe so bright it could be picked up by overhead aircraft and even certain U.S.

government satellites.

Everyone in the Spec Ops community used combat ID marking beacons. It didn't matter if you were American, Canadian, British, or whomever. The goal was to help ID your position so that you weren't mistaken for the enemy. They also allowed downed pilots and operators caught in unfriendly territory to be more easily located and rescued. They were a great way to mark a structure you might want to come back to, you could also use them to track a vehicle, and Harvath even had a small spool of trip wire he could use to set one off if someone crept inside his perimeter. The fireflies were the Swiss Army Knife of night operations, and Harvath was glad to have snatched a couple from the Golden Conex.

Clicking the cubes onto their nine-volt batteries, Harvath placed one on top of the wall at each corner. Then he took up the watch while Fontaine turned on his radio, switched to the Canadian's frequency, and tried to reach Captain West.

"I don't care if it's a glider with water balloons," Fontaine said once he had reached the man and detailed their position and situation. "Get hold of J3 Air at Bagram and tell them to send whatever they've got. Tell them this is an emergency CAS mission for

Roper Six Nine. We're also going to need a medevac. I've got a man down, multiple GSWs."

West put Fontaine on hold while he spoke with his combat controller and then radioed the operations and planning unit at Bagram Air Base who were responsible for air support.

Daoud walked over and stood on the other side of the window from Harvath with one of the AK-47s.

"Do you know how to use that thing?" asked Harvath.

"Yes," replied the interpreter.

"Good. Single shots only. And choose them carefully. We could be here a long time."

Daoud nodded.

"If you want Mr. Gallagher's night vision goggles, go ask. He's not going to be using them."

The interpreter began to walk away, but then stopped. "Mr. Gallagher saved Asadoulah's life. The bullets that hit him were meant for the boy and would have killed him if Mr. Gallagher had not acted. Fayaz too. He is a brave man; a good man. Like you."

"You're mistaken, Mr. Daoud," said Harvath. "I'm not that brave and I'm not that good."

The interpreter smiled. "I think you are. I

470

also think that if we survive this, I will help you find the woman you are looking for. I don't need any more money from you. You can give mine to Mr. Fontaine."

"Don't worry about Fontaine," Harvath replied as he tightened his grip on Gallagher's rifle. "I'll make sure he gets taken care of. Now go get those goggles. I think I see movement out there."

As Daoud walked back over to Baba G, Harvath began to ask Fontaine what the hold-up was, but the Canadian motioned for him to hold on.

"Roger that," he said over the radio. "We've got two IR strobes on top of our position. There's at least seventy-five Taliban along the face of the hill two hundred meters directly west of us. In between us and them are three vehicles, two of which are on fire."

After listening to the response, Fontaine replied, "Copy that," and turned back to Harvath. "We've got a Spectre gunship inbound."

"How long until they're on target?"

"Fifteen mikes."

"How'd you get the call sign, Roper Six Nine?" asked Harvath.

"That's not my call sign," said Fontaine as he shook his head. "It belongs to someone

I know on an American special operations team. He's got high-priority access and we'll get bumped right to the top of the list for air support."

Co-opting someone else's call sign was the kind of outside-the-box thinking Harvath could appreciate. Bringing Fontaine along had absolutely been the right thing to do.

Looking back out the window, Harvath detected movement again. This time, he was certain of it. Massoud's men were closing in. It was going to be the longest fifteen minutes of their lives.

"What about the medevac for Gallagher?" Harvath asked as he flipped up his NODs and focused his rifle on a group of Taliban creeping forward. There were only so many places he and his team could have run and Harvath wasn't surprised at how quickly they had homed in on them.

"West has permission to disengage and roll his company to our location. They're going to establish an LZ at the bottom of the road. A medevac bird is right behind the Spectre."

"Let's do this then," said Harvath, who chose the biggest Taliban member in the approaching pack, took aim, exhaled, and squeezed his trigger.

As the man's head exploded in a shower of

blood, bone, and pink flesh, his associates
hit the ground and began firing their weapons. The fight was back on.

CHAPTER 49

When Harvath finally allowed the three Afghans to start firing, he and Fontaine were running desperately low on ammo.

Enemy tracer rounds lit up the night, and the Taliban machine-gun fire had begun eating away at the little mud hut. Since they retreated to the structure, Massoud's men had fired two RPGs at their position. One had hit the side of the structure and failed to detonate and the other had just missed, detonating against the sheer rock face behind them with a deafening blast and a shower of splintered rock.

The first of their weapons to run dry was Gallagher's sniper rifle. Harvath was now down to half a mag for his MP5 and the AC-130 gunship had yet to arrive.

Massoud's Taliban soldiers had moved their heavy, belt-fed machine guns down from the hillside and had set up on top of the road, not far from the burning trucks. Another contingent had split off in an attempt to flank them, but Harvath and Fontaine had immediately put down that attack.

To his credit, Gallagher repeatedly asked to be propped up in the window so he could get in on the action. He didn't like being sidelined when they were so outnumbered. The first two times, Harvath told him no, but at the third request, he began to seriously consider it. They were going to be down to fighting with their pistols very soon. Harvath would have given his entire fee for this assignment for a box of ammo or a couple of frag grenades.

As they began shooting, the three Afghans amazed Harvath with both their discipline and their accuracy, especially the chief elder. This was obviously not Fayaz's first gun battle. Though they weren't expert marksmen by any stretch of the imagination, the trio had managed to inflict a respectable number of casualties.

Even though it felt like they had been fighting for hours, the Afghans seemed to run out of ammunition way too soon. One by one, their weapons fell silent and the men stepped away from their firing positions and sat down. Whether they were simply trying to stay out of the way of Harvath and Fontaine, who were still fighting, or had resigned themselves to what they felt was the inevitable, Harvath had no idea.

Then his own weapon fell quiet. He leaned his MP5 in the corner next to him and switched to his Glock.

Fontaine continued to calmly relay their increasing need for close air support to the Canadian combat controller in the armored column that was racing to get to their location.

Outside the window, Harvath could see Taliban crawling all over. In another minute, they'd be overrun. Raising his pistol, Harvath fired and nailed one of the soldiers in the throat, dropping him gurgling to the ground.

"One minute," Fontaine finally yelled when he got word the Spectre gunship was almost on station.

"We don't have one minute!" Harvath yelled back.

Suddenly, there was the sound of a pistol being fired behind them. Harvath and Fontaine spun to see that Gallagher had drawn his Taurus and capped two Taliban who somehow, despite the sheer rock wall their structure's missing fourth wall opened up to, had managed to breach the rear of their perimeter.

"Tell the waitress to hurry up with my

beer," Gallagher managed to croak out, before being overcome by a fit of bloody coughing.

Fayaz tried to relieve Gallagher of his pistol, but the Marine would have none of it. "Get your own gun," he said, the red froth building at the corners of his mouth.

The chief elder seemed to understand the joke. Giving the injured man a small smile, he sat down next to him and helped him support the weight of the weapon as they kept watch for any more Taliban who might try to sneak up on them from behind.

"Thirty seconds!" yelled Fontaine.

Harvath surveyed the short distance that separated them from their enemy and, double-tapping another approaching Taliban, he yelled back over the sound of gunfire, "This is going to be close."

"Fifteen seconds! Everyone take cover!"

When the heavily armed AC-130 Spectre gunship joined the fight, the effect was obvious, and instantaneous. Specifically designed for ground attack, the heavily armed aircraft was one of the most devastating pieces of weaponry that could be brought to bear on the battlefield.

When it came to what specific weapons were used, it was "dealer's choice," meaning that Harvath was able to relay through Fontaine and the Canadian combat controller exactly what he wanted. Because the Taliban were not only on the hillside, but also rapidly encroaching on their position, Harvath was very precise. Though the Spectre's 20mm Gatling gun could crank out eighteen hundred rounds a minute, the fire could be wildly inaccurate. Harvath had been in this position before and he knew exactly what he wanted.

The thirteen-person crew of the Spectre, call sign Flash 22, announced their arrival to the party with two ear-splitting 105mm M102 howitzer rounds fired directly into the top of the rocky hillside. It had exactly the effect Harvath had hoped for — a rock slide that sent a mob of Taliban tumbling ass-over-eyelids downhill in a panicked hundred-yard dash to get to safety.

When the Taliban started running, that's when Harvath's second request was put into action.

In the space of thirty seconds, the Spectre's rapid-fire, single-barreled 40mm Bofors cannon rained down a deadly hail of devastating rounds. Taliban soldiers were sliced in half, their bodies left to peel off and collapse in two different directions. Limbs were scattered in multiple directions and the entire hillside, as well as all of the earth up to only a few meters from the structure where Harvath and his team were taking cover, was completely shredded. It looked like a stampede of ten thousand horses, all shod with razor blades, had come barreling through and had cut down everything in their path. The only thing left behind was the smell of burnt earth and charred flesh hanging in the air.

High overhead, the AC-130 flew in a race-track-like orbit.

"The Spectre is going to stay on station, right?" asked Harvath as he crept back to the window with his Glock and peered out with his NODs.

"Are you kidding me?" said Fontaine. "Flash 22 has a brand-new crew. This is the first time they've loosed any steel on the Taliban. Half of them are probably up-loading the video of that first volley to their MySpace pages right now."

"So we're good for another rake?"

"We can have as many as we want tonight until they either run out of ammo or run out of fuel. My money's on their running out of ammo. Are you seeing anything out there I need to draw their attention to?"

Harvath strained his ears once more. "There are definitely people still alive out there. I'm hearing voices just north of us."

"Roger that," said Fontaine as he went back to communicating with Captain West's combat controller over the radio. He repeated that they had "danger close" and that the Spectre crew was clear to use their own night vision to engage any targets outside the mud brick building with the IR strobes atop.

Fontaine then turned back and said, "Thirty seconds."

Harvath instructed everyone to take cover again and crawled away from the window.

When Flash 22 reengaged, they did so once again with a vengeance from their Bofors.

After the Spectre ceased firing, Harvath retook his post at the window. He couldn't hear or see anything moving outside. Fontaine spoke with the Canadian combat controller again and then joined him.

"Flash 22 says we're the only thing they can still see moving, but they're going to remain on station for us," he said.

"Good. How about that helicopter?" asked Harvath.

"West's team is en route. ETA is less than five minutes. They'll have the LZ secured and the helo will be on the ground by the time we get to the bottom of the road. They're sending two LAVs up to meet us."

"With their medic, right?"

"That's affirmative," replied Fontaine.

Harvath looked at Gallagher and said, "Are you ready to rock and roll, buddy?"

Baba G attempted a smile and flashed Harvath a halfhearted thumbs-up. Raising his arm caused him to start coughing pink froth again. They didn't have a lot of time, and while Harvath didn't like the idea of moving him, he liked the idea of wasting what little time Gallagher might have even less.

With Harvath covering him, Daoud crept out the back of the mud hut and retrieved the weapons of the two Taliban Gallagher had killed.

There was no comfortable way to carry Gallagher with his collapsed lung. All they could do for him was to try to get him back up to the road as quickly and as safely as possible. Harvath opted for the superman carry again, but this time, instead of Fontaine manning Baba G's right arm, Fayaz insisted it be him. He considered it an honor.

Harvath nodded, and he and Fontaine switched places. While not exceptionally fast, Harvath figured the old man was probably up to the task. And, for the little amount of speed they were giving up, they were gaining a lot more security. Having Fontaine free to accurately fire one of the AKs Daoud had just retrieved instead of relying on his pistol while carrying Gallagher would make a big difference.

Removing his knife, Harvath cut two strips of fabric from Asadoulah's *patoo.* He then retrieved the two IR strobes and secured one to Baba G and the other to Daoud. He wanted everyone, especially the Canadian troops and the American Air Force crew of Flash 22, to be able to see their party through their night vision devices and know that these were the good guys.

Once everyone was ready, Fontaine radioed the Canadian combat controller that they were about to move and then Harvath gave the actual command to move out.

Five meters outside the mud hut, the carnage was instantly evident. Dead Taliban were everywhere. Had Flash 22 taken even a few seconds more to get there, Harvath and his team would have been totally overrun.

As they moved toward the road, Harvath reminded himself to *scan and breathe, scan and breathe.* Though he found it difficult to imagine that anyone could have survived two passes by the Spectre, it wasn't impossible.

When they finally reached the road, the scent of burnt flesh and scorched earth was replaced by the smell of the exploded vehicles. The noxious black smoke, a stomach-churning mixture of charred metal, flaming tires, and burning gasoline, was carried on the wind to the place where they now took cover.

"How far out is West?" asked Harvath, as he tried to help position Gallagher so he didn't have to breathe the fumes.

Fontaine spoke into his radio and replied, "They've got two LAVs securing the LZ and the other two coming up the road right now."

Harvath collected both IR strobes and used one to mark their exact position; he crept out from behind their cover and placed the second in the middle of the road.

Less than a minute later, he heard the roar of the enormous Canadian LAVs as they thundered up the road.

All of West's men were switched on and ready to fight. The LAV gunners watched for any sign of movement, while the rest of the soldiers poured out onto the road and took up defensive firing positions.

A stretcher was rushed over and Gallagher was placed upon it. Immediately, the medic went to work assessing his injuries. He then took his vitals while another Canadian soldier started an IV.

The medic studied the makeshift tourniquet and, as it was doing its job, decided to leave it in place. He then turned his attention to Baba G's other wound.

Cutting away Gallagher's jacket and tunic, they then removed his armor and the medic cut through his T-shirt beneath, fully exposing Baba G's left side. Though his pulse was thready, the medic gave him a couple of cc's of morphine anyway and then applied a topical anesthetic to the space between his ribs where he was going to need to open him up.

"This is going to hurt," he said to the Marine, and then asked Harvath and Fontaine as well as two other Canadian soldiers to help hold him down.

When the medic used the scalpel to slice between Gallagher's second and third ribs, the man's body seized. He was on minimal morphine, and though the procedure was incredibly painful, he didn't cry out.

The medic worked quickly, inserting the chest tube and feeding it into Gallagher's collapsed lung. As soon as the tube was in place, the medic began his "9 Line" medevac procedure, calling out the patient details to a radio operator, who fed them to the inbound helicopter pilots over the medical freq and told them everything they needed to know about their landing zone, as well as the patient they were going to be transporting.

Once the medic had Gallagher's lung re-inflated, he informed his superior that they were ready to move the patient.

The LAVs were an extremely tight squeeze, but they managed to get everyone inside and once the hatches were closed, they took off for the landing zone at the bottom of the road.

Sitting atop a marker panel with twin door gunners, the two other Canadian LAVs and the balance of Captain West's team for added security, was a UH-60Q Black Hawk. Its rotors were hot and its crew ready to transport Gallagher to the trauma bay of the Craig Joint-Theater Hospital at Bagram Air Base.

Fontaine and Harvath helped load Gallagher aboard the bird. As they did, Baba G opened his mouth and tried to speak. Harvath had trouble hearing him over the roar of the helicopter blades chopping up the night air. He bent down so his ear was just above the man's mouth.

"Get Asadoulah back to his village. Fayaz too," said Gallagher.

"I will," said Harvath as he took his friend's hand and gave it a squeeze.

Baba G squeezed back and added, "Don't be a cowboy. If you can't get Gallo out safely, make the trade."

"Sir," interrupted the flight medic, addressing Harvath. "We need to get going."

Harvath let go of Gallagher's hand and said to the medic, "You take care of him."

"Will do, sir," said the man.

Harvath flashed Gallagher a final thumbs-up and stepped away from the chopper.

Joining Fontaine near one of the Canadian LAVs, he watched as the Black Hawk medevac lifted off and headed toward Bagram. They never saw anyone else from the village. No matter how honorable its inhabitants were, they all knew better than to involve themselves in a Taliban firefight.

Once the chopper was clear, Captain West approached and, pointing at Harvath and Fontaine, said, "I don't know what the fuck is going on, but unless you two have a phone number for a Taliban taxi service, you'd better start talking or I'm going to leave both of your asses right here."

CHAPTER 50

Washington, D.C.

Elise Campbell had several pieces of the puzzle, but no matter how she spun them, she still couldn't get them to fit together.

The night Nikki Hale died, she might or might not have been drinking with the president. Whatever the case, when she left, according to Max Holland, she didn't appear drunk. Todd Hutchinson was the next to see her, and he claimed the same thing. She might have been a little flushed when she left, but she didn't tumble down the stairs or weave on her way out the door, so according to him, he had no way of knowing if she was drunk. This despite the fact that she had apparently been drinking with the first lady.

But the most inexplicable pieces of the puzzle were Porter's accusation that Hutchinson and Hale had something going on between them and the fact that Hutchinson had looked Elise right in the face and lied to her. She was certain of it. Those microexpressions hadn't been a figment of her imagination.

Porter claimed to have seen them groping each other by the garage that night, just as Nikki Hale was leaving. He'd also seen them exchange a very intense kiss. Setting aside the fact that such behavior from a Secret Service agent, especially while on duty, was incredibly unprofessional, if Porter was telling the truth, then Hutchinson had to have known how wasted she was. Even so, he still let her go that night. Why?

And what was the president's role in all of this? What had he done that Stephanie Gallo could threaten to bring down his presidency with?

Somehow, he had not been honest about the events of that night. Elise had hoped she could ferret out the information from witness statements in the police reports, but with Hale dead, none had been taken.

Elise's attention then shifted to the people who could fill in the blanks. As she couldn't directly confront the president, she had approached Max, and he had pointed her toward Hutch, and because of that, another piece of the puzzle had been set on the table by Matt Porter.

Still, Elise's intuition kept drawing her back to the president. Gallo had accused him of being involved in Nikki Hale's death and participating in a cover-up. A cover-up by definition was an attempt to obscure or divert attention from the facts. In the absence of any statements made to the police, there was only one other way Elise could imagine the president might have attempted to conceal what had happened that night.

A forty-five-minute meeting with Nikki Hale, regardless of what they had been doing and even *if* they had been drinking, would not be enough to lose Alden the presidency. And as damaging as an affair's becoming public might be, it wouldn't be enough to force him from office. To lose the presidency, a crime would have to have been committed, and even then, it might not be enough to completely shove him out. For that to happen, the crime would have to be so scandalous that even someone as masterful with the press as Alden was couldn't spin it.

But Elise Campbell still believed that President Alden was a good man. Despite what people wanted to pin on him and the aspersions they loved to cast, having an attractive woman in charge of your Internet campaign wasn't a crime, nor was having a beautiful and powerful donor cum media ally. Just because he had working relationships with attractive women didn't mean he was sleeping with them.

Elise looked down at the telephone number Christine De Palma had texted her from East Hampton. Along with it was a five-word message; *He's waiting for your call.*

Highlighting the digits, Campbell selected the option to dial and waited. Three rings later, Herb Coleman answered the phone at his home in Naples, Florida.

"Mr. Coleman, this is Elise Campbell. Christine De Palma told you I would be calling?"

"Yes, she did," said Herb Coleman. He had a calm and relaxing voice. "I'd ask you what I can do for you, but Chris already explained everything to me."

"I want to make sure that you also know that this is all off the record and you are under no obligation to speak with me."

"But you're operating within your capacity as a Secret Service agent, so this is somewhat official, isn't it?"

Elise took a deep breath. "Mr. Coleman, I wouldn't blame you if you hung up on me right now. Ms. De Palma was very clear that your settlement agreement with Mrs. Gallo and President Ald—"

"*Senator* Alden," corrected Coleman. "He wasn't president yet when all of this happened."

"Correct. He was not yet president when this happened. Nevertheless, as part of your settlement you're required not to talk about the case in any way."

"Agent Campbell, I'm not going to the papers with any of this, and from what I understand, you've got your own reasons for playing things pretty close to the vest. Alden was under oath when he responded to those interrogatories at the beginning of our lawsuit against him. If he lied in any of them, then that's a felony. That's pretty damn serious. But from a court of public appearance perspective, it'll be a supernova if he did so to cover up what happened that night to our son, our daughter-in-law, and our two little grandchildren."

"So you're prepared to read me the president's answers to your interrogatories?"

"I am," said Herb Coleman, "and I hope you're sitting down. I think you're going to find this very interesting."

CHAPTER 51

Nangarhar Province, Afghanistan

The name of the village they were headed to was Dagar, which in Pashtu meant *open space*. It also meant *battlefield,* which Harvath hoped wasn't going to turn out to be prophetic.

As per Captain West, it had been Fontaine's idea to mushroom him, and as much as Harvath regretted having to feed the guy so much BS and keep him in the dark, they had no choice. Until Julia Gallo was recovered, operational security was of primary importance.

This wasn't the first time Harvath had lied to get what he needed. It was just how the game worked. If West had been in his shoes, he would have done the same thing. Sometimes, the ends did in fact justify the means. It was the height of moral folly to play by a set of self-imposed rules when your enemy played by none whatsoever. While Harvath would readily admit that rules were important, there were also times when they weren't, and this was one of them.

Harvath stuck to the same story they had told West in the beginning and kept his embellishments as simple as possible from there. While they did get their interpreter out of the first village, he informed them, the al-Qaeda bomber they were after had fled. They had proceeded to Massoud's village to gather more info on the bomber and his Taliban accomplice only to be ambushed on their way out. Now they wanted to hit Dagar in the hopes of getting up to Massoud's summer grazing pasture to confirm that the bomber was there, and either take the men into custody or call in another airstrike to make sure they never carried out another attack.

Whether West fully believed Harvath was beside the point. Wiping out seventy-plus Taliban fighters and helping to weaken a local Taliban commander was a good thing, regardless of who got the credit for it. Taking out forty or fifty more would only run up the score and make for a much better night. West only wished his men could help.

Understanding that he couldn't roll his armored column right through Dagar and that even if he could, he'd have considerable difficulty actually getting his men to the final objective, Captain Chris West proved that he and the Canadians were true partners in the international war on terror by offering Harvath anything else he needed.

Harvath eagerly accepted the help. West and his team transported them back to Asadoulah's village, where Fayaz provided a Toyota pickup truck and offered to send along as many armed men as the vehicle could carry.

While the idea of having extra men was appealing, Harvath declined. He did, though, accept the truck and promised to have it returned as soon as he was done. It was exceedingly generous of Fayaz, considering the fact that the village had just lost two vehicles in a firefight and would need to return to reclaim their dead.

From the Canadians, Harvath took as much ammo for Gallagher's sniper rifle, the MP5s, and his and Fontaine's pistols as could be spared. He also changed out the batteries in their NODs and was extra-grateful when West handed them several fragmentation grenades.

Daoud knew Dagar, so they let him drive the truck while Harvath rode shotgun and Fontaine sat in back.

"So how do you know Dagar?" asked Harvath as they drove.

"I have a friend there," said the interpreter. "We grew up in the same refugee camp in Pakistan. We used to play cricket together."

"Would your friend be willing to help us?"

"He is a good man," replied Daoud. "He doesn't like al-Qaeda and he does not like the Taliban. He will help us."

"I hope he can help us to some coffee," Fontaine added from the backseat.

Harvath looked at his watch and then rubbed his eyes. It was well after midnight, his back was throbbing again, and he was out of Motrin. Baba G's med kit had gone up in flames with his Land Cruiser. The only things he wanted as much as finding Julia Gallo were a hot shower, a stiff drink, and a soft bed. In fact, despite how grimy he was, he'd be glad to forgo the shower and move right to the drink and the bed.

In order not to focus on his fatigue, he tried to envision again what Julia Gallo was going through. The fact that she had scratched her initials into her previous cell meant that she had remembered her training. That was a good sign. Harvath hoped she also remembered the part about keeping her spirits up and not allowing herself to slip into depression as she imagined the worst that might befall her. It was an easy lesson to teach, but much more difficult to actually put into practice.

As the truck, with its worn-out shocks, bounced and jostled toward Dagar, Harvath closed his eyes and allowed his mind to rest. He knew all too well that the next couple of hours were going to be extremely tense and most likely, extremely dangerous. Fontaine and Daoud seemed to be thinking the same thing, as both men were silent for the rest of the ride.

A deep pothole a kilometer outside the village drew Harvath's mind back to the here and now.

"I'm sorry about that," said Daoud. "I couldn't avoid it."

"That's okay," replied Harvath. "Are we close?"

"Yes, we're very close now."

"Fontaine?" said Harvath looking into the backseat. "You up?"

"No," replied the Canadian.

"Too bad. I think I just saw a Molson sign."

"Well, when you see one for Labatt's, we'll stop. Until then, leave me alone."

Harvath smiled, turned back around, and

checked his weapon, knowing full well Fontaine was doing the same. He was an exceptional operator and, like Harvath, was now 100 percent switched on.

Turning to Daoud, Harvath said, "Are you ready to make the call?"

The interpreter nodded and pulled out his phone. Scrolling through the address book as he balanced it on the steering wheel, he found the number and connected the call. Within two rings, his old cricket pal was on the other end and they were chatting as if Daoud had called him in the middle of the day rather than the middle of the night. At one point, the chubby interpreter began laughing.

Eventually he rang off and slid the phone back into his pocket.

"Is everything okay?" asked Harvath.

"Fine," said Daoud with a smile. "He is waiting for us at his home."

Harvath wondered if Daoud had extended an apology for waking up his friend's wife. Then he remembered where he was. TIA.

CHAPTER 52

Daoud's boyhood friend was a short, whip-thin man named Reshteen. He had widely set brown eyes, a flat, thick nose, and a bushy beard dyed henna red.

He ushered his guests into his home and quickly shut the door behind them. They removed their shoes and entered the living room, where two of Reshteen's young sons were laying out small dishes of cold food and a pot of warm tea. The room was lit by a small oil lamp, which threw off just about as much heat as the old, rusted stove in the corner. They had come up considerably in altitude and Harvath could feel the cold seeping right into his bones despite the clothing he was wearing.

Daoud and Reshteen spoke for several minutes while Harvath studied their faces. He could follow the direction of their conversation simply by their expressions. He had always been good at reading people, but his time at the Secret Service had taken him to a completely different level.

He could tell they were talking about Massoud and the Taliban now. Both men had become very serious. Daoud was doing most of the talking, while Reshteen seemed to respond only with one- or two-word answers.

Turning to Harvath, Daoud stated, "The men passed through here in two groups, several hours apart, but they all went to the same place."

"The grazing pasture," replied Harvath.

The interpreter nodded.

Flash 22 had done a high-altitude pass on their way back to Bagram and had relayed everything back over the radio to Fontaine as they made their way to Dagar. If Reshteen had said that the Taliban weren't here, or that he hadn't seen anything, then they would have had a problem. *So far so good.*

"Did he see Dr. Gallo? An American woman with red hair?"

"In one of the first trucks that came through there were two women in burkas."

Two women? Did the Taliban have more than one female hostage? Had they brought along a woman to watch over Dr. Gallo? Harvath doubted it. Watching Julia was the job of Massoud's retarded brother, Zwak. Most likely, the Russian had put Julia in a burka to disguise her appearance and had dressed up Zwak or one of Massoud's other men in a burka as well. That way they'd be a lot less obvious. People would remember a bunch of Taliban riding around with one woman, but two was less suspicious, especially when they were trying to make their getaway as discreetly as possible. That was what Harvath would do, and he was willing to bet the Russian thought along the same lines.

Just for clarification, Harvath asked, "Do the Taliban normally bring women with them?"

"No, they don't," replied Daoud. "They also never come at this time of year."

That was enough for Harvath. What he needed now was someone to guide them to a position where they could observe Massoud's camp without being discovered. He put the question to Daoud and waited for the man to speak with Reshteen and translate his response.

"He says it is impossible," the interpreter finally responded. "The road passes through a narrow canyon and the pasture is surrounded by sheer cliffs."

"There has got to be some way."

"Only if you come over the mountain from the other side, but even then there are very few places to hide. Massoud chose the location very carefully."

"The pasture abuts part of the Tora Bora cave complex," offered Harvath. "Do any of the caves interconnect? Could we somehow approach that way?"

The interpreter spoke with his friend. After a brief exchange, Daoud reported, "Some of the villagers know the caves, but none of them will go into them for fear of booby traps. They say only the al-Qaeda know which tunnels are truly safe."

On a whim, Harvath asked about the Lake of Broken Glass and if Reshteen had ever heard of it or seen anyone in the area with SCUBA equipment.

"Na," the man answered.

Harvath wasn't surprised. It would have been the ultimate irony if Massoud and the Russian had gone to all this trouble only to discover they'd been sitting atop bin Laden's pot of gold the entire time.

Fontaine nudged Harvath. "What's the Lake of Broken Glass?"

"It's a wives' tale," replied Harvath. "Something that might have to do with where bin Laden hid his money."

"Where'd you hear about it?"

"Like I said, it's a wives' tale," replied Harvath, who, despite all of Fontaine's help, still had no desire to read him in on how he and Gallagher had snatched Mustafa Khan from the Afghan government.

Changing the subject, Harvath ran through their options once more aloud. "Now, since there's only one road into Massoud's camp, that doesn't sound like it is going to work for us. The tunnels are too dangerous and we couldn't find a guide even if we wanted one. There's only sparse cover on the rock faces around the pasture, and to get to those, we've got to come over the mountains from the other side. At this point, it sounds like that is our only option."

"Maybe not," replied Daoud, who had been simultaneously translating as Harvath spoke. He waited for Reshteen to finish saying something to him and then stated, "There may be a way you can use the road."

"What do you mean?"

Reshteen spoke for several more moments and then Daoud said, "As I told you, my friend does not like the Taliban or al-Qaeda. Neither do the people of his village. But they are not stupid. If he helps you, he knows what could happen to him and the rest of the people in Dagar."

"Please tell your friend that I don't like al-Qaeda or the Taliban either, and I am willing to make this worth his while, but we have to keep this quiet. I don't want to run this through his *shura*. We're too close now."

Daoud smiled. "He does not want to run it through his *shura* either."

"So what does he want?"

"He wants the summer grazing pasture."

"Does he want me to help buy it for him?" replied Harvath. "Because it is not mine to give."

Daoud's smile remained as he said, "I have told him of your relationship with Massoud's *shura* and in particular with the elder, Baseer. This grazing pasture once belonged to Reshteen's grandfather, but he lost it to the Taliban when he couldn't pay his debts. Reshteen's family still graze their flocks there in the summer, but Massoud charges very heavy fees for it.

"After what you did to Massoud's men already this evening, I have told Reshteen that I have every confidence you can do so again. If you defeat Massoud, you will be able to convince Baseer to return the pasture to its rightful owner."

"First of all," said Harvath, pointing at his own eyes to emphasize the point, "I only want to go up there to look."

"For the woman," replied Daoud.

"Exactly. Once we confirm that she is indeed there, we'll consider our options and

503

decide what our next move should be."

"*Na, na, na,*" replied Reshteen as Daoud translated.

"What's wrong?"

"He says he has an idea, but you would have to leave very soon."

Something like this was extremely dangerous to rush into. "Let's hear his idea, first."

Daoud spoke to Reshteen and then listened as the man laid out his plan. Then he relayed the information to Harvath. "There are many Taliban up at Massoud's camp. At least forty men. They came in a hurry, with very little supplies. They have no fuel for cooking or heating the buildings there. They have no food and no water."

A smile spread across Harvath's face. "And let me guess," he said. "They asked Reshteen to gather these things and bring them to them."

Daoud's head bobbed from side to side and he turned his palms upward. "They asked Reshteen's cousins, but it is the same thing. Reshteen will be one of the men traveling up to the camp to deliver the supplies."

"Will he take us with him?" asked Harvath.

"If you promise him you will take care of Massoud and that he will get the pasture, he will take you."

Harvath, who was sitting across from the Afghans, leaned forward and said, "Once I have the girl, I guarantee you I will take care of Massoud. And once that is done, I will do everything in my power to get that grazing pasture returned to his family or I will buy him another, even better pasture."

As Daoud translated, Reshteen tugged at his red beard. Slowly, a smile began to form at the edges of his lips.

When the man finally nodded, indicating they had a deal, Harvath said, "Now let's talk about how exactly Reshteen is going to get us up there."

CHAPTER 53

Annandale, Virginia

Elise Campbell took a deep breath and knocked on Todd Hutchinson's faded front door. When he didn't answer, she began knocking louder.

Finally, a shadow passed behind the peephole and there was the scrape of the chain being undone, followed by the sound of the dead bolt unlocking.

Hutchinson must have been down in his basement, working out. "Campbell?" he said, standing there in a pair of gym shorts and a tight T-shirt. "What are you doing here?"

Elise had never before noticed how well built her colleague was. "We need to talk," she said, as she brushed past him and entered his home uninvited.

"Come on in. I guess," said Hutch as he closed and locked the door behind her.

Campbell had purposefully worked herself into a lather on the drive down from D.C. The more emotional she appeared, the harder it would be for him to read her. "Why'd you lie to me?"

"Wait a second, calm down. What are you talking about?"

"I'm talking about you and Nikki Hale."

Hutchinson was about to say something, but then stopped himself. Abandoning his response, he asked, "What *about* me and Nikki Hale?"

"Do you think I'm stupid, Hutch? Did you think nobody was going to know?"

"Know what?" demanded the man. "You're talking in circles."

"The night Nikki Hale died, you had sex with her."

No sooner had the accusation sprung from her lips than the microexpression Campbell had witnessed in Lafayette Park was back on Hutchinson's face.

"You're out of your mind," he stated.

"Really?" bluffed Campbell, removing the Suffolk County medical examiner's form from her pocket. "Not only were you dumb enough to screw her, you were dumb enough to leave your DNA behind."

Hutchinson snatched the form away from her. "That's insane. Let me see that."

"I've got a witness that saw you playing grab-ass with her near the guesthouse."

"Who?"

"Never mind who. Did you and Nikki have an ongoing relationship, or was this just a one-nighter?"

"This is bullshit," said Hutchinson as he crumpled the ME's form and tossed it across the room. "I want you to leave."

"If this is all bullshit, you've got nothing to lose by answering my questions, do you?"

"What's the point? You've already made up your mind."

"The point is, five people died that night and you know something you're not telling me. If I have to drag your relationship with Nikki Hale into the light of day to get some answers, believe me, I'm going to do it."

Hutchinson grabbed the back of his neck with his right hand and lowered his eyes to the floor.

"You've got thirty seconds, Hutch," said Campbell.

"It was a mistake," he said, walking over to his couch and sitting down. "She came on to me. I guess that should have told me right there how wasted she was."

"So you *were* with her," said Elise.

Hutchinson nodded.

"You left Mrs. Alden alone?"

"No."

Campbell remained standing and looked down at him. "You're not making any sense."

"The president's detail was with her."

"How is that possible? You said Alden didn't show up at the guesthouse until after Hale had left that night."

"I lied."

Her read of him had been right. "What else did you lie to me about?"

Hutchinson raised his eyes. "I don't want to lose my job, Elise."

"Right about now, I'd say that's the least of your problems."

"You're probably right."

"Tell me what happened that night."

Hutchinson took a deep breath. "Nikki Hale had been upstairs at the guesthouse with the first lady —"

"Drinking."

"Yes. After a while, things got heated and they began arguing. Right about then, the president showed up."

"What happened?"

"He went upstairs, and the argument got worse. Nikki stormed out of the room. She was mad as hell. The first lady yelled at the president to make up his mind. Either Nikki was history or she was."

"So they were having an affair?"

Hutchinson nodded. "As Nikki came down the stairs, she had a few choice words for both of them. Alden had left his agents outside. I was the only one in the guesthouse. He saw me and told me to take Hale to her car and make sure she got the hell off the estate."

"Did the president know she was drunk?"

"He and Mrs. Alden both did, but they didn't care. They wanted her gone."

"And you had an opportunity to take advantage of her," said Campbell, the disdain evident in her voice.

"No, I wanted to find her a ride home," Hutchinson replied. "I was walking her back to the main house, and the kiss just happened. She was pissed off at Alden and she wanted to get back at him. I shouldn't have let it happen. It was unprofessional."

"About as unprofessional as putting a woman that intoxicated into her car and sending her off into the night," said Campbell.

"I told you. I was *trying* to find her a ride."

She didn't believe him. He would have done anything the Aldens asked him to and now she knew why he'd been allowed to stay on the first lady's detail.

"I'm serious," Hutchinson continued. "We were on our way to the main house when Alden came up behind us. Nikki had left her purse behind. Alden was still fuming and he flung it at her. They began arguing again. I tried to tell him that we needed to get her a ride home and he told me to return to my post or he'd have me fired."

"And you chose to follow orders instead of stopping Alden from sending that girl off drunk to kill herself and the Coleman family."

Once again, Hutchinson lowered his eyes to the floor.

There were a million things she wanted to say to the pathetic excuse for a man sitting in front of her, but she couldn't bear the sight of him anymore. Besides, he wasn't the one she needed to settle this with. The man she needed to confront was President Robert Alden.

CHAPTER 54

Nangarhar Province, Afghanistan

Even though Reshteen had lined the space with blankets, Harvath and Fontaine lay in the bed of his truck freezing to death. They were also dangerously close to running out of time. For their plan to work, they had to get in and get out of the camp before sunrise.

They had been hidden beneath a mountain of carefully stacked gear, which had then been lashed down with ropes. As the truck fishtailed up the icy roadway, it hit pothole after pothole and Harvath began to worry less about being discovered and executed by one of Massoud's soldiers and more about being crushed beneath the ton of Taliban cargo swaying above them.

Theirs was one of three trucks making the supply run up to Massoud's outpost. The Taliban commander had ordered up enough supplies for two weeks. If they didn't take advantage of this opportunity, it was unlikely they'd get another chance.

Remembering the evil eye he'd received from the old, black-turbaned man in Surobi, he knew that no matter how authentic their clothing, there was no way he and Fontaine could pass close inspection as villagers from Dagar. Coming in sight unseen was their only bet. Harvath prayed that Massoud's sentries would be like most soldiers standing post overnight — cold, bored, and hungry.

The security setup along the road was similar to that leading into Massoud's village and involved two checkpoints.

When Harvath felt the truck coming to a halt at the first stop, his heart began to quicken and his hands tightened around his MP5. Next to him, he knew Fontaine was readying himself as well. Neither dared speak and they both knew what they would have to do if they were discovered.

Their bodies tense, each of the men listened for any indication that suggested the sentries suspected something was wrong. Despite the bitter cold, Harvath could feel the sweat forming on his skin as the adrenaline dumped into his bloodstream.

He heard Reshteen roll down his window and speak to the Taliban sentries. This was the first and one of the most dangerous hurdles.

Harvath listened as the Afghan did exactly what he had been told to do. Showing the sentries the box on the seat next to him, he offered them some of the hot tea, warm nan bread, and kebabs he had prepared before leaving Dagar.

There was a lull that seemed to last an eternity. Harvath couldn't tell if the sentries suspected a double-cross or were just examining the contents of the box trying to decide what they wanted.

While the optimist in him said the sentries would take the food and allow the trucks to pass without inspection, the pessimist told him to get ready because all hell was about to break loose.

Suddenly the voices resumed and there was laughter. Harvath's inner optimist had been correct. He felt his tension dissolve, but only by a matter of degrees. While the optimist in him had been right this time, it was by listening to the pessimist and always being ready for the worst to happen that one stayed alive.

One of the sentries pounded on the roof of the cab and the trucks were allowed to pass.

At the next checkpoint the scene was repeated. Hot tea was poured into cups, bread and kebabs were handed out by Reshteen, and the supply trucks from the village were once more allowed to pass uninspected.

While Harvath should have been relieved, at the moment he didn't have that luxury. They were about to roll into the middle of a snake pit. Harvath had given Fontaine every excuse to stay behind in Dagar with Daoud, but the Canadian had refused. In fact, he had accused Harvath of selfishly trying to hog all the fun for himself. The remark had made Harvath laugh. Forty to one odds was not what he would call fun. Forty to two was only slightly better. The one thing they had on their side was that, at least for now, no one knew they were coming.

The truck bumped and jostled along for another five minutes before the steep road finally leveled off. When it swung to the left, stopped, and then slowly reversed, Harvath once again tightened his grip around his MP5 and made ready. They had arrived.

CHAPTER 55

Reshteen backed his truck up to the door of the small, mud brick building that functioned as the camp's kitchen. His two cousins parked their trucks on the opposite side to act as a screen and provide Harvath and Fontaine with as much concealment as possible.

Climbing out from behind the wheel, Reshteen stretched and walked casually into the cookhouse to make sure it was empty. Pushing open its heavy wooden door, he removed a box of matches and lit one of the oil lamps that hung inside. The room was just as it had been left following the first heavy snow the year before.

Stepping back outside, Reshteen called his cousins over and they set to work freeing Harvath and Fontaine from the bed of his truck.

When they had moved enough crates, the men slipped out one at a time and disappeared into the cookhouse.

The cousins continued unloading supplies while Reshteen set up two gas cook stoves and quickly warmed up more tea and nan bread. Filling his pockets with cups and wrapping the bread in a heavy cloth, he exited the kitchen and set off to soften the ground for Harvath and Fontaine.

Fifteen minutes later, he returned. Motioning for Harvath to hand him the sketch of the camp he had drawn back in Dagar, he marked on it where the camp's interior guards were posted and how many of them there were in each group. Harvath counted three groups of three. Nine men. The rest were still asleep.

Harvath pointed at the small storage building that Reshteen had said would be the best place to hold Julia Gallo, and the Afghan man nodded and drew a dark circle around it with his pencil. That was still their primary target. It also, according to Reshteen, did not have a guard posted outside it. Considering the Taliban's habit of relying solely on a sturdy, lockable door, Harvath wasn't surprised, but nevertheless he pointed to all the guard positions on the piece of paper and then back at the storage hut and said, *"Na?"*

"Na, Taliban," he replied.

That was all Harvath needed to hear. Checking his weapons, he tucked his MP5 beneath his *patoo,* and with Fontaine right behind him, he stepped out of the cookhouse into the cold mountain air.

The two men walked with their heads down and mimicked the slow, shuffling Afghan gait.

The camp was not that large and all of the guards on duty were aware of the supply truck's arrival. Being greeted by Reshteen with hot tea and warm nan was an act of hospitality that had not only put them somewhat at ease about the strangers in their midst, but had given Harvath and Fontaine reason to get much closer to them than would normally have been allowed.

Expanding upon the ruse they had used at the checkpoints, Reshteen visited each group of guards, handing out tea and nan and promising to send men back with hot kebabs. The hope was that if Harvath and Fontaine were seen, it would be assumed they represented the kebab wagon making its rounds.

Harvath and Fontaine understood the limits of the ruse all too well. They needed to act as quickly as possible.

Reshteen had shown them on his sketch where the Taliban normally set up their latrine. It was a long trench on the side of the camp away from the buildings. Even though the forty-plus men had not been there long, they didn't need a map to find it. Their noses led them right to it.

The trench from last year was still filled with ice and snow that had only partially melted. That didn't seem to bother the Taliban, who simply urinated and defecated right there as if it was a perfectly suitable latrine.

Harvath and Fontaine tried to ignore the smell as they lay down next to it and readied themselves for the next step.

There had been no way to know how many guards Massoud would have posted. Reshteen had said that Massoud normally had men walking the camp, but had never bothered to count how many. He simply had had no reason to.

Though Harvath's original intent had been to come up and ascertain if Julia Gallo was here, he had also decided that if she was, and he could get her out, that's what he was going to do. If it meant he had to kill a few more Taliban in the process, he had no problem doing that.

Harvath traded Fontaine his MP5 for Gallagher's sniper rifle and got comfortable while Fontaine powered up his NODs and slipped them on so he could function as a spotter.

Flipping down the legs of the weapon's bipod, Harvath then flipped up the scope covers, wrapped his hand around the grip, and got his shoulder comfortable against the stock.

"Ready when you are," whispered Fontaine. "Are you getting enough light through the scope?"

While Harvath would have preferred engaging their targets at a much closer range, the chance that someone might hear even the suppressed report of the rifle and raise the alarm was just too great. The other problem was that they were not going to be able to get anywhere close to the building they hoped was holding Gallo without encountering at least one set of guards. And while Harvath had no problem using a knife and getting his hands dirty, the guards were all out in the open. Sneaking up on them would be next to impossible.

"The light's good enough," said Harvath. "Let's go."

Fontaine guided Harvath as best he could and when Harvath was ready, he exhaled and gently applied pressure to the trigger.

His first Taliban target dropped like a stone, and Harvath quickly readjusted and took out his two colleagues. The first man went down instantly as well, but the next man took two shots before he fell to the ground.

Fontaine tsk'd out loud over the need to take a second shot on the third Taliban. Harvath ignored him.

"Group two," he said as he adjusted his position and reoriented himself.

"One shot, one kill this time," said Fontaine.

Harvath raised his middle finger and readjusted his shoulder against the stock. "Call 'em," he said.

Fontaine did, and Harvath took the three men down in rapid succession, all with bullets through their heads.

Handing Fontaine back the rifle, Harvath pulled out his NODs, powered them up, and slipped them on. Once the men had their weapons hidden beneath their *patoos,* they made a line straight for the storage building.

They were traversing open ground on what remained a relatively bright night. If any of Massoud's men had decided to step outside for a breath of fresh air or a visit to their luxury toilet facilities, that would have been the end of everything. Providence, for the moment, appeared to be on their side.

They made it across the open ground without being seen. Creeping up on the structure, Harvath saw it was windowless, just as Reshteen had said it was. Harvath took a step back and studied the outside of the door. A heavy wooden peg held the lock in place.

With one hand still wrapped around the grip of his MP5, Harvath leaned in toward the door and listened. Not a sound came from the other side.

Reaching down, he gently pulled the peg free. As it came out, Harvath exposed his weapon fully and Fontaine did the same. And then, just as they had done in Massoud's village, Fontaine positioned himself to open the door so Harvath could immediately sweep inside.

Harvath took a deep breath and then nodded.

Fontaine drew back the handle, pulled open the door, and Harvath, weapon up and ready, rushed in.

CHAPTER 56

The room was tiny. So tiny, in fact, that Julia Gallo could not even stretch all the way out. Instead, she sat on the dirt floor with her legs drawn up and her arms wrapped around them while she balanced her head upon her knees.

Other than the two wool blankets Zwak had brought her, the only other item in the room was a plastic bucket she was expected to use for her bodily functions. Upon hearing the door slide open, only her heart twitched, the rest of her body was too sore to move.

"Julia," said a voice in the darkness. "Julia Gallo."

Julia was certain that she was dreaming. Either that or she was finally losing her mind. Besides Zwak, only one other person had been to see her, and he had spoken English with a thick, almost Eastern European accent to ask her four very strange questions about her past. The man had then asked her other questions about Zwak and the boys who had accosted her, but this was definitely not his voice. This voice sounded American. It sounded like home.

Bending down, Harvath lifted the woman's head from her knees and looked at her face. Even through his goggles, with her hair wrapped in her hijab, he could tell it was her. "Julia," he repeated. "My name is Scot. Your mother sent us to get you. We're here to take you home."

Home. She didn't want to allow herself to believe it. "Home?" she said. The men's faces were disguised by something, almost as if they were wearing masks.

"Yes," replied Harvath as he slipped a hand underneath her arm and helped her to stand. "Are you okay? Can you walk?"

Gallo quickly realized that she wasn't dreaming; this was in fact real. "Yes," she stammered. "I think so."

"Good. You must remain absolutely quiet and do everything I tell you. Do you understand?"

"Yes," said Julia.

Harvath looked at Fontaine, who had slipped into the room behind him and closed the door. "We're ready to go."

Fontaine nodded and turned around and cracked the door. Glancing outside, he quickly popped his head back in and said, "We've got a problem."

"What is it?" asked Harvath.

"We've got one of Massoud's guys making a beeline straight for us. What do you want to do?"

"Maybe he's going to one of the other structures."

"Negative," said Fontaine. "He's on his way here and he's going to see that bolt is missing."

Harvath unslung his MP5, handed it to Fontaine, and pulled out his knife. "I'll take him when he comes in. You protect Dr. Gallo."

"Roger that," replied Fontaine, as he gently maneuvered Julia into the corner and then stood between her and the door.

No sooner had they done that than Harvath heard footsteps outside. There was the sound of a hand on the outside of the door and then silence. Whoever was out there had discovered that the peg that held the door closed was missing.

Whether the person was hesitant or confused, seconds passed and nothing happened. Finally, the door began to creak open.

Harvath tightened his grip on the knife and prepared to strike.

The door opened farther and as it did, fading starlight and the dying rays of the moon spilled in. As it opened more, the figure of a man holding a rifle was cast in silhouette.

Just a foot more, thought Harvath as he angled the blade of his knife.

The man moved cautiously and continued forward. When the barrel of his rifle was within striking distance, Harvath lunged.

He grabbed the weapon and pulled the man off balance and into the tiny room. Wrenching the rifle from the man's hands, he let it drop to the ground and slammed him up against wall. With his hand covering the man's mouth Harvath pulled the blade back and prepared to strike, but then stopped.

He had felt something wrapped around the barrel of the man's weapon. It had felt like *tape.* Baseer had said Massoud's brother carried an AK-47 with its barrel wrapped with blue tape to let everyone know it wasn't a functioning firearm.

Sheathing his knife, Harvath held the man tight against the wall and whispered for Fontaine to close the door.

As the door closed, Julia said, "Please. He's mentally challenged. Don't hurt him. He protected me."

Looking over his shoulder at Fontaine, he

said, "Shred those blankets. We'll tie him and gag him."

As Fontaine used his knife to cut the blankets in strips, Harvath held Zwak against the wall and kept his mouth covered. The man's entire body was trembling. Harvath once again thought of the SEAL team that had been discovered by the Afghan goatherds. If he knew one thing about combat it was that you could never second-guess what another man had done unless you'd been there with him. He was thankful that he wasn't faced with the same predicament they were.

If they acted fast enough, he hoped, they could be gone before anyone noticed Zwak was missing. He had also given Baseer, the chief elder of Massoud's village, his word that if he encountered Zwak, he would do everything he could to make sure no harm came to the man.

Once they had Zwak gagged, they tied his hands behind his back and then laid him on the floor and hogtied him.

As they did, Zwak began crying. Julia Gallo bent and stroked the side of his face. She spoke reassuringly to him with her limited Pashtu and thanked him once again.

Once she had finished, Harvath took his

MP5 back from Fontaine, clicked his IR strobe onto a battery, and said, "Let's get the hell out of here."

CHAPTER 57

Mullah Massoud Akhund woke up earlier than usual to the sound of his stomach growling. He rolled over and looked at the empty pallet on the floor beside him. Zwak must have gotten up to check on the American woman. He was like a child with an injured bird, and Massoud feared he had grown too attached to her.

The Taliban commander also feared that his brother was holding a grudge. Zwak had not said a word to him since he had arrived at the mountain camp. Massoud knew his brother was angry at him for taking away his basketball shoes, but that was before the Russian had explained what had really happened with Elam Badar's son, Asadoulah. Even though Massoud had promised to return the shoes once they were back home, Zwak still wouldn't speak to him. But it wasn't just the loss of the shoes that had wounded his pride.

In order to cover their tracks, Simonov had insisted Zwak wear a burka, just like the American woman, as they made the drive to the summer grazing pasture. Massoud understood the Russian's logic. He also understood why Zwak had felt emasculated. Some of the soldiers had teased Zwak afterward and though the Russian had reprimanded them harshly, Zwak felt ashamed and the stern rebuke of the soldiers did nothing to repair his bruised ego.

Massoud wondered how much his brother had slept during the night, if at all. Though he might have stepped outside to relieve himself, he was most likely checking on the woman. He was incredibly protective. Massoud wondered if his brother understood that he felt exactly the same way about him. That was why he found so many important jobs for him to do. *Whether he did or whether he did not,* reasoned the Taliban commander, *Allah knew.*

Rising from his thin bedroll, Mullah Massoud stepped past the sleeping soldiers crammed one on top of the other, quietly opened the door, and slid outside. They had much to do today and he knew he wouldn't be able to fall back asleep. Besides, it was good for his men to see him up so early. It would set a good example.

He walked toward the small hut they were using to hold the woman and looked for Zwak. Except for when he slept or when he prayed, he had not been far from the woman the entire time she had been their prisoner.

Massoud walked around the building and, not seeing his brother, wondered if maybe he was inside with the woman. He knew the two had developed a relationship. And while he didn't think it was wise, he found it difficult to discourage his brother from speaking with her. He knew what his duty was and he also knew that no matter how much kindness she showed him, she would never be able to charm Zwak into setting her free. He was all too aware of the shame that would bring on the entire family. It was far beyond having your basketball shoes taken away or being forced to disguise yourself in a burka.

Completing a full turn around the little outbuilding, Massoud stopped at the door, wondering if Zwak might be inside, but then saw that the wooden peg that held the door locked was firmly in place. Zwak had to be either at the latrine or in the cookhouse trying to get something to eat before morning prayers.

Feeling the urge himself to urinate, Massoud headed toward the trench. If Zwak was there, he hoped that sleep had softened the stone in his heart and that he might be ready to talk.

One of the strange ironies of night was that it always seemed coldest right before the first rays of the sun pierced the darkness to touch the earth. The Taliban commander pulled his *patoo* tighter around his shoulders and readjusted the angle of his AK-47.

Looking up as he walked, he regarded the stars and almost believed he could see them twinkling out one at a time, like tiny lamps being extinguished in the sky as daylight arrived to relieve them. Shifting his eyes away from the sky and back to the path he was walking, he saw something. Though his mind raced for an alternative explanation, he knew even from this distance what he was seeing; dead bodies.

The fear that they had been discovered was surpassed by an even greater fear. *Was one of them his brother?*

Abandoning all concern for his own life, Massoud charged toward the mass of corpses. Two of the bodies were face up with bullets through their heads and he could immediately see that neither was Zwak. Though the third man was obviously too tall to be his brother, Massoud still bent and rolled him over. The lifeless eyes of his lieutenant stared up past him. *Where was Zwak?*

While the kitchen seemed an obvious place to look, Massoud's instincts as a commander were starting to take over and his gut drew him back to the storage hut. If the men from Elam Badar's village had come to make war, they could have begun by quietly taking out the sentries, but that's not what was happening here. This was about the woman. It was a rescue attempt of some sort; he could feel it. And if he was right, the moment she was safely away, the skies would open and all kinds of hell would rain down upon them.

Gripping his AK-47 now, Massoud ran back to the hut, pulled the peg from the lock, and pushed open the door. It took his eyes a moment to adjust, and then he saw his brother bound and gagged on the floor.

The Taliban commander bent down, removed his brother's gag, and set to work on the strips binding his wrists and feet behind his back.

"No crying," he ordered. "Not now, Zwak. What happened?"

The admonition had no effect.

Massoud withdrew a small knife and cut him loose. Helping Zwak to his feet, the Taliban commander grabbed his brother's face in his hands and held it. "It is okay, Zwak. No one is going to hurt you," he said. "You need to show courage. You need to be a warrior now and tell me. Where is the American woman?"

The mentally challenged man's breaths came in short, sharp stabs. "They took her," he managed to choke out.

"How many?"

"Two."

The first thing that came to Massoud's mind was that he had been sold out. Someone in his organization had double-crossed him so they could ransom the woman back themselves. "Did they speak? Did you hear their language? Was it Dari? Pashtu?"

"Na," said Zwak. "They spoke her language. English."

Massoud's heart began pounding even faster, and he willed himself to calm down. That could mean anything. "Did you see their faces?"

"Na," repeated the mentally challenged man. "They had no faces. Only mouths," he stammered as he pantomimed holding a pair of binoculars up to his eyes.

Night vision goggles, thought the Taliban commander. Had he been sold out to an ANA commando unit? Or worse, had the Americans somehow found them and sent in a special operations team?

As quickly as the thought entered his mind, Massoud pushed it away. If this was the work of the Americans, he and his men would be dead by now. Once they recovered the woman, they would have come into the camp and killed everything that moved.

That was another thing; he had not heard any helicopter. Whoever had done this could have only come in via vehicle or by foot.

Removing his cell phone, Massoud turned it on and stepped nearer to the doorway to get a signal. Though many new towers had been built in Khogyani, reception, especially at the mountain camp, could be spotty.

Holding the phone outside, he was finally able to lock on to a tower. Remaining in the shadow of the doorway, he called down to his roadside checkpoint nearest the village.

A man named Mohambar answered on the third ring. The connection was terrible.

"No," the sentry shouted into his phone. "Only the three trucks from Dagar a half hour ago. We have seen nothing since."

"And where are those trucks now?' asked the commander.

"Please repeat?"

"Where are those trucks now?"

"Still at the camp with you."

That had to be it. After ordering his men not to let anything pass, Massoud disconnected the call and slid the phone back into his pocket. He didn't need to press his brother any further. The bodies of the men outside were still warm. Considering the temperature, they couldn't have been dead long. Whoever was behind this had to be connected to those trucks. He had to act fast. They couldn't be allowed to leave.

Making Zwak promise to stay put, he rushed back to the building he'd been sleeping in and woke four of his most trusted bodyguards. Together they moved quickly to the structure next door, where the commander nudged the Russian awake with the toe of his boot.

Rubbing his eyes with the heels of his hands, Simonov sat up and said, "What's going on?"

Massoud signaled for him to be quiet and whispered, "We have a problem."

CHAPTER 58

Reshteen and his cousins had already finished unloading and were busy assembling breakfast when Harvath and Fontaine swept Julia Gallo into the cookhouse.

"Time to leave," said Harvath as he pulled out another IR strobe, attached it to its battery, and tossed it to Fontaine, who walked outside to affix it to the top of Reshteen's truck. Harvath had tossed his other strobe onto the roof of the structure where Zwak lay tied up. Taking him with them was out of the question. The best Harvath could do was to try to shield him from the impending airstrike.

Julia Gallo was looking longingly at the platters of fresh nan and hot kebab, and Reshteen gathered a bunch up and handed them to her.

As the CARE International doctor began hungrily eating, Harvath waved the Afghans toward the door. "There's a 40mm hurricane headed this way and I'd like to beat the traffic. All right by you guys?" he said, though he knew the villagers didn't understand a word of English.

Fontaine returned from taping the strobe to the top of Reshteen's truck and tossed Harvath a heavy black nylon bag. He then stepped back outside with his radio.

Fishing out Gallagher's blood-stained armor, Harvath said to Gallo, "You need to put this on."

He helped her get ready, and as he did, Reshteen and the Afghans went outside to ready their vehicles. Fontaine remained at the door as a lookout.

Harvath had finished cinching up Gallo's armor when Fontaine stuck his head back into the room, said, "Look sharp," and then went back to peering out the doorway.

"What's up?" asked Harvath.

"Company's just arrived."

"More sentries?"

"Negative. I'm looking at a big bushy Afghan with four bodyguards, and either Roman Polanski is thinking of shooting his next film in Khogyani, or I've got eyes on our Russian."

Harvath finished tightening the straps on Gallo's armor and then pointed to where he wanted her to take cover.

Joining Fontaine near the door he asked, "What are they doing?"

"They're having a discussion with Reshteen and his cousins, but they're doing most of the talking. I don't like it."

"Neither do I," said Harvath as he tucked the stock of his MP5 up tighter against his shoulder.

"What's the plan?"

"Let's just relax. Maybe they're only interested in the breakfast menu."

"I doubt that," replied Fontaine.

The two men held their position for several more moments until Fontaine said, "Okay, the bodyguards just raised their weapons and pointed them at Reshteen and the cousins. They're now moving them away from the vehicles toward a wall on the other side. I think they're going to execute them."

Harvath swore under his breath. The last thing they needed was another full-on firefight with the Taliban, especially now, as they were in an even poorer position than they had been before.

"Are you sure?" he asked

"I could be wrong," replied Fontaine. "Let's wait until they pass out the blindfolds and cigarettes."

Harvath was in no mood for the Canadian's sarcasm. "If we open the door far enough for both of us to shoot, can we engage all six targets?"

Fontaine studied the scene outside for a moment. "Negative," he replied. "At this point, I can only see the bodyguards."

"What happened to Polanski and the bushy Afghan?"

"They've stepped out of my line of sight. Maybe they went for reinforcements," said the Canadian. "Listen, the bodyguards are seriously getting ready to wax Reshteen and the cousins. We need to take them out."

"If we take them out, you know what that means."

Fontaine raised his NODs and pressed his rifle against the door frame. "If you're trying to tell me that my application to the Kandahar Country Club might hit a few bumps with the membership committee, I can live with that."

"Just make sure you only hit the bad guys," replied Harvath as he joined Fontaine in the doorway.

"I'll promise if you promise," retorted the Canadian.

Harvath ignored him and gently slid the door open a few more inches. "You take the first two guys. I've got three and four."

"Roger that," whispered Fontaine.

"Now," said Harvath.

Four suppressed shots snapped through the early-morning air in less than two seconds, dropping all four of Massoud's bodyguards. Harvath waited for Massoud and the Russian to step out or return fire, but they did neither. Maybe they had gone for reinforcements. Or maybe they knew what was going on and had wisely taken cover. Harvath didn't care, either way.

"Let's go," he said as he waved for Julia Gallo to join him.

"What about Mullah Shithead and Roman Polanski?" asked Fontaine.

"We don't have the time to wait them out. Go, and I'll cover you."

Reshteen and his cousins were shaken but had enough presence of mind to already be running for the trucks. Harvath admired their courage. Though he didn't speak Pashtu, he knew what Massoud's bodyguards had been interrogating them about. And even though they surely must have known Massoud's men intended to kill them if they didn't get the answers they wanted, none of the villagers from Dagar had cracked. The dignity and honor of the Afghan people never ceased to amaze Harvath.

With Harvath covering them, Fontaine positioned Julia Gallo on the floor of the backseat of Reshteen's truck. "No matter what happens," he warned, "stay down."

Fontaine then got behind the wheel and fired up his truck as Reshteen and his cousins scrambled into the other two vehicles and did the same.

Harvath's NODs were back down now, and noticing movement off to the side of one of the buildings, he let a volley of silenced rounds fly from his MP5 and then hopped into the passenger seat next to Fontaine.

"Hold on," advised the Canadian as he ground the vehicle into gear and punched the accelerator.

The vehicle's tires spun until they were finally able to take a bite out of the frozen road and the truck jerked forward. As they did, the staccato *crack, crack, crack* of automatic-weapons fire filled the early-morning air.

CHAPTER 59

Harvath returned fire through his open window and then, leaning back inside, stated, "We need to call in that CAS right now."

After conducting their high-altitude reconnaissance of Massoud's mountain camp, Flash 22 had marked its location and had returned to Bagram to refuel and ammoup. Seeing how many Taliban were crawling around down below, the Spectre's captain had guaranteed Fontaine that they would be back for more.

No matter how things went down, Harvath had seen the air support as the world's best insurance policy. If he swept the camp and Julia Gallo wasn't there, he could decide whether to call for a strike. If Julia was there and he could pinpoint her location, he could designate it with a strobe and have the AC-130 rake everything else. And, if they were lucky enough to take positive control of Julia and needed somebody to kick the back door shut for them, there wasn't anything the Taliban had that could compete with heavily armed aircraft.

Fontaine kept one hand on the steering wheel and lifted up his radio in the other. "I'm not getting anything," he said.

"Nothing?" replied Harvath, looking back out the window, knowing the Taliban were going to be on their tails any second. "Not on any of the channels?"

Flash 22 had promised to be on station, ready to shower steel at 5:00 A.M., thirteen minutes before sunrise.

"Nothing," responded Fontaine. "We're surrounded by solid rock. The radio isn't powerful enough to get out."

"How about a phone?" said Harvath as he pulled his Afghan cell phone from his pocket. "Do you have a direct number for J3 Air?"

Fontaine rattled off the digits and Harvath punched them into his phone. He hit *send,* but the call failed to connect. The signal strength wasn't strong enough.

"No joy," said Harvath as he punched the *end* button on his cell phone and tucked it back in his pocket.

"What's going on?" asked Julia from the floor behind them.

"Don't worry. Everything's going to be okay."

"You picked a great night not to bring a sat phone," said Fontaine.

Harvath was about to tell the Canadian he had brought one, but that it had been barbecued along with Gallagher's Land Cruiser, when two trucks came up on their three-vehicle column from behind and begin firing. The results were instantaneous.

"We've lost the rear vehicle!" yelled Harvath as he watched the truck one of Reshteen's cousins was driving slide to the side of the road and come to a stop.

"We can't do anything for him now," said Fontaine as he kept his foot on the gas. "We're almost at the first checkpoint. Get ready."

As the MP5 was an easier weapon to shoot one-handed, Harvath traded it to Fontaine for Gallagher's LaRue. Positioning the sniper rifle out the window, Harvath looked once more into his side mirror. "Damn it!" he cursed. "Reshteen's going back for his cousins."

"There's nothing we can do about that," replied the Canadian. "We're going to have that checkpoint in sight in less than a minute."

Underneath them, their bald tires were

skidding and slipping over the icy road. "Go back," said Harvath.

"Are you fucking crazy?" replied Fontaine. "There are at least forty Taliban back there."

"Who are going to execute three men who risked everything to help us if we don't help them."

"Goddamn Afghans," Fontaine growled, as he stepped on the brakes and the truck fishtailed back and forth. "How the hell am I supposed to turn around?"

They had just left the valley area of the pasture and entered the narrow canyon with its single-lane road that led down to the village.

"Reverse it," ordered Harvath.

The Canadian shook his head and slammed the truck into reverse. Its tires spun until they finally caught and they went hurtling backward in the direction they had just come.

Harvath jumped into the backseat, opened the rear window, and pushed the barrel of his rifle through. Pulling his Afghan cell phone from his pocket, he dropped it to Julia Gallo and said, "Keep redialing the number on there and don't stop until you get through."

Fontaine continued to speed backward. Thirty meters out, Harvath could see Reshteen's vehicle, as well as that of his cousins. He could also see the two Taliban trucks just beyond, which were closing fast and firing at them with everything they had.

"What are we doing here, Scot?" yelled the Canadian as errant rounds began pinging off their truck.

Harvath took several shots at the approaching Taliban vehicles as he quickly studied the situation.

Although Reshteen's cousins wouldn't be happy about losing their trucks, the way they were now parked, side by side, made them a perfect roadblock. There was only one thing that could make them better.

"Stop!" yelled Harvath.

As Fontaine brought the vehicle to a halt, Harvath leaped out, raised his weapon to engage their attackers, and yelled for Reshteen and his cousins to come to him.

The men ran right toward him, and as Harvath examined their vehicles, he could see that both trucks had flat tires and were inoperable.

"Get in the truck!" he yelled as he pointed over his shoulder. Despite their inability to speak English, they had no problem understanding him.

Harvath continued to return fire, until he got within a few meters of the trucks. As he dropped to a knee, he could see beyond the two Taliban trucks rapidly approaching, to an armada of headlights right behind them.

Breaking off his assault, Harvath fished two fragmentation grenades from his coat pocket. He pulled the pins, pitched one underneath each of the disabled vehicles, and yelled, "Frag out!" as he ran back to his pickup.

Leaping into the bed, he slammed his fist against its side and yelled, "Go, go, go!"

Immediately, Fontaine stepped on the gas and Harvath ducked down. When the frags detonated, they lifted both of the disabled vehicles off the ground and sent a bright orange plume of flame into the air. Shrapnel pockmarked their tailgate and skipped across the roof of the cab.

They had been driving for only a few hundred feet when Fontaine saw something up ahead and stepped on the brakes yet again. Before Harvath could ask what it was, the Canadian yelled, "RPG!"

He managed to grind the vehicle into reverse but ended up spinning the tires so fast that he couldn't get any traction.

Harvath jumped from the bed yelling, "Everyone out!" as he scrambled to make it to the passenger side door in time. With no choice but to abandon ship, Fontaine did the same.

As the Afghans and Dr. Gallo poured out of the vehicle, there was an ear-splitting *pop* as the RPG was fired and hissed toward them.

Grabbing Julia Gallo by the shoulder, Harvath pulled her behind a narrow outcropping of rock and yelled for everyone to take cover.

No sooner had he said the words than the RPG hit their truck and detonated, sending another towering fireball into the sky.

Harvath pressed Gallo into the rock, covering her body with his as the charred remains of the vehicle rained down around them.

It took what felt like a lifetime for the ringing in his ears to subside. When it did, he could hear Fontaine calling out his name.

"Over here!" Harvath yelled back, and soon they were joined by the Canadian and the three Afghans.

Fontaine was just about to speak, when they all heard a tremendous crash from up the road.

"They're trying to ram their way through the trucks I fragged," said Harvath.

"What are we going to do?"

"Fight," replied Harvath, who was suddenly interrupted by Julia Gallo.

"It's ringing!" she cried as she held the

phone out.

Fontaine took it from her as Harvath leaned out toward the road and took aim.

After three attempts at ramming into the wreckage, the men above them broke through. At the same moment, the sentries from the checkpoint below them pinpointed their position, and they immediately began taking fire from both directions.

Harvath very quickly burned through his magazine and yelled for Fontaine to hand him another. As he did, the Canadian relayed their situation to J3 Air at Bagram, which patched him in to Flash 22.

With their strobe gone, all Fontaine could do was give their approximate location in relation to their burning pickup.

As the string of Taliban trucks came rushing down the road toward them, Harvath alternated trying to slow them down and engaging the sentries from the checkpoint who were now coming up the road.

There was a distinct clap as the final round in Harvath's magazine was fired. He had just called for a fresh mag, when Fontaine yelled for everyone to drop and take cover.

CHAPTER 60

Mullah Massoud grinned as he and Simonov barreled down on the men who had stolen the American woman from him. Their vehicle had been destroyed, but there were still survivors returning fire. He prayed that he would find the woman there. He didn't care if she was injured, as long as she was alive. He and the Russian both had too much invested in her to allow her to slip through their hands.

As they drew closer, the accuracy of the person shooting at them improved. Whoever it was, he was very good with a rifle. Massoud pounded the roof of the truck and yelled at his soldier to make sure he didn't shoot the woman or their fellow Taliban down below.

The commander was going to teach whoever this was a very painful lesson. You didn't steal from a man like Massoud Akhund. All he had to do now was to keep them pinned down until they ran out of ammunition; then he and his men would move in.

Simonov slowed their truck to a crawl to allow the soldiers from the checkpoint below to move up and apply pressure. Hot shell casings tinkled onto the roof of the cab as Massoud leaned against the roll bar and kept firing in short bursts.

It was during a break in the shooting, when the soldier ejected his spent magazine and fished for another, that Massoud realized that the marksman near the flaming wreckage below had stopped shooting at them. It was also at that time that he heard an explosion from behind.

Looking into his side mirror, he saw the trucks behind him erupting in bright yellow flashes. "Move! Move! Move!" he yelled at Simonov.

The Russian, who had been transfixed by the spectacle behind them, popped the clutch and leaped forward. Though neither of them could see any aircraft, they knew they were under attack from above.

Simonov pushed the truck as fast as it would go, as the hand of death came racing up behind them.

Both he and the Taliban commander were so mesmerized by what was happening in their mirrors that they didn't realize how quickly they had closed with the burning hulk of the truck in front of them that had been RPGed.

The Russian tried to brake but lost control. The truck bounced against the high rock wall on the right side of the road and then slammed into the flaming wreckage.

The last thing that went through Sergei Simonov's mind as he went through the windshield and was killed was his son Sasha.

Mullah Massoud was ejected from the passenger window as the vehicle flipped over and rolled several hundred feet down the road.

He regained consciousness for only a moment. Blood poured from his nose and ears. Though his eyes refused to focus, he thought he could see daylight. Off in the distance he heard his brother calling him to prayer.

As the sun's rays grew brighter, his body was beset by cold and grew numb. Zwak's voice seemed to move farther away as the life drained from his body.

Standing above him were two shapes. They were men with guns, foreigners; probably Americans. Massoud Akhund opened his mouth to tell them that they would never triumph in Afghanistan.

The Taliban commander wanted to mock

them for their arrogance, but nothing came. Nothing but deep, impenetrable, bottomless darkness.

CHAPTER 61

Washington, D.C.
Two days later

Carolyn Leonard cleared White House security on West Executive Drive and then found a parking space. It was one of those perfect D.C. days — warm with a bright blue sky and barely a trace of humidity.

"Are you sure you want to do this?" she asked as she turned off the car's engine. "Maybe you should take some more time to think about it."

Elise Campbell turned to her, "Carolyn, I didn't bring you along to talk me out of my decision. I brought you for moral support."

Leonard smiled. "I'll be waiting right here when you come out."

"Thanks," said Campbell as she unbuckled her seatbelt and opened the door.

As she stepped out of the car, she was greeted by the scent of magnolia blossoms drifting across the grounds. Max Holland was waiting for her in front of the West Wing entrance.

"Are you sure about this, Campbell?"

Elise nodded. "I'm sure."

"Okay," he replied. "The president is waiting for you in the residence. Are you okay if we walk this way?" he asked, pointing toward the North Lawn. "It's a nice day, and I'd like to enjoy what's left of it."

"That would be nice. Thank you."

As they walked, Holland said, "The night Nikki Hale drove off the estate, I'd been on break when Alden went to the guesthouse. I never knew the details of what happened until you asked me to set up this meeting. I'd like to think that if I'd been there that night, things might have turned out differently."

"Me too," replied Elise.

They covered the rest of the distance in silence. On the third floor of the executive residence, Campbell followed Holland down the hallway to a carpeted ramp that branched off to their left. At the top was a room most Americans didn't know even existed; the White House solarium.

Constructed by William Howard Taft in the early part of the twentieth century as a sleeping porch, it had originally been intended as a place to catch a cool breeze on hot nights and had been a favorite of first families ever since. President Eisenhower barbequed outside on its promenade, while his wife, Mamie, hosted bridge parties inside. The Kennedys used it as a kindergarten for Caroline and other children, President Nixon gathered his family here to break the news of his resignation, and President Reagan spent weeks in the solarium, recuperating from the assassination attempt on his life.

"The president will be here in a minute," said Holland. "Make yourself comfortable."

As he left, Elise took in the solarium.

It was an octagonal room, composed almost entirely of windows. The décor was bright and the tasteful furnishings plush and comfortable — exactly what one would expect to find in a sun room meant for relaxed family gatherings.

Its most striking feature was its view. In the foreground was the Washington Monument and beyond that the Jefferson Memorial.

"Best view in all of Washington," said a voice from behind.

Surprised, Campbell turned around. "Hello, Mr. President," she said. It was the first time she had ever seen him on time for any meeting, much less early.

"Elise," he said as he crossed the room

to shake her hand. "I understand you were quite insistent about seeing me."

"I was. Thank you, Mr. President," she replied as she accepted his hand.

Alden pointed toward one of the over-stuffed couches. "Please sit down. Can I get you anything? Something to drink?"

"No thank you, sir."

"Okay," said the president, taking a seat in the armchair just adjacent. "I'm all yours."

Elise knew there would be no perfect segue or preamble for what she had come to say. The only way to say it was to say it, and when she did, the color drained from Alden's face. "Mr. President. I wanted to tender my resignation to you personally."

"Excuse me?"

"I know what happened the night Nikki Hale killed the Coleman family. She had been drinking with both you and the first lady. The three of you quarreled, and despite the fact that she was drunk, you insisted she get in her car and leave the estate. Then you lied about what happened that night under oath."

"What are you talking about?"

"I'm talking about your answers to interrogatories in the civil suit. You lied about everything that happened that night. As if your involvement in Hale's death wasn't enough, you perjured yourself in trying to cover it up."

"You wait just a second," snapped the president indignantly.

"No, you wait, sir," said Elise, cutting him off. "You lied to protect yourself and you lied to protect your candidacy, and I can't work for you anymore."

Standing up and buttoning his suit jacket, Alden said, "Agent Campbell, you simply don't have your facts straight. I don't know what's ailing you, but I think you need to take some more time off and come back when you're feeling better."

"I feel fine, Mr. President. And I'm not coming back," said Elise as she stood up as well. "Where this goes now is up to you. And for your information, Herb and Janet Coleman will be taking a very keen interest in what you decide to do going forward."

"The Colemans? Is that who's behind this?" said Alden contemptuously. "I should have known."

"Yes, you should have, Mr. President. Lying under oath is a felony."

Alden glared at her and tried to shift the blame. "So this is how divisive politics have become? Even when the people have spoken, you won't stop until you find a reason to force the duly elected president of the

United States out of office, even if you have to make the reasons up?"

"This has nothing to do with me, or politics. I voted for you. I *believed* in you. But you're unworthy of your office."

"I guess I made a mistake asking to have you assigned to my detail."

Elise had had it with the man's arrogance. "You politicians want to blame everyone but yourselves when you screw up. Your mistake wasn't having me assigned to your detail. Your mistake was lying under oath. In fact, now you've got me talking like a politician. Lying under oath isn't a mistake, it's a reflection of a very deep character flaw. The office of president and the people of the United States deserve better. The Colemans and I will be expecting you to announce your resignation shortly. Good-bye, Mr. President."

Elise left the president and exited the solarium. Max Holland was waiting for her outside. "How'd it go?"

"C'mon, Max," said Elise. "You're telling me you heard none of that?"

"Our job's to protect the president, not to eavesdrop on his conversations."

Campbell was silent.

"That said, sometimes you can't help but hear things," replied Holland. "You're a good agent, Elise. Don't quit the Service just because of him. We'll get you reassigned. In fact, there's a position open on the first lady's detail."

"Hutch resigned?"

Holland nodded. "Ten minutes ago."

Removing her credentials, she handed them over to him. "Thanks, Max, but I've got other plans."

Holland knew better than to argue with her. Reluctantly, he accepted her creds and slipped them into his pocket. "So what are you going to do?" Max asked. "Are you just going to give up on law enforcement?"

Elise smiled, "I think I'm going to become a detective."

"You're going back to the Virginia Beach PD?"

"No. I've been offered a job in East Hampton."

CHAPTER 62

Kabul, Afghanistan

With the convoy of Massoud's soldiers taken care of, as well as those he had posted along the road, Harvath knew it was safe to call Daoud in to pick them up. As a courtesy, Flash 22 stayed on station until they were all safely back in Dagar.

Reshteen and his cousins mobilized the other men of their village. Arming themselves, they established a perimeter around Dagar just in case any stray Taliban happened to wander down from the mountain camp or travel over from Massoud's village looking for revenge.

Out of appreciation, Harvath had allowed the Canadians to be credited with the success of the operation and the recovery of Julia Gallo. He neither needed nor wanted the publicity, but more than that, the Canadians had been integral to their success.

Without them, things could have turned out very differently. They more than deserved the credit.

When Captain West and his team arrived, they helped reinforce the village and establish a secure LZ. Twenty minutes later, a UH 60 BlackHawk, accompanied by two AH-64 Apaches, landed to transport Julia Gallo to Bagram.

Once the helos had lifted off, Fontaine led Captain West and his team back to Massoud's camp to gather as much intel as possible about the Taliban commander and his Russian counterpart. In the truck that Fayaz had loaned them earlier that night, Harvath and Daoud followed.

Most of the Taliban vehicles were still smoldering as the column made its way up the narrow mountain pass. Though it took some doing, the heavy LAVs were able to clear a wide enough path for everyone to make it up without having to permanently dismount.

Once they arrived, the Canadian forces swept the camp. Only one survivor was found; Mullah Massoud Akhund's brother, Zwak.

Though Zwak had been untied, he had remained in the storage building beneath the protection of the IR strobe Harvath had thrown on the roof. Though the man had no idea that it had been there, it had saved his life.

Daoud spoke to him quietly and tried to calm him down, but Zwak kept asking for his brother, saying he wanted to go home. With Captain West's blessing, Harvath and Daoud were granted permission to return the man to his village, providing Harvath didn't tip them that it was their next stop. The Canadians planned on taking Massoud's compound apart, as well as all of the other houses that the Taliban had been using. Harvath, of course, agreed.

Harvath and Daoud drove Zwak home and remanded him into the care of Baseer, who thanked Harvath for being a man of honor who kept his promises. He also gave his assurance that he would deal with young Usman personally.

Harvath and Daoud then drove to Bagram, on the outskirts of Jalalabad, and Gallagher's Shangri-La guesthouse cum fortified compound. There, after arranging to get the truck back to Fayaz and his village, Harvath paid the intrepid interpreter and, though the man politely attempted to refuse, gave him a significant bonus. Daoud had more than earned it.

Harvath then took a long hot shower,

poured a stiff drink, and popped a much overdue Motrin. He then slid into bed, closed his eyes, and didn't wake up for twelve hours.

When he awoke, he checked the email account he was using for this assignment. Waiting for him was a two-word message from Stephanie Gallo. It read simply, *Thank You.*

Out of sheer curiosity, he surfed over to his bank's website and logged in. Mrs. Gallo had already deposited the balance of his fee. She was a woman of her word, and though he disagreed with much of her politics he had to give credit where credit was due. While he didn't really care either way, he couldn't help but wonder if maybe her opinion of people like him and the other brave men and women in the world who risked all to protect the innocent and take the fight to the bad guys had maybe now changed.

Next he logged in to the personal account he used to communicate with Tracy and found six emails, all with photos of their dog, Bullet, attached. Harvath smiled as he read through them, but felt an odd sense of melancholy. He loved his dog, but a dog wasn't the same as having children. There was no bond stronger than family, and he was ready to start one of his own. Considering how much money he'd just banked, Tracy couldn't argue that kids were too expensive. And he wanted to have a ton of them.

His optimism returning, Harvath smiled and typed a quick reply to the last email she had sent. *Done having fun. Wish I was there. Be home soon.*

Borrowing the Shangri-La's other Land Cruiser, Harvath drove himself back to Kabul, alone. He slowed in Surobi and hoped to see the little old man who sold the Jackie Collins book standing outside his shop, but the store was closed. It was prayer time, and even in a village not "officially" controlled by the Taliban, repercussions for not strictly adhering to Islamic laws could be harsh.

Harvath did see, though, the same man with the same black Taliban turban he had seen the last time he had passed through Surobi. The man's eyes were still filled with hate, and he threw Harvath the same blood-chilling stare. *Fuck diplomacy,* thought Harvath as he flipped the guy the finger.

He drove to the safe house in the Shahr-e Naw and called Flower from his cell phone to come outside and open the gates.

"Mr. Scot, I am not there," he said. "My wife had the baby. A beautiful little girl."

Harvath was glad to hear Flower so excited about having another girl. "Congratulations.

I wish you and your family much health and happiness."

Flower thanked him and said his cousin was at the house and he would call him and have him open the gates.

Less than a minute after they hung up, the gates opened. Harvath drove the Land Cruiser into the courtyard, parked, and entered the house.

The large plasma television was on in the living room. Hoyt was sitting on the couch with his back to him.

"I hope you bought enough beer, Mei. We're going to have half of the NGO community here for this party tonight."

Harvath was about to reply when Hoyt turned around, saw him, and said, "Or maybe not."

"Nice try."

Hoyt smiled. "Now that the job's done you're finally lightening up. Better late than never."

"How's Midland?"

"Fine."

"And our guest?"

"Mustafa, Special K, Khan? Still a creepy pain in the ass, but on the right side of the grass, which is only because I like you so much. Now that Gallo's safe, Mark wants to hang him from his ankles and beat him like a fucking piñata for what he did to his ear."

"First things first," said Harvath, who then glanced up at the TV. "What are you watching?"

Hoyt looked at the plasma and then back at Harvath. "What? You couldn't get a fucking newspaper in Nangarhar? Alden just announced his resignation."

"President Alden?" said Harvath as he stepped closer to the couch.

"Yup. Second-shortest presidency in U.S. history. William Henry Harrison is first. He served for only thirty-five days, and also coincidentally gave the longest inaugural address. Guess who gave the second-longest inaugural address?"

"Alden?"

Hoyt nodded. "Spooky, huh?"

"Why is he resigning?"

"Nobody knows. He made a brief statement and evaporated."

"Well something must have happened. No one runs for office as hard as he did just to give it up," replied Harvath, bringing his mind back to the work they still had to do. "We've gotta get Khan ready to roll."

"Where are we taking him?"

"Bagram."

Hoyt smiled. "Scot Harvath! Aren't you thoughtful."

"What are you talking about?"

"Next to cold beer, there's nothing Baba G loves more than a piñata party."

Harvath smiled. "That reminds me. I need you to pack a cooler."

CHAPTER 63

Bagram Air Base, Afghanistan

"If this guy's not at the gate," said Harvath into his cell phone, "I'm gonna cut Khan loose."

Seven thousand miles away in Langley, Virginia, CIA operative Aydin Ozbek tried to put his friend at ease. "My guy is already there waiting for you. Don't worry."

Hoyt motioned to the cooler on the backseat.

"And nobody searches the car either," added Harvath.

"For fuck's sake, Scot. You're driving onto an American military base in the middle of a war zone. If they want to search your car, they get to search your fucking car."

"You know what, Oz? You're right. I don't know what I was thinking. We're going to turn around and hand Khan over to the Afghans."

"All right, all right. No inspection. I'll let them know. Now, are there any last-minute bites at the apple I need to bend over for?" asked Ozbek.

"Let me think a minute," said Harvath. "Considering how I'm giving you, and by *you* I mean the Agency, one of the highest-ranking al-Qaeda operatives since Khalid Sheik Mohammed —"

"Whom, I believe, you stole from the Afghan government," Ozbek clarified.

"Hey, if you don't want him."

"Scot, you know we want him. We also know that the Afghans didn't really catch him, so we consider him fair game."

"Okay," said Harvath. "What happens after you're done with him?"

"When we've wrung him out like a damp dishcloth? We'll arrange for the Afghans to *recapture* him."

"That's good enough for me. That plus a month's worth of drinks at a bar of my choosing in the D.C. area."

Back at Langley, Ozbek began laughing. "Feel free to grab my dick and shake the money tree."

"Oz, you and I both know you're going to jump at least two pay grades because of this. If I want to drink Macallan 1926 you're buying."

"For a month? You're out of you're fucking mind. I'll buy you a case of Johnnie Green and we'll call it even."

"Johnnie Blue and I want it on my doorstep by the time I get home."

"Deal. Now drive onto that base and surrender that prisoner so I can go home and beg American Express to raise my credit limit."

"And all of the deals we made with the Afghans get honored, right?"

"Yes," said Ozbek. "I will see to it personally."

"I'm going to hold you to that, Oz," said Harvath. "These people risked everything for us. If we don't live up to our end, we deserve all the problems they can cause for us, and believe me, even small villages like theirs can cause problems."

"Don't worry."

"Oz, these villages have lived with the Taliban. They know them and they can be huge treasure chests of intel; don't let the 'failure factory' fuck this up."

"I'm going to make sure these villages get taken care of. The projects they want are within the scope of the budgets that have been proposed for their province. Everything is good."

"I gave them my word," said Harvath. "So

I am going to make sure every single project happens."

"Scot," said Ozbek. "You've already blown half the budget for these projects on cell phone minutes. Would you just hump to Bagram and dump the prisoner already?"

Ten minutes later, Hoyt drove the Land Cruiser up to a little-used gate on the far side of the air base.

"Can I help you, gentlemen?" asked one of several American soldiers at the guard booth armed with very atypical weapons.

"We seem to be a bit lost," replied Hoyt. "Is this the road to Sea World?"

As the sentry smirked, Harvath leaned across his friend and, using the front name for the Agency's air transport unit, said, "We've got a perishable cargo delivery for Polar Air."

The sentry nodded and, stepping back inside the guardhouse, raised the gate and lowered the bollards.

Thanking the guards, Hoyt smiled and drove forward. Thirty yards inside the base they were greeted by a tall man with short, dark hair in blue jeans and a TAD Gear jacket. "You must be Norseman," he said, using Harvath's call sign as Harvath rolled down his window. "My name is Jude."

Harvath smiled, "Nice call sign. The patron saint of lost causes. Well, it just so happens that I have someone who is a follower of a very major lost cause here with me."

"I'm glad to hear that."

Harvath pointed at Hoyt and said, "He thinks the Dolphins are definitely going to go to the Super Bowl this year."

The man in the blue jeans didn't laugh. "Where's the other guy?"

"Oh, *that* guy," replied Harvath. "We've got him wrapped up in a rug in the back."

Opening the rear passenger door, Jude hopped in and said, "Hang a left at the first road and keep going until I tell you to stop."

"Are we going to see Shamu?" asked Hoyt, who loved to fuck with humorless intel people. When Jude didn't respond, Hoyt put the Land Cruiser in gear and started driving.

Jude led them to a dark aircraft hangar where several men in blue jeans helped unload Mustafa Khan from the back of the SUV.

"Don't forget to read him his Miranda rights," yelled Hoyt. When Jude didn't respond, he added, "On second thought, fuck it. Who cares, right?"

Harvath put his hand on Hoyt's shoulder and he drove the car out of the hangar and made his way across the tarmac and over to the Craig Joint-Theater Hospital.

Parking the Land Cruiser, he and Harvath pulled out the enormous Igloo cooler that had been spray-painted on the side with a red cross and the words, *Rush: Human Blood Plasma*.

As he was less than thirty miles north of Kabul, Hoyt had already been to see Gallagher multiple times since he had been admitted and knew exactly how to get to his room.

As he entered, he identified the other soldiers in the room and said, "Fell out of a jeep. Fell off a ladder changing a lightbulb. Slipped taking a piss. And our own Baba G, who apparently broke off his dick jerking off."

A chorus of "Fuck you!" erupted in the room, complete with multiple middle-finger salutes.

"I'm sorry," responded Hoyt defiantly. "We only brought beer for warriors."

Once again the "Fuck you" chorus rose until Hoyt waved his arms to calm the men down. "Okay, okay," he admitted. "This isn't exactly the paper-cut ward. There may be one or two warriors sucking up some easy medical leave within these four walls, but as I'm not a guy to point fingers, I ain't

575

saying nothing."

Harvath bumped Hoyt out of the way and introduced himself around the room, meeting three Army Rangers and a Green Beret.

He blamed not having come to the hospital earlier on having to mop up after Gallagher and killing another forty-plus Taliban, which roused cheers throughout the room.

"Tom, I think all of these men deserve a beer," said Harvath, upon which Hoyt flipped open the lid of the cooler and delivered cold beer to everyone.

Baba G smiled. "How's your back feeling?" he asked.

"Not great," replied Harvath.

"You still taking those Motrin even though I warned you to be careful?"

"I've upped it," said Harvath, holding up his bottle of beer. "Vitamin M and vitamin B."

Gallagher pulled a plastic bag from beneath the pillow propping him up and said, "I had one of the nurses pick this up in PX for you."

"I should have guessed," said Harvath as he pulled a PEZ dispenser with a Marine Corps drill instructor's head out of the bag.

"Now, while you're frying your liver and kidneys you can think of me."

Harvath laughed and opened his beer. "To a successful mission," he said as he raised his bottle.

There was a television on in the corner running a story about President Alden's resignation and the swearing in of the VP as the new commander in chief. One of the Army Rangers raised his beer and said, "To the United States of America."

With that, all of the men in the room raised their bottles and in unison said, "To the United States of America."

ACKNOWLEDGMENTS

This part of the book is where I get to thank all of the people who make it possible. At the top of my list are you, my wonderful readers. Thank you for your letters, emails, participation on the BradThor.com forum, your appearances at my signings, choosing my novels for your book clubs, and for turning so many of your family, friends, and coworkers on to my work. Nothing builds a successful author like good word-of-mouth and you all have been incredibly generous to me. Thank you.

The next V.I.P. group I want to thank are the fabulous booksellers who have been supporting me since my very first book. From Peoria to Paris and San Antonio to São Paolo, whether you are a national chain, an independent, an online retailer, a warehouse club, or any other type of bookseller, please know that you have my deepest appreciation for everything that you have done and continue to do for me.

My literary agent par excellence, Heide Lange, of Sanford J. Greenburger Associates, Inc., is hands-down the best agent on the planet. An author could not hope to have a more dedicated, principled, and enthusiastic powerhouse in his camp than Heide. Thank you, Heide, for all that you do for me.

I have called Simon & Schuster's Atria and Pocket Books home since my very first novel. There's a reason for that. They are not only the best people in the publishing business, they have become like family to me. My deep gratitude goes to the brilliant men and women in the Atria/Pocket sales staff, the Pocket/Atria art and production departments and the Simon & Schuster Audio family. Thanks as well go to Lisa Keim and Michael Selleck, as well as Laura Stern, Sarah Branham, Mellony Torres, and Irene Lipsky.

My editor, Emily Bestler, is the type of editor whom authors dream of someday working with. I have been fortunate enough to have been with her since my very first novel. Not only is Emily brilliant and incredibly talented, but she is funny as hell and keeps me laughing so hard that it can be easy to forget that what we do is called work. Thank you, Emily.

Carolyn Reidy, Louise Burke, and Judith Curr are the titans who captain the S&S, Pocket, and Atria ships. Thank you for your ongoing support, wisdom, and, most of all, friendship. It is truly a joy to be working with all of you.

David Brown, or "Conan the Publicist," as I like to refer to him, is the best P.R. person I have ever met, and I appreciate him more than I think he will ever know. Thank you for everything, David.

I also want to thank Jennifer Linnan, Alex Cannon, and the rest of the fabulous team at Sanford J. Greenburger Associates for all that they do for me all year long.

Now for my thanks to the people so intimately involved with the writing of this novel.

This novel would not have happened if not for the man it is dedicated to, James Ryan (not his real name). If you want to know whether or not our country has real-life Scot Harvaths out there in the field, away from the flagpole, taking the fight to our enemies, the answer is yes. Do we need more of them? Do they need to be better equipped and better funded? Do they need better leadership? Do they need better management? Do they need more respect and less red tape and bureaucracy? Do we need to better trust them to slip off into the dark of night to do the jobs which so desperately need to be done? Yes, yes, and yes ad infinitum.

I chose the Orwell quote at the beginning of this novel as my way of honoring James Ryan for how invaluable he has been to me throughout the writing process. I chose to dedicate the novel to him, though, because of how invaluable he has been to this nation. I have a love and admiration for this American patriot that I will never be able to fully express, as there is so much of who he is and what he does that cannot be spoken of. Suffice it to say that he personifies American exceptionalism and that never in my life have I been more honored than the first time he called me friend.

Once again, my very good friend and patriot Scott F. Hill, PhD, was a key sounding board and wellspring of creativity in writing this novel. Whenever I have a new idea for a novel, he is the first person I turn to. The example he continues to set as a selfless American and one of the best friends a person could have is a daily reminder to me of the good mankind is able to achieve in this world. Thank you for all of your help and thank you for everything you continue to do in service of our great nation.

I round out the literary triumvirate so crucial to this novel with my dear friend and patriot Rodney Cox. Rodney's tactical expertise, excellent sense of humor, and deep military experience in Afghanistan were key resources I drew upon repeatedly throughout the writing process. Thank you for everything, including equipping me for my trip to Afghanistan and for making sure we continue to turn out the world's most formidable warriors. We're looking forward to seeing you and Steph real soon.

My family and I also owe a special debt of gratitude to Tim Lynch and Walter Gaffney. You gentlemen know what you did for me, and I am deeply grateful. Thank you.

I also want to thank my friend Glenn Beck. Congratulations on your success and thank you for everything you, Kevin, Chris, Stu, Dan, and everyone else have done for me. Nice guys do finish first, and you and your team have proven it.

I also want to thank the key group of warriors who not only influenced and assisted in the writing of this novel, but are also very good friends: Chuck "Eagle Eye" Fretwell, Steven Bronson, Jeff Chudwin, Shawn Dyball, Thomas Foreman, Frank Gallagher, Rob Hobart, Steve Hoffa, Carl Hospedales, Cynthia Longo, Ronald Moore, Chad Norberg, Gary Penrith, Rob Pincus, the real Roper 6-9, Jonathan Sanchez, and Mitch Shore — as well as all the people out there who asked that they not be named in this book, for their own safety. Thank you for all you do for us. Stay safe.

For their invaluable assistance I am also indebted to Chief A. M. Jacocks, Jr. — Virginia Beach Police Department, Captain Edwin Ecker — East Hampton Town Police Department, Michael Foreman — Point Blank Solutions, Steve Tuttle — TASER International, the National Executive Institute Associates (NEIA), the Major Cities Chiefs (MCC), the Major County Sheriff's Association (MCSA), author Kathy Reichs, Jason Kohlmeyer, Esq., Stephanie Dickerson, Tom and Geri Whowell, and John Giduck (who provided several key back office elements for my trip to Afghanistan).

In Washington, D.C., I continue to be grateful for the assistance of my friends Patrick Doak and David Vennett.

Friends Richard and Anne Levy always do the voodoo that they do so well with the assistance of a beguiling young woman known from Kolkata to Kowloon simply as Alice. Thank you for everything. We'll see you in Munich.

Thank you to all the members of BradThor.

com forum, aka the Thorum. There are too many of you to thank by name, but please know that I appreciate you all so much and love conversing with you online every day.

My attorney, Scottie Schwimer, continues to amaze with his magical powers in Hollywood. In a town where beauty is only skin-deep, Scottie's beauty and talent go right to the bone. Thank you for all you do for me, my friend.

Finally, none of this would be possible without my gorgeous wife, Trish. I cannot count the nights and weekends she backed me up at home so I could stay in my office and get this novel completed. For those of you who want to know the secret to a happy marriage, marry someone kinder, smarter, funnier, and more patient than you are. You will never regret it. I know I haven't. . . .

Thank you, my love.

I'll be back next year with an all-new Scot Harvath adventure. In the meantime, I highly recommend reading the authors of the International Thriller Writers Association. Visit their website at www.Thriller Writers.org.

ABOUT THE AUTHOR

Brad Thor, a graduate of the University of Southern California, has served as a member of the Department of Homeland Security's Analytic Red Cell Program and is the #1 *New York Times* bestselling author of *The Lions of Lucerne, Path of the Assassin, State of the Union, Blowback, Takedown, The First Commandment,* and *The Last Patriot.* Visit his website at www.BradThor.com.